Prey

E.M. Taylor

Copyright© 2024 by E.M.Taylor

All rights reserved. No part of this publication may be reproduced, stored or transmitted in any form or by any means, electronic, mechanical, photocopying, recording, scanning, or otherwise without written permission from the publisher. It is illegal to copy this book, post it to a website, or distribute it by any other means without permission.

This novel is entirely a work of fiction. The names, characters and incidents portrayed in it are the work of the author's imagination. Any resemblance to actual persons, living or dead, events or localities is entirely coincidental.

E.M.Taylor asserts the moral right to be identified as the author of this work.

Designations used by companies to distinguish their products are often claimed as trademarks. All brand names and product names used in this book or on its cover are trade names, service marks, trademarks and registered trademarks of their respective owners. The publishers and the book are not associated with any product or vendor mentioned in this book. None of the companies referenced within the book have endorsed the book.

First edition

In memory of Nala
2016 – 2022

Prologue

Lydia's feet pounded the forest floor as she raced wildly through the trees, her heart hammering in her chest. She strained her eyes, trying to make out the way ahead, but the thick, damp fog made it impossible to see more than a few inches in front of her, and the faint, silvery moonlight streaming through the branches did little to help. Instead, it cast a dull, ethereal glow that sent a shiver down her spine.

She leaned against the rough bark of a tree, her shallow, raspy breaths a cloud in the air as the cold bit through her chest. Alone in the darkness, her eyes widened, adjusting to the sparse light, while she tried to make out the shadowy figures surrounding her.

Snapping twigs broke the stillness of the night, like a gunshot echoing in the distance. Lydia gasped at the sound, the cold stabbing her lungs, before clamping her hands over her mouth, desperately trying to quiet the cough rising in her throat.

She had to be quiet. She had to stay as silent as possible, or *it* would find her.

Her head whipped around at the thought, searching for those glowing red orbs, but finding nothing but the startled, yellowish eyes of a deer amongst the endless shadows. It bolted at the sight of her, and she released the breath she'd been holding, her eyes fluttering shut in relief. But only for a moment.

After another quick glance around, she darted from her cover.

"Lydia!"

The voice cut through the quiet like a knife, and she jolted in surprise, her head jerking around in response.

"Will? Is that you?" she breathed out her words in a whisper.

She scarcely dared believe it, but Will's voice was unmistakable, seeming to come from her left. A rush of relief washed over her, causing her knees to buckle.

He hadn't abandoned her. She was safe now.

Her eyes tried to follow the sound, but all she could see was a blur of darkness. In the deep blackness between the trees, she couldn't make out a thing, and all she could feel was the dampness of the night air chilling her bones. And now, a horrifying thought struck her.

Had she imagined it?

The idea turned her stomach, and she shut her eyes tight, a soft sob escaping her.

"Lydia, where are you?!"

Her eyes flew open.

His voice again. She was certain of it now.

She had left her cell phone in the cabin when they had set out on their hike. Will said he wanted to take her to the lake to look at the stars. He shone almost as brightly as they did when he was talking about the heavens, and she hadn't wanted anything to distract her from listening to him. From watching him. But now, without her cell, she had no idea how long he'd been gone. It felt like hours, but could that be possible? Nothing made sense.

All she knew for sure was she had spotted an owl, its golden eyes piercing through the darkness, and she had wanted to take a picture, forgetting she didn't have her phone with her. She didn't call out to ask Will to wait, because she didn't want to startle it away. Besides, she wouldn't take long, and she could still *hear* him. He wouldn't get ahead by much.

But she startled the animal anyway. She must have gotten too close, because it had swooped down at her, its talons scratching at her forehead before it took off into the night, leaving hot, sticky blood to drip down into her eye in its wake.

Will didn't like blood, but there hadn't been much. Just a graze, really. A warning from the bird, rather than an attack. Still, it had shocked her, and she had shrieked and ducked her head in case it circled back. Then she had stayed like that, head down, listening for the sound of his footsteps running back to her, for his voice cooing apologies for leaving her behind. She had waited to feel the familiar warmth of his arms enveloping her, holding her safe, the way they had done since the night they left.

If she'd been looking, if the damned owl hadn't distracted her... they probably wouldn't have gotten separated at all. It was all her fault. But it had happened so quickly. Him, telling her to run, and then a screech piercing the tranquillity of the forest. And then Will was gone, and all Lydia could see was a pair of huge and horrifying red eyes. Eyes that seemed to paralyse her.

They had vanished as quickly as they had appeared; the creature retreating, leaving behind a putrid stench of decay and rot that made her stuff her fist into her mouth to stop herself gagging. Lydia didn't know where it had gone, or if it would be back, but she knew she had to hurry. She had to run.

She had run blindly, the darkness closing in around her, the silence so heavy it felt like a physical weight on her chest. But she hadn't given up. She had kept going, because if she could find the road, then she could get help. The cops would have guns, tranquillisers... whatever they needed to handle that thing. *She* didn't have anything useful. Everything they'd packed was still where she had left it. Back at the thicket where she had last seen him.

Bringing herself to a halt now, she spun around and leaned against a massive oak tree, concealing herself from view. Saliva pooled in her mouth, and she swallowed it back before cautiously glancing around the side of the tree.

There was no sign of the creature anywhere.

Stepping out from her cover with clenched fists, she braved the open clearing, her senses alert as she listened.

"Lydia!" Will's voice echoed again, and this time, it sounded closer. She traced the sound along a rocky path, going as fast as she dared. "Answer me!"

But she didn't. She didn't dare. She could hear the fear in his voice as he spoke again, making her grip her palms tightly to suppress the impulse to cry out his name. That would be too dangerous, and he was close now.

He hadn't abandoned her.

She crouched under a low-hanging branch and stumbled into a glade, the giants that lurked there soon transforming into trees as the moonlight cast a soft, dreamlike sheen on them.

Lydia's eyes widened as she frantically scanned the area, her heart racing with the desperate hope of seeing him. Because he had to be there. Yet the forest stood in complete stillness, broken only by the whispering of wind among the trees.

He wasn't there. *How* wasn't he there? Maybe it was the wind, or the echoes of the mountains playing tricks on her, distorting the sounds, but she had gotten it wrong. She scanned her surroundings, but nothing looked familiar, and the truth of her situation hit her like a punch to the gut: she was lost.

She took a deep breath and looked up, only to find the sky hidden by a sea of treetops. A shiver ran down her spine, and the hairs on the back of her neck stood at attention, as if sensing something in the air.

At a sound, she whirled, her lungs burning while her breath caught in her throat. The sound grew louder and louder, and her blood turned to ice as it coursed through her veins. Because she knew what it was. She had already heard it once tonight.

She gasped for air, her chest heaving with each desperate breath.

The rustling branches were a ghostly whisper in the wind.

She should run. She knew that. Just run as fast as she could. But her feet felt anchored to the spot while the earth trembled beneath them.

It was too late.

The air was foul with the rotten smell of death. *It* paused at the edge of the clearing, its eyes seeming to penetrate her soul as they glowed a sinister red. Sharp fangs protruded over snarling lips, blood dripping from the clumped fur on its chin.

Her mouth formed the shape of a scream, but only a soft whisper came out, carried away by the chilly breeze. Her knees twitched, and she almost buckled under the weight of her own body. She gasped for air, relieved that she could finally move again. The snap of a twig echoed as she stepped on it, and she squeezed her eyes shut, holding her breath for the attack, but the beast remained motionless. She exhaled slowly, daring herself to look once more, her heart racing as her eyes confirmed it still lurked at the edge of the clearing, and...

She spun. Without hesitation, she turned right, her instincts telling her that the sparser trees would give her a better chance of getting away.

Adrenaline rushed through Lydia's veins as she readied herself to bolt, the sound of her pounding heart filling her ears.

She didn't even hear it move. Not until she felt the hot, foul breath crawling down her neck. As the creature emitted its deafening howl, the sound reverberated through the forest, and she found herself rooted to the spot once more, a solitary tear rolling down her cheek. The sound of wings beating filled the air as birds took flight in the distance, escaping while they still could. Leaving her there. Trapped. Alone.

She closed her eyes...

Then it pounced.

1

Ten, nine, eight...

I could hear the truck approaching, even with music blasting through my headphones. A bonus to having superhuman senses, I supposed. As it came nearer, I sat up to slip my feet into the pair of slippers beside my bed. And then I waited.

Seven, six, five...

The truck's engine cut out. I repositioned my headphones, letting them dangle around my neck.

Four, three, two...

The sound of a car door opening, swiftly followed by it slamming shut. Then footsteps.

One...

A firm rap at the front door.

I jumped up with a grin, yanking off my headphones and tossing them on the nightstand. Then came a crash as they bumped into the photo frame that was standing there, tilted just right for me to see it when I woke up. A photo of us before the homecoming dance. Him in his tux, and me in the black dress he liked. He had his arms around my waist, grinning widely for the camera, while I gazed up at him. *Sickeningly* cute, really.

I adored that picture, but nothing could beat the real thing, so I didn't hang around to fix the frame. It could wait.

By the time I reached the front door and tore it open, my smile was so wide my cheeks ached.

And there he was: Carter Johnson. *My boyfriend.*

He stood on the doorstep, one shoulder resting against the garage wall, arms crossed over a black puffer jacket, and his tight brown curls peeking out from under a bright orange beanie hat. It was mid-afternoon, so the sun was still up, and it was a surprisingly mild spring day for Havencrest, but that didn't mean busting out the sandals and swimsuits. Besides, even if it was warm enough, the beanie was Carter's signature look, and he knew how much I loved it, how it brought butterflies to my stomach. He knew it was happening right now. I could tell by the grin he shot my way.

"Madison Stone, you are a sight for sore eyes."

I glanced down at my outfit of grey sweats and a tank top, suddenly self-conscious. "Shut up." I grumbled. "I thought we were just hanging out, or I would've—".

"We are. And I don't care what you're wearing. You're beautiful."

A blush crept over my cheeks. "Shut up." I grumbled again, because I didn't know what else to say. I never did when he said things like that. "You're the one who's been driving for six hours, and yet you still show up looking like the hottest guy this side of the Piscataqua."

He chuckled. "Hardly. Also, I wasn't the one driving. Guess it was handy having my dad tag along after all."

He tried to deflect the compliment, but he couldn't hide his beaming smile, which was so contagious that I couldn't help but return it. It was impossible not to. Carter's smile had the power to make his entire face light up, and it *still* sent a thrill through me every time I saw it.

He stepped forward and planted a gentle kiss on my cheek, his arms enveloping me in a warm hug. "Damn, I missed you." His soft sigh drifted through my hair.

"It's only been a couple of days." I said, like I hadn't been up since daybreak just waiting for this moment. At the thought, my arms tightened around his waist, as if he might disappear again if I gave him the chance.

Even though he'd only been out of town for a couple of days checking out colleges in New York, it was the longest we had been apart since he tiptoed back into my life a little over a year and a half ago. He'd done it so quietly, so unassuming, that I barely noticed until he'd burrowed his way into my heart; a piece of me I could no longer survive without. So I'd be lying if I said I didn't miss him like crazy, too, no matter how short a trip it'd been.

"I'm glad you're home." I admitted, almost sheepishly. "How was it?"

"It was *awesome*, Mads." He gushed as he pulled the beanie from his head and shook his hair out, while I kicked the door closed behind him to block out the chill. "Honestly, you'll love New York. There was always something going on. Tons of clubs, and parties, and... man, it was just so awesome. I can't wait to take you there."

I just smiled in response, because I knew I wouldn't 'love' New York. It was too busy, with too many people, always rushing about. There was no open land to run through, or forests to hunt in. And the smells... *ugh*. I shuddered to think about how NYC must smell to a werewolf. Even the New York pack stayed out of the city as much as they could.

Werewolves struggled to be in close quarters with humans for too long. We weren't driven to frenzy by the light of the full moon – that was just a tale told to frighten children – but our noses were more sensitive than humans, and our ears were so powerful they could capture even the softest of sounds. Being around people was an assault on our senses, and it was mentally draining. That was why the pack had settled down in the most off-the-map part of Maine they could find, surrounded by its own private patch of breath-taking forest… and two miles as the crow flies from the rest of society.

Carter, however, was blissfully unaware of that. He didn't know I was a werewolf, and I intended to keep it that way, so I didn't argue.

"So, that's it, then? Your mind's made up? NYC?" I asked, leading the way down the hall towards the den.

Once we'd settled on the couch, he shrugged. "Not for sure. I mean, I think I'd really like it there, but St John's seemed cool, too. Columbia… Well, that's Ivy League. I only visited because my folks insisted. It's not like I stand a chance."

My lips formed a tight line as I shook my head. "You don't know that. They'd be lucky to have you."

"You sound like my mom." He chuckled. "And, like her, you're blinded by my charm and good looks. Sadly, it takes more than that to get into an Ivy League."

I rolled my eyes, smirking. But then, more seriously, I said, "You've got a good GPA. *And* you've got extracurriculars. Basketball opens up a lot of opportunities. Just look at Henry."

"I'm the small forward for a team no one has heard of, that hasn't won a championship in over a decade. Barton got a scholarship because, even with the Hawks' lack of trophies, he's still the best shooting guard this county has seen in years. And it wasn't exactly easy for him, either. D'ya know how many strings Coach had to pull to even get that Berkeley scout to travel up here?"

I opened my mouth to argue, but he clamped his hand over it to stop me before rushing on. "Besides, basketball is more of a hobby for me. I'm not sure it's something I even want to continue after graduation, so a sports scholarship is out of the question." He shrugged. "Maybe I'll change my mind. Who knows? But either way, Columbia isn't on my radar. NYU is my first choice so far."

"So far?" I asked once he dropped his hand from my mouth. "You have other schools you wanna visit?"

"I'm not sure. I'm waiting to see what *you're* doing next year before I decide. There's still UMaine. Did you know Stephen King went there?"

I managed to resist sighing and instead gave a noncommittal response that he could take however he wanted. It wasn't because I didn't care about Carter's future. Quite the opposite, in fact. I didn't want there to ever be a time when I didn't know all of his plans, or when I wasn't the first person he called when one of them fell into place. It was just that we'd had the same conversation over and over since the start of senior year, and I still didn't know what the hell I wanted to do after graduation. Everything since the attack, since losing Ryan... it was all still so raw, and I wasn't sure if I even wanted to *go* to college, much less one in a whole different state.

He wasn't the only one who refused to drop the topic. Dad was lecturing me pretty much constantly these days about how it was his job to worry about me, not the other way around. That might be true for normal families. It wasn't that simple for supernaturals.

Still, I hadn't totally ruled it out. Going to college had always been part of my plan. Ryan had been a professor of history at the University of Maine, and I always found it fascinating listening to him recount his multiple research trips in Europe. I'd just never really considered it as a viable path before. But now, in the wake of his death, the idea seemed a little less ridiculous. It felt like a nice way to honour him.

Carter was still speaking, and I suddenly realised I hadn't heard anything he'd said in the last few moments. I smiled and nodded along, hoping he hadn't noticed, as I refocused.

"Anyway, forget about that. I've been thinking—"

"I've warned you about that." I said, seeing an opportunity to distract him. "You'll hurt that pretty head of yours one of these days, and that would be a real shame."

He let out a fake, exaggerated gasp. "Ouch. You're very mean, Stone, d'ya know that?"

"I know. But do you know why?"

He raised his eyebrow. "Why?"

I shifted on the sofa, reaching out to grasp the front of his shirt and pull him closer. His eyes closed instinctively, his lips puckering in anticipation of a kiss, but I didn't give it immediately. Instead, I leaned towards his ear, the racing beat of his heart sending a wave of heat pulsing through my body.

"Because then I get to make it up to you." I whispered, before our lips finally met.

2

"If that's the welcome home I get, I'm gonna leave town more often."

As he collapsed onto the mattress beside me, Carter let out a satisfied sigh, his chest rising and falling rapidly as he tried to catch his breath. I turned onto my side so I was facing him. "Um, nope. You're never leaving me again."

"Aw, Stone. You really did miss me, huh?" He chuckled before planting a kiss on the top of my head, while I snuggled into his side. "But you should know – as much as I enjoyed it – it's not gonna work on me every time."

"What?"

"Distracting me with your womanly charms."

"Womanly charms?" As I tilted my chin so I could look up at him, I let out a quiet chuckle, my fingers gliding mindlessly over the tufts of hair on his chest. "I thought you said you were the one with all the charm?"

His eyes fluttered closed, and one arm stretched up above his head while the other went around my shoulders. "I didn't say I had *all* the charm. I simply said I *had* charm. But, after *that*, I'm not so sure. I think it might be all you."

"Oh, you have plenty yourself. Trust me." I laughed, and Carter gave a lazy smile without bothering to open his eyes. Then silence fell for a beat, until I said, reluctantly, "My dad could be home any minute."

With a groan, he tugged the comforter up over our heads, hugging me closer to him.

"*Carter.* Come on, I'm serious!" I tried to sound stern, but I couldn't suppress another laugh. He met my eyes again, then he huffed, sulking, before squashing my mouth with an over-the-top kiss, complete with a '*mwah!*' sound to finish it off.

"Fine." He grumbled finally, and he didn't stop me when I untangled myself from him, but he didn't follow, either. Instead, he just sat up against the headboard, letting out a heavy sigh. As he shifted, the sheet slipped down until it draped across his lap, exposing his toned chest and abs, and his tousled hair stuck up in all directions. His cheeks took on a soft pink flush, and his lips, still slightly swollen from our kisses, had a rosy hue. I bit my lip, feeling a rush as I looked at him.

My boyfriend was incredibly attractive. Sure, he didn't have model good looks - he had a pimple or two, and he sometimes left it a little too long between shaves. But his flaws just made him even more attractive, and it still blew my mind that I got to call him mine.

He caught me checking him out, and his cheeks burned even brighter as he raised an eyebrow.

"What?" He gave a low laugh, not making eye contact as he swept his sweaty hair away from his forehead.

"Nothing. Just admiring the view." I grinned. "You gonna get dressed? Or do you actually *want* my dad to catch you naked in my bed?"

"You know, we wouldn't have to worry about this if—" He started as he finally stood up, taking the pile of clothes I was holding out to him, but then he cut himself off.

"If?" I prompted as I moved to my dresser, grabbing my hairbrush.

He cleared his throat. "Well, I was just thinking. Y'know, about college. And I thought maybe... only if you wanted to, I mean. And not right away. But, well, we could get a place together."

My hands froze with the brush mid-stroke, and I swallowed back the saliva in my mouth, my stomach churning. Silence stretched for what felt like an eternity, but couldn't really have been more than a few seconds, while I scrambled for the right thing to say.

"That sounds nice." I finally managed.

It was the only thing I could think of, the only thing I could say that wasn't a lie. It *did* sound nice – the thought of a future together. But it wasn't possible. Not for someone like me.

Sometimes, I couldn't help but think about how, in another life, maybe Carter and I would be soulmates, if such a thing existed. But not in this one. Because I was a werewolf, and he was human.

We weren't going to have our happily ever after in a cramped New York City apartment. We weren't going to have that anywhere. I already knew how our story ended. I'd known ever since our first kiss by the riverside.

It ended with me losing him, and no amount of wishing would change that.

"Did you ask your dad about spring break while I was away?" Carter asked once we'd returned to the den.

I paused my search for a movie to turn a playful glare on him, and he threw his hands up in surrender.

"I know, I'm sorry. I told you I'd leave it up to you, and I don't mean to put any pressure on you. It's just... if there's any chance you might actually *want* to go to Daytona with the guys... well, there's only one room left at Ethan's beach house. He's been hanging on to it for us, but Jack has been on his ass about it. We gotta let him know soon."

"Jack?" I asked, raising an eyebrow, not recognising the name. I might've been dating a basketball player, but that only meant more people said 'hey' in the halls at school. I still wasn't *one* of them.

"He's Ethan's cousin." Carter clarified. "He graduated two years ago, so you probably don't remember him. But he's dating Faith Green – y'know, from English class?" He paused but, seeing my blank expression, he hurried on. "Not important. The point is, Ethan *really* wants us to go, but he can't dodge Jack's calls forever. Faith even cornered him after gym class last week to ask about it."

I clamped my lips together, suppressing the groan that was rising in my throat, and sank back into the couch cushions. "Ethan doesn't even like me. He could care less if I go."

"What're you talking about? Sure he likes you! Why wouldn't he? You're smart, sexy, beautiful—"

"You don't have to sweeten me up, you know. If you want to go to Florida with your friends, then you should go."

"Oh no. Don't do that, Stone."

"Do what?"

He let out a frustrated sigh and rolled his eyes. "Tell me to go without you. Because I don't *want* to go without you. I want to spend the break *with* you. Plus, if I were to do that, we both know you'd only sulk the whole time."

I pursed my lips. "I wouldn't sulk."

"Fine. *I* would sulk. Being without you."

I laughed, but before I could respond, the low rumble of a car engine caught my attention. It stopped moments later, replaced by footsteps up to the porch, before the front door opened, sending a chilly blast of air shooting down the hall and into the den.

"Hey Dad." I called, just as he appeared in the doorway, flashing a warm but exhausted smile. "Good day at work?"

"Long one. If I ever find out who decided it was a good idea to open on Sundays, I'm gonna kick their ass." He shook his head, stifled a yawn, and then greeted Carter with a nod. "You here for dinner, Cart?"

"If that's okay, Mr Stone."

Dad sighed. "How many times I gotta tell you to stop calling me that, huh? It's Robbie, for crying out loud. You've been coming around since you were knee high to a grasshopper, well before you started canoodling my daughter, so I reckon we've moved to a first name basis, don't you?" He shook his head, and I couldn't help but giggle when Carter's cheeks flushed pink. "Anyway, I'm gonna hop in the shower. Sierra dropped some food over earlier, but it's not enough for the three of us, and I'm too beat to cook. You wanna order pizza? There's cash in my wallet."

He threw the black leather pouch at me and then left the room before I could respond.

"Pizza it is, I guess." I said, grabbing my phone to order.

"Don't go thinking the conversation about spring break is over." Carter said, relaxing now we were alone again. He swung his legs up and around, resting them across my lap while he lay his head on the arm of the sofa. "I honestly don't care where we are, as long I'm spending it with you, but, I mean…" His words faded away as his attention flickered towards the door. As he looked back at me, his voice grew quieter, almost a whisper. "It *would* be pretty cool to have some time to ourselves, right? An entire week without worrying our parents might walk in on us."

"Oh yeah. Just swap them out for Ethan. You know, I wouldn't be surprised if one morning we woke up and found him right there with us. In our bed." My lips curved into a smirk, even as I rolled my eyes. "Very romantic."

Carter chuckled. "We'll barricade the door."

"Ah, so you've already thought about this, huh?"

"Have I thought about the prospect of a week in Florida, with my sexy as hell girlfriend, strutting her stuff in tiny little bikinis the whole time? Um… *yes*!"

"You realise I can wear bikinis here, right?"

"It'd be kinda cold."

"You could warm me up." His eyes widened slightly in surprise, and I responded with a playful grin. "What?"

He licked his lips once. "Goddamnit, Stone. Just… *ugh*, goddamnit."

I laughed again, and for a moment, I wasn't worried about the future. I wasn't anxious about what would happen next. Because he was grinning that trademark smile of his, beckoning for me to lie with him so he could hug me close as we settled to watch a movie and wait for our pizza. And for that single beautiful moment, nothing else mattered. I loved him, and he loved me, and that was enough.

At that moment, I wasn't a werewolf, and he wasn't a human. We were just *us*. We were just *happy*.

3

By the time Friday finally rolled around, it was a relief to inhale the fresh air in the forest behind Vineyard Manor.

It was almost four thirty, but the sky overhead was still a clear and welcoming blue. Everywhere I looked I saw trees full of vibrant green leaves, pin cherry buds that hadn't bloomed yet, and the promise of fruit that would be ready to harvest in the fall. A chill lingered in the air, but nowhere near as biting as winter had been. Usually, I was fine with the cold, especially after a Change, but I preferred the more temperate climate for hunting. The forest was a cornucopia of food when animals woke from hibernation.

It was strange to hunt without Henry, and it was more challenging than I'd thought it would be, getting used to following my own instincts, rather than deferring to him all the time. It was getting easier, but I still missed the company. Not that I was *always* alone. Sometimes Dad would come out, if he wasn't busy with other things, and Jackson too. Today, though, after a crazy week, I just needed some alone time, so I headed straight to mine and Henry's old hangout without dropping by the house first. Once there, I stripped off my clothes, leaving them on the uprooted tree we'd repurposed into a seating area, close to the old campfire we were forbidden to light anymore. Then I got down on all fours, focused on my breathing, and waited until I felt the familiar tingling in my extremities that warned the Change was beginning.

After it ended, I stood, panting, claws digging into the dirt, until my heart rate returned to normal. Then I lifted my snout to the sky. Almost immediately I sensed a grouse about a half mile east, and a deer close by that. Tempting, and certainly easy hunting... but that wasn't what I wanted today. Today, I needed a break from all the noise in my head, even if only for a little while. The forest was already helping, but a five-minute pursuit of small game wouldn't be enough to still my thoughts completely. I needed more.

And then I smelled it - the unmistakable scent of a moose, just a few miles west. Close enough for a decent chase, but not so far that the reward wouldn't be worth the effort.

My lips pulled back into a grin before I bolted, my paws pounding the forest floor as I followed the scent. I slowed down to a gentle lope when another gust of wind hit me, letting me know I was getting close. The last thing I needed was to startle the beast and send it fleeing in the opposite direction. I wanted a challenge, but I didn't want to chase it all the way to New Hampshire.

As I manoeuvred through the dense undergrowth, the damp earth muffled my steps, until a sudden creaking branch above brought me to an abrupt halt. My heart raced, and adrenaline surged as I looked upwards at the looming treetops, their jagged outlines contrasting against the darkening sky. And there, amidst the branches, a pair of piercing yellow eyes glared down at me.

Even before my brain identified the shape, a guttural snarl erupted from within me, reverberating through the silence. Black spots on tawny fur, with tufted ears camouflaged against the tree trunk...

A lynx sighting was rare, but not unheard of in the forests that surrounded Havencrest and Silveroak. *This* one had been a particular nuisance for months, getting way too close to headquarters. I'd love nothing more than to chase her off once and for all, but I wasn't dumb enough to pick a fight I wasn't absolutely certain I could win.

The moose was *so* close, though. I could try to make a break for it. Maybe snatch it before the cat even realised I'd moved. If a lynx was sniffing around it, that probably meant it was just a calf, so it wouldn't be difficult to take it down. Normally, I wouldn't go for young prey, but I'd already come this far…

I didn't do that, because there was a reason it wasn't doing more than stare at me. It had the advantage, and it knew it.

There was only one viable option, even though it left a bitter tang on my tongue. Frustrated, I let out a huff and shot one last glare at the cat before backing away from the clearing, and only when I felt a safe distance away did I dare turn my back.

The unmistakable smell of barbecued meat as I approached the forest's edge softened the blow of missing out on the moose.

Coming here always put me at ease, because even though it wasn't where I actually lived, Vineyard Manor still felt like home. Our actual house, just like Henry's, was smack dab in the middle of Havencrest, although his family lived in a way fancier neighbourhood than Dad and me. Not that any of that mattered. Vineyard Manor, the two-storey timber building before me, with its cosy, homely interior, the sound of laughter ringing out from the wraparound porch and the lush green of the sprawling land, was where the pack spent most of its time. The old building had been the headquarters of the Maine werewolf pack for generations, its walls steeped in history, and so it was home.

After adjusting my shirt and securing my sweaty locks in a ponytail, I made my way across the grassy patch that connected headquarters to the untamed wilderness of Maine's woodlands. Passing the grill, I snatched a steak and stuffed it into my mouth. Dad playfully swatted my hand with the spatula he was using to flip burgers, and I gave him a smile around the mouthful of food.

Jackson shook his head and laughed as I settled into the deckchair next to him.

"Damn, girl. You look like you haven't had a bite in forever. Hey Robbie, why aren't you feeding this kid?" He shouted to my dad, who just shrugged and returned to grilling.

Jackson was still chuckling as he popped the cap on a beer and handed it to me.

"Damn lynx." I grumbled, as if that was enough to explain everything, before I took a swig from my drink and carefully placed the bottle near my feet.

"Ah." He nodded, while I tore another chunk from my steak. "She's back, huh? Ain't seen her for a while, but Trevor said there was no way she'd have moved on so easily. He thought she might be pregnant."

I shook my head as I swallowed my food. "Don't think so. She didn't seem stressed. I guess she could've already given birth, and left the litter in the den while she hunted, but…"

"She'd have chased you off to be sure you didn't run straight towards her kittens." Jackson finished for me, and I nodded. "Well done for walking away. It's not always easy, but knowing when you're outmatched is a great skill to have. One I didn't have when I was your age."

"Thanks, I guess. Damn thing is still an asshole, though." I grunted as I leaned my head back against the chair and closed my eyes, while Jackson snorted with laughter.

"Asshole, huh? Sure hope you aren't talking about me, Mads."

My head snapped up in surprise at the unexpected voice, unsure if it was real or just my imagination. I knew it wasn't Jackson, but I still instinctively glanced at him, just to confirm. He only shrugged, lips pressed together, but I could tell he was trying not to smile, and then I knew I hadn't imagined it.

Scrambling to my feet, my eyes darted around, searching for him, but I saw nothing. Until he spoke again.

"'Cus if you are, I can soon leave again."

He emerged from around the corner of the house that led to the front driveway, his tight black jeans hugging his legs and one hand casually tucked in his pocket, while the other gripped a half-empty beer bottle, a mischievous smile playing on his lips.

Henry freakin' Barton.

Henry was home?!

"Dude! What the hell?!" I yelled, and he was about to say something, but I didn't let him finish. I bolted towards him and then tackled him with a hug. He grunted at the impact, his body tensing up as if caught off guard and uncertain how to respond. Heat flushed my cheeks, but just as I was about to let him go, I felt him awkwardly hugging me back.

Things had been weird between us ever since *that* night. The night he told me he had feelings for me. We had promised each other we would still be friends, that we wouldn't let it affect our relationship... but then he'd moved to California, thousands of miles away. We hadn't hung out much since then, and I wasn't sure how he felt about me anymore. But this... this was a good sign.

"How are you here? I thought you weren't coming back for another few months! I mean... Is this really happening?" I asked as I stepped back.

"You know I've only been in California, right? Not Timbuktu." He used one hand to push his hair back before crossing his arms in front of him. "And the three hundred bucks I just dropped on a plane ticket felt pretty real to me."

"Why didn't you tell me you were coming home?" I demanded.

"I didn't know." He shrugged. "Spur of the moment, I guess. I finished the semester early and figured I'd surprise you all. Had nothing better to do since my roommate is still drowning in whatever the hell it is he studies, so I booked a last-minute flight. Got in a few hours ago, drove home to drop my shit, and then came straight up here."

"It sure was a surprise, son." Dan declared when he joined us on the deck. He patted Henry's shoulder as he went past. "Made your mom's entire week when you walked through the front door."

Henry shook his head and rolled his eyes again. "Anyone would think I hadn't been home in two years. I was literally *just* here for the holidays."

"Yeah, and that was *four* months ago, kid. That's like four *years* in mom-time."

"Mom-time? You trying to say you didn't miss me, too, old man?" Henry said, earning a chuckle from Dan.

Seeing them together like this, it really hit me how much Henry looked like his dad. With their towering heights, strong muscular builds, and jet-black hair, they were nearly identical. But there was one distinguishing feature that set them apart: Dan's piercing blue eyes were the complete opposite of Henry's, which were like dark shadows, deep and haunting. He got those from his mom.

"Danny, lay off the kid, or he might not visit again." Dad's booming voice carried across the yard as he called from his spot by the grill. "I reckon those two have got a lot to catch up on. If it's four years in mom-time, then how long is four months in teen-years?"

"Way too fucking long, Robbie." Henry chuckled. Then he grabbed another beer from the cooler, threw his arm around my shoulders, and led me inside.

4

"Stop it."

"Stop what?" I asked, raising my eyebrow at the back of Henry's head. "I'm not doing anything."

He turned from the cupboard, clutching a bag of chips, and shot me a look. "You're staring at me, and it's weird. So knock it off."

I raised my eyebrow. "How would you even know? You grow eyes in the back of your head?"

"No. But I can feel you watching my every move."

I sighed as I heaved myself up onto the countertop. "I just... I can't believe you're here, H. I missed you! It feels like forever since we've had a good talk."

I saw a flicker of something in his eyes as he leaned against the counter opposite me, but it was gone before I could identify it. Then he stuffed a chip in his mouth, crunching it loudly before saying, "Yeah... Sorry 'bout that. I've been slammed. Between basketball and y'know, actually studying. College is fucking hard. They should warn you about that."

"Um, I'm pretty sure they *do*. You just don't have the teachers wrapped around your little finger anymore. That cheery attitude of yours not winning over the cool Californians, huh? *Bro?*"

"Shut up." He threw a chip at me, and I caught it with a smirk, shoving it into my mouth. "And you're saying it wrong. It's *'brah'*. Or at least, that's how Ty says it when he gets back from hanging out with his dumb surfer buddies. '*Hey brah – hit some gnarly waves today!*' He's not even a Californian! He's from fucking Washington!"

I couldn't help but laugh as he grimaced, but when he didn't so much as smirk back, I stopped. "Everything okay, H?" I asked gently.

He was silent for a moment, and so was I, like he was a cornered animal, and I didn't want to make him bolt. Then, finally, he shrugged. "Yeah. Fine. Berkeley is awesome."

"You sure?"

"*Yes*, Madison. Jeez." He snapped, slamming the bag of chips down on the counter with force enough that I flinched. He noticed, and his eyes widened. "Sorry. I'm just tired. It's been a long day. But I swear, I'm fine. Cali is cool. I'm just still getting used to it, y'know? Everything is different there. And I sure as hell never imagined I'd be sharing a place with a pot-smoking, veggie-loving hippie, so that's taken some getting used to. But Ty is pretty cool, I guess." He took a swig of his beer, then added, "Yeah. It's great."

I wasn't sure why, but I felt a stab in my gut at that. "So great you can't find the time to call anymore, huh?"

He shot me a look. "Well... it's tough, y'know. With the time difference and everything."

I arched my brow. "It's literally three hours."

"Yeah, but by the time I wrap up practice and get back to my dorm, it's pretty late here. Besides, aren't you usually with your boyfriend? My mom says you two are inseparable."

I blinked at that. Had he *asked* Sierra about Carter and me? It didn't seem like the type of thing she would bring up otherwise. But why would he even care? Still, that was less important than the way he referred to Carter. It wasn't by name, even though we'd all been friends since we were kids, or even 'Johnson', which was what Henry normally called him. Just my '*boyfriend.*' As if Carter, as a person, was irrelevant. And it pissed me off.

Eighteen months had gone by since that night in Henry's car, and in that time, we had both gone on with our lives. I was happy in my relationship, and Henry certainly seemed to enjoy dating around, judging by all the tagged photos I saw on his Instagram. Yet he still held a grudge against Carter, and that was the reason he barely called, even if he wouldn't ever admit it.

Henry Barton was used to getting anything and everything he wanted without ever having to try. I mean, the entire pack knew Ray was mentoring him to take his place as Alpha one day, even though he hadn't officially said so. Even his days at Silveroak High School had been a breeze compared to the average student. Not only was he obviously extremely attractive, looking more like a guy in his mid-twenties than a teenager, but he also had the reputation of being the best basketball player to wear a Silveroak uniform in years. It was a lethal combination that made him an unstoppable force both on and off the court, so he could be a huge jerk and still have his pick of any girl. *Everyone* wanted to be associated with Henry freakin' Barton.

But then *that* night happened. For all of five minutes, Henry had decided he wanted *me,* and I'd said no. Because I knew, deep down, he didn't really mean it. I'm sure he *thought* he meant it, but in reality, they were words spoken by a frightened boy who had done the unthinkable to save his family and still blamed himself for not doing more. For not saving Ryan. It didn't matter that he was just a kid and did everything he could, or that I couldn't protect Ryan either. The guilt ate away at him, messing with his head.

Even after, when he told me he wasn't giving up on us, I knew it was more about the competition than anything else. Henry's feelings towards me weren't love. Not in the romantic sense, anyway. There was a time – a long time – when I wished they were, but not anymore. Oh, he loved me in his way, as a friend. As a pack mate. But that night, all he really wanted was comfort. To lose himself in the feeling of being truly understood by each other, like only he and I could.

Except, it was all an illusion. Once the fog of grief cleared, we would have realised our mistake, and by then, it would be too late to fix it. Our relationship would never be the same. How could it be after that? Henry and I had a connection deeper than friendship. No one else understood me like he did. He was my confidant, my ally, my pack. We couldn't exist without each other, and losing him would mean losing a part of myself. It wasn't worth it for a quick escape from reality.

Plus, there was Carter. *He* wasn't an illusion. He was real, and sincere, and had captured my heart without me ever really noticing. And he was probably the first person to, at least in Henry's eyes, beat him at something. Everything else might have been fake, but the defeat was real, and Henry, being stubborn as always, wasn't giving up on it easily. Me, though? He gave up on that easily enough. Just like I knew he would.

Our friendship might be going through a rough patch right now, but I knew we would work it out... once Henry pulled his head out of his ass. That meant I had to swallow my frustration at his remark about Carter. After not seeing him for months, I really didn't want to start fighting with him right away.

"Carter actually cares about you, you know. And you guys used to be friends. Remember?" I said after a moment.

Henry rolled his eyes and mashed the salsa-covered chips between his teeth, leaving a salty residue on his lips that I fixated on as I anxiously waited for his reply. He took his time, licking his fingers, then his lips, before he downed his beer and finally spoke. "Yeah, well, the phone works both ways, Madison. You weren't hitting me up either."

"I, um..." I frantically tried to think of a comeback, but my mind drew a blank. He was right. I hadn't made the effort either. But that was *his* fault.

"Okay, yes, you're right. But can I be honest?"

"Are you ever anything else?"

I shot him a stern glance, but he wasn't looking at me. "I got the feeling you didn't want me to."

His eyes narrowed almost to slits as he looked up. "That's bullshit."

"Is it? You've been avoiding me ever since..." I noticed his jaw twitch, so I hurriedly said, "since you started college. You skipped out on Thanksgiving! We *always* do Thanksgiving together. The whole pack. Even *Joe* showed up, and you didn't. And it was the first one since..."

He sent another piercing glare in my direction. "I don't need the reminder. But it's a long flight from Cali just for the weekend, and I had assignments to do."

"Alright." I said, voice lowering a bit. "But what about Christmas? It kinda seemed like you were avoiding me then, too. And we hadn't seen each other in months!"

"What the hell are you talking about? You literally came to my house for Christmas dinner."

I let out a long, heavy sigh. "Because your *mom* invited us. *You* snuck off to Pete's the first chance you got."

He clenched his jaw again, as if he was trying to keep his anger in check, and when he spoke, his voice was unexpectedly soft.

"That wasn't about you." He said, shuffling and crossing one ankle over the other. I could tell by his expression he considered that explanation enough. Case closed. When he realised I *didn't*, he sighed. "Honestly, Mads. It's just... kind of overwhelming being back here. What with... you know. And I love my family, but jeez, it's crazy how quickly you get used to living on your own. You'll understand next year."

I felt a twinge of anxiety at the reminder of the decisions I still had to make about my future, but I tried not to let it show on my face. It must have worked, because he continued.

"My mom's been driving me insane every time I've come home. Seems to think I've not *'processed my trauma'.*" He rolled his eyes, and I bit my tongue against the impulse to tell him I agreed. "I just needed a break, so when Pete asked me to come over for a beer..." He left the sentence hanging and shrugged. "I would have asked you to come, but you said you were seeing Johnson. Figured he'd be expecting to cosy up in front of the fireplace, not spend the night sitting in Pete's garage watching reruns of fucking *Golden Girls*."

"Well, I just think—" I was about to argue, but then what he said hit me and I completely forgot my anger, my eyebrow shooting up instead. "Wait... did you just say Golden Girls? *That's* what you and Pete were doing?"

A slight tinge of pink spread across his cheeks. "Yes, alright? It's a classic. But if you tell *anyone*, I'll fucking deny it, *and* tell everyone about the time you pissed the bed. I might not be *at* Silveroak anymore, but I still have connections."

"Hey, tell them whatever you want, dude. I was nine. You're nine*teen*." I couldn't suppress a laugh as I hopped off the counter and grabbed the bag of chips, which were now mostly crumbs. "But don't worry. I'll keep your secret." He shook his head, but his lips twitched with a smirk, and I knew that was it. We'd had our fight, cleared the air, and now we could move on. That was how me and Henry worked.

"So, how long are you back for, anyway?" I asked.

"Couple of weeks. Maybe a month, if I can make it that long without my mom driving me completely crazy. You'd think she never heard from me. It's not like we don't speak almost every damn day when I'm at college. We probably talk more now than we did before I left." He sighed. "Y'know, I fell asleep one afternoon while studying. Woke up to *fifteen* missed calls, and campus security knocking at the door to check I wasn't dead. She called *campus security*, for fuck's sake!" He shook his head as I sputtered a laugh.

"She just cares about you. Especially after... everything."

He grunted, because he knew I was right, but it didn't mean he had to be happy about it. Then, after a beat of silence, he said, "Anyway, most of my classes are done. Just catch-up stuff, y'know? I gotta get back for my finals in May, but I can do the rest online, so I'm gonna stick around for a bit. Probably get more done without Ty's incessant goddamn seventies playlist. Plus, I've actually kinda missed this place. God knows why. I mean, there's obviously forests down in Cali but... I dunno. No place like home, I guess."

"Well, Dorothy, you're the one who ran off to the west coast to 'discover yourself'. When you had all this right here." I shook my head before I swept my arm around the room. "And you didn't even have to tap your heels together three times to get it."

I expected Henry to roll his eyes or shoot back with something sarcastic, but my joke was met with complete silence. Instead, he only gazed out the window, as if captivated by the sight of the wooden deck and the forest beyond.

After a few moments had passed, I cautiously asked, "You are happy, though, aren't you? At Berkeley, I mean."

"Huh?" He mumbled, then blinked and tore his eyes from the window, like he'd just remembered I was even in the room. "Oh. Yeah. I told you, I'm fine. The semester has just been exhausting, and it's been a long day. That's all." He straightened up away from the counter. "I'm not really feeling barbecue. You wanna get out of here?"

I narrowed my eyes at him, like it might help me figure out what was going on in his head. But whatever it was, he'd shut the door again, locked it down tight, and there was no use pushing him. So, with a shrug, I simply said, "What did you have in mind?"

5

At nine o'clock, there were only two businesses still open in Havencrest: Luigi's restaurant, and the takeout pizza place. Without asking, Henry steered towards Luigi's, and I eased back in my seat, tapping my foot to the tunes on the radio, and admiring the blur of trees outside the window.

We were getting close when Henry turned down the radio and glanced across at me. "So, got any big plans for the weekend?"

"Nothing exciting. We've got racoons nesting under the deck, so Dad wants help to flush 'em out and then fix it up. As well as someone to hold his hand at the hardware store." I gave a dramatic eye roll. "Your dad gave him a list of what he needed to get, but you know how hopeless he is with DIY."

Henry chuckled. "Oh, hell yeah I do. I'll never forget the mess he made of that deck the first time. Took Dad and me weeks to put it right."

As he made his way around the corner onto Havencrest's main strip, the smell of food from the restaurant drifted through the air vents and made my mouth water. When my eyes landed on the fluorescent 'Luigi's' sign moments later, my stomach rumbled.

Henry drove the car into the parking lot and I was relieved to see it wasn't too crowded. Hopefully that meant our food wouldn't take too long, but I sat back to wait, pulling out my phone to keep myself busy, while he went inside to grab the order I had called in on the way there. Right away, the small, recognisable icon of a text from Carter popped up on my screen.

> *hows ur night? <3*

It was time stamped around seven-fifteen – almost two hours ago, and right around the time Henry had shown up. A twinge of guilt ran through me as I quickly typed a response.

> *Hey! Sorry I'm so late texting back. It's been nice! Hung with dad a while, went for a run. Pretty chill. How's yours? Xoxo*

After I pushed the send button, I placed my phone on my lap, and within a moment, a reply popped up, as if he had been eagerly expecting my response. I couldn't help but smile at that.

> *Not as gd as if you were here. R u home now? <3*

As I read the text, my leg started trembling uncontrollably, my teeth piercing into my lower lip, although I had no idea why the question freaked me out. Carter knew about my past with Henry, but he was never possessive or jealous because he knew I didn't have those feelings anymore. He'd always been cool about our friendship, so there was no reason to think he'd react differently now.

I shook my head and pushed the thought away, then started typing my reply.

> Nope. You won't believe this but Henry's home! And he asked me to hang out. That's cool, right? Xoxo

Ugh, that damn jittering again as I waited for his reply...

As soon as the three little dots showed up to let me know he was typing, only to be gone a second later, my pulse quickened. When his response eventually came, though, I let out a breath of relief.

> Vry cool!!! Sounds fun! Tell him I say hey and I'll c u 2moro. With an answer about sprng break ;)

> Promise. Hope you're having fun with the guys. Stay safe. ILY Xoxo

His response came right back, followed almost immediately by another.

> Love you more <3<3<3

> Plz let me no when ur home safe. Might not reply... but do it anyway, ok? Will call u after wrk

He ended the message with a string of alcohol themed emojis, then, within seconds, a third buzz sounded. This time, the message simply read '*MWAH!!!*', followed by three kissing emojis. I laughed as I quickly replied.

> Dork xoxo

I was so glued to my phone that I didn't even notice Henry coming back, so when he slammed his car door, I jumped and dropped my phone into the footwell by the driver's seat. I tried to grab it, but Henry was faster.

"Jeez, he's checking up on you now? He sure keeps you on a short leash."

I reached out to snatch the phone back, and his grip loosened without resistance. "I don't see how it's any of your business, but he was just wondering what I was up to."

Paying no attention to me, he imitated Carter's message, his voice dripping with sarcasm. "'*Let me know when you're home safe*'. Seriously? What's his damn problem? What does he think I'm gonna do?"

A wave of frustration hit me, making me roll my eyes. "It was nothing to do with you. It's natural to want to check in on the people you care about. Not that you'd have any idea about that."

My words came out harsher than I intended, but it was the second swipe he'd taken at Carter in as many hours, and I was tired of it. I shot him a glare that could cut through steel before turning my attention to the view outside the window. There was a brief pause, the air thick with tension, before he let out a snide laugh.

"Are you fucking serious right now? So, what, because I don't text you every damn day to ask what you had for dinner, I suddenly don't care?"

I bit back a sigh, because I knew he'd react this way. I guess I brought it upon myself for finally biting back.

Turning back to face him, I said, "No. That's not... ugh, I didn't say that. Can we just drop it?"

"You didn't have to say it. I got the idea. Let's just hope Johnson's around the next time you need saving from a madman in the woods, huh? Oh, wait..." He trailed off, leaving his unfinished sentence to linger in the air, and I clenched my jaw in annoyance. "You'd have to tell Prince Charming what you are, wouldn't you? Damn. That's a pickle."

"Knock it off." I said, almost through gritted teeth as I tried to hold back my anger.

Henry ignored me. "But, hey, at least you've got those texts of his, because that's what really counts, right? I'm sure they'll bring your dad a lot of comfort when he's burying you in an unmarked grave."

While he ranted, he turned the key, and the car came alive, the sharp scent of gasoline and exhaust fumes stinging my nose. It just fuelled my anger even more, and I clenched my fists tightly, the crack of my knuckles echoing like gunshots in my ears.

"I said knock it off!"

My raised voice got his attention, and his head snapped in my direction. "Jeez, relax! I'm just messing around."

"No, you're being a jerk. And I know you're beat from all the travelling, but that's not an excuse. It's not funny, so stop it!"

He put the car in reverse, his arm brushing against my chair as he craned his neck to look out the rear window. "Wasn't meant to be funny. It's just the truth."

And then, I couldn't hold it back anymore, so I shoved the bag of food onto his lap and unbuckled myself before I even had time to think. He slammed on the brakes, jolting me forward, but I didn't stop. I could feel his wide-eyed stare without even looking at him.

"What the hell? I'm driving here!"

I said nothing, because I didn't trust myself not to say something I'd regret once I'd calmed down. But I knew I couldn't be near him anymore, not right now, not stuck in such a tiny space, so I flung my door open, the cool night air brushing against my skin. It was a relief compared to the burning feeling inside me, but I still hugged my arms as I walked away from the car.

I still didn't stop when he got out of the car and started shouting at me to get back *in*. I just needed to get away from him, so I kept walking towards the street. His string of curse words echoed in my ears. Then I heard the door slam, so I knew he was back in the car, and only then did I finally breathe a sigh of relief.

As I walked, I could hear the faint hum of his car engine approaching from behind, inching closer and closer on the road beside the sidewalk. I pretended not to notice when his window opened with a creak, but I automatically slowed down in spite of myself.

It was pathetic, but all he had to say was sorry, and I'd get back in the car. He wouldn't even have to really mean it. Oh, I'd convince myself he did, to stop feeling like such a loser for letting him get away with being a jerk all the time. But that wasn't Henry. He'd just wait for me to get over it, to give in, and then he'd act like nothing even happened. Some things never changed.

But some things *did. I'd* changed.

"Come on, Maddie. Would you quit being such a brat and get in the car?"

"Not until you apologise." I snapped, my gaze fixed straight ahead.

Even without looking, I could sense him watching me. Then he cursed under his breath again before saying, "Would you just stop for five fucking seconds?"

Jaw clenched, I came to a halt and gave him a fierce look, arms tightly crossed. A moment passed that felt like an eternity, though it couldn't have been longer than a few seconds, before he finally took a deep breath, and...

"You still owe me twenty bucks for your food." He said, a smirk playing on his lips.

A shriek of anger burned up my throat. "Screw you, Henry!"

My head felt like it was about to explode but, not wanting to give him the satisfaction of seeing my reaction, I bolted across the road, the screeching tyres echoing in my ears as he sped away.

6

"You're very quiet, cub. Everything okay?"

"Hmm?" I muttered as I followed Dad through the hardware store parking lot the next morning.

He paused just outside the door, his concerned gaze settling on me. "I said, is everything okay? You didn't talk much on the ride here. Did you and Carter have a fight?"

"No. I didn't really speak to him last night. He went to a party and then had to work today. I'll catch up with him later."

Dad pushed the door open, the bell tinkling above, and then stepped back, letting a rush of cool air hit me as I went through first. "Ah, I remember when I could do that. Be out all night and still turn up for work in the morning. Man, those were the days." He shook his head, a wistful smile on his lips. "What about Henry, then? Everything good? Gotta say I didn't expect to beat you home last night. I half expected a message to say you were spending the night over there."

"We're too old for slumber parties, Dad." I answered, offering a friendly wave to Trent, who stood behind the counter. He nodded to us, the weight of his gaze lingering for a moment, before returning to his paperwork, leaving Dad and me to navigate the untamed wilderness that was his store.

"Really? Does Carter know that? He's always spending the night. You need your old man to have a word?"

"Ha-ha." I said, rolling my eyes. "Henry and I are fine. He was just tired, so we grabbed dinner and he went home."

Dad headed to a shelf filled with hammers and nails, the metal tools clanging against each other as he ran his fingers over them. "I've always told you, cub, that you can be whatever you desire in this life, no matter our, um... *unique* circumstances. But if I could just offer you one piece of advice? Steer clear of acting. It's not your forte." He shook his head as he pulled Dan's shopping list from his jacket pocket, focusing on it while continuing to grill me. "So what was it about this time? Even for the two of you, that's gotta be some sort of record."

I finished playing with the bundles of cable ties on the rack near me and gave him a hard look. "What's that supposed to mean?"

"Oh, please. When you were kids, all it took was one wrong look and you were ready to throw down. The way you two fought... it was more like siblings than friends. Mind, I suppose you kinda were." He let out a small chuckle. "O'course, it never lasted long. You guys couldn't go a day without talking."

"Pretty sure that was only true for me. Henry could care less how long he goes without speaking to me."

Dad shook his head. "Nah. As I remember, it was usually him coming round first. Always inviting you to the ice-cream parlour as his way of apologising. Y'know, Sierra was sure you'd end up getting married. I kept telling her she was crazy. The two of you are both so damn stubborn, it'd never work."

I ignored the part about Sierra, because it left me wondering just how much she'd noticed going on between Henry and me. The idea that she might know about our history was mortifying so, instead, I just scoffed.

"Henry apologising first? That's ridiculous. What about..."

My words vanished as I realised I had nothing to support my point. Dad was right; Henry was always the one who made the first move. Well, until he went to high school and pretty much gave up on me altogether. When we were kids, though... He never actually said it, but he didn't have to - whenever he'd show up at my door, clutching his allowance, and ask me out for ice cream, I got the message. Henry's apologies were more about what he did than what he said.

Guilt settled in my stomach, a lump forming in my throat, though I couldn't really understand why. It was *Henry* who'd hurt *me*, and worse than that, he'd *meant* to. He knew his words would sting. That was why he said them. Maybe Dad was right about him always making the first move when we were kids, but it didn't change anything. A thousand past apologies didn't change that my best friend had taken my deepest fear and used it as a cheap shot against me. There wasn't a mint chocolate chip sundae big enough to make it up to me this time.

Still, I couldn't say that without admitting there *was* something wrong, and I didn't want to get into it with Dad. But I didn't attempt to finish my denial, either. There was no point. Instead, I quickly grabbed the shopping list from him and concentrated on deciphering the messy handwriting as I headed to the other side of the aisle.

I could feel him watching me as I searched for the right size nails, trying to decide if he should force the subject. Thankfully, he decided not to, and when I went to throw the packet in the cart, he quickly looked away, pretending to be suddenly very interested in the cable tie display that had grabbed my attention before.

"We aren't fighting, okay?" I said again, if only to ease the awkwardness. "I told you, he just had a long day yesterday and wanted to get some rest. Can we change the subject, please?"

Dad made a gesture of surrender with his hands. "Whatever you want, cub. So what's the plan for spring break, then? Did you and Carter settle on something?" When I groaned, he raised his eyebrow. "What did I say wrong now?"

"Nothing. It's just complicated."

"Everything from waking up to going to sleep feels complicated when you're eighteen, Maddie. This still about Florida? Because I say just go and enjoy yourself. What's the worst that could happen?"

"Um... any number of bad things could happen. A panic attack, for starters. What happens if I set off a Change and can't stop it? Go rabid and eat everyone in the house?"

"When has that ever happened to you? You've only been shifting for five years, and, I swear, you have more control over it than I've ever had. But if you *do* eat someone, they probably had it coming." When I glared at him, he gave a hearty laugh and squeezed my shoulder. "Look, I know it can be overwhelming, cub, but you're forgetting one very important detail — Carter's gonna be there. I've never seen you more relaxed than when you're with that boy. He'll look after you."

Taking a deep breath, I moved further up the aisle to the back of the store and a pyramid of stacked paint cans. Dad quietly walked behind me, giving me a moment to think about what he'd said. I knew he was right, that Carter would do his best to help me stay calm, but I just had this feeling it wouldn't be enough, not for a whole week. And I wouldn't even be able to tell him why.

Dad sighed as he grabbed a can of paint from the top of the display and dropped it in the cart. "Listen, if it's bothering you that much, I can be the bad guy and say you can't go. Carter can't blame you then. But I really think it could be good for you to try something new, cub. You're graduating soon. Hopefully heading off to college." I shot him a warning glance at that, and he raised his hands in surrender again before continuing. "All I'm saying is time goes by too damn quickly, and life sends people in different directions. Don't miss out on the chance to have fun with your boyfriend and your friends."

"Carter's friends. Not mine." I grumbled, internally squirming as I heard the sulkiness in my voice.

"They're your friends now, Maddie. That's what happens when you date a jock. If you wanted to stay an outcast, you should've gone for a guy from the chess club."

"You make it sound so easy. But it's not, and you know it."

"Maybe not at first. But it will be, eventually. Breathe through your mouth, pack earplugs. Whatever you need to do. You remember after your first Change? You *begged* to be home-schooled. Said you couldn't handle being in there all day. You got used to that."

We continued around the store as we talked, picking up our supplies, and before I knew it, we were at the checkout. As we reached the counter, I let out a growl of frustration, earning a raised eyebrow from Trent.

"Uh... is my store really that bad? 'Cus if it is, please don't mention that in your Yelp review." He smiled. "Everything okay?"

Dad sighed, while I emptied the cart onto the counter for Trent to ring up. "Teenage woes."

"Ah. Say no more." Trent chuckled. And I didn't.

7

An hour later, we were back home and unloading the trunk, just as Dan pulled his Chevy Silverado onto the driveway behind us. I raised my arm to wave, but I stopped, my face contorting into a scowl, when I saw Henry in the passenger seat.

"What are you doing here?" I asked once he was out and walking towards us. I tried to mask the anger in my voice, but I still felt Dad's gaze swing our way.

Henry shrugged. "Hell if I know. Not what I had planned for my Saturday."

"Since none of your buddies are on break yet, all you were planning to do was lie around playing video games and eating your mother and me out of house and home. While you're here, you can damn well earn your keep. A decent day's work won't kill you." Dan said, slapping his son on the shoulder as he came up behind him. "You get everything on the list, Robbie?"

"Ayuh. Gimme a hand carting it round back, would ya?"

Engrossed in conversation about the new deck boards Dad had bought, they made their way towards the back gate, leaving Henry and me to complete the task of emptying the trunk. I focused on stacking the last few decking boards across his outstretched arms, purposely avoiding eye contact.

Just as we were about to reach the gate, Henry's voice broke the silence.

"You got home alright, then."

I turned to glare at him, and the smug curl of his lips made me want to swing the can of paint I was holding at his head. "No thanks to you."

"Let me get this straight. You threw food at me while I was driving, bailed out of the car, and disappeared into the night like a freaking lunatic, and you're angry with *me*?"

I snuck a quick look over my shoulder to confirm my dad and Dan weren't paying attention, but they were too busy on the other side of the yard, going over plans for the deck. Then I pivoted back to Henry, feeling my fury ignite again. "*Yes.* 'Cause you were being a jerk!"

"You're not seriously still upset about that? Jeez, Madison, I was kidding!"

"Whatever. I'm not into doing this now, okay? Not here. So let's just forget about it."

"Fine by me." He grunted, rolling his eyes. I had to bite down on the inside of my cheek to stifle my response.

Even though we had been working without a break for hours, the backyard looked worse than it had before we started.

We hadn't exchanged more than a few sentences between the four of us. Dan's directions were the only words that broke the peaceful silence, occasionally accompanied by Dad's tuneless singing and the twang of a steel guitar, thanks to the country music that was softly playing on the radio.

As afternoon arrived, I stopped for a swig of water and noticed Henry trying to get my attention from the other side of the deck. When I caught his eye, he pointed at Dad, who was down on his knees with a trowel, lost in some Johnny Cash song blasting from the speakers, and oblivious to Dan scowling behind him.

Even though I was still angry with Henry, I couldn't help but laugh. My dad heard, and he turned, his eyes flitting between Henry and me, before he gave me a triumphant glance and a knowing wink. I knew he was silently saying '*I told you so!*' I just shook my head and kept going with my sweeping, while Dad used my laughter as a sign to take a breather from his work.

"So, Henry. How's college going?"

Henry shrugged and passed his dad the deck board he'd just cut. "Not bad."

"You still seeing that girl? I forget her name. The cheerleader?"

Henry shook his head. "Nah. That was over a long time ago."

"Probably for the best. You don't wanna be taking baggage with you to college." A nudge from Dan got him busy with the trowel again, but only for a few seconds before he froze up and looked at me with a horrified expression. "Oh, cub! I didn't... What I meant to say was... Ah, you and Carter are totally different, kiddo. It's just that for a guy... crap. I mean – no, not for *any* guy, but for someone like—"

Dan snickered as he clapped my dad on the back. "Hey Robbie, better to focus on digging that hole instead of digging a deeper one for yourself, yeah?"

Dad opened his mouth to respond, but suddenly seemed lost for words, so I faked a little laugh and shrugged my shoulders, as if it didn't bother me. Unlike Henry, Dad wasn't *trying* to upset me, and so there was no point in making him feel bad about it. Besides, it's not like I hadn't considered it a hundred times already. Once Carter went to college, everything would be different. While it didn't mean we'd break up straight away – I was pretty sure ending your relationship wasn't a prerequisite for accepting a college offer – I wasn't stupid. I knew it was just a matter of time. I wasn't exactly prepared, but at least I wouldn't be caught off guard when it happened.

If Dad wanted to say more, he didn't get the chance, because the familiar rumble of an old engine sounded out front and, moments later, Carter appeared at the gate, as if summoned by the mere thought of him.

"Knock knock." He grinned as he held out a brown paper bag that smelled *amazing*. My stomach rumbled, and I suddenly remembered that I hadn't had anything to eat since the steak I'd grabbed at headquarters last night, since I didn't stop to grab my food before ditching Henry outside the restaurant.

"What're you doing here?" I asked, setting my sweeping brush against the wall, and wiping my hands on my pant leg. "I thought you had to work. Did you call out? Last night too much to handle?"

He grimaced, blushing, his ears turning bright red. His free hand came up to rake through his hair. "Nah. I made it. I was kinda late, but I blamed it on a flat tyre. Think I pulled it off." He smirked. "That does mean that, sadly, this is just a pit stop. Owen sent me to Silveroak to grab a part for the truck he's been working on, so I gotta get back. But I was passing the diner, and I figured you guys might appreciate this." He gave me the bag of food and I smiled in thanks. "It's probably cold. *But* I made it the whole way here without stealing even *one* fry, so I'm feeling pretty good about that."

I laughed. "Wow, I'm proud of you. And thank you. You didn't need to do that, though."

He gave a nonchalant shrug and then greeted the others. "Brought enough for everyone. Onion rings too, Mr St—" He cut himself off and then shook his head before correcting himself. "*Robbie.*"

The trowel fell from Dad's grasp. "I knew I liked you for a reason, Cart. And now is as good a time as any for a break." He cast a quick glance around the yard, only standing when Dan set his tools down, too. Then he sauntered over and swiped the bag from me. "Appreciate it. I'll take this inside while you give Carter here a proper thank you. Somehow, I don't think he'd enjoy it quite as much coming from me."

My face grew hot at that, and he gave me a sly smile before heading for the back door, Dan and Henry following in his wake.

8

I thanked Carter, and then he left, with his face rosy and lips plump from the impromptu make-out session on the front porch, and the promise that he would be back as soon as work was over for the day. I watched his taillights until they vanished from view, a trail of smoke billowing in the truck's wake, before turning back to the gate.

When I returned to the yard, my dad, Dan, and Henry were still inside, so I followed them to the kitchen. There, I found them sitting around the table, with the diner bag ripped open, the smell immediately making my mouth water.

"I hear Carter's thinking of NYU for the fall, huh?" Dan said as I pulled up a chair and grabbed the last burger.

"Yup." I didn't even look up as I answered, just tore into the wrapper and took a big bite, like a starving animal that hadn't eaten in forever. Grease dripped down my chin, and I wiped it away with my sleeve while everyone else fell quiet for a minute, until Dan spoke again.

"You know, that's where my sister went to school. She lives in England now, but I'm sure she'd answer any questions he's got. Want me to give you her contact info?"

Dad chuckled. "Be careful, cub. He's just trying to butter you up."

"Butter her up for what?" Henry cut in before I could.

Dan ignored the question, his eyes narrowing at my dad before he shifted his gaze back to me. "Alright. Guess I'm getting straight to it." He shook his head. "I've got a proposal for you, Maddie. You and Carter doing anything over the break?"

I glanced around, puzzled, looking for any clue as to why he asked, but Dad just smirked and Henry shrugged, as confused as I was.

"Um... well, we haven't decided yet, but maybe we'll go to Florida. Ethan's parents own a beach house in Daytona, and they're letting him stay there with a few friends, so—" A snort from Henry cut me off, and I raised an eyebrow at him. "What?"

"Sorry. Just trying to imagine you playing spin the bottle and slammin' tequila shots with Johnson's buddies." He paused, his breathing the only sound in the room for a beat, before finally shaking his head. "Nope. Can't see it."

I was about to bite back when Dan jumped in. "Henry, can you just stop being a jerk for like, five minutes?" He sighed, before slouching back in his seat and meeting my eye again. "Sure, Daytona sounds cool. But your dad said maybe you weren't that into it, so I got something else to offer."

Henry interrupted again before I could say anything. "What're you talking about?"

"Christ, Henry. I wasn't talking to you! But since you won't let Maddie speak for herself, Uncle Sean is taking a business trip soon, and I thought of letting Maddie and Carter use his cabin while he's away. Is that alright with you, huh?"

"Sean?" This time, I managed to butt in before Henry. "Is he the one who lives way out in the sticks? Didn't we used to go to that place in the summer?"

"Ayuh, that's the one." Dan said, relaxing as he focused his attention back on me. "The place is gonna be empty for a week or so, and with the spring break tourists around there..."

"They hardly get a rush of people." Henry scoffed, but shut up again when Dan gave him a look.

"*Anyway,*" Dan continued, "Sean's kinda paranoid. All those years living alone out there, I guess. You learn to expect the unexpected. So he wants someone to keep an eye, ya know?"

Dad let out another laugh. He'd been keeping quiet while Dan and Henry argued, just watching and eating, but then he said, "And Danny don't wanna do it."

Dan threw his head back and groaned. "Would *you*? It's a four-hour round trip! Between work and Cady..." He trailed off and shook his head, as if that was all the explanation needed. "Look, if you're not into the idea, that's fine. I just thought you guys might want some alone time. You'd have the place all to yourselves. It's right near Chibouwood, ya know? That ski place? I know it's no beach house in Daytona but, damn, if I could've taken Sierra to a secluded cabin in the woods when I was your age..."

I felt my cheeks heat at the suggestion, and I nibbled on the end of a fry to avoid meeting anyone's eye, since all three of them had theirs trained on me.

"Hold on," I said after a second. "Doesn't that place not have any power or running water? I definitely remember Sierra taking us to a creek to wash and me getting a fever from a tick bite."

"He's got indoor plumbing now. And it always had power. It was just... spotty. But Sierra *assures* me he's sorted that out now. I'll be honest, there's no Wi-Fi or anything. Hell, he barely gets a radio signal. You'll find something to keep you busy, though, I'm sure." He winked, his eyes crinkling with amusement, but then, seeing my unsure expression, he added, "Take your time, no need to decide right away. Talk to Carter about it and let me know in a couple of days. Yeah?"

I nodded my agreement. For sure, I'd think about it – it *would* be nice to have some time alone with Carter before we graduated, after all. *Really* alone – without having to fight his friends for his attention the whole time. But being almost completely off the grid for an entire week? Just imagining it made me feel sick to my stomach. What if something happened while I was gone? Suppose they needed me but couldn't reach me? A secluded cabin was definitely more my style than Daytona, but I would at least have cell service at the beach. If something came up, I could be back in Havencrest in a few hours. Sean's cabin didn't even have a *landline*. When I visited with the Bartons, Sierra would always take me to town so I could call Dad using a payphone, since that was the only option. Even Ray, if he needed to get in touch, would write a letter, and Sean would collect his mail once a week from the little post office counter in the grocery store. In an emergency, someone would have to physically go there, because that was the quickest way to reach him.

Dad's hand on my shoulder, and his voice in my ear, brought me back to the room, stopping the spinning in my head. "I can tell what you're thinking, cub. But whatever you decide – Florida or Chibouwood – I just want you to have fun. Stop worrying so much. That's my job, not yours."

"But—"

Henry's snicker filled the air, stopping my protest. "You're both wasting your breath. Theres no chance Maddie is gonna agree to that, and Johnson's got about the same odds for Daytona. Fucking *zero.*"

"Excuse me?" I demanded, pushing to a stand, the chair legs scraping against the tiled floor hard enough to make Dad wince.

Dan's voice was a warning, "Henry—", but his son didn't pay him any attention, instead just scoffing and rolling his eyes in my direction.

"Oh, come on. Admit it. You *hate* trying new things. I'm not saying it's a *bad* thing... you just like what you know. What's *safe*. You don't take risks. I mean, take college, for example. Have you even applied yet? And before you get mad, I'm not trying to be a jackass. I'm just saying that..."

Anger made my pulse thud louder with every word he spoke, until I could barely hear him over the noise. *How dare he?* How dare he act like he knew anything about me anymore, when he'd been ignoring me for eighteen months?

But that wasn't really the problem, though. The thing that got me really angry was that it brought up all the stuff I thought I had let go of, like feeling the need to prove myself to him. To prove that I was strong enough, smart enough, even bold enough.

A part of my mind was telling me I'd regret it later. The same part that warned I'd be angry at myself for letting his words get to me at all. But I wasn't listening. My mouth moved faster than my mind, and the next thing I knew, words were tumbling from my lips.

And that's how I found myself agreeing to spend my spring break in a creaky, decrepit cabin deep in the woods...

Shit. Carter was going to kill me.

Henry gave me the silent treatment for the rest of the afternoon.

I couldn't decide if I should be pleased or mad about that. I mean, I probably should've been relieved not to hear him complain all day, but it bugged me he felt he had any right to be angry at all. He still hadn't apologised for what he said last night, and now I had to tell Carter I wasn't going to Daytona. And it was *his fault!*

Still, no matter how mad I was, the more he acted like I wasn't there, the more I wanted to make things right. But I also knew that's exactly what he was waiting for, and I wasn't about to give him the satisfaction. Not again.

As soon as I could, I made an excuse and snuck away, muttering about needing to clean myself up. Honestly, though, I just wanted to hide in the bathroom until Dan and Henry left. Thankfully, I didn't have to wait long before the sound of Dan's engine roared to life and slowly faded away down the street. I breathed a sigh of relief, washed my hands, opened the door, and...

"*Holy crap!*" I yelled, clutching my chest as I walked headfirst into Henry. "You scared the life outta me. What the hell are you doing, anyway? I heard you leave."

Henry just shrugged. "You heard my dad leave. And yours too. He told me to let you know he's heading to the store." Then he paused, and we locked eyes, before he said, "I wanted to talk to you."

"Finally ready to apologise?" I gave him a sharp look and pushed past him into the hall, feeling his stare burning into my back as I headed to my bedroom.

He trailed after me into the room. "What the fuck was that about earlier?"

I let out a sigh before I faced him. "Your dad asked for my help and I agreed. What's the big deal?"

"The big deal is that I know it's not what you want. You're just doing it to get at me."

"Do you hear yourself right now? You think me wanting to spend time with my *boyfriend* has *anything* to do with you? Seriously?"

He made a sound suspiciously like a growl, but he didn't respond to my question. Instead, he continued with, "He shouldn't have fucking asked you to begin with. I don't know what the hell they were thinking. Does everyone need a refresher on what went down last time Robbie left you unsupervised? That psycho's son stalked you, and we had to bury *two* bodies." I tried not to flinch at that, but he didn't seem to care. "And now you want to go off the grid for a week? Alone?"

"I won't be alone. I'll have Carter."

I hoped. Although I kept that thought to myself.

I crossed my arms over my chest in defiance. "Besides, what exactly do you think is gonna happen, huh? I'm not an idiot, Henry. If I wake up to find a bear in the kitchen, I'll be sure to run far, far away. Does that make you feel better?"

His nostrils flared, and his eyes burned with anger as he stared at me. "Don't be a smartass, Madison. I know you think you're all grown up now, but Lavoie wasn't that long ago. He might be dead, but do you seriously think there aren't people out there who still believe in him? Rogues just biding their time until they can finish what he started? The pack beta's daughter would be a damn good bargaining chip. And after what happened last time, sorry if I don't trust Johnson to keep you safe."

"How about you just trust *me*?" I snapped, but I kept going without waiting for his answer. "So what do you suggest? I stay in Havencrest forever? Where it's '*safe*', just like you said. Or maybe...

oh! I know! You can just follow me around forever. Watch out for dumb Madison so she doesn't screw up again. Does that suit you?"

By the time I finished, my chest was heaving, and I struggled to catch my breath. Silence settled over us for a moment, but he didn't have to say anything for me to know what he was thinking, and his raised eyebrow sent a wave of unease through me.

"Henry, *no*."

"If that's what it takes to keep you safe." He said, then pivoted towards the door, the wooden floorboards protesting under his weight as he made his way back into the hall.

"I was kidding! I don't need a babysitter!" I yelled, but when he didn't reply, I mumbled a string of colourful curse words and ran after him. "*Henry!*"

But it was too late. I rushed into the hall just as the front door slammed shut, and then he was gone.

9

If I had ever needed proof of how incredible Carter Johnson was, and just how lucky I was to call him mine, that came when he took me out for dinner that night.

Agreeing to house-sit the cabin for spring break without asking him first had been a risk, and although I'd been hopeful, there was still that seed of doubt about whether he'd be willing to give up on Florida for me. Yet Carter had once again proven that any worrying was just wasted energy. Yeah, it kinda bummed him out not to go to Daytona with his friends, but he flat-out refused to even think about going without me.

"And let you go out to that cabin alone? What d'ya take me for?" He said as he poured us both a glass of water from the bottle the waiter had just set in the centre of the table. "Besides, skiing sounds fun. *Especially* when it ends with snuggling up in front of the fire with you."

He winked at me as he set the bottle back down, and I looked down quickly, pretending to focus on stirring my soup, since my insides were all twisted up thinking about how to tell him the rest. But there was nothing for it but to rip off the bandaid, so I sucked in a deep breath and blurted it out.

"Henry's coming too."

Looking up, I imagined seeing his jaw clenched, his soup spoon suspended in disbelief, but there was only a split second of silence before Carter raised his eyebrows in surprise and simply said, "Is he? Neat."

"I tried to talk him out of it." I offered in explanation, my words tumbling out in a rush.

Carter chuckled. "I'm sure you did, and I can imagine how Barton took that. But it's fine. It'll be fun! I didn't even know he was seeing anyone."

"Oh... um... he's not. It'd just be him."

I noticed him hesitate, his glass of water lingering against his lip for a moment, before he quietly said, "Oh." Then he sat back in his chair. "Really? That's, um... I mean, why?"

I gulped. "Well, um, I don't know, really. I guess because it's his uncle's place? He seemed a little put out that Dan didn't ask him first. And his mom smothers him when he's back. I think he's glad for the excuse for a break."

"The other side of the country isn't far enough?" Carter asked, and I met his eye, my stomach twisting, but I relaxed when I saw the smirk on his face. "Kidding. I get it. I love my brother, but when Noah comes home from college, it drives me insane. Can't wait for him to leave again to get my room back to myself."

"Me too." I smirked, remembering the time Carter had invited me to his place for the night, and his brother had come home without warning...

Clearly, he was also thinking about it, because he chuckled. "There's two bedrooms at this place, right?"

"Right."

"Then I'm good with it." He said, then went back to eating his soup.

The rest of the week seemed to crawl by, yet somehow still pass in the blink of an eye. I was really looking forward to being with Carter, but I had hardly spoken to Henry since Saturday. Last I heard, he was still planning on coming… and I was dreading it.

"She's good to go."

The slap of Carter's hand on his truck startled me, snapping me back to reality as he made his way up our driveway. Until then, I had been relaxing on the porch, enjoying the unexpectedly warm morning, and now I stood up to welcome him.

"She, like me or the truck?" I joked.

"Oh, definitely the truck. I know better than to presume you're ready to go, my love." When he reached me, he smirked, then bent to give me a quick kiss.

"Hey! I've been sitting here for, like, five minutes already."

He arched an eyebrow. "Is that so? Good thing I meant the truck then. It was quiet in the shop yesterday, so Owen let me work on her. Replaced the alternator. It was on its way out, so I thought I'd better fix it now. We don't wanna break down halfway to Chibblewood."

"Chib-*ou*-wood." I corrected him with a laugh, handing over my bag when he gestured for it. "That's probably a wise choice. I doubt there'll be a functioning garage out there if we need it."

"Ayuh… I checked out the place online. As did my mom. Which is why there's a weeks' worth of groceries back there. If we're stranded, at least we won't starve."

I chuckled. "You can get groceries in town. It's a ski resort, remember? A shitty one, but a resort nonetheless. From what I remember, it's quite a hike from the cabin, but it's doable if it's an emergency."

The rumble of an engine stopped his reply, and we craned our necks over the top of the truck to see Dan's silver Chevy emerging around the bend onto our street. I suppressed a groan as my eyes landed on it.

Did I seriously think Henry wouldn't show up? Not at all. But I couldn't help but hope, so when I saw the Chevy and the two guys inside, I clenched my fists so tight my nails dug into my palms.

If Carter saw me tense, he didn't say anything. Instead, once Henry hopped out of the car, he gave him a warm greeting and took his bag before stowing it with ours. While he was busy fastening the tarp to prevent anything from flying out during the drive, Dad walked out of the house and made his way over to us.

"You guys all ready to hit the road?" He asked.

I shrugged as Carter said, "Yeah, I think so."

Dan had joined us as well now, and he cleared his throat before saying, "I really appreciate you guys doing this. I know it's not exactly Palm Springs out there, so I owe you guys one. Just try not to kill each other, alright?" He jabbed a finger at Henry. "I'm looking at you, son."

Henry raised an eyebrow. "I'm just gonna have a nice week with my friends, Dad. What the hell do you think is gonna happen?"

"Yeah, that's what I'm worried about." Dan shook his head. "'Nice' has never quite meant the same to you as it does everyone else. And as much as I'd understand it, I'd rather neither of these two killed you off."

As I turned from giving Dad a hug goodbye, my gaze shifted to Dan. "I promise not to smother your son in his sleep, but I can't promise he won't come home with a few bruises. I'm only human, after all."

Dan just shrugged and laughed. "Fair enough. That's all I ask."

To give Henry some credit, he was pretty pleasant on the drive.

Well, pleasant when measured by Henry Barton standards, at least. All that really meant was he didn't grumble when Carter and I sang along – badly – to the road trip playlist we'd put together, but he didn't join in, either. I was grateful he made an attempt to talk to Carter, though, even if it was just about basketball. Maybe, *finally,* he was feeling a little guilty about the way he'd acted.

It was silly, seeing as we were gonna be together all week, but I felt a wave of disappointment wash over me when we passed the town sign, followed by the same stone statue that'd welcomed visitors for as long as I could remember – some ugly thing with huge antlers, that Henry used to joke must've been a tribute to the first mayor of the town, since Chibouwood was so off the grid it felt like a whole different universe where animals ruled.

Honestly, being in the truck for the past few hours had kinda felt like a whole other world, too. But I knew once we left, things would go back to normal. Back to tense and awkward. I wanted to soak up the last moments, knowing it'd be over soon.

Carter slowed down as we passed the statue, whistling through his teeth while he took it in. "Well, that's an, um... interesting way to welcome people. What's it meant to be? A werewolf?"

I looked at him and couldn't help but laugh. "You really think that's what werewolves look like?"

He quickly glanced at me from the corner of his eye. "Sure. I've seen movies."

"Of course." I laughed, shaking my head.

"Alright then, if you're such an expert. What is it?"

My mind drew a blank, even though I would have asked the exact same question when I was younger and first saw the hideous thing. "Um... I actually don't know." I admitted. "I'm sure Ryan told me once, but I don't remember."

"AHA! So it could be a werewolf, huh? I *knew* it!" Carter's grin was so contagious that it made me smile involuntarily, even as I rolled my eyes in mock annoyance. Ignoring Henry's snort, I just looked ahead as Carter parked the truck on Main Street.

"Okay, okay. You win." I laughed as he turned to plant an exaggerated kiss on my cheek.

'*Main Street*'. That was laughable. That's what the sign tacked to the wall of the end building said, but, honestly, the town looked like they abandoned it mid-construction. It barely qualified as a 'town'. Main Street was the only way to get through Chibouwood, a singular road splitting it in half. Townhouses lined both sides of the street, their grubby windows and weathered paint revealing their age. A few showcased signs of life and activity, but they had converted most into store fronts, leaving empty parking bays in front.

No one in their right mind was heading to Chibouwood for a shopping trip, but it had the basic stores you would expect for a ski resort. There was a grocery store that took over two units on one end of the high street, a coffee shop at the other, and a ski rental place across the road with a gaudy neon sign that proudly stated '*OFFICIAL PARTNER TO CHIBOUWOOD HEIGHTS*'. Alongside them were a couple of empty units that still held the signage for a pizza joint and a bakery, and some others with shutters down, so I couldn't tell what was inside, but judging by the rest of the amenities, I was pretty sure none of them were hiding a fancy restaurant. Still, Chibouwood Ski Resort had a certain appeal. I never got much choice about coming out here with the Barton's, because Dad was working and there was nobody to look after me during the summer breaks if Sierra was away visiting her brother, but honestly, I never used to mind that much.

A gentle tinkling sound caught my attention, and I looked around for the source, spotting metal wind chimes hanging above almost every door. A few had decorative gems that sparkled in the midday sun, while others had silver pinwheels and spinners like the ones used in gardens to scare birds away. Over the rooftops, the snow-topped mountains peeked out, and I smiled to myself, relishing the peacefulness that washed over me. It was always quiet during those summer visits, and today was no different. That's what was cool about Chibouwood. No luxury hotels with outdoor hot tubs and mountain views to lure in the usual crowd, just quaint, secluded cabins dotted around the edge of the forest.

With Carter's mom making sure we had everything we needed, we didn't need to buy groceries. However, since it wasn't even two in the afternoon, I thought it would be nice to take Carter to town and show him around. No one argued, but once we hit the sidewalk, Henry mumbled something about needing to stretch his legs and took off before I could respond, and I watched his retreating form until I felt Carter come around the bumper to stand beside me.

"Barton fed up with us already?"

I chuckled. "Probably. But that's his fault for gatecrashing. So, where d'ya wanna go first?"

Carter looked around and raised his eyebrow, rubbing his chin like he was thinking hard. "Hmm... I dunno. It's tough to decide when I have so many options."

"*Don't*." I playfully jabbed him with my elbow, chuckling. "That place down there might have the best coffee ever. You won't know until you try."

"Alright. Let me taste this 'best coffee ever', then. Lead the way."

"Hey! I didn't say—"

"Nope, too late. I'm expecting big things. No way to squirm out of it. Come on, let's go." He grasped my hand and entwined his fingers with mine, leading me down the street. After a few steps, though, he cleared his throat. "So, just now in the truck, you mentioned Ryan. He was your dad's friend, right? The one who passed away?"

The question caught me off guard, leaving me with a knot in my stomach and a lump in my throat. Carter noticed, his grip on my hand tightening.

"Sorry." He said. "I don't mean to pry. It's just... You never really talk about him. And I know you were really close. I just wanted to say, if you ever wanted to, then I'd love to hear about him. Okay?"

"Thank you." I shot him a quick, grateful smile. He gave a little nod, but didn't push it, and a peaceful silence came over us as we strolled down the quiet street.

My eyes wandered over the shop fronts as we passed, taking in the flyers displayed in the windows. Most of them were sun-faded and unreadable, like they'd been up there forever, but a couple were still clear: a torn flyer for last year's circus in the next town, and a 'FOR SALE' poster advertising a truck. It was the one below that that really caught my eye, though, the bright red, bold letters standing out amidst the sea of black and white.

MISSING

Local girl Lydia Kennedy and her boyfriend, William Porter, were last seen in Chibouwood on April 23, 2023. We urge anyone with information to contact the Berkton County Sheriff's Department.

I couldn't stop looking at the photograph that came with the brief write-up. They seemed to be our age - a girl with vibrant, curly crimson hair pinned to the side and flowing over her shoulder, flashed a wide grin to the camera, while the boy, who looked slightly older, affectionately placed his arm around her shoulders, a mischievous smirk directed at something just out of the frame. He wore a tuxedo, while she had on a beautiful, shimmering sea-foam green dress, with a corsage adorning her wrist. It reminded me of the photo I had of Carter and me, sitting on my nightstand.

"Do you reckon they found them?"

Carter's voice made me shift my gaze from the window, and I frowned at him before I saw he was looking at the same flyer I had been.

I took one last glance at the photo. "Let's hope so."

He let go of my hand and wrapped his arm around my shoulders instead, like he was trying to comfort me, so I let out a breath and put on a smile. "Anyway, coffee?"

He nodded, and we continued on to the shop.

10

Henry met up with us at the coffee shop about half an hour later.

I wanted us to reach the cabin before dark, so we didn't hang around for him to order anything. We did him a favour, really, because the coffee was as bad as the service, tasting as though it'd stewed in the pot all day. Although, that wouldn't have surprised me, since we were the only customers, and Main Street wasn't exactly bustling.

The girl serving started cleaning the counter the moment we sat down, eyeballing us as she did. We quickly got the hint she wanted us to leave, and the door had just shut behind us when we heard the tap of the plastic sign in the window flipping to 'closed'.

Thankfully, we didn't have much trouble getting to the cabin. The biggest challenge was finding the turnoff, since Sean had camouflaged it so well. He *really* didn't want anyone stumbling upon his place, so he had strategically placed branches and shrubs to hide the old wooden gate, making it difficult for even my heightened werewolf sight to locate. Then, after *finally* spotting it, we spent five minutes clearing away – and then replacing – the foliage to open the gate wide enough for Carter to drive through. From there, though, it was just a quick and easy ten-minute drive on a straight road until we saw it.

The place hadn't changed a bit. Even after six years, the dark oak timber logs remained vibrant, sheltered from the sun's bleaching rays by the dense canopy above. The little light that got through bounced off the small window in the bedroom where Henry and I used to sleep. I knew the other window was to the main bedroom, but the curtains were closed, so I couldn't see what was beyond.

The faint smell of weathered wood filtered through the air vents, intermingling with the natural, earthy fragrance of the surrounding forest, and it sent a wave of nostalgia through me. Sean hadn't done anything to bring his home up to date, preserving the timeless charm that had always defined it. Well, that's what Sierra used to say when Henry and I whined about the electricity being out, anyway.

Carter drove up to the side of the cabin, the engine purring to a stop. Henry didn't hesitate. He swung the door open and hopped out, and I followed him, now able to see the building more clearly.

The enclosed porch, covered with a fine mesh insect screen, held two rocking chairs that faced outward, towards where I knew the creek should be, though it remained hidden from view in the dense forest. Despite the slight breeze in town, the air here was so still that the chairs didn't move. Between them, a worn metal bucket sat on the floor, emitting the unmistakable stench of stale cigarette smoke and ash, making me scrunch up my nose and turn my head in search of fresh air. And then, I spotted something new. An open-air deck, almost hidden by overgrown shrubs at the forest's edge, emitted a faint electrical hum. The new generator that Dan promised me. At least he hadn't lied about it.

Inhaling deeply, I turned my back on the cabin and let the sweet scent of wildflowers, plants, and pine fill my lungs. The familiar odour of animal waste hung in the air, but I had become so used to it I hardly noticed anymore. Besides, being surrounded by creatures made the place feel even more familiar, like my forest back home.

A calmness washed over me, making me smile. Carter and Henry were getting along, and we had made it, and it was going to be an amazing week. If I kept thinking it, maybe it'd come true, and it'd be a nice memory of our time together when Carter left for college. When I was no longer in his life.

But right now, none of that mattered, so I pushed the thought aside as I turned to Carter, taking a step towards him, and...

Nausea rushed over me, my stomach sending a warning I hadn't yet processed. My body tensed, eyes flickering nervously, ears perked up for any unexpected sounds, but there was only the lively melodies of chirping birds and the constant hum of insects. Still, suspicion nagged at me, like a loose thread demanding attention.

What was I missing?

Shifting my position, I glanced over the entire length of the building once more. The windows, all firmly closed. The rocking chairs on the porch, undisturbed and motionless. Wisps of smoke rising from the makeshift metal chimney...

Realisation made my stomach lurch and stole the breath from my lungs.

Smoke from the chimney.

My mind raced with possibilities as I stared up, mesmerised by the smoke drifting ominously into the evening sky.

Did Sean forget to put out the fire? No, that was ridiculous. He left yesterday. It would've burned itself out already without someone to stoke it.

So, did he have someone else start the fire before we arrived? That didn't make any sense, either. If he had someone he knew well enough to ask, we wouldn't be here at all. He could have asked them to watch the place until he came back.

There was nobody in Chibouwood he'd trust enough. That's why he'd asked Dan and Sierra. Why *we* were here.

A low, menacing growl rumbled from my left, and I knew Henry had realised it, too. I glanced at him, but he kept his eyes fixed, unwavering, on the exterior wall of the cabin, closest to the porch. I briefly shut my eyes and focused on the internal sounds, desperately trying to recall the layout.

If nothing had changed, the living room would be on the other side of that wall, with the old sofa bed that Dan and Sierra always slept on, its mattress springs creaking whenever one of them moved.

Right on cue, the same creaking noise confirmed my suspicions. I held my breath, and in the stillness, I finally heard what Henry caught onto the moment Carter shut off the engine: the rapid thud of a pounding heart.

Someone was in the cabin. But it wasn't Sean.

11

No matter what I did, Henry remained oblivious to my attempts to get his attention. His eyes were fixated on a spot on the wall, his body tense and ready for action. Until I took a step towards the cabin. Then he growled again, his deep rumble echoing through the air, warning me to stay away.

I should've known he was still watching, somehow. He seemed to have a sixth sense specifically tuned to me.

He still didn't turn to face me, but he motioned towards the back porch. I nodded my agreement, before subtly gesturing towards the front door. A quick dip of his head confirmed his understanding. Entering through the front would effectively cut off their escape route, leaving them with no choice but to flee via the back porch... the exact spot where Henry would be waiting.

As plans went, it was far from perfect. I sensed multiple heartbeats, three to be exact, which made the thought of splitting up nauseating. The safest option was to stay together. However, with the dense forest providing ample hiding places, we couldn't afford to let them slip by us, because we'd have a tough job finding them again. And we'd have to find them, because it was way too suspicious that intruders had turned up at Sean's house the second he went out of town.

Cutting off their escape was the only choice.

I looked back at the door. The deck steps were so old and rickety, I knew they'd give me away immediately. I cringed at that, but soon realised it didn't actually matter. My job was to be the distraction, so the creaking of the steps was the least of my concerns, considering I was about to throw open the damn door.

I shook my head, took a deep breath, and prepared myself for what was about to happen. Then I took a step forward and...

"Any chance of a hand?"

Even without shouting, Carter's voice had a booming effect in the silence, making me jump. I had completely forgotten he was there, and now my stomach tightened as I turned to look at him. His eyebrows shot up as he peered at me from behind the truck bed, clearly surprised by my jitteriness.

How the hell did I forget he was there?

It didn't matter. The only thing that mattered was getting him *out*.

"Barton already scoping out the best bed, huh?"

As I approached him, Carter shook his head with a smirk, his eyes gleaming with amusement, completely oblivious to the terror that was surging through me.

Scrambling for a response, I quickly manoeuvred him behind the truck, hoping to shield him from view in case someone glanced out of the cabin windows. It didn't really matter, but it was all I could think to do.

"No. He's... um..." I whispered, then realised that seemed more suspicious. Chances were high they'd already heard us, and trying to stay quiet now only let them know *we* knew they were inside. "He's just..."

I trailed off, a flicker of an idea teasing my thoughts, suggesting that maybe this could work to my advantage. There really was no point trying to disguise ourselves now; it would only jeopardise my cover. And maybe it was nothing. Maybe there was a good reason three people broke into Sean's cabin, but was I ready to take a chance with Carter again?

That didn't need much deliberation. The answer was no. A firm, resounding no. Better safe than sorry - if it was nothing, then no harm done. But if it *was* something and Carter got hurt...

My skin prickled with sweat at the mere thought of it, but I ignored my rising panic. I needed to stay calm if I was going to talk him into getting back in the truck and driving away, even if only for a short while. Not only would it guarantee his safety, but it would also make it seem like I hadn't detected the intruders. If I thought there was someone lurking in the cabin, I wouldn't dare send my boyfriend away.

I cleared my throat when I noticed Carter looking at me curiously, realising how long I had been silent. "He's getting firewood. Gets so cold inside, it's best to do that straight away. But, um, Cart, I... I just realised I've lost my cell. I think I might've left it on the table at the coffee shop. Could you go back and check for me?"

The lie escaped effortlessly from my lips, and a wave of regret washed over me as I felt the bile creeping up my throat. They were becoming easier and easier to tell, and even if it was for his own good, I still felt suffocated by them.

He made a little pout with his lips, then let out a breath. "Of course. Not like I've been driving forever or anything." He rolled his eyes, but then a mischievous smirk appeared on his face as he caught me nervously biting my lip. "You're so freakin' lucky I love you, Stone. C'mon then, before it gets too late."

"Um…" I started, stealing a quick glance behind me to confirm that Henry hadn't moved. It would've ruined the plan if he had, but Henry was impatient, so it wouldn't have shocked me if he had taken matters into his own hands while I was stuck chatting with Carter. Thankfully, though, I could still detect him just past the porch - his breaths loud and huffy, urging me to hurry.

"It's just that I'm so tired." My heart was pounding when I faced Carter again, and my mouth got so dry I had to gulp before I could continue. "And I'm guessing you are too, right? I can stay here and get everything ready for when you come back. What do you think? If I tag along, we'll only have to start dinner when we get back, and you must be starving."

I hated lying to him. I also hated how easily he believed the lies. Carter told me once that he trusted me and didn't need to know all my secrets. He'd never made me doubt that. But it didn't make me feel any better. It made me feel worse, like I was betraying his trust.

Wasn't that exactly what I was doing? Even if it was to keep him safe, it wouldn't lessen the pain if it ever came out. For either of us. It's why I had to keep it hidden – my big secret. If he ever found out how much I'd lied to him, he'd never look at me the same. Even knowing it would come eventually, the thought of losing him was like a weight on my chest, but I held onto the hope that our friendship would endure. If he knew the whole story, he would have every right to hate me, and I just couldn't deal with that. It would destroy me.

"You want me to go back without you? Leave you alone out here?" He asked, glancing around at the trees that surrounded us. "If Barton's out picking up wood, let's wait 'til he's back. Then I'll go."

My chest tightened, but I tried to ignore it.

"It's almost dark. It's gonna be harder to find your way back then. And Henry won't be long, I promise. I'll make the place cosy ready for you getting back." I explained as I tried to usher him into the truck. When he still resisted, I forced a laugh. "What d'ya think is gonna happen, huh? The cabin's just over there. I'm gonna head straight inside and lock the door, okay?"

His eyes searched my face, and I bit the inside of my cheek to stop myself from squirming under his gaze. The seconds seemed to stretch forever as we watched each other, and I was all too aware of how exposed I was with my back to the cabin. An easy target. I kept my body still, but my fingertips lightly grazed over Carter's forearms, as if it might ease his concerns.

"Why does it feel like you can't wait to get me out of here?"

The sadness in his voice was impossible to ignore, and I could almost feel my heart shattering. "I-I'm... That's not... I didn't mean it like that. I just..." I trailed off, not sure what I wanted to say, so instead I sighed. "Y'know what, it doesn't matter. If I left it, then it'll still be there in the morning, right? Sorry I asked."

I turned away, hiding the fear in my eyes, as a wave of sickness washed over me. Now what was I going to do? I knew Carter wouldn't let me and Henry handle the intruders alone. He'd want to protect me. Which was why I needed him to *go*—

His groan cut off the thought. "No, no. *I'm* sorry. You're right. It doesn't take two of us. I'm just tired. But I'll go. Of course I will."

As I bit my lip anxiously, I quickly stepped aside, allowing him to access the cab of the truck. Relief flooded through me as he reached for the door handle, but then a sharp breath caught in my throat when he paused. His eyes locked onto something behind us, his brow arching, and I knew instantly what he'd spotted. The cloud of smoke rising from the chimney. It just took a moment to register, as it did with me, but I saw it reflected in the shine of his eyes, and my stomach dropped.

Almost instinctively, I pulled him close by the waist, positioning ourselves with his back toward the cabin and mine against the truck. "I'll make it worth your while."

His hand came to rest on the hood of the truck, just above my head, as he leaned down towards me, teasingly close to my lips but not quite touching. "You better."

It seemed absurd, given the circumstances, but I couldn't deny the heat that spread across my cheeks. "You're being pretty assertive, aren't you? I'm kinda into it." I joked, feeling a tingle of anticipation as I reached behind me to grasp the cold, metal door handle, then quickly sidestepped out of his way before I could lose focus. He grinned mischievously and then, finally, pressed his lips briefly to my cheek, leaving a tingling sensation of warmth before he climbed into the truck.

"Oh yeah? Noted." A chuckle escaped him as he took hold of the door handle, ready to pull it closed, but I called his name before he could.

"I love you. You know that, right?"

His eyebrow arched in surprise, while the corners of his lips twitched, fighting back a smile. "I'm only going to look for your phone, babe. I'm gonna be back before you know it."

"I know. But I do. And, um…" My voice trailed off as I felt the familiar flush of embarrassment creeping up my cheeks. "I just wanted to tell you."

"Well, ditto." He gave a playful wink and a salute before revving the engine, the pungent smell of gasoline lingering in the air as he zoomed off.

I watched his taillights until they disappeared into the sea of green, and then I turned, my legs feeling heavy and unsteady as I approached the porch. Since I assumed Henry was already watching, I didn't give any sort of signal to tell him I was in position and, as I climbed the deck, the creaking of the boards had my palms sweating. As the truck's engine noise faded, I could hear the intruders' voices getting softer, so I knew they had heard me, although my heart was thumping too loudly in my ears to catch what they were saying. If they were making a plan to attack me, I just had to count on Henry to have my back.

Sierra had told us about the key under the cigarette bucket, which I found odd because Dan said his brother-in-law was super paranoid about security. But I guessed being so far out in the forest, there wasn't much risk of getting robbed. At least, you would think that, but I suspected our current situation proved Sean's paranoia was justified.

Sierra's key, with the huge pink pompom chain, was in my jacket, but I left it there and pretended to look for the spare – *loudly*. My foot collided with the metal bucket, creating a resounding clang that echoed through the air as it toppled over and rolled towards the edge of the deck. I crouched down, pretending to reach for the key, only to retract my hand swiftly when I found nothing there, just as I had predicted.

A panicked whisper echoed from inside, immediately followed by a hushed '*Shh*!' from another voice. They knew the key wasn't going to be there. So did I. I was just playing my role.

"Huh." I muttered, my voice carrying enough volume for the trio inside to catch my words. "That's weird."

Taking a deep breath, I ran my hands along my pants to remove any dirt, and then I retrieved the bucket, placing it back between the chairs. It wasn't necessary. I was just stalling.

Reluctantly, I made my way back to the door, grabbed the handle, and then paused as if something had pulled my attention away. I waited a few moments, hoping to unsettle them. The fear in the air was almost tangible, its taste lingering on my tongue with each passing moment, and I wasn't even sure how much of it was coming from me.

A growl emanated from the rear of the cabin once again. Henry was getting antsy, so I knew I had to suck it up and get it done. Just *open the damn door!*

I inhaled deeply, feeling the air rush into my lungs, and nervously bit my lip before finally pressing down the handle... and the door opened with a soft whoosh.

12

The door swung inward, and the screech of worn-out hinges echoed around me. I couldn't help but cringe, even though they definitely heard me when I first stepped onto the deck. Probably since we first pulled up in the truck.

But, inside, there was nothing but a ghostly silence, interrupted only by the whisper of my footsteps and the distant rustle of their breath, coming from the darkness, deeper inside the cabin, where I knew the living area was.

A kitchen unit obstructed my view from the doorway, so I couldn't see much. That meant that, if not for my heightened senses, they'd have the upper hand, because the rapidly fading sunlight streamed through the doorway, lighting me up like a damn Christmas tree. But little did they know I didn't need to see them to know they were there.

Then it hit me. Even though a minute had gone by since I opened the door, nobody had budged. Nobody ran towards me or tried to throw down. They stayed huddled up in the living room, not saying or doing *anything*.

So, what was their plan? Were they just waiting for me to leave? Hoping I wouldn't notice them? The cabin was so small, there was nowhere to hide. Just two more steps forward and I would see them. They'd cut the lights – probably as soon as they heard the truck approaching – but all I had to do was flick the switch and they'd be the ones under the spotlight.

I didn't do that, because my only advantage was that they didn't know *I* already knew about *them*. If surprise was my only weapon, I had to use it. So, I stepped further into the kitchen, leaving the door ajar behind me. As I twisted my body around, the fireplace came into view, and I paused at the sight of the flames dancing, as if caught off guard. Although, I kinda was. Yeah, I saw the smoke and knew there had *been* a fire, but they were quick enough to switch off the lights when they heard us coming, so I thought the smoke rising from the chimney was from extinguishing it. Trying to cover their tracks. But it still burned, clearly forgotten about, and I had to fight to resist rolling my eyes at their stupidity.

I moved my hand towards the light switch, but halted inches away when I heard a faint rustling, my muscles tensing in anticipation. Still no one ran at me, and besides a squeak of terror from the darkness, the only discernible sounds were a sharp '*shh!*' and a subsequent harrumph, as though the second person had jabbed the first in the stomach to silence them.

I gulped, telling myself it was all part of the act, but truthfully, I wasn't sure it was *completely* theatrical. I could tell by their scents they were human, but human didn't mean harmless. Humans could be more dangerous than any species.

"Who's th—"

Before I could even finish the question, I felt a gust of wind rush past me, a blur of movement darting from the living area. I stumbled back out of its path, my hands instinctively reaching for something to hold on to, finding the door frame. It took a second to figure out they weren't aiming for me. Instead, they were charging right past me and making a beeline for the kitchen. Towards the back door.

Everything happened so fast. The two guys in the living area were yelling at their friend to stop, but he wasn't listening. I wasn't sure he could hear them at all. I'd seen that kind of panic before, in animals, when Henry and I were hunting. They always knew when it was game over for them. We would use the same tactic - Henry peeling off while I pursued it. And then, while it still had a glimmer of hope, thinking it might outrun me and get away, I'd send it straight into Henry's path. Just like this guy.

I rushed forward so I could see down the hall. As he reached for the handle, the door swung open, as if by itself. Henry's silhouette came into view, and the guy, noticing it as well, stopped dead in his tracks, his breath catching in his throat. For a moment, no one moved a muscle. All five of us were still. Silent. No one wanting to make the first move.

The guy caved first. He tried to backpedal, spinning on his heel. I darted forward, blocking his path back to the kitchen and trapping him between Henry and me.

The sound of Henry's knuckles cracking echoed through the entire cabin as he stepped across the threshold, his face twisted in a scowl. As soon as our eyes met, his jaw hardened, and his eyes sparkled with rage. Then, in a movement so fast I almost missed it, he grabbed the guy by his collar and slammed him into the wall.

Someone gasped. Maybe it was me, but I wasn't sure. It *was* shocking. The guy wasn't small, but Henry lifted him like he weighed no more than a rag doll, and as he held him, pressed against the timber wall, the guy let out a high-pitched squawk, triggering a chorus of shouts behind me. Voices clashed together, followed by the thumping of footsteps getting closer. Turning, my heart raced as I caught sight of the other two guys, emerging, finally, from the shadows of the living area.

Both looked around our age. One had shoulder-length dirty blonde hair, partially hidden by a baseball cap adorned with a college emblem I didn't recognise. He was a little taller than me, and his shirt clung to his body, hinting at a fit build without the bulky muscles of someone who spends all their time at the gym. But what really stood out was his scowl. It was so intense, almost rivalling Henry's, and I could practically hear the tension crackling between them.

When Baseball Cap growled and lunged, it took every ounce of self-control not to flinch. Henry was distracted with the runaway, so he didn't notice, and there was nothing he could've done if he had. All I could do was brace for impact... but then the third guy shot out his arm to stop him.

"*Don't.*"

I thought he was talking to me at first, and a retort flew to my lips, but I realised just in time that he wasn't even looking my way. He was looking at Baseball Cap. They locked eyes in a tense standoff, and I could see by Baseball Cap's expression he couldn't believe his friend seemed to be taking *our* side. I couldn't either, really, but I seized the opportunity to examine guy three while he wouldn't catch me sizing him up.

The first thing I noticed was he was pretty short. Much shorter than Henry and Carter, at least, but I doubted that would make a difference if it came down to a physical fight. One glance at his arms, the muscles straining against the tight sleeves of his tee, warned me not to underestimate him because of his small stature. The determined set of his jaw, and his buzz-cut hairstyle didn't make him look any less intimidating, either.

My stomach churned. Even with supernatural strength on our side, a fight with these three wouldn't be a walk in the park.

Before I could panic over that too much, Baseball Cap shouted again, this time at Buzz-Cut. "Are you serious? They fucking attacked Colton!"

It took me a second to understand what he was talking about. Colton had to be the runner's name. But once I realised, a snort of laughter burst from me. It sounded so out of place it even shocked me to hear it, and I immediately felt four pairs of eyes turn my way.

"*Attacked?*" I repeated. "Really? Your guy nearly knocked me out trying to run away after you *broke into our cabin*. What did you expect?"

A snarl curled Baseball Cap's lips as he hissed, "The place was deserted."

I sighed, setting my hands on my hips, where I could quickly throw them up if he came at me again. He didn't, so I rolled my eyes, hoping I seemed more confident than I actually felt. Trying to avoid a fight by making ourselves seem more threatening. "*No*. It was temporarily vacated. But, regardless, you think that's a good enough reason to commit a felony?"

He ground his teeth together as he glared at me. "Are you serious? Your psycho boyfriend is squeezing the life out of Colton, and you're talking to *us* about felonies? We should call the fucking cops right now. Before he kills him!"

I shrugged. "Go ahead. But FYI, in Maine, we have the right to use force to protect our property from trespassers. Even *deadly* force."

He clicked his tongue before saying, "How do we know it's even your place?"

My eyebrows raised in surprise at the question, and Henry sighed in exasperation behind me. "Oh for fu—" He began, but another voice interrupted him. Buzz-Cut.

"Jamie, *cool it*."

Jamie, the guy with the baseball cap, clenched his teeth again, but surprisingly didn't argue.

"It's obviously their place. She has a key." As Buzz-Cut spoke, his attention shifted to my hand, where I clutched the pink pompom keyring from Sierra. I couldn't remember taking it out, but there it was, the key clenched in my fingers like a blade. My face turned beet red as I quickly shoved it back into my pocket.

Buzz-Cut's gaze shifted, now focusing on my face as he continued. "We're so sorry for the trouble. Although... technically speaking, we didn't really '*break in*'." In the soft evening light that spilled through the doorway, I saw him raise a piece of metal and then casually toss it in my direction. Recognising it was the missing spare key, I quickly put it in my back pocket. "But I realise that's splitting hairs. Bottom line – we shouldn't be here. Any chance you could talk your boyfriend into releasing my buddy? It's kinda tricky to get out of your hair when he's stuck to the wall like that."

Henry snarled, gripping Colton and refusing to let him go. "Like hell I will."

He didn't bother correcting him on the 'boyfriend' comment, so I didn't either. It wasn't important right now. "*Not* until you've explained why you're here. But Henry won't hurt him. You have my word."

Henry's snort prompted me to shoot a stern look in his direction, silently scolding him. He only rolled his eyes.

"No offence, but we don't know you. Your *word* isn't worth much."

I took a deep breath and tried not to sigh as I looked back at Buzz-Cut. "Ah, the criminals are doubting *my* honour? Figures."

Wait, did I imagine it, or... did Buzz-Cut just *smirk* at that?

I glanced at Henry once more and gave a quick nod. The way he frowned at me, I could almost hear him saying *'hell no'*. As I shrugged my shoulders, Henry's jaw clenched, but he eventually released his grip on Colton's throat, placing his hand on his chest instead. He looked at me, almost daring me to ask for more, but I knew that if I asked him to release Colton completely, he would only *tighten* his grip out of pure spite. And I really wanted to avoid that.

Turning back to Buzz-Cut, I said, "There. Happy?"

This time, he *definitely* smirked. "Ecstatic."

Jamie's eyes grew wide with a mix of shock and anger as he faced his friend, scowling again. Or *still,* more like, because he'd had the same expression since I first laid eyes on him minutes before. "You can't be serious!"

Buzz-Cut's piercing stare silenced him instantly, before he said to me, "This is all just a misunderstanding. Truth is, we got lost out there and stumbled upon the place. We didn't mean to cause any trouble. Just let Colton go, and you can get back to your evening."

My body instinctively tensed as he reached into his pocket. He noticed, and when he pulled his hand out again, he did it slowly, holding his wallet up like I was aiming a gun at him. While holding it above his head, he opened it and pulled out a fresh twenty-dollar bill.

"Take this as a peace offering. We're really sorry for messing up your plans, so here's something to make it up to you. Consider it a small thank you for your... *hospitality*."

"Or a bribe to keep us from calling the cops?" I asked.

"I doubt twenty bucks would buy your silence. I'm guessing you'd want at least fifty. Am I on the mark?"

As a snort of laughter escaped me, I could feel the heat of Henry's glare piercing the back of my head. I ignored it.

"I just have one question. Before I decide about the cops, y'know." I crossed my arms as Buzz-Cut eyed me curiously. "If it was pure coincidence that you stumbled upon this place, why did he bolt when I showed up? Why not just tell us what's going on? We could've helped you out."

Buzz-Cut and Jamie shared a look. It was like they were talking without *actually* talking - just like Henry and I did sometimes. Whatever was going on, Jamie was clearly not happy. His scowl deepened, and he clenched his fists so hard I could smell the metallic scent of blood in the air from where his nails dug into his palms. But Buzz-Cut seemed unfazed, exhaling heavily before diving into his explanation.

"Colton's just a little edgy right now. He was only here because I convinced him, so when you showed up... I guess it freaked him out."

I took a little time to consider that before replying. "Why's that? Is he like, scared of the woods? 'Cause I hate to break it to you, but it's all around you out here."

His gaze shifted towards Jamie, a hint of uncertainty in his expression, but it didn't last long before he resumed speaking. "No, it's not that. It's just... look, he swears he saw something out there."

"I *did!*"

As I heard the voice behind me, I spun around in surprise, my eyes landing on Colton. *His* eyes widened in disbelief, as if caught off guard by his own words, and I couldn't help but notice Henry's knuckles turning white as his fingers clenched the front of the guy's shirt.

"What? What did you see?" Henry demanded, but Colton just gulped, and I knew that was all we were getting from him. He had retreated back into his shell.

"Some creature." Buzz-Cut said after a brief silence. "I have no idea what it was, but it scared him so much that he ditched his stuff and ran. We must've chased him for a mile before he'd slow down."

When he finished, my mind was racing with thoughts. Did I actually buy his story? I wasn't sure. The woods were teeming with animals that most people probably didn't know of, and these guys definitely didn't look like experienced explorers. Seeing a grizzly up close was absolutely terrifying even to me, and I'd practically *lived* in the wilderness my whole life. But running away from a monster and finding an empty cabin to hide in? That was a bit *too* convenient.

Still, if he was lying, there was only one way to know for sure. Henry would hate it. He'd also try to stop me. But I was hoping he'd realise it was the only option.

I'd made mistakes in the past, and the weight of them hung heavy on my shoulders. I had a tendency to trust people before they had proven themselves worthy of that trust. But I wouldn't make that same mistake again. I knew better now.

Besides, the forest was my kingdom. I was in control here. Nothing to be scared of. So, before I could talk myself out of it, I locked eyes with Buzz-Cut.

"Show me where."

13

"What exactly are you hoping to find out here? Proof I lied?"

We were in the forest, just Buzz-Cut and me, following a path that felt weirdly familiar, even though it'd been years since I was last in Chibouwood. It was the most direct way from the cabin, so Sean's scent was everywhere, but where the guys' trail continued in a straight line, his turned right, toward the smells of freshwater and algae. It triggered a memory of Sierra corralling Henry and me down this path when we were kids. The creek we used to bathe in must be nearby.

With the daylight already fading quickly before we set out, to say Henry had been unhappy about letting me go was one hell of an understatement. The only reason he hadn't blocked the door was because he knew I could track better than him, and the alternative was leaving me alone with the other two. It was either that or we *all* went searching for this so-called 'creature', but that'd just give them a chance to escape. Of the three, Buzz-Cut seemed like the best bad option, so Henry reluctantly agreed. Though not without threatening to kill his friends if anything happened to me, of course.

My eyes briefly darted to Buzz-Cut before settling back on the woodpecker diligently tapping at a tree just ahead of us.

"Why? Will I *find* proof?" I asked.

"No. Well, I mean... No promises you'll find proof either way, but definitely nothing to show I'm lying. But Colton..." He trailed off, and I saw him stumble and his eyes widen, like he suddenly realised what he had said. "I mean, I don't think he's *lying*. Something definitely freaked him out. But... shit, I dunno. Let's just say his imagination is pretty wild."

His words made me raise an eyebrow, but I said nothing. Maybe he didn't trust Colton, or maybe it was some kind of trick. Either way, if I wanted to know more, I wasn't gonna get it by pushing Buzz-Cut too far and making him shut down completely.

"What were you up to out here to get so lost, anyway?" I asked, steering the conversation in a safer direction.

I took a few steps before I realised he wasn't beside me anymore, and when I did, a shiver ran down my spine. I stopped dead, not daring to turn around, even though I knew, logically, I was being ridiculous. What did I expect to see? A gun, loaded and pointed at the spot between my eyes? Impossible. Henry made me pat him down before we left, so I knew he didn't have any weapons. I was just being paranoid, my nerves still on edge from the surge of adrenaline after stumbling upon them in the cabin.

Holding my breath, I pivoted to look for him, and...

No gun, of course. He was just staring at the ground, the toe of his boots kicking up the pile of leaves at his feet. I let out a breath.

"You okay?"

"Yeah. It's just... well, it's pretty embarrassing, honestly." His lips curled into a sheepish smile as he looked up again, and all it took was a raised eyebrow for him to let out a sigh. "Ugh, *fine*. Believe it or not, we were trying to get to the town. We rented a cabin right by the lake. Or *a* lake... Not sure if there's more than one.

It was the cheapest option we could find last minute. The listing called it secluded, but... *dang*. It was a miracle we found it in the first place. Jamie was right, *obviously*."

I watched expectantly as he unclipped a bottle from his backpack and guzzled down some water. After he had reattached it, he was quiet for a moment, and then shook his head.

"He said we should've gone to Cape Cod like everybody else. We're freshmen at Boston University. Did I mention that already?" He asked, but didn't wait for a response, brushing away his question with his hand before he started talking again. "Everyone seems to go to Cape Cod for spring break, but I wanted to do something different, y'know?"

I nodded. I knew it all too well. If you switched 'Cape Cod' for 'Daytona Beach', it'd be like the exact same problem me and Carter had for spring break, until Dan offered us the cabin.

"My brother... He's an 'outdoor enthusiast', shall we say. He passed through Chibouwood recently and said it was cool. I think he was more charmed by the girls he met out here, honestly, because otherwise... I don't really see the appeal." He shrugged as he met my eye. "No offence."

It took me a moment to understand what he was implying, but then I remembered he still believed the cabin was ours - Henry's and mine. That we lived there, together. I figured it wasn't worth correcting him, so I just waved it off and gestured for him to keep going.

"My point is, we aren't from around here, as you already guessed. But we wanted to hit the slopes and spotted the ski rental place on the way in. We were headed there when we got turned around, I suppose." When he finished, I said nothing, and we continued for a few yards in total silence, until he added, "We really didn't expect anyone coming home. It was locked up tight."

I snorted. "Yeah. There was a reason for that."

"Fair. But come on... spare key under the bucket? You're asking for trouble."

I wanted to argue, but I couldn't, because he was right. It was a dumb place for anyone to leave a spare key, let alone a werewolf who lived alone. *Especially* one who was so nervous to leave his cabin for a week that he agreed to three teenagers watching the place. So, instead, I met his comment with even more silence as I continued along the path.

A couple of minutes passed by before he spoke again. "My turn to ask a question. Or repeat one, anyway, since you didn't answer me before. What *do* you expect to find out here?"

I thought about it for a moment, but only one word came to mind: *nothing.*

That was my honest answer, but I couldn't very well admit that to him. I was only investigating because trusting strangers at their word had bitten me on the ass one too many times. I needed to know why they broke into the cabin, and to see for myself what – if anything – sent Colton running, because I wasn't about to take Buzz-Cut's word for it.

"Your friend's bag, for a start." I responded. It was the only thing I could think of, and, when I really considered it, it wasn't actually a bad idea. "You said he left it behind when he ran. If there's food in it, it could attract something."

"Like a wolf?"

I suppressed a smirk and settled for a shrug. "Maybe. But I was thinking more along the lines of mice, 'cause they'll attract snakes.

Whatever your friend saw, I'd rather not leave anything out here that doesn't belong."

Maine didn't have any venomous snakes, but I took a risk that he didn't know that, and I knew I got away with it when he didn't argue. Instead, he asked, "So, you don't believe Colton saw anything?"

"No. I, um... well, I believe he *thinks* he saw something."

His laughter erupted with such force that it sent the birds nesting in the trees above us scattering into the sky. "That's just a polite way of saying '*hell no*'."

I didn't deny it. Instead, I just stayed quiet as we neared the area where Colton had abandoned his backpack. I knew we were getting closer because, even mingling with the usual smells of the forest, their trail was getting more potent by the second. Still, if I let my mind wander, it would be easy to veer off onto the wrong trail, so I had to stay focused.

I slowed down, allowing Buzz-Cut to get a few steps ahead as I discreetly tilted my nose up and took a slow, deliberate breath. Looking around, everything seemed normal, with only a faint hint of a coyote, so weak that it had probably been hours since it had passed through. No trace of a bear, either...

"It's just over here, I think." Buzz-Cut said, turning to glance at me over his shoulder. "I recognise that tree."

I raised my eyebrow. "You mean the one that looks exactly like every other tree we've passed on the way here?"

"True. But there's also the X that I carved into it while we were waiting for Colton to finish peeing." As I threw him a look, I saw his cheeks tinge pink. "What? You gonna yell at me for vandalism?"

"Normally yes. But right now, it's actually very helpful." I reluctantly confessed.

His eyes flickered with doubt for a moment, before a wide grin spread across his face. Then, without another word, he veered from the path towards an obviously trampled section of bushes. I trailed behind him into a clearing, my eyes landing almost immediately on the rucksack abandoned near the base of a tree across from us.

I motioned towards it. "Colton's?"

"Yup." Making his way to the tree, he reached out and grasped it, then lifted it up as if it were a trophy. "So I guess we're good now. This shows I wasn't lying, right?"

"Does it, though? 'Cause I don't see any paw prints from where I'm standing. So, what spooked your buddy? The bogeyman?"

Buzz-Cut opened his mouth to say something, but then his eyes darted to the ground, as if expecting to see some kind of print, and his lips clamped shut when he didn't. He was quiet for a moment, his eyes narrowing as he locked his gaze on me.

"Listen, I don't know what to tell you, but I didn't lie. Do you really think I'm out here, trudging around this damn place when I'm freaking tired just to... what? Mess with you? I told you what went down, and we were gonna take off. You could've just pointed us in the right direction and sent us on our way."

The irritation in his voice was unmistakable, making the corners of my mouth twitch, and I had to bite my lip to suppress a smirk. "Sure, I could've. But I had to make sure there wasn't a flesh-eating monster at my doorstep. It's happened before, y'know. Not in Chibouwood, but nearby. You ever heard of the Maine Mutant? The Turner Beast?" I let out a sigh as he shook his head. "Look that up later. And you won't believe how many Bigfoot sightings there've been in these mountains, too. When someone says they saw something out here, better be on your guard."

Silence stretched out for what felt like an eternity, and I was about to crack when he narrowed his eyes. "You're messing with me."

"Maybe a little."

"And here I was thinking you were the nice one. Maybe I should've stayed back with the big guy."

"That was your first mistake," I said as I turned away, back towards the main path. "I never claimed to be nice, and you can't always judge by appearances. The Maine Mutant thing is true, though. Turned out to be a wolf-dog mix that was going after pets and farm animals. People were convinced it was a demon."

"People are dumb."

"I don't think so. They're just scared of things they can't make sense of, you know? Then their imagination takes over."

"You mean, like Colton, right?" He asked, and when I nodded, he added, "You know, he's been totally obsessed with these weird stories lately. Legends and things. I guess it got into his head, huh?"

"Yup." I agreed. "He was probably a bit dehydrated, too."

In my peripheral vision, I saw Buzz-Cut shaking his head. "Come on, give us a little credit, will ya? We're not total morons. We all brought our water bottles. Colt drank so much, he even had to refill his. He definitely wasn't dehydrated."

At his words, I froze, feeling my muscles tighten, before I slowly shifted my gaze towards him. "What do you mean he had to refill it?"

His own bottle was in his hand again, but he just held it, his eyebrows furrowing in confusion. "Well... he drank it all, so he filled it up from a pond. It was clean. No fish or anything." The sound of liquid sloshing inside the bottle echoed in the air as he brought it to his lips. My arm acted on its own accord, shooting out and knocking it from his grasp. It hit the ground with a loud thud, causing water to splash out from the open lid, and he quickly jumped back. "What the *hell*?!"

"You guys really don't know jack, do you? You can't just drink water from a pond without purifying it first! Do you have any idea what's in it?"

He drew in a breath. "Well, *that* was water from your damn kitchen, genius. I refilled mine when we got there."

I felt a blush spread across my cheeks. "Oh. Well... sorry, I guess. But we gotta go back and make sure your friend doesn't get a fever. He'll probably get sick, but there's not much we can do now. You definitely didn't have any?"

"Scouts honour."

I glared at him. "Well, that's something, at least. I don't wanna have to carry you if you pass out."

He let out a snicker, but he quickly stifled it, transforming it into a cough when he caught my expression. "Oh, you're for real? Thank God I didn't, then, 'cause I don't think you'd make it very far with me on your back, little one."

"Little one?" Irritation seeped into my voice, giving it a sharp edge. "You're assuming I couldn't do it? Well, maybe I'm stronger than I look."

"Doubt it."

I was about to fire back when a sound in the distance made me freeze once again.

Was that..?

"Madison!"

Yup. *Shit.*

"CARTER?" I cupped my hands around my mouth, trying to make my voice travel far enough for him to hear, although I doubted it'd do any good. His voice had sounded close enough, but that must've just been the forest skewing it. Most likely he'd just gotten back to the cabin, seen I wasn't there, and set off to find me. I had hoped to be back before him, with the guys gone, so he wouldn't have a clue about anything, but I guessed that ship had sailed. At the very least, though, I expected Henry to stop him from following me if I wasn't.

Jerk.

Frustration bubbled up inside me when no reply came, and I cursed under my breath, picking up the pace as I hurried towards the gap in the bushes that led back to the path. I'd almost forgotten about Buzz-Cut until his thunderous footsteps echoed behind me.

"You hear something? Is it a bear?" He asked, panting slightly as he caught up.

"Huh? Oh. No. Just my boyfriend, but I'd rather he didn't come looking for me and get himself lost as well. It's been a long enough day already."

Buzz-Cut whistled. "I thought he was playing guard dog to Colton and Jamie. He doesn't trust you very much, does he?"

"Is that another assumption?"

"That depends – is it wrong?"

"Yes, actually. *Henry* trusts me just fine. It's strange guys who break into our cabin he doesn't trust." I shot him a sharp glare from the corner of my eye. "Also, *he* isn't my boyfriend. We're just friends."

He said nothing for a few steps and, when he finally opened his mouth, I wished he hadn't. "Huh. Does *he* know that?"

When I gave him a hard stare, he responded with a deep, throaty chuckle. "I'm just saying... you know how it looks, right? He's obviously into you. And you're out here in the middle of nowhere, alone in a cabin with him? Talk about leading a guy on."

I felt heat rise in my cheeks once again, a mixture of anger and embarrassment, as I stopped and rounded on him. "*Excuse* me? Not that I have to justify myself to you, but we're not alone here. My boyfriend just had to run to town for something. And now he's back."

"Sure, sure." He said, a smirk playing on his lips, accompanied by a knowing wink.

I opened my mouth to argue, but the smarmy look on his face made my blood boil, and all that came out was a screech of frustration. He threw his head back and laughed, the sound seeming to echo through the trees, following me as I spun around and stormed away.

"Oh c'mon. I was kidding!" He called after me, but I ignored him. I just wanted to get back to the cabin, to see Carter. Plus, maybe I kinda wanted to prove to Buzz-Cut he was real, that there was nothing going on between me and Henry. I knew it was ridiculous. Who was this guy? He was no one. I didn't even know his name. But it mattered to *me*. *Carter* mattered to me.

I practically ran along the trail, and he soon stopped calling after me. I wasn't even sure if he was trying to catch up. All I knew was I wanted to put enough distance between us that I wouldn't have to see his stupid smirk anymore.

14

"It's Ansel, by the way."

I cast a sidelong glance at Buzz-Cut, my gaze lingering on the sweat droplets that dotted his forehead, eyes narrowed.

I *did* manage to escape him, at least for a little while, but his racing heart and heavy breathing made me feel guilty enough to slow down and let him catch up. Not enough to make small talk, though, so we had been walking for about ten minutes without speaking, and I was completely okay with that. There was a part of me that thought about picking up the pace to prove a point, but he would soon see I wasn't breaking a sweat, and that would only lead to questions. Instead, I let him walk beside me, while ignoring his presence completely.

"What?" I blurted without thinking, then silently scolded myself for engaging with him.

"My name. It's Ansel. I know you didn't ask, and I would be mad, but I didn't ask yours either. Didn't really have time to introduce ourselves while we were cowering from your bodyguard, huh?"

I clenched my teeth, then said, "Or all the unwanted psychotherapy afterwards?"

Even though I was looking straight ahead, I could feel him staring at me. I fought against the urge to glance over my shoulder, and after a pause, he let out a sigh. "Did that actually bother you? Because it was a joke. But if it did, then I'm sorry."

"I think that was the least genuine sounding apology I've ever heard."

"I mean it, seriously. Cross my heart. I mean, what do I know, right? I just met you, so I obviously misread the vibes between you."

I shot him a fierce glare. "There's no *'vibe'* between us. He's my friend, and he was just looking out for me. You guys *broke in*, remember?! And Colton tried to run, which, let's be real, was kinda sketchy."

"He's got a fever from that gross pond water. Not thinking straight."

A snort of amusement escaped me. "Maybe. But we didn't know that then. Neither did you."

"Well, you know... Oh, look, we're getting off track. Can't we just let bygones be bygones and start over? Tell me your name." As I glanced sideways, I caught a quick glimpse of him, a sly smirk playing on his lips. "Or I could just keep calling you *'cutie-with-the-brown-eyes'*, like I've been doing in my head. But something tells me your kinda-sorta-not-really boyfriend wouldn't be cool with that."

Despite its ridiculousness, a blush crept up my cheeks, but I brushed off what was obviously a poor attempt to flirt his way into my favour. "My *friend's* name is Henry. And as for the other... I've just been calling you *'Buzz-Cut'*."

His sudden burst of laughter echoed through the forest, causing a squirrel to scurry from the undergrowth and up a nearby tree.

"*Ouch*. I always thought I was kinda decent looking, but..." He trailed off while shaking his head. "Seriously, that's all you noticed? Not my forest green eyes, or my devilishly handsome looks?"

"I didn't mean... It was just the first thing I noticed, so it stuck. I didn't mean to offend you."

"Don't worry, I'm not upset. Feeling a bit rejected, maybe..." I cast a quick glance his way, hoping he wouldn't notice, but he responded with another laugh. "I'm *kidding!* You're even cuter when you blush, you know? But if you don't wanna tell me your name, I guess I'll have to stick to the nickname, *cutie-with-the-brown-eyes*. Or maybe just *'C'* for short. Whaddya think?"

"I think you're an idiot." I bit my lip to stop a smile, not wanting him to see it. "But it's Madison."

"Madison." He repeated slowly, as if he enjoyed the sound of it, like the name was special, not one of the most popular in the country.

Unsure of what to do, I continued walking, only realising he had stopped when I glanced back and saw him wiping his palm on his pant leg. He came closer, reaching out his arm to me. I raised an eyebrow in surprise, but eventually accepted his gesture, and he beamed as we clasped hands.

"It's a pleasure to meet you, Madison. And thank you for being such a gracious host, letting us into your home."

"Huh, didn't realise I had a choice." I couldn't resist rolling my eyes. "Luckily, it's not actually *my* home, so maybe I'm not as upset as I could be."

There was a second of stillness, like he was thinking about what I'd said, and then his eyes widened in disbelief, nearly popping out of their sockets. "Whoa, whoa, whoa. Hold up. Are you serious?

After all the crap you gave us for breaking in, you guys did the same thing?!"

"What? No!" I shook my head. "That's not what I meant. The cabin is Henry's uncle's, and we're just watching it for him. You really dodged a bullet not getting lost yesterday, by the way. If Sean had found you? He's not very welcoming to trespassers."

"If he's anything like his nephew, then I believe you." He said, relaxing a little at my explanation. "But, come on, who could blame him? What kind of jerk trespasses on someone else's property?"

"Beats me." I chuckled, and he responded with a smirk.

It was only when I heard the roar of an engine echoing through the trees that I realised how close we were to the cabin. It took a moment for my brain to register the familiar rumble, and then I heaved a sigh as I realised it belonged to none other than Carter's truck. Ansel stopped abruptly, his brow furrowing.

"Who's that?"

"My boyfriend." I said, shaking my head.

What was Carter thinking, trying to follow me in the truck? He knew that, past the dirt road to the cabin, no car would make it through the dense forest. He'd barely get a few feet before he'd get stuck, tyres in the mud or the bumper in a ditch, and then what? Who knew if we'd get a tow truck around here to pull it back out. And Henry should've known better than to let him try.

My fists clenched tightly as I quickened my pace, while calling to Ansel over my shoulder. "We're almost there, so I'm gonna go ahead before he does something dumb. Just follow this path, okay? It's so easy, even you can't mess it up." Then I darted off, leaving his profanity-laced retort echoing in the air behind me.

The truck's engine sounded steady as I hurried along the trail, a reassuring rumble that made me feel more confident, because it meant Carter hadn't gotten himself into any trouble yet. A couple of minutes later, my eyes finally caught sight of the cabin amidst the thick foliage. Relief washed over me, and I exhaled, feeling the tension melt away. Then I reached out, my fingers grazing against a branch, its rough texture tickling my skin, and...

A flash of red caught my eye, standing out against the backdrop of the clearing, about half a mile down the dirt path connected to the highway. I blinked and squinted, trying to see the outline, but the thick canopy quickly hid it, and it disappeared again. But the rumbling grew louder and louder until it was deafening, and then, out of nowhere, the truck emerged from the shadows.

Carter pulled over by the cabin, beaming a smile and waving at me through the windshield. I waved back to him while making my way to the driver's side door.

"I made it to the coffee shop just in time." He said as he jumped down from the cab. "But your cell wasn't there. And that girl behind the counter was *not* happy to see me again, let me tell you."

It took me a sec to get what he meant, but then I remembered the lame excuse I made up to get him out of the way, and guilt coursed through me.

"Oh, um—" I coughed to clear my throat when my voice came out croaky. "I actually found it. Sorry. I must've dropped it when we got here. I spotted it on the ground after you took off. I tried calling you to tell you, but... no bars here. Are you mad?"

"You mean to tell me I had to deal with Little Miss Sunshine back there, and it was all for nothing?" His eyes narrowed, and I felt a knot in my stomach as he stared at me for what seemed like forever. Finally, he sighed, and I glimpsed a smile in his weary eyes. "Nah. Glad you got it back. I should've looked around the truck before I left, but oh well. I did as you asked. You owe me now, and I'm expecting to be paid in full for my services." He winked playfully. "Also, I gave your dad a heads up that we arrived safely. Just in case we can't send a message from here."

"That's... not the direction I thought that conversation was going. But thanks for doing that. All of it." I rose on my tiptoes, leaning in to place a gentle kiss on his cheek, but he turned just in time, and I felt the warmth of his smile press against my lips. I couldn't help but giggle as I took a step back. "Cheeky. But I guess you deserve a kiss."

"Do I also deserve dinner? 'Cause I'm starving." He declared, straightening up and turning towards the driver's door to close and lock it.

Shit. Shit, shit, shit...

"Um..." My throat felt dry as I swallowed hard. When he faced me again, I anxiously bit my lip, and he responded with a deep groan.

"You're joking, right? Stone, we had a deal! What've you been doing while I was gone? Redecorating?"

He followed it up with a laugh, but I saw a hint of seriousness in his eyes. It wasn't exactly an accusation, but close enough, and it made my stomach churn.

Avoiding his gaze, I nervously tugged at the bottom of my jacket. "It's kind of a long story..."

"Okay... Mads, what's wrong?" The moment those words escaped his lips, his entire demeanour shifted, and he pulled me closer, his hands firmly gripping my waist. His eyes widened with a mixture of shock and curiosity as he glanced behind me before looking back at my face, and I watched his expression change as he realised. "Hold up. Why were you coming from over there? Were you out in the woods? Where's Henry?"

I was about to explain, but then his words hit me like a ton of bricks. "Henry? He's... he's inside, isn't he? Didn't you speak to him?"

"No... I just got back, like, right now. Why? *Should* I have talked to him?"

I didn't respond right away. Instead, I twisted my head towards the cabin, immediately catching the unmistakable sound of Henry's growl, silencing the other two guys.

But if he was still inside, if nothing was wrong, then what...

"You weren't looking for me?" I blurted, the words tumbling out before the thought had a chance to fully form.

"In the truck?" Carter asked, his brows furrowing in confusion. "Not likely. Plus... hold up — did you say *looking* for you? Why would I need to go looking for you? What's going on? Are you okay?" His voice kept getting louder and sharper with each question, and I could sense the panic radiating from him.

Crap. I was totally screwing this up, and I had to get it together before he freaked out. Obviously, there was a logical explanation – I just hadn't thought of it yet. It was probably just a bird, its chirping somehow sounding exactly like Carter calling my name... Or maybe it was just the wind whistling. I was so worried about Carter getting to the cabin before me, it made sense I heard something and convinced myself it was him. No biggie.

I inhaled deeply, feeling the crisp air fill my lungs, and then I looked him in the eye, trying my best to muster a smile. "I'm fine! We just had a little situation, and—"

The crunch of leaves behind us interrupted me mid-sentence. Carter's body became even more tense, his breathing quickening. Before I could add anything else, he stepped in front of me, his hand softly guiding me against the truck.

Despite his stocky frame blocking my view, there was no mistaking who was approaching. Carter's body language said it all - his shoulders stiffened, and his hand immediately moved to my hip, even though he had his back turned to me, shielding me. Guilt surged again, but I didn't have time to worry about it, so I shoved it aside and dodged past him to see Ansel, his silhouette framed by the trees. When he saw me, he nodded hello.

"Guess you weren't lying about him." He said. "So, you're the boyfriend, huh? I've heard a lot about you."

Carter's piercing gaze burned into the back of my head for a long moment, until he replied, "Sorry, but I can't say the same."

Ansel's eyes narrowed as he glanced between the two of us, and I knew he could feel the tension, but before he could say anything that might make it worse, I jumped in.

"This is Ansel." I blurted, pointing my arm towards Buzz-Cut, as if there was any doubt about who I was referring to. I spun around to face Carter again, my heart pounding in my chest. "I tried to tell you there was a situation. And... well, we need to talk."

"*Ayuh*." He said, licking his lips slowly, the calmness in his tone only making me feel worse. "I think we do."

15

I waited until Ansel had disappeared inside, the sound of the door clicking shut behind him, before I turned my attention to Carter.

"That wasn't what it looked like, I promise. He just—" Breaking off mid-sentence, I glanced back over my shoulder, suddenly very aware of our proximity to the cabin. Then I bit my lip and gestured to the truck. "Should we…"

He nodded, his hand turning the key in the lock, and then he held the door open for me to climb into the cab ahead of him. Once we were inside, we had some privacy, but Henry could still eavesdrop if he really wanted to. It wasn't ideal, but it was the best I could do, so I sucked in a breath, held it for a second, and then I told Carter everything.

Nearly everything, anyway. I skipped the part about already knowing someone was inside when I told him to leave, because there was no way to spin it that wouldn't make him furious. By the time I finished, I was out of breath, and Carter's eyes seemed ready to pop out of his head.

"Anyways, we were coming back with Colton's backpack when I heard you, and now we're here."

I laughed nervously as I finished my story, my eyes bouncing between Carter and the window, feeling butterflies in my stomach as I waited for him to make eye contact. But he didn't reply, and the air was so thick it felt like it was suffocating me, making me wonder if he even heard me at all.

"Carter?" I prompted, my voice trembling. He just nodded and mumbled, "yeah," before the silence took over again.

That proved it – he was mad at me, and it totally threw me off, coming from Carter. He didn't get mad. Not at *me*. And now it felt like there was this huge wall between us, and I had no clue how to get over it. Before I could even try, though, he cleared his throat, gave my hand a quick squeeze, and then hopped out of the truck, leaving me staring after him.

Truthfully, I was almost relieved, because it felt like I could finally catch my breath. But that feeling didn't last long. Not when the reality set in, which was that I knew him walking away didn't mean everything was fine. It was just his way of saying he'd drop it, if that's what I wanted. He wouldn't push. But that wasn't fair, because he was upset, and I knew that if the tables were turned, he wouldn't just brush my feelings under the rug. I shouldn't either, regardless of if he was offering me a way out. He came back to find me with some random guy in the forest, so I couldn't blame him for being upset. It wouldn't be fair to just act like I didn't see it.

My eyes stayed fixed on him as he made his way to the deck, the sound of creaking boards echoing in the quiet. As he propped his elbows on the weathered wooden fence, flecks of old paint chipped off and floated to the ground. Seeing him, his usually soft features now hardened, made my stomach twist, but I followed him anyway.

"Carter," I said as I walked closer, but he didn't even glance my way. "I swear, nothing happened with Ansel. I just needed to be sure their story checked out. That's all."

"I know, Mads. It's not that. It's just..." He sighed, his gaze fixated on the swaying branches of the trees across from the deck. But I didn't miss the way his grip tightened over the fencing and his knuckles turned white until, with a sharp shake of his head, he released his hold. "Nothing. Forget it, okay? I'm just tired."

I let a beat of silence pass between us before I said, "No, it's more than that. You forget how well I know you, Carter Johnson." He laughed when I nudged him, but there was no genuine amusement behind it, so I sighed and carried on. "If it's about Ansel... Henry wasn't thrilled about the situation either, but we had no choice. If you'd come back to an empty cabin, you'd have freaked out, wouldn't you? It just made more sense for him to stay put, since there were two of them. You know he wouldn't have let me go if he thought Ansel was gonna do anything. Henry had my back the whole time. No doubt about it."

He snorted. "Yeah. He always does, doesn't he?"

And bam, there it was. The crux of it. It was like a punch in the gut, and all I could do was stare at him in disbelief, wondering if I actually heard what I thought I heard, because the voice... for sure, that was Carter's. But the words? The swipe at Henry? That *wasn't* him. At least, I'd never seen that side of him, and I had no clue how to react. *Again.*

He seemed surprised by it himself, his eyes widening as he turned to face me. "Shit, Mads. I... That's not what I meant. I'm glad he was here. Of *course* I am. If you were alone..." He shuddered. "It's just that..."

"What?" I demanded, unable to keep the frustration from my rising voice. He heard it and cringed, gripping the fence tightly again as he stared at the trees.

"I should've been here! *I* should've been the one looking out for you. But instead, I was hunting around under the tables of the damned coffee shop for a phone that wasn't even there. It feels like I'm never there when you need me. If anything had happened to you..."

He couldn't even finish the sentence. His voice faltered on the last word and, in an instant, my anger vanished. I opened my mouth to speak, to reassure him, but there was a lump in my throat, and all that came out was a garbled mess with no actual distinct words. So, instead, I inched closer and nestled my face against his shoulder blade, my arms going around his waist. He tensed at first, but only for a second, before his body relaxed, and he melted back into my embrace.

I wasn't sure how long we stayed like that, but it felt like it ended too soon when he mumbled, "I'm sorry."

"I know. Me too."

He twisted so he was facing me instead, then gently placed his hands on my hips. "I mean it. It's just... when I think about what could've happened..." As he took a deep breath, his grip tightened, and he briefly closed his eyes. "I shouldn't have left. I should've gone in myself and checked it out. Made sure it was safe. I know you don't need me, that you can take care of yourself, but I'm your boyfriend, Mads. Your dad trusts me to take care of you, and I wasn't here." He paused again, glancing away, before he added, "But Henry... he never misses a thing, does he? And I feel like I'm always playing catch up to him."

"Carter, that's not—"

He shook his head, his hair ruffling in the breeze. "Please, just don't, okay? You did nothing wrong. You *or* Henry. I just..." He let out a shaky breath. "I know it's selfish, but... *ugh*. If you insist on getting yourself into trouble, then I want to be the one who saves you sometimes."

"Carter—" I started, but he cut me off again with a groan.

"Mads, please. I'm begging you. Admitting this is hard enough without you trying to pacify me like I'm a toddler throwing a fit. I just wanted to explain why I was such a jerk. Just explaining, not making excuses. So, now that's done, how about we just make out instead?"

The suggestion was so out of the blue that I burst out laughing. But it worked like a charm in diffusing the tension, so I wrapped my arms around his neck and pulled him closer to me. "As tempting as that is, I'm not sure that's the healthiest way to wrap this up. We should probably talk more."

He shrugged and kissed the tip of my nose gently. "I'm tired of talking. I just want to kiss you."

His breath, warm and smelling faintly of coffee, caressed my face as he leaned in, but right before our lips touched, I stuck out my tongue and pulled away. Our eyes met, and his mouth fell open in surprise, while I couldn't suppress the mischievous grin that spread across my face.

"Oh, that's how you wanna play it, huh?" He asked while shaking his head. But before I could answer, he lunged at me, his fingertips grazing my arm before I dodged out of reach, leaving him groaning in frustration.

I laughed and carefully backed down the porch steps, putting more space between us. "That all you got?"

"You just wait, Stone." When he spoke, his eyes sparkled with a promise that made me almost eager to surrender. *Almost.*

"Oh, I'm waiting." With a playful wink, I spun around and sprinted to the end of the truck, shivering as the cool metal pressed against my skin when I grasped the side panel. Seconds later, he was there too, holding onto the opposite side. He took a quick glance at me, then started checking out the pickup. He was trying to figure out which way I'd go, his eyes quickly scanning the two paths, hoping for a clue about what I would choose. Left or right.

A smirk played on my lips. "Huh. Would ya look at that? Deadlock."

"Ayuh. Sure seems that way." His eyes narrowed as he fixed his gaze on me, like he was trying to read my mind. Then he moved to the right, and I followed suit, creating a distance between us, much to his annoyance. I waited until he took another step... and then I bolted.

I was just steps away from the porch when a soft rustling sound in the undergrowth made me pause. I glanced in that direction, my eyes darting back and forth, straining to catch even the slightest twitch, but the bushes were still again. It must've been a squirrel or something. Satisfied, I continued forward, although I purposely slowed down my pace to give Carter a chance to catch up. Our spontaneous game of tag had been a welcome distraction from *that* conversation, but he had suggested an even better alternative, and now that the tension had faded, I was more than happy to comply.

In an instant, his hands were on my hips, pulling me away from the steps. I laughed as he twirled me around, the world blurring around me. "Gotcha!"

"Oh no! Whatever will I—"

At a blur of movement in the forest, my breath hitched. I glanced past Carter to the trees as goosebumps rose on my skin, although I couldn't explain why. There was nothing there except for the rustle of the wind.

"Everything okay?" Carter leaned in closer, his voice right in my ear as he strained to see what had caught my attention.

Reluctantly, I tore my gaze away from the forest and locked eyes with him. "Yeah. Just thought I—"

And that's when I saw them, and a shiver ran up my spine.

Huge crimson eyes, still and unblinking. Staring right at me.

16

A chill ran down my spine, and the world seemed to fade into the background, leaving me all alone with those eyes. Lost in their unblinking stare.

Fear rose in my chest, skin prickling as the hairs on the back of my neck stood up. My wolf woke up, too, hackles rising, as if she sensed something was wrong, but couldn't tell me what. There was probably a logical explanation, but I'd have to take a closer look to be sure. After all, I'd ignored my gut feeling once before, and both Carter and Ryan had paid the price. I would *not* make the same mistake again.

My mind raced frantically through all the possibilities. Could it be a rabbit? Even as I thought it, I knew that was ridiculous. Sure, some had red eyes, but this was on a whole other level: two massive, unwavering orbs that seemed to peer into the depths of my soul.

An owl, then? The porch lamp cast a dim glimmer of light across the lawn, just enough to illuminate an owl's eyes if one was hanging around. I'd spotted a few of them in the trees near headquarters, always seeming to appear whenever I was on garbage duty after pizza night. I'd stroll out into the pitch darkness of the grounds at the back of the house, not really paying attention, and then the blood red peepers would pop up in the corner of my eye and scare me to death.

But this seemed different. All those other times, I felt myself being looked *down* at, from high up in the trees. That's what I would expect here, too, if it *were* an owl. Unless they were searching for food, they tried to stay hidden, to not become something else's meal. Even if this one *had* been looking for something to eat down on the ground, Carter and I weren't exactly being quiet. It should've taken off when it heard us, so it didn't make any sense.

My dad used to joke that I was more like a were-owl than a wolf, since I had little patience for people and would rather be alone than hang out with a bunch of strangers. Owls were loners, too, almost always by themselves, staying out of human sight most of the time. Which made it weird to find one lingering near the cabin, especially while Carter and I were goofing around so loudly...

But if it wasn't an owl, then what? Definitely not a rabbit. Unless it was some crazy mutant species only found in Chibouwood. Although... considering everything, mutant rabbits might have actually been the least strange thing to happen in recent years.

What the hell was it?

My thoughts raced around my head like a pinball, anxiety sending my mind into free-fall. But *why?* It made no sense. Yeah, anxiety wasn't anything new to me, but usually, I had a good sense of *why* I was so worked up - like a noise from outside or a comment that sent me into a panic about how I might've upset someone. It usually ended up being nothing, but I had never freaked out over an animal before, and honestly, not knowing why my heart was pounding so fast just made it even harder to calm down.

It was stupid, really. It wasn't that weird that I had no clue what the animal was. Knowing creatures by sight was Henry's thing. He could tell a field mouse from a woodland mouse in two seconds flat. He had eyes like an eagle, while I had a nose like a bloodhound, so I'd catch the scent before I—

It hit me all at once. The reason I was so freaked out...

There was no scent.

Was that even possible? I inhaled deeply, straining to catch any sign I might have missed... but all that greeted me was the sharp scent of pine, the lingering odour of the cigarette can, and the smoky aroma of the fire burning inside. Shifting my focus beyond the cabin, the earthy fragrance of the woods mingled with the delicate scent of wildflowers. Faint traces of the animals that had passed by reached my nostrils, too, though the scents were so weak it must have been hours since they had left. Anything that had been lurking around had vanished when Ansel, Colton, and Jamie arrived. It was obvious from the multitude of tracks that led away from the cabin and disappeared into the woods. There were no new prints leading *towards* it.

Even with all the other smells blended together, it *should* be easy to identify that one. To separate that strand from the rest. But I couldn't. With my gaze fixed on the creature, I took in deep breaths, filling my lungs with air, and... *nothing*. As though it were a ghost.

I shivered as a fresh wave of coldness enveloped me, raising goosebumps on my arms. I had a faint sense of Carter's presence behind me. He said something, his voice barely a whisper, lost in the soft rustle of the wind. He was there, but I still felt alone. Like a fog had enveloped me, blocking out the world. All but those eyes.

My legs moved involuntarily, carrying me closer to the edge of the forest. Closer to the creature. I was almost there, and still all I could make out were those deep red orbs peering out from the shadows. Nothing else. They didn't even seem to be attached to a head. As I extended my hand, my fingertips grazed the rough bark of a branch, gently pushing it aside to clear my path. I steeled myself, ready for the animal to pounce on me. But it didn't budge. It didn't even blink, just kept staring, like it wasn't scared at all. Which made no sense, because it should smell the wolf on my scent, yet I felt sure I could just walk up to it, and—

"*Madison!*"

Carter's hand on my arm made me gasp, my muscles instantly tensing from the sudden pressure, and as I blinked, reality flooded back in.

"Can you hear me? *Mads*?"

My mouth opened, but instead of words, a harsh, hacking cough escaped, seeming to echo in the quiet. Finally, I made a sound that he must've taken as a yes, because he let out a deep breath and pulled me into a hug.

"Thank god." His breath brushed against the top of my head, leaving a tingling sensation, while the thunderous pounding of his heart filled my ears.

I let him cradle me until his heart stopped racing, then I asked with a tremor in my voice, "You see it too? What is—"

My words evaporated into nothingness as soon as I turned to look back at the trees.

There was nothing there.

Heart pounding, I took a step forward, frantically scanning the forest, as if I had somehow missed it in my panic. But there was nothing, save for the faint whisper of the wind as it danced through the air.

My stomach inexplicably filled with dread, the weight of it so heavy it made me nauseous. I spun on my heel, crashing right into Carter, who had been following closely behind me. The impact shocked me, almost knocking me off my feet, so it was a relief to feel his arms around me again. His voice, soft and comforting, echoed in my ears as he mumbled, "hey, hey, hey", but even the familiar scent of his cologne mixing with the crisp air couldn't ease my anxiety.

"Breathe. Take a minute. Are you okay?"

"I... I..."

I couldn't think of what to say, desperately needing some breathing room to gather my thoughts. The air felt heavy, suffocating, as I raised my hands in a feeble attempt to create distance between us. He complied, albeit reluctantly, moving back a couple of steps while still within arm's reach, as if he was afraid I might suddenly collapse.

After a deep breath, I finally managed to say, "I saw something. But I don't know—"

He shifted slightly while I was talking, and that's when I saw four sets of eyes staring at me from behind him. Henry was just a few steps away from us, but he'd stopped dead in his tracks, frozen mid-step on the lawn, his fists clenched so tightly they had turned white. Ansel, Colton, and Jamie stood on the deck, their gazes flickering between me and each other.

How hadn't I heard them when they came outside?

My cheeks flushed with embarrassment, my palms sweating, as I leaned in closer to Carter, trying to keep our conversation hushed. I knew Henry would hear me, but the other three didn't have to.

"What's everyone doing out here?"

Carter's eyes widened as he looked down at me. "Mads... you just like... flaked out. And then you tried to make a run for the woods. I had to stop you, so I screamed your name and grabbed you. They all came out to see what was going on."

With every word he spoke, an icy feeling coursed through my veins.

I shook my head, but it wasn't very convincing. "No. That didn't... I mean, there was something there. I was just checking it out. That's all. You didn't see it?"

Carter's eyebrow twitched a little. "I didn't see anything."

"Oh. Well..." I let my words fade, and then I attempted a laugh I didn't even believe myself. "It was probably just an owl. Those things always give me the creeps."

Henry looked at me skeptically, like I knew he would. But he didn't push, at least not in front of everyone else. He obviously wanted to have a conversation, but when Carter suggested getting food because *'being hungry wouldn't help'*, I was relieved to find he didn't try to stop me walking away.

Carter guided me to the cabin, my legs trembling with each step, and the shrill creak of hinges cut through the air as Ansel threw the door open for me. Carter's arms held me up as I climbed the steps to the deck, and I was almost at the cabin door when a voice interrupted the silence.

"I know you saw it."

My arms erupted in goosebumps as I spun around, searching for the source of the unfamiliar voice. It took me a moment to recognise Colton, since I'd barely spoken to him. I'd heard him say a few words earlier, but that had been in the midst of all the chaos, so it hardly registered.

A lump formed in my throat as I nervously asked, "Saw what?"

He took a step closer, and Carter immediately planted himself in front of me, arms forming a barricade across his chest. Colton stopped, his body tensing. He kept looking at me, but thankfully didn't come any closer. He didn't need to. His next words, even from a distance, struck me like a blow, sending fresh waves of dread through me.

"You saw the monster."

17

"**M**onsters aren't real."

That's what I said to Colton, and I meant it.

Was that me splitting hairs? Probably, all things considered. Werewolves, vampires, witches... They were all real, and society would classify them as 'monsters'. That's why we had to keep our lives a secret. Horror movies made it *very* clear how humans felt about anything supernatural, and there were historical records to back it up. They didn't trust us, and when that turned into fear, it was dangerous. It wouldn't matter that we were supernatural beings, *not* monsters, or that most of us just wanted to live a normal, quiet life. Sure, there were those who thought they were above everyone else because of their powers, but they were the exception. They didn't define an entire race of people.

Humans had done some awful things to each other throughout history, so it was ironic that they labelled *us* as monsters, really. Still, if they ever found out about us, the best we could hope for was a swift death. Rather that than risk being captured and experimented on.

The point was monsters, like from the movies, or the ones Colton was imagining, didn't exist, meaning there wasn't one lurking outside our door. But that didn't mean we were safe. There was something out there, eyeing me like I was its next meal. If that's what Colton saw, too, then it must have followed them to the cabin and been waiting out there for hours. It wasn't safe for anyone to be outside, especially not at night, until we knew what it was and if it was dangerous.

And that's how we ended up with three total strangers crashing in the living room.

Henry was definitely not on board when I brought up the idea of Ansel and his buddies crashing for the night. Carter wasn't thrilled about it either, but at least he didn't just storm off. After hearing me out, he eventually agreed I was right. Yeah, he'd prefer if they left, but he knew why they had to stay and he wouldn't make it weird for anyone, which was more than I could say for my best friend.

Regardless of Henry's whining, there was no alternative. Those fools couldn't find their way back in daylight. Anything could happen to them now it was dark. Carter offered to drive them back to their rental, but I could tell he was kind of unsure about leaving me again after I flaked out, and the day had been exhausting for him as well, so I said no.

Honestly, I wouldn't have been okay with him going out alone, even if he wasn't so tired. So, their only option was to stay put until morning when we could safely take them back to their cabin.

"How're you feeling?"

I felt the mattress dip next to me as Carter plopped down, and his voice cut through my thoughts.

After a few hours of tense conversation with the group, we had finally escaped to our bedroom. If it hadn't been for Henry's disapproving presence, the night wouldn't have been so difficult to endure. But he *was* there, sadly, and seemed determined to make it as awkward as possible.

Luckily, I managed to avoid being alone with him for the rest of the evening, so he couldn't grill me about what happened. I didn't have a clue what I'd tell him. The minute I laid eyes on it, there was something really weird and almost supernatural about the creature, and even though it sounded ridiculous, I couldn't shake the uneasy feeling in my stomach. Henry, though, had this annoying habit of downplaying my concerns, and I didn't feel like being laughed at for being spooked by a rabbit, mutant or not.

Shifting my attention to Carter, I settled against the headboard and flashed him a smile, crossing my fingers that he'd believe it.

"I'm all good. It's been a long day, huh?"

"Ayuh." Our fingers interlocked, and there was just the sound of our breath for a while, the air thick with things left unsaid, until he finally, almost unwillingly, blurted it out. "You scared the crap out of me earlier."

"I'm sorry. It won't happen again, I promise."

He rolled his eyes, sighed quietly, and then gave a half-hearted smile. "Yeah, it will. You can't help but do it."

Raising my eyebrow, I asked, "Do what?"

"Put everyone else first, even if it means you starve to death."

"I wasn't about to starve to death." I laughed, but his expression stayed unchanged, and I could tell that didn't make him feel any better. Honestly, I wasn't even sure anymore if my spacing out was because of hunger, and maybe he was thinking the same thing. If Colton saw what I saw, it couldn't have been a hallucination; we couldn't have shared the same vision, even if I was half-starved or losing my mind.

When he didn't reply, I sighed. "I'm *fine*. Everything turned out alright. Just a crappy end to a long and crazy day. Now I'm just happy to *finally* be alone with you, like we planned." I gave his hand a firm, reassuring squeeze. "Anyways, I had as much to eat as you and Henry did. It could've happened to either of you."

His thumb, which had been grazing the side of my hand, stopped, leaving a tingling sensation on my skin. "Except neither of us were taking an evening stroll through the woods, were we?"

His voice was so harsh, it almost made me flinch, but I just turned to face him again. "Carter..."

He let out a groan and stared at the ceiling. "Sorry. It's just been a rough day. We should get some sleep." A heavy silence hung in the air as he paused, then slowly turned his head to meet my gaze, his stare intense and piercing. "Can you do something for me? Promise you won't do this again - no more wandering the forest with strangers."

Nodding my agreement, I brushed my lips against his, hoping the kiss would tell him everything I couldn't put into words. How much I loved him, and how important he was to me. How I'd do anything for him. When he kissed me back, I could tell he felt the same way. It wasn't sweet or playful, but it also wasn't passionate like those heated kisses we had outside. It was a sensation unlike anything I had felt before. As his tongue brushed against my lips, there was no hunger or longing, only a desire to be near me. I could feel the tension in his body as he held me tight. His touch was gentle, but also desperate, like he had to physically connect with me to make sure I was okay, even though I was *right there*.

I had no idea how much time passed while we stayed like that, our hands intertwined and our lips pressed together, but when he finally broke the kiss, I just wanted to drag him back in. He didn't even realise, just smiled at me before snuggling into the blankets, leaving me to stare at the back of his head and his tousled curls until he started breathing deeply in his sleep.

I wanted so badly to snuggle up with him, but I knew I couldn't, or I wouldn't do what I *needed* to do. Instead, I just watched the shadows from the moonlight moving across the room, my mind going to the dark depths that I couldn't get away from at night.

Lately, every word I spoke felt like a knife piercing deeper, chipping away his trust. That's why it was better to end things sooner rather than later, as well as why, while he had no idea, I was memorising every single detail about him. His scent and, hell, even the taste of him. Capturing everything about every moment, before he saw through my lies. If — no, *when* that happened, he'd never forgive me, no matter my intentions.

Once again, I tried to ease my guilt by telling myself I wasn't totally lying. Even though I wasn't sure I believed it, I kept repeating the mantra to myself, or else I would've stayed in bed, feeling the warmth of his body against mine until morning. But no matter how badly I wanted to, I just couldn't. I needed to figure out what I saw in the woods to be sure Carter was safe. And if that meant going toe-to-toe with a bear, or a mountain lion, or whatever the hell that thing was, I'd do it in a heartbeat, whether he liked it or not.

I really wasn't breaking my promise. I'd agreed not to go into the woods with a stranger again, and I meant it...

But I never said anything about going alone.

18

Carter's deep and rhythmic breathing resonated throughout the room, occasionally accompanied by a thunderous snore.

When he was that exhausted, I could throw a party and he wouldn't notice. He'd crashed at our place a few times after a super tiring day at work, and Dad would stumble back home after a night out with his buddies, reeking of booze, yelling and slamming doors while trying to get to his bedroom. Carter never even flinched. If I snuck out of bed now, he'd never know.

But *he* wasn't the issue. It was all the others.

While Carter was out cold, our surprise guests took ages to fall asleep, arguing about whether they could trust us not to kill them while they were out. Well, Ansel and Jamie argued, at least. Colton hadn't said a word since his comment about '*the monster*'. Mostly because every time he tried to talk, he had to rush to the bathroom to puke. I didn't enjoy seeing him suffer, but I had to admit to being kinda glad when he started feeling sick from that pond water he drank. He was too busy throwing up to bug me about what I saw outside.

The odds were high we'd seen the same thing, and if he wanted to pretend it was a monster so he had an exciting story for his friends back in Boston, that had nothing to do with me... I just wasn't about to feed into it, so it was best to stay away from the conversation, at least until I had more information.

Not surprisingly, Jamie was the last one to doze off. Despite being annoying as hell, I had to respect his determination to survive. He battled with it for over an hour until he finally crashed.

Henry... well, he was trickier.

It had already been a few hours since he shut himself away in his room, yet the steady thud from his headphones told me he was still awake. Part of me wanted to wait a while longer, to see if he'd eventually give in, but it was hard to keep my eyes open with Carter's warmth beside me, and every second that went by gave the creature more time to run deeper into the woods. Assuming it wasn't already long gone, of course, but even then, the sooner I got on its trail, the better my chance of getting answers.

Besides, I doubted Henry would get any sleep at all. Not with three strangers on the pullout in the living room. My only option was to sneak out of the cabin, hoping his music would be loud enough to drown out my footsteps.

Taking a deep breath, I closed my eyes and slowly shifted away from Carter, carefully sliding his arm off my stomach and onto the mattress. When he mumbled in his sleep, my heart leapt into my throat, my breathing quickening as I froze, but he just turned towards the window before settling again. Holding back a sigh of relief, I stepped back from the bed, my toes curling on the cold, creaky floor. But Carter was knocked out, snoring like a freight train and masking the sound of my hurried steps to the door.

With a swift yank, I opened the door, not daring to glance back. Just one look at him and I'd wanna go back to our cosy bed and forget about everything. To pretend nothing was wrong. But I couldn't, no matter how badly I wanted to. I was pretty sure my late-night investigation would be a waste of time, and I'd end up finding some animal I just hadn't recognised. But if there was even a tiny bit of doubt, I couldn't ignore it.

Trying to ignore the guilt that hit me again, I cautiously stepped around the door into the hall and...

"Everything okay?"

"Jesus!" I jumped almost out of my skin at the voice, my gut lurching as I clutched my chest. "What the hell?" I hissed, trying not to look back at my room. I didn't need to check to know Carter was still asleep. If he'd woken up, I would've heard it before I saw it.

Henry's brow arched. "What?"

I closed the door, the gentle squeak of the hinges sounding ten times louder in the silent cabin. When no sound of movement came from within, though, I guided Henry a few steps backwards down the hallway, the floorboards groaning softly under our weight, until we reached the back door where our hushed tones wouldn't wake anyone.

"I thought you were in your room." I whispered.

"Nope." He crossed his arms over his chest. "Is something wrong?"

I had to clench my jaw and dig my nails into my palms to keep myself from biting my lip. If I did that, it would be a dead giveaway, and there'd be no chance of me sneaking past him. For a second, I felt frozen like a deer in the headlights, my mind scrambling for a response. Then, at last, I said, "No. You just startled me, that's all. I gotta go to the bathroom. Would you excuse me?"

As I started down the hall to the bathroom, a tight grip on my arm stopped me in my tracks. I didn't turn back straight away.

Instead, I closed my eyes and inhaled deeply before mustering the courage to face Henry again.

"What's up?" I asked, attempting to sound casual, but my voice betrayed me with a slight tremble. I crossed my fingers he wouldn't notice.

"That depends. Anything you wanna tell me?"

My heart was pounding so loud there was no way he wouldn't hear it, but I still tried to disguise it with a nervous chuckle. "Um… I really gotta pee?"

He said nothing. Instead, his narrowed eyes bore into me, and the sharp click of his tongue sent shivers down my spine, sure he knew the truth. Why did I even think this would work? It was a ridiculous idea. No one on earth knew me like he did, so of course he'd figure me out. And now I had to confess - about what I saw and what I was gonna do - and just brace for his wrath.

I told myself I was keeping it quiet so they wouldn't freak out, but I knew there was more to it. Maybe that was true for Carter, but with Henry, it was more complicated. Truthfully, I didn't want to tell him because I was scared of how he would react. He was my best friend – maybe even more, once upon a time – but there was still a part of me that felt like a shy kid tagging along, hoping he'd notice me. Wishing he'd see me as his equal, see what I was capable of. But he only ever saw the girl he had to look out for.

The silence was so loud, and my anxiety was skyrocketing, but I didn't look away from him. My heart pounded in my ears as I waited for him to confront me. To call me out for lying. But then he released my arm, and I glanced at the spot where he had grabbed me, half expecting to still see his fingers on my wrist, feeling a surge of excitement when they weren't there anymore.

"Right. Well, goodnight, I guess." He grumbled.

"Yeah. Night." I said, fighting the urge to bolt immediately. Instead, I turned slowly, feeling his intense stare burning holes in the back of my head as I made my way down the hall.

It felt like an eternity to get to the bathroom, even though it was only a few steps away in the tiny cabin. As I inched closer, the door seemed to move further away. But I finally made it and, once inside, I turned on the faucet, the room filling with the soothing sound of running water and masking my heavy breaths. I leaned back against the door, feeling its coolness against my hot, sweaty skin as I listened. Henry hung around in the hall a little longer, but then I heard his door thump closed.

Relief washed over me, making my legs buckle. My gut screamed at me to bolt out of the bathroom before he caught on, but that would be too obvious. So, I just stood there, hands shaking as I pressed them against the door, until enough time had gone by for me to flush the toilet and turn off the water without him getting suspicious.

Back in the hallway, I hesitated outside Henry's room, my ears tuned in for any sign of activity inside. I was half expecting him to rip the door open, shout 'aha!', and drag me in to give me a piece of his mind, but thankfully that didn't happen. Carter's snoring was so loud that it was hard to make out anything else, but the cabin stayed still, and Henry's music still thundered on through his headphones.

Feeling pretty confident no one would stop me, I snuck to the backdoor, wincing as the floor kept groaning. I grabbed my sneakers, then ran my fingers over my jacket before taking it off the hook, holding it in one hand while gripping the door handle with the other. Clenching my jaw, I felt the jolt of the old mechanism reverberate through my hand as I released the lock, the click echoing through the hallway. This time, I didn't stay to find out if anyone would come running. Instead, I ventured outside onto the deck, and the crisp night air wrapped around me, bringing with it the scent of dewy grass.

Making my way across the deck towards the lawn, the rustling of the leaves in the trees caught my attention, and I turned to check out the edge of the forest, a smile tugging at my lips. If I stayed close to the trees on the edge, in their shadow, I could move around without anyone spotting me. Even if someone glanced out a window, I'd be invisible. Completely out of sight.

With each step I took, a surge of excitement bubbled in my stomach, and a smile spread across my face. I couldn't believe Henry fell for my story, but he did, which just proved how exhausted and disoriented we all were. I felt a little bad for taking advantage of that, but what choice did I have?

Seeing as I had made it this far without any trouble, I took a moment to stop and slip on my shoes. Then I straightened, turned my back on the cabin and...

"Going somewhere?"

His voice shattered the silence like a clap of thunder, jolting me to a standstill.

Crap.

19

"Dammit, H. You trying to give me a heart attack or what?" I said, clutching my hand to my chest.

He totally ignored my question and fired one right back. "What're you doing out here?"

I let out a shaky chuckle. "You spying on me now? 'Cause I'm pretty sure I heard you go back in your room."

"Don't be a smartass, Madison. What's got you so out of it you didn't realise I came out here? Pretty fucking dumb move, all things considered." Without giving me a chance to respond, he abruptly broke away from the wall he had been leaning against and moved closer to me. It took everything in me not to flinch away. "You're hiding something, so just fucking spill it."

"Don't be so dramatic." I said, rolling my eyes, despite the tension like a coiled spring in my stomach. "I didn't realise you came out here 'cause I wasn't paying attention. It's late, I'm beat, and Carter's snoring like crazy. Oh, and in case you didn't notice, there are three people passed out in our living room. Strangers who've been wandering through the woods all day and haven't showered or changed their clothes. I just needed a sec, alright? To get some air."

His eyes zeroed in on the jacket in my hand, and as his eyebrow twitched, the heat of a blush crept up my cheeks.

"It's cold." I mumbled in explanation.

"Nope, not really."

"Well, y'know, temperature is subjective."

He didn't reply straight away, and we just stood there in silence for what felt like forever until he finally laughed.

"You must think I'm real fucking stupid." The fury in his voice made me glance towards the back door, half-expecting the sound of approaching footsteps. Henry didn't seem to care. "You suck at lying, you know that? So just tell me. What the hell happened earlier, huh? Something obviously freaked you out."

"Keep it down!" I hissed, then grabbed his wrist and pulled him away from the deck. Once we were at a safe distance, I let out a deep breath. "Nothing happened. Everything's fine."

His nostrils flared as he snorted. "Bullshit. Madison, I'm not playing around. And I'm damn sure not taking any chances - not after what happened back home. So you don't wanna talk to me? Cool. Maybe you'll talk to your dad. Or Ray. I bet either of them would be real fucking interested to hear about your plan to sneak away into the woods alone. I should probably just wake Johnson up now and save us all some time, right? We'll be back in Havencrest by morning, and then you can tell everyone what the hell is going on with you. Does that work for you?"

"You can't do that. Ansel and—"

"I could care less about those assholes."

Since I had no idea what to say to that, I said nothing, but soon realised that was the wrong thing, because he clicked his tongue, whirled around... and stomped back to the cabin. I let him walk a bit, hoping he'd glance back. He didn't. He was almost at the door when I had to accept that he wasn't kidding.

"*Wait.*" I sighed. There was no need for me to raise my voice. It was loud and clear in the silence of the night.

He came to a stop, arms crossed over his chest, and silently rotated towards me, the only sound being the faint hooting of an owl in the distance. I waved him back to where I was standing, and he rolled his eyes, but came over anyway.

"Well?" He snapped.

I shot him an icy stare. "I'm not doing this if you're gonna be pissy."

"Trust me, I'm way past pissy. Now, explain."

"Ugh, *fine.*" I groaned. "It's probably nothing, but I..." I started, but my mind went blank on how to even begin explaining it all.

Henry's jaw clenched, and after a long pause, he let out a growl. "But *what?*"

I glared at him again, then said, "*But* Carter and I were talking—"

He rolled his eyes, making it clear he knew we weren't just 'talking'. My cheeks turned red, but I pushed through with my explanation.

"I heard something. And I know what you're thinking – '*it's the damn forest*'. Right?" I paused for his argument, but the silence that followed was more uncomfortable than anything he could've said. It felt like being judged. "Anyway, I looked over and there were these crazy bright red eyes just peeking out of the bushes. Right over there."

I pointed at the spot, and when Henry looked, I saw him visibly relax, his shoulders dropping from their tense position. Right away, and even before he said anything, I felt myself getting defensive. I knew it was stupid, because I was the one who said it was probably nothing to worry about, so I should've been happy he was confirming that. But there was something about how he blew it off without even thinking twice, even though I knew he would, that bugged me. It wasn't worth fighting with him, though. I never won.

"Madison, this is the forest." He said, almost repeating me word for word. "That's totally—"

"Normal? I knew you'd say that, which is *exactly* why I didn't tell you. But you're right, I guess. I'm just a bit off today."

"That's not even *close* to a good enough excuse for coming out here in the middle of the night by yourself. It's fucking dangerous."

Gritting my teeth against a snarky response, I simply said, "I get it, okay? You're right. I'm sorry."

"Why do you always have to be such a pain in the ass?"

That... that took me by surprise, and I raised my eyebrow, eyes wide as I stared at him. "*What?* You're actually mad at me for *not* starting a fight with you for once?"

"No. I just don't buy it. You never give in that easily. So what's the catch?"

My breath made a cloud in the air when I sighed. "No catch. It's just... now that I think about it - really think about - I bet Sean's been giving food to the animals, so they came looking for more. It's gotta be the only way to make friends here, right?" I tried to lighten the mood with a laugh, but he wasn't up for it, so I cut it off by clearing my throat. "I should've said something earlier. I know that now. I just didn't want to freak anyone out, that's all. It was probably just an owl or a deer or something. No big deal."

"Uh, no. *It's a huge fucking deal.* I don't care if it was a goddamn unicorn. Next time you wanna be Dora the fucking Explorer, you let me know, okay?"

The mood was heavy, but I couldn't help but smirk at the reference. "Sure thing, Boots."

All I got in response was a blank stare, so I just mumbled a *'never mind'*. Ugh, if I was cracking jokes about cartoon pet monkeys, it meant I'd been hanging out with Henry's little sister *way* too much. I loved Cady like she was my own sister, but that was another reason I'd been so stoked about this trip with Carter. Basketball season was over, but he was still crazy busy with work, college visits, and applications. I barely saw him these days, and since I had nothing else going on, I had plenty of time to take care of Cady while Sierra was at work. I was usually happy to help – it was way better than just moping at home, stressing about what would happen after graduation – but I missed being able to goof around with my boyfriend. Still, after all the Bartons had done for me over the years, saving them a few bucks on childcare was the least I could do.

I shook my head and waved my hand in the air as if to brush away the comment. "Look, the point is I didn't think it was gonna be a big deal, so I didn't want to stress anyone out. Besides, it's not like I was going far. Just a quick look, that's all. There's really no need to make a fuss."

"Didn't you say the same thing when Blondie showed up out of nowhere? How'd that go?"

His words hit like a punch to the stomach.

Had he actually just said that?

It had been eating away at me for a year and a half that *I* was the one who trusted Ben. *I* was the one who bought into his lies, who let him get close, and practically handed control of Vineyard Manor over to him and his dad. Henry wanted to send him packing when we first met, and if I had just listened... Carter would never have ended up kidnapped. Ryan might still be alive.

I'd forgiven Ben. Ryan would've wanted me to. I mean, he was just a messed-up kid who got taken advantage of by the one person who was supposed to love him no matter what. And he helped us in the end. Knowing what Ben had been through, it was too difficult to hold onto anger, so I had to let it go.

But I never figured out how to forgive myself.

I couldn't believe Henry was throwing my biggest mistake in my face. His words were like a knife to the chest, stirring up all the pain I had only just begun to heal from. And I didn't have a clue how to react.

He always said it wasn't my fault. They all said it – him, Dad, Sierra, Ray. Even Jackson, when we went for a hike together at White Mountain. He probably thought going back there would bring up bad memories, but it didn't matter where I was. Images of Ryan's bloodied face and the hiker's pallid complexion haunted me, and no matter how much they reassured me, I couldn't rid myself of the guilt.

Had they all just lied to me? Did everyone secretly blame me for Ryan's death? Hate me for it? Not that it really mattered. Even if they did, it couldn't be any more than I already hated myself.

Tears welled up in my eyes, but I bit my lip to hold them back. I wouldn't let him see me cry. I wouldn't let him know he got to me.

In the soft glow of the moonlight, I noticed his cheeks blushing, but he wouldn't meet my eyes. The silence around us felt heavy, as if time was holding its breath, until he broke it with a cough.

"Well, we're here now, and you went to all that trouble to sneak out, so we might as well have a look. Just to be safe." He mumbled, his fingers combing through his once sleek black hair, now a wild and unkempt tangle.

He was trying to brush off his outburst, and though I wanted to confront him, a part of me just wanted to pretend it didn't happen, too. If everyone was lying to me about Ryan, I wasn't ready to face the truth. I just wanted to stay in my bubble, where the only anger I had to battle was my own.

Besides, even if I wanted to confront Henry, it was too late. He had already taken off, heading towards the edge of the forest. If I wasn't so relieved to be free from the conversation, I would have been furious that he didn't give me the opportunity to defend myself. As it was, though, I was more than happy to table it for another day. Or, you know, for*ever*.

It was only when he stopped and looked back at me over his shoulder, eyebrow raised, that I realised how long I had been just standing there, watching him go. At first, he didn't say anything, but then he sighed, before following it up with probably the best apology Henry Barton had ever given me.

"And for the record... fucking *Boots?* You've gotta be kidding me. I'm *obviously* Diego."

20

"This is a waste of time. There's nothing here." I grumbled, while Henry crouched to investigate yet another bush. "Just a bird that's flown off now. That's why I didn't wanna bring it up. I don't need you mocking me."

I didn't go into more detail, like how the creature seemed to have no smell at all, or that the eyes were too big for it to be an owl. Carter said I was totally out of it, so I must have been imagining things, or at least blowing them *way* out of proportion.

Henry scoffed as he straightened. "Why do you always make me out to be such an asshole?"

"Because you *are* an asshole, ninety-nine percent of the time."

"Oh, Mads, you flatter me." He grinned. "But I'm not mocking you. This is serious. It's weird you'd flip out over '*just a bird*', don't you think?"

Ridiculously, I felt myself getting defensive again. "It wasn't *just* over a bird. I was also hungry. And tired." When he said nothing, I bristled. "You don't believe me?"

"Didn't say that."

"Well I didn't lie, either, if that's what you're getting at."

"Nope."

I narrowed my eyes at him... and then it clicked. "Oh, I get it. You don't *really* think it was a big deal, do you? You're just using it as an excuse to escape the cabin for a bit."

"Didn't say that." He said again, and I clenched my jaw, my scowl deepening. But, if I was honest, there was a surge of excitement that coursed through me at the same time, because, truthfully, I felt the same way.

I didn't need a break from Carter, despite his thunderous snoring; in fact, I found it oddly comforting. No, it was the three strangers in our living room. They made the cabin feel so small that I almost regretted not taking Ethan's offer of the spare room at his parent's beach house. At least that was designed to accommodate a bunch of people, whereas Sean's cabin was only meant for him and maybe the occasional overnight visitor. Definitely not six people all at once. It was okay when we were kids, but as I stood, breathing in the crisp night air, I realised how stifling it had been inside. My heart longed for the sensation of my paws pounding against the earth. It craved the sense of freedom that accompanied running through the one place where I truly felt alive.

There was just one thing holding me back.

"What about Carter? We can't leave him there by himself."

Henry arched his eyebrow. "Why not? You're the one who invited them to stay. You told me they weren't a problem, right?"

"Yes, but..."

My voice trailed off, leaving an awkward silence in the air. I couldn't quite put it into words, but I had a gut feeling that they weren't a danger. There wasn't any real reason for it. Colton was an odd character, but I guessed it was to be expected. He'd be even worse tomorrow, when whatever bacteria were in that pond water settled into his body. As for the other two... Jamie had a short fuse, and he didn't trust anyone, so really, he was no different from Henry, but Ansel seemed friendly enough. Of course, after what happened with Ben, I wouldn't take *just* that as evidence of their innocence. It was Henry's reaction that confirmed it.

I knew him, and his tells, so I knew he wasn't worried. He wouldn't have agreed to them staying if he was. He might act like he didn't give a damn, but deep down I knew he cared about Carter, in his own way. He wouldn't intentionally put him in danger. *That* was why I felt safe enough to be out here, while Carter was still inside, unaware.

Besides, they were all still sound asleep. We could sneak off to the woods, explore, and be back before anyone even realised we'd gone.

I looked over at Henry, but he just shrugged his shoulders. It was up to me. If I wanted to go back, he'd be right behind me. But I *didn't* want that. Not yet.

Admitting that, even if just to myself, sent a wave of guilt crashing over me, even as I reminded myself it wasn't about Carter, or wanting to get away from him. It was just that, up close, the forest was hard to resist. Plus, it's not like I hadn't wanted him to come with me, or I'd avoided him specifically. Truthfully, I hadn't wanted *anyone* to come with me. It was supposed to be a secret mission. A quick look around to confirm whether I was losing my mind. I'd tried to avoid Henry. It wasn't my fault he found out and tagged along. Carter would understand. He always did.

"Okay. But, not too far, alright?" I said finally. "We've been out here long enough already. If Carter wakes up and comes to find me before we're back... I just don't want—"

Before I could finish my sentence, a noise nearby silenced me. Our eyes met, and I could tell from Henry's expression that he'd heard it too. It was so loud and chaotic that it was hard to miss, but I couldn't trust my own senses anymore, so it was a relief to know I hadn't imagined it.

It took me a moment to separate the barrage of noises enough to realise it was voices, and then another for me to recognise who the voices belonged to. But it was a single word that struck me like a dagger.

My legs reacted instinctively, propelling me towards the cabin, the word echoing in my mind.

'Gone.'

21

Sprinting through the woods, my eyes barely registered the trees and rocks in my path, yet somehow, I avoided them all. Henry called out to me a few times, but I brushed him off because talking would have slowed me down. Eventually, he gave up, but I could still feel his silent presence trailing behind me.

We must have gone way farther than I thought, because no matter how hard I pounded my feet on the ground, the cabin just wouldn't get any closer. As I looked ahead, I could see the clearing, and the sound of the generator was a constant buzz in the air, but it felt like it was far away. I pushed on, my face slick with sweat, my vision blurring where it ran into my eyes, and the branches punishing my cheeks with sharp stings. I didn't care. All I cared about was the echo of that one word running round and round my head - *'gone'*.

It was Jamie who said it, and even though I didn't know him well, the fear in his voice was unmistakable. The high-pitched tone was a stark contrast to the deep, gruff grunt he had spoken with before, and it sent shivers down my spine. All the words sort of merged together, except for that one, which just dangled there, taunting me.

Despite my werewolf ears, I couldn't hear the rest over my pounding heart. But it didn't really matter. The only thing that mattered was that something was up, and I'd bailed on Carter - again. If something bad happened to him, it would be all my fault.

Images of Ryan's battered body flashed in my head with each step I took, and black spots danced across my vision until I had to depend entirely on my nose to find my way. My foot kicked against something on the ground, and I stumbled for a moment, but quickly got back on track and didn't bother to check what it was. Like Henry, it would only slow me down, and I couldn't afford to waste time. I just had to get back to him.

After what felt like forever, I finally made it out of the dense forest and...

Carter, with his eyes still glassy from sleep, stood on the deck. I could see the confusion etched on his face, but he was safe, and the overwhelming relief brought tears to my eyes and a lump to my throat.

His eyes locked with mine, and suddenly, the world felt dizzying, my legs turning to jelly. I stopped, mesmerised by his face and the way he softly whispered my name. And then, I was gone, my feet pounding the grass once more, running around the truck in a blur, before I flung myself into his arms.

The impact made him stagger back, but he didn't let go of me, and I took a deep breath of his familiar scent, making sure he was really there. That he was okay.

He murmured against my hair, "Hey, hey. You're okay. I've got you."

"I heard Jamie. Heard him say... and I thought—"

"Just breathe, okay? Are you alright? I woke up to yelling and when you weren't there I—"

I backed away a little, but I kept my hands on him, as if he might vanish if I let go. "I'm fine. I'm sorry. I just... What's going on?"

"They're saying Colton's missing. That's all I know. Where were—" His voice trailed off as his eyes darted behind me, his eyebrows knitting in confusion. He saw Henry, and I watched as it hit him, the realisation washing over his face. Then he tensed up and took a step back, putting more distance between us, until I couldn't reach him anymore. "What were you doing out here, anyway?"

"Um..." I struggled to find the right words, my mind drawing a blank, so a surge of relief flooded through me when the door to the cabin opened and Ansel stepped out onto the deck, his presence shifting the spotlight away from me. Seizing the chance to dodge Carter's question, I redirected my attention to Ansel, inwardly cringing at the over-the-top perkiness in my voice. "Hey. What's going on?"

Ansel flopped onto one of the deck chairs, making the wood groan. "Honestly? No idea. I woke up to Jamie freaking out, saying Colton was gone. And then—"

Jamie's sudden emergence from the forest on the opposite side of the clearing silenced Ansel's explanation. Charging forward, his face twisted with fury, he made a beeline for the deck, his finger jabbing accusingly at something.

"You! What the fuck have you done to him?"

"Am I supposed to know what the hell you're talking about?" I heard Henry sigh, and I spun, silently begging him to stay calm when I saw the finger was pointed right at him. But he only squared his shoulders and positioned his arms firmly over his chest as Jamie came to a halt just inches away from him.

Their height difference was pretty stark when they stood face to face. Jamie barely reached Henry's shoulders, but he didn't seem to notice, or care. He gave Henry a shove, hard enough to throw him off balance if he was anyone else. Henry's eyes barely flickered, though, like Jamie was just some annoying gnat, not worth his attention. But even though his face looked blank, the bulging vein in his temple gave away just how angry he was, and I held my breath, waiting for the explosion.

"What've you done to him, huh?" Jamie demanded, raising his hands as if to push him again, but Henry grabbed his wrists just in time.

"Try putting your hands on me again and see what happens." His expression was still a blank canvas, but Henry's voice carried a distinct warning. A warning that, judging by the look on Jamie's face, he had no intention of heeding.

We all stepped forward together – Ansel, Carter and me – ready to intervene. But then Jamie tore his gaze from Henry to face me, his scowl piercing through me like daggers. His finger shifted, and it was suddenly pointing my way instead.

"And you too! Acting all nice and friendly. I knew what you were about from the get-go. What the fuck have you and your boyfriend done to Colton?"

I could feel Carter moving next to me, and then he stepped around, his back to me and facing Jamie, just like he did with Colton earlier. Shielding me from his wrath. His hand rose slowly, palm outstretched, as if to ward him off without startling him. Then he said, "Hey man. Can you back off a bit? We didn't do anything to your friend. I mean, I was sleeping. And Maddie—"

He had this way of being both authoritative and gentle, something only Carter could pull off, and Jamie's face softened a little when he looked at him. But it was only a brief flash before he scowled again, cutting off Carter and gesturing towards Henry. "Not you. *Him.*"

It was ridiculous, considering we were being accused of… well, I wasn't actually sure what Jamie was accusing us of. Abducting Colton? Killing him? Whatever it was, it didn't matter to me as much as what he just said about me and Henry. I looked at Carter, standing in front of me, and a knot formed in my stomach. His arms hung loosely by his sides now, like the statement had knocked the fight out of him. But I noticed the slight quiver in his hands, so I reached out to him, our fingers barely brushing before he snatched his hand away. My heart sank.

So, this was it. Carter was finally opening his eyes to the person I really was – a liar. Alright, so I didn't hook up with Henry, but that's what he thought, and I couldn't even blame him. Especially when I couldn't tell him what was really going on. He had every reason to doubt me, and it was crazy he hadn't done it sooner.

Knowing I deserved it didn't make it hurt any less, though.

It was a relief to hear Ansel's voice fill the void of silence, because I had no idea where to start.

"Jay, c'mon. This isn't helping anybody." He sighed. "Madison was right before. He's sick. Got a fever. I'm sure he just woke up, got confused about why you were spooning him, and wandered off somewhere. But I just took another look inside and his shoes are still there, so he can't be far."

Jamie's laugh was cutting – icy and with no hint of amusement. "You seriously believe that?"

"Do I believe our friend, who has spent the entire night puking his guts up, could've wandered off in some sort of fever dream? Yeah, Jay, I do. Because it makes a lot more damn sense than these folks hauling him out here and killing him. If they'd done that, don't you think they'd have tried something with us as well?"

Jamie's nostrils flared, and the only sound between us was the grating of his teeth as he struggled to find a reply. Finally, he settled on, "They were going to! They were coming back to finish us off but didn't count on us being awake. Ain't that right?"

"Jesus Christ." Henry groaned.

Ansel walked closer to his friend and put his hand on his arm, as if to calm him down, but it just made Jamie tense and then flinch away. He had the scared look of a deer in headlights, and even though he'd been a jerk all night, I still felt bad for him.

Either Ansel didn't notice Jamie's reaction, or he simply didn't care, but either way he took another step towards him. Again, Jamie tensed, but didn't back away a second time. I couldn't tell if that was because Ansel was gripping his arm like a vice now, not giving him a chance to escape, or if Jamie was just too defeated to try. Maybe both were true.

When Ansel spoke again, his voice was much softer. Soothing, almost, and I got the impression he was used to Jamie losing his temper. "I know you're worried, Jay. But right now, Colton is out there, confused and possibly hurt. He needs our help, and we're wasting time arguing with these people when we should be out there looking for him." He shifted his gaze to me then. "Any chance you'd be up for helping us? I know it's real late, and you don't owe us anything, but—"

I nodded. "O-of course. Yes. Anything you need."

He gave me a small, half-hearted smile. "Thanks. Okay, well then, Madison, you're with me. We'll take that way." He gestured towards the trail Henry and I had just returned from. Then he looked at Carter, Henry, and Jamie. "You three can take the other side."

"*What!?*" My eyes widened at the same time that Henry snarled, '*fuck no*'. Carter said nothing. "No! I- I mean... Why? Why can't you two stay together, and then the three of us? Doesn't that make the most sense?"

Ansel let out a long breath, as if the reason was obvious. "It's Henry's uncle's place, right? So you guys know the area better than we do. We'll cover more ground by splitting up, but Jamie and me... we need someone who knows the way. It's pitch black, and as you may recall, we didn't really have much luck when the sun was still out."

He was obviously right. I hated it, but we weren't in some ninety's horror movie, where someone always died within five minutes of the leader telling the group to split up. Besides, I wouldn't feel comfortable with them wandering the woods in the dark. I told them they could spend the night for that reason, didn't I? But I still wanted Carter with me. It wasn't just about keeping an eye on him, or making sure he stayed safe, since I knew Henry would take good care of him. I just needed to talk to him. I had to make sure he knew there wasn't anything going on between Henry and me before Jamie put any more ideas in his head.

"Okay." I finally agreed. "We split up. But I want Carter with us."

Ansel snorted. "Do you actually *want* for there to be bloodshed tonight? He needs to go with those two to mediate, or they'll murder each other within five minutes, and then where would we be?"

I opened my mouth to argue, but Henry beat me to it. "No fucking way."

Ansel turned to him, fists clenching at his side and his pulse quickening slightly. It was just for a moment, though, before his friendly mask slid back into place. "What do you think I'm gonna do? I've had plenty opportunity today to hurt her if that's what I was planning. You know this is just practical."

"Practical? Like hell. Why're you so desperate to get her alone, huh? You just want—"

Another voice cut him off before he could finish. It seemed out of place at first, and it took a moment for the words to sink in, but when they did, it felt as if someone was physically twisting my heart, crushing it with their bare hands.

"Quit wasting time and just do what he says. I'll grab some flashlights."

Then Carter turned and headed into the cabin, letting the door slam shut behind him.

22

I didn't wait for Carter to come back with the flashlights.

Was that cowardly? Absolutely. A better girlfriend would've waited. Actually, a better girlfriend would've gone in after him and wouldn't have left until it was all worked out. But I wasn't a good girlfriend. I knew it, Henry knew it. Hell, *everyone* back home knew it. The only person who hadn't realised it was Carter, but now even he was seeing the truth about me as well.

I always knew he'd stop seeing me through rose-tinted glasses one day. When every other word you said was a lie, it was bound to happen, and Carter wasn't stupid. He knew I had secrets, he just loved me enough to look the other way. But everyone had a limit, and it seemed like Carter's was his girlfriend sneaking out of his bed in the middle of the night to go on an adventure in the woods with the guy she's been crushing on her whole life. And who could blame him?

He deserved better. I knew that. He deserved an explanation, and I knew that too. But there was no way to put it into words. How could I explain that the secret I'd been keeping from him all this time was that I was a *werewolf?* How could I put that on him?

No matter what, I was confident Carter wouldn't betray me. At least not on purpose. But with a secret that huge, he'd surely want to confide in someone. Ethan was his best friend, so it would probably be him - and while I had complete faith in Carter, could I say the same of Ethan Hawkins?

No. I couldn't. Which raised the biggest problem...

Ray had been Alpha my whole life, and I'd never heard of him getting rid of a potential threat, although it'd happened before. Even so, it was too risky to bring Carter into that. So I lied to him, day after day, knowing one day he'd have enough. But if he had to hate me to ensure his safety, then I was prepared to make that sacrifice... *eventually*. Just not right this second. If I didn't face him, then he couldn't say the words, and then I could live in the fairy tale for at least a little longer.

So was I cowardly? Yes. But only because I wanted to cling to him, to *us,* for as long as possible. Surely, nobody could blame me for that.

It didn't take long for Ansel to catch up, his flashlight casting long shadows on the ground as it waved around while he ran. Honestly, it surprised me to have gotten as far as I did without Henry hauling me back. Maybe he tried, but I didn't notice because I was so wrapped up in my head. I doubted that, though. If Henry really wanted to stop me, he would've, but he stayed quiet, probably realising it wasn't the time to question if I could handle myself. Apparently, he could make smart decisions occasionally. Who knew?

"Would you slow down?" Ansel huffed behind me, and I did, if only because I realised I was charging through the forest in the pitch black, when I shouldn't have been able to see even a hand in front of my face without the flashlight to guide me. He jogged to my side, his chest heaving, and said, "So... that was kinda intense back there, huh?"

I ignored the question, trying my best to squint past the light Ansel was shining ahead of us. It would be easier without it, where I could let my night vision lead the way, but it wasn't like I really needed to see, anyway. This part of the forest was becoming too familiar for my liking, since I'd taken this trail three times today already. I'd memorised the paths so well I could find my way around with my eyes closed.

As we walked, the sound of animals scurrying away from us was the only thing to disrupt the silence, but soon Ansel seemed to tire of it, breaking the quiet with a cheerful whistle. I snuck a look at him, but he was too busy looking at the ground to notice. Or so I thought, but he must have felt my gaze, because he stopped whistling soon after.

"Are you doing okay, Madison?" He asked.

The question totally caught me off guard, especially because he seemed genuinely worried, which was unexpected given our circumstances. Almost as unexpected as his cheerfulness. "Considering I'm trampling through the forest with you on the first night of my spring break? Not what I planned, but I guess I'm doing okay."

"Seems like you weren't exactly snuggled up with your boyfriend, either." I shot him a look, but he just chuckled. "Relax, I'm just kidding. What's the story with you and the big guy, anyways?"

I sighed. "I already told you - we're friends. And speaking of friends, you don't seem all that worried about yours."

He didn't say anything right away, and I wandered a few steps before I noticed the shadows had grown longer. When I glanced back, I saw Ansel had paused a few feet behind me, the flashlight beam pointed at the ground.

"Ansel?" I said, and when he still said nothing, I felt my heart rate quicken slightly.

Had I read him all wrong? If I had, and he tried to come at me now, I knew I could easily handle him. But honestly, I was more worried about proving Henry right the first time he actually trusted me. It would be the cherry on top of a goddamn wonderful day.

When I spoke again, I made sure to keep my voice steady, so he wouldn't catch on that I was onto him. "Is there something you wanna tell me?"

The quiet stretched on, making my skin prickle with unease. Sweat dripped down my back, my body tensing, until he let out a tired sigh. "Listen, let me first say that Colton is a good dude, okay? One of the best I know. But he's going through some stuff right now. And, well... he's done this before."

"Done what before?"

"The taking off without a word thing. Ever since..." He faltered, and for a moment, I considered prodding him for more details, but I resisted the temptation, not wanting to make him shut down entirely. "I didn't wanna bring it up earlier 'cause, well... Jamie's not exactly level-headed when it comes to Colton, if you catch my meaning."

"Ah."

"Yeah... He thinks I don't know, so don't say anything. But Jay worries. Probably more than he should, all things considered. But whenever Colt's gone before, it's always been back home in Boston or at least somewhere he can hail a cab once he pulls his head out of his ass, y'know what I mean? Out here..." He gestured at the trees surrounding us, his gaze darkening. "I'm sure he's fine, really. But after today... it's just that something really bad could happen to him. That's why I didn't mention it before. Figured you wouldn't help us look if you knew."

I wanted to deny it and give him a piece of my mind for not being honest, but I stopped myself. If I'd known the truth, would I have been so willing to help? I wasn't sure. Henry definitely wouldn't. But Ansel was right – if Colton normally skipped out back in their city... The forest was a whole other level. Chances are he would be okay, like Ansel said, but it was also possible he could run into something that wouldn't be too happy with him in its territory, so we needed to find him before anything else did. Especially considering how sick he was.

"I was around here with Henry. Colton didn't come this way. But we should check out the creek. He could've gone around us. Heard us talking and avoided passing us altogether?" And, going in that direction would have positioned him downwind, ensuring that neither Henry nor I would have detected his scent as he slinked around us.

Ansel gave me a sceptical look, like he wasn't sure if I was teasing him, but I could tell from his face he was telling the truth. He didn't lie to get me alone out here and attack me. He was just scared for his friend and willing to do anything to find him. Once I accepted that, I felt myself unwind, and I gave Ansel a little, comforting smile.

He hesitated for a moment longer, but then finally he smirked and gave a short nod before saying, "Whatever you say, boss."

And though we may have met under unusual circumstances, I was pretty sure Ansel and I just became friends.

———⚭———

There was no sign of Colton by the creek.

I hadn't expected there to be, despite what I'd said to Ansel. That was mainly to let him know I was taking him seriously. But Colton was still passed out when I snuck out of the cabin. At least, I was relatively certain he was, even if I hadn't actually checked. I heard three heartbeats in the living room, and that made me confident I could sneak out without getting caught. Maybe I was wrong, but did it even matter? I didn't think so at this point, since he *was* gone, no matter when it happened. It was just that knowing if he was still there when I'd left could've given us a clue about how far he might've gone. Honestly, though, with how sick he was, I doubted an hour would give him much of a head start.

The point was, wherever he'd run off to, I was pretty sure it wasn't in this part of the forest. While he could've snuck around Henry and me by keeping downwind, we'd have still heard him. We might not have realised it was *him*, but we would have still heard *something*. Colton had been dumb enough to drink the untreated water, so I highly doubted he'd be careful when slinking through the woods at night. If he had been anywhere near us, we would have noticed... as well as every other animal within a two-mile radius. We hadn't heard anything, though, which meant he hadn't come close.

He must've gone the opposite direction. It made sense – following the dirt track would eventually bring him to the highway, and if he'd heard Henry and me, he'd know it would take him further away from us, where he wouldn't get caught. It was the easiest way to escape if, in his fevered mind, he believed he was in danger. If we'd been paying attention, we still might have heard him, even if he had gone that way. But when you're accustomed to being in the wilderness, the noises faded into the background, like elevator music. We were both so caught up in looking for the creature I saw that we might have overlooked any movement from the other side of the cabin.

Of course, I couldn't tell Ansel any of that, so I was stuck pretending to search for clues where I knew there were none. It didn't help that he'd been leading us around in circles for the last thirty minutes, either.

On our third - or was it the fourth? – return to the creek, he groaned, before striking out at the nearest tree with his fist, prompting some creature to scurry away. I bit back a sigh.

"He obviously isn't here, so why don't we go and find the others?" I suggested. Then, noticing his expression, I quickly added, "I don't mean give up. It's just... Well, maybe they've had better luck?"

I didn't really believe that – Henry would've found some way to let me know if they had – a whistle, or a shout, or, hell, he'd probably just ditch the guys and come find me if he needed to. But Ansel didn't need honesty right now. He needed hope.

Ignoring me, he leaned against the tree trunk he had hit a few moments ago, head back and tilted up towards where the sky should be, if not for the canopy of leaves above us. He stayed like that for so long that I started to wonder if he even heard me, until he finally straightened up and gave me a tired look. He let out a long breath, scratched his fingers over the little hair he had on his head, and then nodded in agreement.

"Yeah, you're right. Let's head back." He said, gesturing – in completely the wrong direction – for me to lead the way. I didn't comment on that, but when I turned away from the creek and towards the path that actually *would* take us back to the cabin, he said nothing, instead just silently falling into step behind me.

As we walked, the only sounds that broke the silence were the gentle rustling of leaves in the breeze and the satisfying crunch of the forest floor beneath our feet. There was a chill in the air, but it wasn't too bad, so it was a pleasant enough walk, even if I'd rather have been in bed. Ansel obviously wasn't a fan of the quiet, though, because after a while, he cleared his throat to get my attention.

"Sorry 'bout earlier." I turned my gaze towards him, noticing the slump of his shoulders and the sadness reflected in his eyes. He was more worried about Colton than he was letting on. "Y'know... Flipping out. I'm not usually like that, I swear."

It was weird seeing him so vulnerable, especially since I barely knew him. It made me uncomfortable, so I hurriedly looked away, but then I felt a little tickle on my cheek. A spiderweb. *Ugh.* I swatted it away, holding back a shriek, while my other hand went to my hair to make sure it was gone. The whole thing took only a moment, but it distracted me just long enough for my foot to snag on a vine. As I stumbled, my arm reached out, fingers frantically scrambling for a lifeline, until they latched onto a nearby branch, stopping the fall. It did nothing to help the embarrassment though, as my cheeks flushed with heat.

I braced myself, half-expecting to hear Ansel's laughter echoing, but there was only silence. He didn't rush to help me, either, which both relieved and pissed me off, but it wasn't a big deal, so I pushed it to the back of my mind and regained my balance.

Once I'd recovered my footing, I said, "It's a stressful situation. Don't worry about it. But you mentioned he's done this before, yeah? So it's gonna be okay. The guys will have something, I'm sure of it."

Another lie, but this time I wasn't sure it was completely for his sake. I wanted them to find Colton safe, but with the anticipation of seeing Carter again at the forefront of my mind, I had to admit I was hoping for something that would divert attention from the awkwardness between us. I got why he was mad at me, but I'd never seen him react like that. I wasn't sure I could handle it again, even if I knew I couldn't avoid it forever.

I kept walking, waiting for Ansel to reply. When he didn't, I looked over my shoulder again. "Everything okay, Ans—"

His name caught in my throat, a shiver running down my spine. Because Ansel wasn't there. There was no one on the path except for me.

What the hell?

"Ansel?" Fear made my voice tremble as I called out, desperately trying to suppress the rising panic that threatened to overwhelm me.

There was a logical explanation. There had to be. He probably just went off the trail to take a piss or something, which was rude – and really stupid, since he already got lost in this forest earlier today – but it wasn't a big deal. No need to freak out.

Even though I tried to stay calm, my voice still shook when I repeated his name, holding my breath while I waited for a response. Nothing came. At a sudden noise to my left, my heart leaped in my chest. I whipped my head around, desperately hoping to spot Ansel, but all I saw was a lone deer grazing in the distance. Heart still pounding, I tore my gaze away and took a small step back towards the creek, feeling the hair on the back of my neck stand up.

And then it hit me - the scent, so distinct, engulfing me as I stood amidst the trees.

Blood. *Human* blood.

23

A torrent of images flooded my mind immediately. At first, a flashback: Ryan, dead in his car, drenched in blood. But then it wasn't Ryan anymore. Instead of his face, it was Carter's. I blinked, and suddenly it morphed into Henry. Then I imagined both of them, completely motionless, their blood pooling beneath their bodies, blending together before flowing into the grass at my feet, as I helplessly looked on. Jamie standing over them, a knife in his hand, laughing maniacally.

My stomach churned, a wave of nausea engulfing me.

Just when I thought I couldn't handle the weight of it any longer, a gust of wind blew down the abandoned trail, bringing a fresh wave of the scent with it, and...

Tears welled up in my eyes. Because it wasn't them. The blood – it didn't belong to Carter *or* Henry.

It must have only been for a second that terror gripped my very soul. Where I thought the worst, imagining my entire world being obliterated. If anything were to happen to Carter or Henry, that's exactly how it would feel. But even though it was short, it felt like forever. Now, as I breathed in that scent, savouring the rush of air filling my lungs, relief threatened to floor me.

They were okay! For now, at least. But that brief moment was enough to throw me off, and now I needed to see for myself they weren't harmed. That was the only way to really get rid of the fear that had settled in my gut. So I had to find Ansel, quickly, and—

The realisation hit me like a lightning bolt, sending a shockwave through my body. I was so worried about Carter and Henry that my brain just took a moment to catch up. But once it did, I knew it right away.

Colton.

Suddenly, it felt like his smell was all around me, and I wondered how I hadn't noticed it before. Maybe the wind had changed, but with a scent that strong, I should've picked up *something*. It didn't really matter, though, because one thing was certain — there was nothing I could do for Colton now. He was gone. Nobody could lose that much blood and survive.

My legs turned to jelly as I thought of him, and tears spilled over to race down my cheeks. But I couldn't let myself go there. Not when I could still help Ansel. I could stop him from being the one to find his friend's body. Nobody should have to see something like that, especially not when it was someone they cared about. I had to find him. Find him and go back to the cabin. Carter would have to drive me to town, because this couldn't wait until morning. We needed to call the cops.

As I turned to head back down the trail, I called out Ansel's name, hoping to hear a rustling or response amidst the silence, but all I heard was the sound of my breath. Did he go too far off the path and get lost? No way that was true. Even assuming it was, there was no way he could have gotten far enough away for me to not hear him. I was a werewolf, for crying out loud. I could hear clearly for miles, so unless Ansel had grown wings and flown away, there was no way he was out of earshot.

So, was it all just a big joke? I didn't think so. There was no way they could fake that amount of blood. The nauseating stench polluted the air, leaving me no choice but to breathe through my mouth to avoid it. But if Ansel had no clue, if he didn't know what happened to Colton, then maybe he just thought it'd be funny to hide from me in the woods at night. I mean, he'd straight up confessed they had zero hiking experience. Maybe he didn't take my warning about the woods seriously. Just a dumb, but ultimately harmless, prank—

Unless...

No. No way. Ansel and Jamie hadn't killed Colton. *Had they?* But then, why was he so insistent on separating me from the guys? That was weird, wasn't it? I'd only agreed because Carter had made it *very* clear he didn't want to speak to me. I still thought that was really weird, too, even if it wasn't undeserved. It was just so unlike him. He'd never reacted like that before. I'd only heard Carter lose his temper once, and he didn't even know I knew about it. We hadn't been 'official' for long – just a few weeks – and I'd been hanging around outside the boy's locker room, waiting for basketball practice to finish, because we were going to the diner after school to work on a history project together. I *shouldn't* have heard, and I didn't mean to eavesdrop, but supernatural hearing makes it pretty hard not to. So I heard every word when one of the guys started ragging on him for dating me. Carter had tried to tell him politely to back off, but the guy had continued bating him until Carter snapped.

I didn't even know who he was – some kid a couple of grades below us. Certainly no one important, yet I remember Ethan had to step in to stop it turning into an actual fight.

I could recall that afternoon like it was yesterday. When Carter had finally come out, I'd noticed the flush in his cheeks and the tight lines around his eyes that relaxed as soon as they looked at me. But I never mentioned it, and neither did he. Instead, he just took my hand and led me to the truck, not even stopping when Ethan called after him to see if he was okay. I soon forgot about it, because over dinner, he was just Carter. *My* Carter – sweet, warm, beautiful. As if nothing had happened.

Just that one time. Even then, it wasn't directed at me, so his reaction now felt completely unlike him. The not giving me a chance to explain, and being okay with us being separated like that, given the circumstances. Ansel and Jamie must've said something to him. Got in his head to push us apart. I had no idea why they would, but it was the only thing that made sense. And we'd fallen for it. All of us. But now I'd figured them out, and I had to get back to them, to warn them—

A faint whisper of a thought had been lingering at the back of my mind, but I'd ignored it until now, because it was an elusive thread that slipped through my fingers whenever I tried to grasp it. But it finally materialised, crystal clear. The forest... it was quiet. *Too* quiet. I strained my ears, listening for *anything*, but heard only silence in reply. *Dead* silence. Like a graveyard.

Was that even possible? There should be noise - animals and insects chattering, owls hooting, deer lapping up water. In the forest back home, no matter how far I was from Vineyard Manor, I could always hear the sounds of life. I got so used to it that the sounds just blended together, like a constant soundtrack in the background that I didn't always notice but was always there.

I noticed it now. Or, more like, the complete lack of it. My ears were on high alert, but there was nothing to hear. There was no melody. Just silence, as if every creature was holding its breath.

Something felt weird, and I suddenly wanted to run away, but my feet wouldn't budge. I didn't even know why I was so freaked out. There wasn't anything obviously wrong, not that I could see, and I still needed to find Ansel. I couldn't just ditch him, no matter how much I wanted to go back to Carter and Henry.

Swallowing hard, I forced down the sour taste of bile that had crept up my throat and took a step forward. Just one step. Then one more, and...

A sudden scuffling sound made me spin around, heart pounding, but there was nothing in sight, only a cool breeze on my skin that sent shivers down my spine. I paused for a second, taking a deep breath to fill my lungs with the earthy scent of the forest, before continuing on my way.

"Ansel?" I called out again after a few steps. "Come on, this isn't funny!"

More silence. I knew it was a long shot, but I had to try anyway. Crouching down, I let my fingertips explore the leaves that littered the ground, before bringing a handful to my nose... only to recoil at the repulsive smell.

Bile crept up my throat once more, and I folded in half, my body convulsing while I desperately tried to hold it back. The leaves slipped through my fingers, falling to the ground, and I inhaled deeply, allowing the fresh air to cleanse my lungs and relieve the nausea that had come so suddenly. Gingerly, I kicked at the pile of twigs and leaves to scatter them, hoping I wouldn't find any unpleasant surprises, like a decomposing critter, considering the stench. But when the mound was gone, all that remained was a sad patch of dirt and a few wilted blades of grass.

That should've made me feel better, but it didn't. Instead, it had anxiety coiling in my gut. Animals lived in these woods, which meant that death and animal carcasses were an inevitable part of the landscape, no matter how unpleasant it was to see up close. If it wasn't some animal I'd smelled…

There's no way it could be Colton. The smell on the leaves was super strong, so the decomposition must have been pretty far along. He'd only been gone for a few hours, tops. But then I remembered something – my thoughts drifting to the poster of the missing red-headed girl and the dark-haired boy, their haunting faces standing out among the faded advertisements in the abandoned storefront back in Chibouwood. Above their photo, the word 'MISSING', emphasised in bold capital letters.

Before I could even determine if it was animal or human remains, another wave of nausea hit me, only this time I couldn't control it. I bent over as the vomit burst its way up my throat, splattering onto the grass that lined the trail. But it didn't really matter if the victim was human or animal. Not when Colton's blood still tainted the air. What was important was figuring out what – or who – attacked him, before anything could happen to Carter.

And I was all alone, with no weapons, or even a way to Change without leaving myself exposed. Completely defenceless.

24

Panic took over, dark spots clouding my vision until I could hardly see at all. Desperate for stability, I summoned an image of Carter in my mind, holding onto it like an anchor until, gradually, my racing heart began to slow, giving me the chance to take a deep breath and steady myself. I sucked in the cold air, bracing myself for the disgusting smell that was about to come, and...

A mixture of sweet wildflowers, the crisp scent of pine, and the cool sensation of early morning dew enveloped me instead.

What the hell? How was that poss—

And that's when it hit me - none of this was real.

I was dreaming. *Obviously* I was dreaming, and I should've known right away. This happened a ton when I was a kid. My therapist said they were 'lucid' dreams, which I didn't really understand at the time, but my dad was still worried. He kept waking up at night to find the back door wide open, and I'd be wandering around the woods behind our house, totally out of it, according to him. But it felt real to me. Like there was an entire other universe in my head.

When I had my first Change, it was as if the wolf in me woke up and fixed a part of my brain that had been messed up for ages. The lucid dreaming stopped, and so did the sleepwalking. Until now, apparently. *Ugh*, of course it had to start up again when I was in a cabin in the damn woods, with my boyfriend, my overbearing best friend, and three strangers, one of whom already thought I was crazy.

But there was still something bothering me. Some piece of the puzzle that didn't quite fit.

Every time before, back when I had these dreams... it felt different. I couldn't really explain it, but I always had this sense that I was dreaming. That it wasn't reality. This... it felt just as real as it did when I was a child, but without the same certainty that it wasn't. Maybe it had something to do with the fact that I was a werewolf now. It's not like there had been extensive research into how lucid dreaming affected supernatural creatures, after all. It was quite possible that this was entirely normal for someone like me.

I was flipping out over nothing. I'd just fallen asleep, still in bed, cuddled up with Carter. Everything was fine. It was just a dream.

And since it was all happening in my head, there was no harm in looking around, finding out what my subconscious was trying to tell me. Right?

Decision made, I looked around at the moonlit branches, taking it all in before heading back toward the creek, feeling more confident now. Not having to wait for Ansel had its advantages - I reached the fork in the path quickly. There, the trees started to thin out as the ground sloped downwards, leading to the creek below.

Carefully moving downhill, the moonlight pierced through the trees, creating haunting shadows on the ground. I was about halfway down the embankment when I paused, a flash of metal catching my eye, just a few yards to the left of my path. I thought about ignoring it, but my gut said it was important. My mind wouldn't have put it in the dream if it wasn't.

I moved towards it, struggling to maintain my balance as I tripped over tangled roots and vines, but miraculously stayed on my feet. It was only when I was nearly upon it that I realised the object was a flashlight, half-buried in the earth.

No. Not just any flashlight. It was *Ansel's* flashlight. The one he had before he vanished.

I bent down, grabbed it, and gave it a quick look over, flicking the switch to make sure it was the same one. Not that I had gotten a good look at it before, but as soon as I held the shaft, his scent wafted up to my nose, the lingering traces of palm sweat revealing how tightly he had gripped it.

I clutched onto it just as tightly, feeling the weight of it in my hand as I continued my descent down the bank. There were no other signs of Ansel as I walked. He wasn't waiting for me by the water either, grinning or shouting "gotcha!". Did I actually expect anything else? Not really. I didn't even know why I bothered coming back or what I was expecting to find. It just felt like some invisible force was dragging me here, and it didn't make much sense, but I had no other option but to go along with it.

It wasn't a steep descent to the creek, really, but the path above definitely provided a good vantage point. I didn't like that. It felt like being at the bottom of a cage, where anyone could look down and watch you, but you couldn't see them. Which was stupid, because who the hell would be watching me? It was the middle of the night, miles from anywhere, and Ansel complained the first time we came this way. I couldn't picture him willingly coming back, and I definitely would've heard if he did, considering how badly he was puffing and panting by our third time cutting through here. But I just had a gut feeling I was in the right spot. This was where my dream wanted me to be.

"MADISON?"

I jumped at the voice, coming out of nowhere and sounding out of place amongst the dead silence of the night. Within a second, though, I knew exactly who it was. I'd recognise that voice anywhere.

"Henry?" I said, mostly to myself, as I spun around, trying to figure out where the heck it was coming from. But the clearing made his voice echo, sounding like it was coming from everywhere, making it impossible to pinpoint. "HENRY?" I shouted even louder, accidentally dropping the flashlight as I cupped my hands around my mouth. "I'm over here! By the creek!"

"Madison?!" As his frantic shout echoed back, I realised he hadn't heard me. He must've been upwind, the breeze carrying both my scent and my voice away from him, so he had no idea where I was, either. "Where are you?!"

The panic in his voice was so genuine, it was almost believable. Maybe I was totally wrong, and this wasn't a dream. But even if it wasn't, that didn't explain why he'd be so scared. He knew I was with Ansel, and it hadn't been that long since we split up to search for Colton. He had no reason to freak out.

Unless...

I thought back to the blood I'd smelled, so sure it belonged to Colton. But how would I even dream about that if I didn't have any memory of it? Dreams are just your subconscious mind playing tricks on you, bringing up old memories, even the ones you forgot about, like a random person you saw on the bus. That's what my therapist used to say. I racked my brain, but couldn't remember Colton bleeding last night, not even a tiny cut. Which meant—

Nope. I refused to go there. I was so wrapped up with Carter last night that I wouldn't have noticed if Colton had a little cut, but the smell would still stick with me, whether I realised it or not. No reason to stress, whatsoever. I was still in the dream, so there was nothing to be scared of. I just had to keep going until I figured out what my subconscious was trying to say. And then I could wake up.

I pushed that thought aside and turned my attention back to Henry. The second time he called, his voice was quieter, like he had moved down the embankment. It was a weird way to come since there was a well-worn path up the hill that would've led him directly to me, but dreams often had a way of defying logic, so I didn't dwell on it.

"Henry?" I called out again. "Stay where you are. I'll come to you!"

The ground around the creek was a thick, slippery sludge, making every step a challenge. I took it easy, because if I didn't, then I was sure I'd end up on my ass in the mud, but I eventually stumbled my way to the tree-line on the south side, where I stopped for a second to wipe my shoes against the grass. It was no use, though, because the thick, sticky mud just clung to them. Frustrated, I let out a loud grunt before finally giving up and taking a step into the dark abyss beyond the trees, when...

"MADISON?!"

I stopped dead, pivoting on my heel to look behind me. Henry's voice again. But this time it had come from the northern side of the creek. *What the hell?* How did he get around so quickly? Even with the slipping and sliding, it couldn't have actually taken me more than a couple of minutes to make it across—

A scratching sound interrupted the thought. Wait, no... not scratching. Dragging? Yes. That was it. A low, scraping noise echoed through the air, as if a massive weight was being dragged across the forest floor. And then the scent that had assaulted me earlier was back, hitting me just as hard as before. Rotten flesh. Nausea engulfed me, and I could feel the acidic bile rising in my throat, yet I was paralyzed, unable to take a single step.

Shit. I couldn't move. *Why* couldn't I move?

I focused all my attention on my legs, feeling the strain in my muscles as I desperately tried to regain control of my body, my heart pounding in my ears. I realised then that I'd never had to think about it before – moving. My body just effortlessly obeyed my commands without me even having to ask. But now, I couldn't remember how. I begged my body to respond, but it wouldn't listen, and with each passing moment, the waves of panic washing over me grew fiercer, leaving me feeling more and more helpless.

Just a dream. Just a dream. Just a dream...

Though everything else refused to budge, my eyes still darted around, searching for something, anything, to help. As I scanned the area, they landed on a quivering tree branch across the water, and a surge of relief flooded through me. It had to be Henry. He hadn't heard me telling him to stay put, and he'd found me, and now he'd get me out of here. And I'd never been so happy that he never did a damn thing I asked him to, even in my subconscious mind.

Anticipation filled me as my eyes anxiously trained on the cluster of trees, hoping to catch sight of his shaggy black hair or to hear his voice, spewing curses, as he shoved aside branches to get to me. With a final rustle, the branches parted, and a figure came into view, accompanied by the unmistakable sound of cracking twigs.

The words were on the tip of my tongue, and my lips parted, ready to release them into the air. To tell him I was stuck. That he was right, obviously. I needed help.

"Thank G—"

The words disappeared into nothing. Just a breath on the air. Because my stomach had dropped, and now a cold sweat ran down my back.

At first, my brain couldn't process what I was seeing. Only that it wasn't Henry. But then it hit me — it was the same thing as before, hiding in the trees near the cabin. Stalking me.

The creature with glowing red eyes that pierced the darkness.

Except, this time, it didn't just lurk in the shadows. I could feel its penetrating stare fixated on me, until, without warning, it unleashed a snarl so sudden and fierce that it sucked the air out of my lungs. And all I could do was stand there as it leapt towards me.

25

I wasn't sure at what point I regained control of my legs. All I knew was one second I was stuck, and then suddenly I wasn't, and I sure as hell wasn't hanging around to figure out why. Not with that *thing* rapidly closing the distance between us.

There was no other way to describe it than that – a *'thing'*. I'd never seen anything like it, which made me even more sure it wasn't real. That might seem cocky since I could transform into a wolf at will, but that's not what I meant. I just recognised that there was a scientific reason for the Change. Something about atoms, molecules, and the changing states of matter. I was always curious as a kid, and thankfully I had Ryan to pester with my endless questions about the supernatural. Of course, that didn't mean I always understood the answer. Despite Ryan's efforts, I was too young to grasp it. Still, I trusted him, so just knowing there *was* an explanation was good enough, even if I couldn't wrap my head around it.

Even Ryan would have a hard time explaining this.

Across the water stood a being with the body of a human, but as large as a grizzly bear. It looked like a corpse from far away - all dark and leathery skin stretched over protruding ribs. But then I saw the huge antlers and skinny arms as long as tree trunks dragging on the ground, and I realised it wasn't a zombie at all... and I wasn't sure if I should be relieved by that or not.

Ben used to joke about us being like Mystery Inc from Scooby Doo, and I would crack up because Henry would get so annoyed when he called him 'Freddie', after Fred Jones. But now it seemed like he'd hit the nail on the head, and if I just got close enough, I could reach up and pull off a mask to reveal a man sputtering about how he '*would've gotten away with it if it wasn't for us meddling kids.*'

Shit. I was spiralling. But, even with my mind in a frenzy, I still kept an eye on the creature. It was almost at the water's edge, looking straight at me. I took a step back, heart pounding, trying to make sense of it all but failing. It didn't seem real. More like one of those horror movie monsters than an actual beast. I felt tiny compared to it, like a mouse standing off against a lion. The thought sent a shiver down my spine.

I needed to get to the other side of the creek. That was the quickest way back to the trail. But the creature was blocking my way, and I didn't want to risk getting too close to it. Plus, what if it chased me all the way back to the cabin? To the others? I didn't wanna get caught, but I'd prefer that than it being anywhere near Carter.

A thought struck me then, and my stomach tightened. *Henry*. I'd heard his voice. He was close by.

Shit! No... He wasn't just close. He was somewhere on the other side of the water – *behind the creature.* If he came charging out of the woods...

I stopped the thought, shaking my head to get rid of it because I knew it couldn't happen. This was all just a dream, wasn't it? So, even if Henry showed up, it wouldn't really be him. The actual Henry was back in his room at the cabin, perfectly safe. That thing posed no danger to him. But, me? It couldn't physically hurt me, but it would *feel* real, and I had no intention of experimenting with it.

Like it knew what I was thinking, the thing took a deliberate step forward, its tree-like arms scraping against the ground. My gut told me to run, but I knew I couldn't make a break for it. The sight of a fleeing prey was an irresistible trigger for any predator, like a red rag to a bull.

Our eyes met, and it moved forward, but it didn't come charging at me. The movements were deliberate and slow. It was like a game, one that made me feel sick to my stomach.

Another step. Then another, and another, until the creature finally stopped at the edge of the creek, taking a moment to lower its head and study the water. I held my breath, taking a cautious step back when...

A sharp crack echoed through the air as a twig snapped under the weight of my step. I froze in horror, but it was already too late. Without warning, the creature threw back its head and let out a piercing shriek of rage.

The sudden noise startled me so much that I lost my balance and stumbled, falling to the ground. My hair cascaded over my face, blurring my vision, and I hurriedly brushed it aside, desperately trying to regain focus on that *thing*.

It wasn't hard to spot it again, and as soon as I laid eyes on it, I couldn't help but smile, even though it felt ridiculous in the circumstances. But the creature was still standing at the creek's edge, and so I couldn't stop the smirk.

It couldn't cross the water.

The creek was narrow – only about twenty feet across – so I couldn't really tell if the creature *couldn't* cross or just didn't want to. But honestly, I didn't care about the reason. All that mattered was the chance it provided, a precious opportunity to escape. Yes, it could loop around the water to catch up with me, but that would waste precious seconds. Seconds that made all the difference. Henry and I had spent countless hours running through the woods, and I knew those runs had prepared me for this moment. Alright, so those times were with four paws, not two human legs, but I still knew I could get away. This was my chance.

My instincts kicked in and I broke into a full sprint, paying no attention to where I was going. My groggy legs protested, but I pushed myself to run faster, determined not to give up. I *couldn't*. Branches snapped back in my path, slashing at my face and arms, while the uneven ground threatened to trip me up with every step. But, somehow, I stayed on my feet.

My heart raced in my chest, and the quietness of the forest intensified the ringing in my ears. Was it in pursuit? I couldn't tell, what with the sound of my breathing drowning out everything else. I'd have to stop and make sure, and there was absolutely no chance I was gonna—

I saw it too late - the figure just appeared out of nowhere, blocking me. With no time to switch paths, I just smashed into it, and immediately felt a pair of arms wrap around me, tight and suffocating. A scream fought its way up my throat, but I clamped my mouth shut, terrified of leading that *thing* right to me. Because this definitely wasn't the creature. I hadn't had a chance to turn away, but I could immediately see it was only half the size of the beast.

I'd escaped one danger, only to become trapped by another. It was almost ridiculous enough to be funny.

Whatever this new danger was, it had me in a vice-like grip, and I struggled to break free. Imprisoned in darkness, I frantically flailed my fists, hoping for a lucky strike. Finally, I felt the satisfying contact of my knuckles meeting flesh, accompanied by an unmistakable 'oomph' sound. Gearing up to land another blow, I pulled back, my muscles tensing with anticipation, when...

"What the *fuck*, Madison?!"

The voice made me freeze, my brain registering the familiar but faint smell of sandalwood, failing to mask the stench of sweat. But I still knew it. It was as recognisable to me as popcorn or freshly cut grass.

He loosened his grip slightly, but didn't release me completely, like he thought I'd still bolt given half a chance. But it was a good thing, really, because without his arms to lean on, I felt sure my legs wouldn't have been able to hold me up.

Finally, I looked up and saw a face staring back at me, dark eyes wide with terror.

Henry.

"What the fuck is going on?" He repeated.

I knew this was just a dream, and he wasn't actually there. Everything was an illusion. Yet, his appearance was so lifelike that I felt an overwhelming sense of relief and instinctively grabbed onto his shirt, burying my face in his chest to keep from losing my balance.

It surprised me how long he held me, his embrace strong and safe, almost too strong to be make-believe. But he'd never hold me like this in reality. Henry Barton was the last person to show vulnerability, and true to form, he was the first to pull back.

"I... um..." After escaping the creature, my mind was all over the place, so I took a deep breath to clear my head. Then I bit my lip, ran my hand through my hair, and said, "Nothing's going on. Can we just get out of here?"

"Don't give me that shit, Madison. You know I know you better than that. So we'll stay right here until you tell me what's got you so jumpy."

At a noise, my head snapped around so fast that I felt a twinge in my neck, but there was no sign of the creature. Everything in the forest was still and silent, as if trapped in time.

"*Please.* Can we just go? Before it comes." I begged.

"Before what comes?" When I didn't answer, he let out a low, menacing growl. "*Madison!*"

My anger surged as I shot him a glare. Even in dreams, he was a colossal pain in my ass.

"*Henry!* Goddamnit, you're not in control here. I'm the boss this time. My head, my rules."

"The fuck does that mean? Your head, your rules? Madison, you're making zero sense right now."

As a noise sounded again – scratching – his voice faded to the background. My spine tingled with dread, and I stood motionless, ears alert, as the nauseating stench of rot overwhelmed me once more. "It's not real. It's just a dream."

As I mumbled to myself, trying to drown out the noise, my hands instinctively covered my ears, but Henry's voice still penetrated my thoughts. "A dream? Madison, what the—"

"A dream. Just a dream." I scrunched my eyes closed tight, and my legs jittered as I repeated the words over and over. *Wake up, Madison. Just wake up!*

A gentle touch grazed my cheeks, jolting my eyes open while my hands instinctively clenched into tight fists. But I only saw the pools of Henry's eyes and felt his hands gripping either side of my face. He was so close his hot breath tickled my skin, yet I still struggled to focus on his voice. Until one word broke through the fog - sleepwalking.

He thought I was sleepwalking? How was that even possible? He wasn't the real Henry. If I already knew I wasn't awake, why would my subconscious go through the trouble of creating a version of him just to convince me I was sleepwalking? That made zero sense. Not unless...

My eyes widened in alarm as I quickly backed away from him. As a child, my therapist taught me techniques to differentiate between dreams and reality. She called it 'reality checks'. It had been forever since I needed them, so I couldn't remember the specifics, just something to do with my hands...

I fixed my gaze on my palms, studying the intricate lines that intersected across them, then flipped them over to examine the backs. A faint memory stirred at the back of my mind, almost catching, until – *Yes!* That was it.

With my left hand up, I moved two fingers from my right hand towards it, hoping they would go right through, like a ghost, to prove it was all in my mind. I held my breath as the tips brushed against my skin. And then... *shit.* Resistance. The pressure against my palm made my fingers curl over the two pushing, clamping down like a claw.

That reality check *never* failed. Which could only mean one thing.

As the cold, harsh reality of the situation hit me like a tidal wave, my stomach plummeted. The stench of Colton's blood – the metallic tang that had made my stomach churn. The sight of the creature's twisted, misshapen form, and its grotesque features, burned into my mind's eye. My chest was heavy with the weight of it all, each breath a struggle.

It wasn't a dream. It was all too real.

My heart raced, and I struggled to catch my breath as my mind raced. I spun around, my eyes scanning the path I had just taken, desperately searching for any sign of trouble. "I have to find Ansel!"

I had barely gone two steps when Henry's grip on my hand stopped me in my tracks. Facing him again, anger flushed my cheeks. Because, no matter what he felt – or didn't feel – for Ansel, Henry had no clue what was in these woods. Hell, I didn't even know myself, and I'd *seen* it. But if that beast was *killing* people, then I couldn't just leave Ansel out there to fend for himself. I wouldn't have another death on my conscience. I wouldn't be able to live with myself.

The argument was on the tip of my tongue, but Henry interrupted me before I could speak.

"Ansel is fine, Madison. We got back to the cabin an hour ago, and he was there. Just fucking sitting on the damn deck like nothing..." He dragged his hand through his hair, his nostrils flaring. "Said you'd just disappeared. And – *fuck* – I should never have let you go with him. I shouldn't have let you out of my sight. I'll kill him. I'll fucking kill him."

My lips parted, the denial prepped and ready. I wanted to explain to him about the creature and tell him that Ansel was innocent. But then his words hit me properly, and suddenly nothing seemed certain to me anymore.

Ansel was back at the cabin. He'd left me behind.

A chill ran down my spine. "N-no. That's not—" I started, but I couldn't form the words, because I knew, deep in my gut. I knew Henry was telling the truth.

But... how? *How* had I been out here for over an hour already?

It wasn't a dream. I knew that now. But did that mean it was real? Did Ansel drug me? He insisted on separating me from Henry and Carter, and I didn't really put up a fight because I was too scared to face my boyfriend after everything that went down. Had I really been so stupid? Made it *that* easy for him?

I went over every little thing in my head, from when I left the group until Ansel vanished, trying to find any proof of his guilt or any details I might have missed. Because people didn't just disappear. And that thing I saw... my brain had been so quick to accept that I was dreaming because it was so surreal. It could have been a hallucination just as easily as anything else. Just like I thought had happened to Colton, leading them to the cabin.

My mind strained to connect the dots, but the puzzle pieces refused to interlock, and I could practically feel Henry's impatience drilling into me as he waited for me to provide an explanation.

"I... I think—"

"MADISON!"

The voice interrupted me mid-sentence, coming from behind Henry. My gaze instinctively fell to our hands, still intertwined, and I immediately snatched mine away just as Carter emerged from the shadows of the forest.

My body tightened the moment I saw him, but all the tension disappeared when I caught a glimpse of his expression. I could see in his eyes he wasn't thinking about what had happened earlier. I had no idea what to even call that. *'Fight'* didn't seem quite right, but it was the closest Carter and I had ever come to arguing, and I hated that it was my fault. But now he only rushed towards me, arms stretched out, and I let go of my worries as I melted into his embrace.

"I'm so sorry. So, so sorry. Are you okay?"

Wait... *he* was apologising to *me?* My heart swelled with a mixture of emotions, but I forced the guilt to the back of my mind. Now wasn't the time.

When I pulled away, his gaze lingered on my face, just like Henry's had, looking for any traces of injury, as intense as if he could see right through me to my soul. Without thinking, I reached out and touched his cheek to let him know I was okay in every other way, too. *We* were okay.

"I'm good." I promised, then I shifted so I could see both of them, eyes darting back and forth between them. "But we better not hang around here. We need to get back to the cabin, where it's safe."

"Safe?" Carter asked. Henry's poker face didn't budge, but his raised eyebrow gave away his nerves.

Swallowing a lump in my throat, I averted my gaze, fixating on the branches swaying behind them. "There's something I need to tell you."

26

"You really think he drugged you?"

Carter's voice, so sudden in the stillness of our bedroom, startled me. I knew he wasn't asleep, but neither of us had spoken for ages. Obviously, his mind hadn't been so quiet.

Twisting onto my stomach, I rested my hands on his chest and nestled my chin on top, savouring the comforting sensation of his heartbeat pulsating beneath my touch, while I studied the contours of his face.

We'd been back at the cabin for a couple of hours now, and there was no sign of Ansel and Jamie.

No big surprise. Sure, my theory could be wrong, but the fact remained that Ansel had abandoned me in the forest, in the dead of night, after insisting I go with him. Me being missing distracted Henry long enough for them to take off, and I honestly didn't blame them for not wanting to face him after that, even if I was way off about everything else.

I didn't want to believe Ansel was a bad guy, or that he'd used me, but the evidence was right there, staring me in the face. I didn't know what it proved - that he killed Colton? That he was the one who made those other two kids disappear? It was too much to believe, but no matter why he did it, his actions were shady, and that I didn't see it before just showed how careless I was, and how easily I could put everyone I loved at risk.

Both Henry *and* Carter had wanted to go after them, but I didn't see the point. It wouldn't achieve anything. Better for them to be gone, so we could get on with our week. I should have known it wouldn't be that easy, though. Henry demanded an immediate explanation, then insisted we return to the creek once I told them about the creature. He said he just wanted to check it out, but I knew that was code for '*checking Maddie hadn't lost her goddamn mind*'. Still, I couldn't really fault him for it. I was starting to think maybe I *had* lost my mind.

As expected, there was absolutely nothing to find. Not so much as a footprint that didn't belong to me or Ansel, which only made me more confident that I had been hallucinating all along.

Before responding to Carter, I took a deep breath and exhaled slowly, trying to gather my thoughts. "I don't want to believe it," I finally said, "but I can't think of any other explanation." I waited for his reply, but as his silence continued, I shifted onto my knees and gave him a quizzical look. "You don't agree?"

"Nah, it's not that. Not really. It's just..." He trailed off with a sigh, his eyes searching the room as if trying to find the perfect words. I kept my mouth shut, not wanting to interrupt him, and in the end he admitted, "Maybe you really did see something out there."

I tried to contain it, but a sudden burst of laughter still broke free. "You were listening when I described it, right? It was like something straight out of a horror movie. No way that was real."

He averted his gaze, the tips of his ears turning pink, and I immediately regretted my words. But then, after what felt like an eternity, he spoke again.

"Do you ever think that... I dunno. I mean, all the stories have gotta start somewhere, don't they? What if they're actually true? You ever think that could be possible?"

His words seemed to hang in the air, and it took a moment for them to sink in. When they finally did, my heart skipped a beat.

"I..." I felt a lump in my throat as I tried to speak, and my mouth tasted like it hadn't had a drop of water in days. "Um... I don't..."

Was he actually saying what I thought he was saying? Did he *know?* Maybe this was it. If I wanted to be with Carter - actually, there was no *if* about that. I had never loved anyone like I loved him, and I didn't think I would ever feel the same way about anybody else. But for us to work, he'd have to know the truth.

I always believed that keeping him in the dark was the best way to protect him, but what if I was wrong? Wherever he went, danger was always right behind him, no matter what I did. This time, though, there was nothing paranormal about it. Ansel, Colton, Jamie... they were all human, and yet he still could've gotten hurt. It might be safer for him to know everything.

No. I was out of my mind if I was actually thinking about telling him. He'd be in New York in a few months, and then he would *actually* be safe. Safe from me, safe from all the crap I brought with me.

But the question just kept nagging me, and honestly, I'd probably never have a better shot at finding out...

"Carter, I—"

His chuckle interrupted me as he sat up, his face flushing with embarrassment, and my stomach churned with disappointment as my opportunity vanished. "Shit, I don't even know what I'm talking about, Mads. I guess it's easier to believe it was real than to admit I screwed up. That all of this was my fault."

That made me freeze, my eyes going wide, and any idea of confessing disappeared, suddenly feeling unimportant. He'd been so mad at me earlier, and I'd been so relieved that he *wasn't* anymore, that I hadn't even considered anything else. And now he was saying he didn't blame me at all?

Somehow, that felt worse than anger.

"What are you talking about?" I couldn't help myself and reached out to touch him, lightly grazing his arm with my fingertips. I half expected him to pull away, but he didn't. "It's not—"

"Yeah, it is. We all know it, and I should count my blessings that Henry hasn't kicked my ass yet."

I shook my head, my fingers instinctively curling around his hand. "I was the one who—"

He chuckled again, but it sounded empty. "Mads, I love you, but would you stop? I know you're going to say what you think will make me feel better, but I don't deserve it. I shouldn't have let you go alone with him. I'm your boyfriend, for crying out loud. Your dad trusted me to look out for you, and I..." He trailed off, clawing his free hand through his hair. "I was an asshole. It's not an excuse, but when I woke up and you were gone, I was so scared. And then I found out you were hanging out with Barton, and man, I got jealous. But I screwed up and put you in danger, and I'm so sorry. It's unforgivable.

"I don't know what came over me. All I know is I was so pissed, and it was like I couldn't see anything past it. I wanted to come find you the second you were out of my sight, but he wouldn't let me. I get why. It wouldn't have done anyone any good if I got lost out there. But... shit, I don't know. I just... I guess I'm trying to say I get why you wanted Barton to come with us. It's because you didn't think I could look out for you. And before you say it, trust me, I *know* you can handle yourself just fine, but you shouldn't have to. Not all the time, anyway. And he does that for you, right? He makes you feel safe. And the worst thing is... Dang, I wanna be mad about it, but how can I when it's true? I can't protect you like he can. We aren't the same."

His words landed on me like a blow to the stomach, making me instinctively flinch away. It took me a moment to find my voice again.

"Is that really what you think? That I don't feel safe with you?" He barely met my eye as he shrugged, so I squeezed his hand tighter. "I already told you I didn't invite him up here, that he invited himself, and it was the truth. He's my best friend, Cart, and I've missed him since he's been at college, so yeah, it's nice to have him here. But that's it, okay? *Not* because I need him to protect me. Not when I'm with you. And earlier... I'm really sorry. I just... I couldn't sleep, so I went out to get some air. I guess Henry was still awake, so he came to see what was up. We didn't plan it, and noth—"

I didn't even notice he was moving closer until his kiss cut me off, the beat of his heart racing in my ears and merging with my own until they were indistinguishable. I gasped, breathing him in, and a hunger ignited inside me, deep in my gut, so suddenly it was as if it had only been temporarily contained after our game in the clearing earlier. It had never fully extinguished, and now the fire raged again, and I eagerly kissed him back. His hands moved to my hips, grip tightening as he effortlessly pulled me onto his lap. Immediately, I felt his desire pressing against me, and my arms instinctively wrapped around his neck, fingers tangling in his hair and tugging him nearer. After everything that'd happened, his lips were a lifeline, an anchor in an inky black sea. I hadn't realised I needed one until this very moment, but now, I clung to it like my life really did depend on it, savouring his intoxicating taste that had lit a fire that coursed through my veins as our bodies entwined.

The rest of the world faded to nothing, leaving only that moment, our bodies doing all the talking. I heard a door close in the distance, but I wasn't really paying attention. Because we needed this. So desperately needed it. And for the first time since we'd arrived in Chibouwood, I felt calm.

Afterwards, I snuggled against Carter's side, savouring the silence while my fingers lazily traced patterns on his bare chest.

He let out a long, happy sigh, and I craned my neck to see him, smiling when he looked at me with a relaxed grin that made butterflies dance in my stomach. Without a word, he leaned over to plant a gentle kiss on my forehead, before laying his head back on his pillow. Soon after, his breathing slowed, and the sound of his snores filled the air instead.

Sleep wasn't so forthcoming for me. The whirlwind of thoughts in my mind wouldn't stop, bouncing between Ansel and the creature. To drugs, and then to Colton and, finally, the two missing kids. I just couldn't shake the feeling that there was a connection between them.

But mainly, I couldn't stop thinking about Carter. As his words echoed around my head, doubts swirled, and I couldn't help but wonder if I had missed my chance to reveal everything.

'The stories have gotta start somewhere, don't they? What if they're actually true?'

Just how much had he already figured out?

No matter how hard I tried to ignore it, the sun's beams blared through the curtains, leaving a faint orange hue dancing on the backs of my closed eyes. By six in the morning, the persistent chirping of birds outside my window made it clear that sleep was no longer an option.

Even though I was tired, I loved being up before Carter. I couldn't help but smile as I watched him, softly snoring with his mouth slightly ajar and one arm lazily stretched above his head. It was truly amazing how he could sleep so soundly, oblivious to everything happening around him, as if he had no worries at all.

Although I didn't want to leave, I knew I couldn't stay there all day, so, after a few moments of watching him, I dragged myself out of bed, the chill of the wooden floorboards making my toes curl as I hurriedly grabbed his jacket from the floor.

It was even cooler in the hall, and when I stepped out of the cocoon of the bedroom, softly pulling the door closed behind me, the crisp morning air nipped at my skin. A shiver ran through me, and I pulled Carter's jacket tighter around my shoulders.

The only sound in the cabin, other than Carter's snores, was my footsteps. No sign of Henry.

I made my way to the door in the kitchen and found him sat outside on the deck, his eyes closed, head tilted towards the sunshine that filtered through the mesh screen, and a shabby looking patchwork blanket across his lap. At first, I thought he'd dozed off, but he looked up as soon as I stepped outside, watching me as I settled into the empty seat beside him.

"Morning." I said, getting a grunt from him in response. "Anything to report?"

"Nope."

"Good. Want to sleep for a bit?"

As he shook his head, a single strand of his dark hair gently fell across his eyes. He flicked it away as he said, "Not really tired."

I thought about arguing, but what would be the point? I wouldn't win. So, I just sighed. "Carter wants me to talk to the cops about everything. What do you think?"

Henry scoffed. "I think it's amazing you found the time to talk at all." I shot him a look, and in return, he rolled his eyes. "Jeez, chill out. I'm messing with you. But these walls aren't soundproof, just so you know."

"Sorry." A sudden warmth spread across my cheeks.

"Yeah, well, I knew what I was getting myself in for when I invited myself along, right?"

His words made me tense, but when I looked at him again, I noticed he was smirking, and my shoulders instantly relaxed. "You did kinda gate crash." I laughed. "I'm glad you're here, though. Really. It just might've been better if you'd brought a plus one, y'know? Three's a crowd, as they say."

"Not in my experience." He said, his expression deadpan, but a twinkle of something in his eye. It took a moment to sink in – I blamed lack of sleep – but when it finally did, my eyes widened.

"*Henry!*"

He snorted a laugh, before turning serious again. "You really think getting the cops involved is a good idea?"

I quickly glanced over my shoulder at the door, trying to catch any sounds of movement from Carter, but he was still sound asleep. Still, I lowered my voice anyway when I answered. "I mean... it's not like we're dealing with something supernatural, so this is the best move, don't you think? A guy is *missing*, H."

"That's assuming he wasn't in on the whole damn thing. That jerk is probably laughing at us from his cabin as we speak."

"Maybe." I let out a heavy sigh. "But if not? If he's actually missing? If Ansel and Jamie report it first... Well, they could really screw us over, and we don't need that. I just think we need to stay ahead of this. Last time..."

I trailed off, letting the sentence hang in the air. We both knew what I meant. We'd tried to handle things ourselves before, and Ryan ended up dead.

Our eyes connected then, and I could feel the reluctance radiating from him. He shifted in his seat, and I braced myself for an argument, but none came. He only let out a groan and slouched back into the chair, shoving his hands in the pockets of his jacket.

I waited for a few seconds, but he didn't say anything else. "So, I'm assuming your silence means you're not gonna give me a hard time about this?"

He was silent for a few more seconds, and when he did speak, I *heard* the eye roll in his voice, before I saw it on his face.

"What's the point? You'll just do whatever the hell you want, anyway." My fists clenched tightly as he stood up from his seat. Then he looked at me again. "Better wake Sleeping Beauty, then. Looks like we're going for a drive."

27

"Let me get this straight... You wanna file a missing person's report for a kid when you don't even know his last name?"

My fingers tapped nervously against the wooden armrest of the chair while I listened to the police officer, stealing quick glances at Carter beside me. No matter how hard I tried, I couldn't make my fidgeting stop since, as each second ticked by, my anxiety grew, and I regretted my decision to come more and more.

It took about thirty minutes to drive south from Chibouwood to Rowland, where the county sheriff's office was located. After talking to Henry, I woke up Carter, and then we quickly grabbed breakfast and hit the road. We arrived in town so early that the stores on the main street were still closed, and the sheriff's office was quiet enough to assign us an officer right away. Officer Horton, or at least that's what the name plaque said, sat across from us, jotting down notes while we told our story.

Carter's fingers intertwined with mine, his firm grip easing the rapid beat of my heart. I shot him a smile to say thanks.

"I know it's not much to go on, Officer, but—"

The officer cut off Carter with a dismissive snort. "Not much? Kid, it's *nothing* to go on." He tapped his pen on the paper and looked down at the notepad. "Young adult male, brown hair, below average height. You know where you are? Almost half of the tourists around here in spring match that description. So, what's the deal? You thought it would be fun to bother the local sheriff as part of a dare or something?"

Carter tensed up next to me, his voice tight as he replied, but the officer didn't notice. "Absolutely not, sir. It's like we told you. We got here yesterday to house sit for our friend's uncle. Sean Barton."

"DeWitt." I cut in. Sean was Sierra's brother, not Dan's, so he wasn't a Barton. I didn't think it would really matter for our case, but just in case Officer Horton actually checked our story, I didn't want to risk him dismissing us if he couldn't find any record of a Sean Barton nearby.

Carter gave a nod of acknowledgement. "Right. Sorry. Sean DeWitt. Anyway, he's got a cabin near Chibouwood and he's out of town for work, so he asked us to watch it. Except, when we got there, someone had beaten us to it. Like I said, Colton was acting weird straight away. A little jittery, I guess. Then he disappeared while we were asleep. Isn't that odd to you?"

"Actually, what *I* find odd is that you allowed the people who broke into your place to stay the night." Horton shook his head in disbelief before muttering, under his breath, something about idiot tourists wasting his time. Then he cleared his throat and said, "If you wanna file a report about the break-in, I can do that. But, based on what you've told me, I'm not sure how far you'll get. Hosting a slumber party for intruders isn't exactly a good look. Unfortunately, I can't do anything about this supposed disappearance. You can't give me enough information on this kid, and according to your timeline, it hasn't even been twelve hours yet. That's not really an emergency. Besides, if he had two buddies with him out here, wouldn't they have reported him missing themselves?"

"Not if they're the ones who *made* him disappear." Carter shot back, earning a raised eyebrow from Officer Horton.

"And what makes you say that?"

"One of those assholes *dru*—"

I shut Carter up by giving him a kick. I said I'd come and report the break-in and Colton being missing, but that's all. I wasn't completely sure if Ansel had drugged me - it was more of a gut feeling at this stage - and they would probably need to perform some sort of sample test to check. *That* would raise more questions than it would provide answers.

Carter redirected his focus to the officer, exhaling and scratching his head before carrying on. "Nothing. I just... got a bad vibe from them."

Officer Horton let out a sigh, the sound reverberating through the room, as he folded his arms and leaned back in his chair. His bulging belly strained against his already-tight belt, the buttons of his shirt looking about ready to pop off. With his bushy moustache, the stench of stale coffee clinging to him, and a half-eaten donut on his desk, he looked like the stereotypical small-town cop. The moment I laid eyes on the man, I knew it was gonna be a challenge to convince him, and I wished I hadn't walked through those doors at all. Now, not only did he know our names and faces, but he also knew exactly where we were staying. And since he clearly didn't believe us, no doubt the entire sheriff's department would be on high alert for any misstep we made throughout the rest of the week. The idea of anyone paying attention to us made me anxious.

Officer Horton sighed as he shuffled the papers on his desk into a neat stack, signalling that our time was up. "If you come up with any more *useful* information – more than a *'bad vibe'* – then come back and see me. Otherwise, I suggest you go back to your day before I decide to charge you for wasting police time. Now get outta here."

Carter held the door open for me as we left the sheriff's station, and I blinked in the bright sunlight bouncing off the busy high street windows. The delicious smell of freshly baked bread and steaming coffee from the café next door greeted us as soon as we stepped outside. We couldn't have been inside the station for quite an hour, and yet in that time the street had transformed from a quiet lane to a lively shopping district, with people rushing around and all the shops opening for the day.

As my eyes adjusted to the brightness, I saw Henry sitting on a bench by the truck, his eyes glued to his phone screen, but before I could go over to him, Carter bumped my shoulder.

"How about a coffee break before we hit the road? I'll even sweeten the deal with a muffin." He nodded towards the café.

"Oof, you sure know the way to my heart, Johnson."

"I like to think of that as my superpower."

"And I would agree." I grinned. "Let me just grab Henry and I'll be there."

He bent down to give me a gentle kiss, and his hands held onto mine tightly, like he didn't want to let me go when I pulled back. The reason became clear quickly.

"Hey, can I just ask you something?"

My stomach lurched in response, but I quickly masked it with a smile. "Sure."

"So, um... why didn't you want me to tell him about the drugs?"

I paused, taking a deep breath and weighing my words before finally answering. "I... I don't know. I guess I just didn't wanna mess up this week anymore by opening up a whole can of worms. Not when I'm not a hundred percent certain that's even what happened."

"They could've tested for it. We would've known for sure then. Made certain there are no side effects. That you're *okay*. Shit, Mads... Who knows what could've happened to you because of that jerk. If Henry hadn't—"

He abruptly cut himself off, like he couldn't even finish the sentence, but I knew exactly what he was thinking from the way he tightened his grip on my hand and flared his nostrils. He shut his eyes for a moment, took a deep breath, and then glanced at me again. "It's your call since it happened to you, not me or Barton. But the idea of him getting away with it... I could kill him. If I ever see his goddamn face again, I just might."

"Oookay, let's maybe not make threats of violence outside of a literal police station, Carter. As attractive as bad boys are, I'd rather you stayed *out* of jail." I winked, hoping for a laugh, but when that failed, I gently touched his cheek. "Hey, I'm good. I promise. In fact, I feel totally fine, so either Ansel had some seriously weak roofies, or I was totally wrong."

"First off, that's not funny. Plus, I know you don't actually believe that. You don't have to lie to make me feel better. This isn't about me. I only care about you."

I bit my lip, and the silence became suffocatingly heavy, lingering in the air while I waited, hoping he'd say something more, so I didn't have to. When he didn't, though, I exhaled in defeat. "And I love you for that. But I don't want them to steal more from us than they already have. We had to at least give the Colton thing a shot, but that officer was right. It hasn't even been twelve hours yet, and I'm starting to think it was just a prank. A dumb one, but nothing for us to worry about. I'm sure Colton is fine. Come *on,* Cart. It's our *spring break.* The last one before we graduate. Let's just enjoy it, okay?"

I paused, studying his expression before playfully adding, "Now, didn't you promise me a muffin? I'll take a chocolate chip, please and thank you. You go ahead and order, and I'll be right in."

I knew he had more to say, but the resignation in his eyes told me he realised it wouldn't make a difference. The cops didn't give a damn, and we had no idea how to find Ansel and Jamie. All we knew was they were from Boston and staying in a cabin 'by the lake'. None of us really knew Chibouwood that well, so I wasn't even sure if there *was* a lake. We had *nothing* to go on.

Anyway, I wasn't stupid. If I had drugs in my system, Officer Horton would likely think I took them willingly, and then panicked and tried to blame someone else. After all, Ansel never actually touched me. He just left, and even though it was a crappy move, it wasn't against the law. I knew what Horton's conclusion would be if we told him: a teenage girl meets another guy while being away from home for a week. Add a drug plot to the story, and it's a perfect fit. *Clearly,* she cheated on her nice boyfriend and will do *anything* to avoid fessing up. You know, like lying to the cops.

Horton was a jerk, but I reminded myself that his opinion didn't matter. It only mattered that *Carter* knew better.

I stayed on the sidewalk, my eyes fixed on the café window as Carter made his way inside. He wasted no time and headed straight for the counter and the display fridge of snacks, leaning so close that his breath immediately fogged up the glass. Watching him made me smile, but I forced myself to look away and went over to meet Henry.

As I walked over to him, he looked up at me and smirked, his grin getting bigger when he saw my face.

"Haven't seen any squad cars rushing out of here. Something wrong?"

"Shut up." I stopped in front of him, grunting in frustration as I crossed my arms. "You could've joined us, ya know? Helped us convince him."

"Nothin' I could've said that wouldn't have sounded better coming from Prince Charming. If he couldn't do it, then I had no chance. Also, making myself known to the cops? Dumb as hell, if you ask me."

I clenched my jaw tightly and shot him a glare. "Whatever. Just wanted to let you know that Carter's grabbing us coffee. You can join us if you want. Or are you gonna turn that down too?"

He thought about it for a moment, like he had a ton of other options, before he finally stuck his phone in his pocket. "Nah. I suppose I can grace you with my presence. Just this once."

With an eye roll and a sarcastic '*lucky me*,' I turned around and went back to the café.

"One chocolate chip muffin, as requested." Carter grinned, sliding a plate over to me as I sat down at the table in the corner of the cafe. Then he glanced at Henry and motioned to the other two plates. "Wasn't sure what you'd want. I remember you being a blueberry guy as a kid, but just in case, I got cinnamon, too. You choose."

Henry shrugged. "Blueberry is good, man. Thanks."

Carter nodded, his eyes shifting between Henry and me, and then he said, "So... that didn't exactly go to plan, huh?"

Just as I was about to reply, the waitress arrived, a girl around our age, placing a tray of hot coffee mugs between Carter and me.

"Hey there, welcome to Lil's! Here're your coffees – the best in town." Her voice was dripping with fake enthusiasm, like they made her say it to every customer, even though she clearly didn't believe it.

As she passed out the steaming mugs, her eyes swept over each of us, her smile lingering a little longer on Carter. He didn't even notice, too busy tearing into a packet of sugar.

"You guys new in town?" The waitress said when the tray was empty, tucking it under her arm. "Haven't seen you around here before, and I'm usually good with faces."

"Just passing through." I said.

"Ah. So, what brings you to Rowland?" Her eyes quickly shifted back to Carter as she asked.

After he finished making his coffee, he finally glanced up at her and gave a polite smile, saying nothing. She tried to hide it, but I still saw her disappointment when I responded instead of him.

"Just checking out the area, I guess. Actually, we're staying in Chibouwood. Spring break trip."

That got her attention, and she laughed out loud as she flipped her sandy blonde hair over her shoulder. "Damn. Did y'all lose a bet?"

Carter chuckled, shooting me a knowing look. "Yeah, something like that. But they promised me sick slopes. Got any recommendations?"

As she started talking excitedly about the mountains with Carter, I couldn't help but check her out. She was drop-dead gorgeous, no denying it. With her curvaceous figure and makeup that made her look ready for a night on the town, she seemed out-of-place working in a coffee shop, bussing tables. And she was clearly interested in my boyfriend.

Under the table, a sudden thud against my ankle startled me – Henry, trying to get my attention. Suppressing a laugh, he tilted his head and raised an eyebrow at the waitress and Carter, silently asking, "*Are you seeing this*?'. Then he cleared his throat.

The waitress quickly glanced at him before straightening up, her body subtly brushing against Carter's arm. He smoothly dodged her touch, but she didn't seem to care. She just shifted the tray under her arm, adjusted her apron, and stepped back to check out Henry, without a hint of embarrassment. Honestly, I had to give her props for being so bold.

"Oh, and if you need it, my cousin can help you out with lessons. He's a skiing instructor." As she spoke, Henry snorted, spitting out the sip of coffee he had just taken. "But if you get tired of all the tourist crap, then some townies are having a party tonight. Out by the lake. You should come."

"Townies?" Henry repeated, a hint of a sneer in his tone.

She raised an eyebrow at him, as if it was totally obvious. "Like, locals? It's nothing crazy. Just something we do every spring break. A bonfire, maybe some moonlight swimming, and *definitely* beer. It's fun. You gotta come, seriously!" She yanked a notepad from her apron pocket and scribbled something, and I had to stop myself from cringing. "I'm Jen, by the way. Here's my number. Just to, y'know, sort out tonight. If you wanted to come."

She placed the torn piece of paper in front of Carter, and I deliberately avoided meeting Henry's gaze, even though I could feel it burning into the side of my head. Carter just stared at the note for a sec, but then he cleared his throat, reached out for it... and casually slid it back to her.

"Thanks, but we're good. We've got a pretty packed week already."

When he said that, Jen's face fell for a moment, but she quickly pulled herself together. "Sure, no problem. Well, can I get you guys anything else?" She motioned to the coffees and muffins, her smile not quite genuine as she resumed her role as a server, returning to the counter when we said no.

We sat silently, sipping our coffees, until Henry couldn't keep quiet any longer. "*Dude,* are we gonna talk about the fact she was just *hitting on you*?"

Carter almost choked on his muffin. "No, she wasn't. She was just being friendly."

"She gave you her *number*, for fuck's sake."

Carter's head snapped towards Jen, who was busy behind the counter, and then towards me. I watched as panic spread across his face, his eyes widening as his mind connected the dots.

"I didn't... I mean, I don't—" As he tried to stammer out an explanation, I noticed his hand trembling on the table and reached out to give it a reassuring pat.

"Hate to say it, but H is right. She was definitely flirting. I was getting kinda jealous."

As I smirked, he noticeably relaxed and a teasing smile appeared on his lips. "You never have to be jealous of anyone, Mads. You know that. But I still think you're both way off base. She just gave us her number for the party info. Besides, she probably meant for *you* to take it, Casanova."

He nodded towards Henry, but it was half-hearted, because he knew we were right – he just didn't want to admit it. He tried to hide it, but his face turning tomato-red totally gave it away. I couldn't resist teasing him even more by giving him a playful nudge under the table and a mischievous grin, and he scowled in response.

"You really think so?" Henry replied, shifting in his seat to get a better view of the counter. "Let's see, shall we?"

Carter cast a quick glance in that direction, his eyes widening. "Dude, *no.*"

Henry chuckled and shook his head, amused. "What's the problem? If she's just being friendly, why not go to a party?" He ran his tongue over his lips. "And hey, if she really meant that number for me, then I'm game for a good time." His eyebrow shot up at Carter, who shifted uncomfortably in his seat. "Unless you don't *really* think that?"

Carter gave me a pleading look, and I sighed. "Alright, H. You've had your fun tormenting him. That's enough—"

But it was too late, because he'd already called her name. Jen turned abruptly at the shout, accidentally bumping into a tray of croissants on the counter. She scrambled to save it from falling, then moved it to a less risky spot before heading back to our table.

"Yeah?"

"Is that invite still good?" 'Cus we changed our minds. We'd *love* to come."

Jen's face lit up, but Carter's expression turned grim as he shot Henry a glare.

"Absolutely! It kicks off at eight." While Jen was speaking, the door chime rang through the café, grabbing her attention as a family walked in. Flashing a grin at Carter, she dropped her number on the table again before heading off to greet the new customers. "See you there!"

28

We didn't stick around for much longer. Just enough time to finish our coffees and muffins. Henry insisted on getting a box of goodies to go, but I had a feeling it was more about annoying Carter than having a particular desire for breakfast pastries. It worked, too – Carter yanked me outside before Henry even made it to the counter. From there, I couldn't make out what he was saying to Jen, but she looked out of the window in our direction, so I had a pretty good hunch.

Once Henry finally came out, box in hand, we took a stroll down the high street. There wasn't much to see. It was a lot like Havencrest, with mostly boutique stores aimed at tourists and people who hadn't figured out the internet yet. But there was a convenience store, bigger than the one in Chibouwood, so we stocked up on food for the cabin, and then headed back.

It was still only early afternoon by the time we got home, but after a crazy start to our trip and no sleep the night before, we were all too tired to ski. Instead, we opted for a lazy day, which consisted of dumping candy in a bowl, hunting through Sean's extremely limited movie collection, and then settling down on the sofa to watch *The Lord of the Rings*. Although, how much of the movie any of us actually watched was anyone's guess, because I woke up hours later to the cabin bathed in only the soft light from the TV, the DVD reset to the menu screen, and the gentle chirping of birds outside filling the silence. Oh, and Jen's voice running round and round in my head.

I couldn't understand why her words kept playing on a loop, so I pushed the thought away and looked around to get my bearings after the nap. I was lying on the sofa with my head in Carter's lap, one leg hanging off the edge onto Henry's shoulder as he sat on the floor. The sight made me smile - Carter snoring softly with his head against the cushions, and Henry nuzzling against my foot. He grunted and moved to lean on the sofa arm when I pulled my leg up, but he was still fast asleep.

I wriggled until I could grab my cell phone and see the time, its screen shining in the evening light, forcing me to squint until my eyes adjusted. It was already way past six, and the party was supposed to start at eight. I hated doing it, but I knew I had to wake them up if we wanted to be in Rowland on time, so–

Wait.

It hit me like a lightning bolt, and I scrambled to sit up. Jen's voice in my head again...

'*Some townies are having a party tonight. Out by the lake.*'

I let a few more minutes pass, giving my groggy brain a chance to catch up, before I gently nudged the back of Henry's head with my foot. When he didn't react, I nudged him again, this time with a bit more force, until his eyes slowly opened, and he glanced up at me with a bewildered look on his face. Then he grunted again, crossed his arms, and fell immediately back to sleep.

"Henry!" I swung my leg to hit him again, but he was too fast, catching my ankle before I made contact.

"Do that one more time and I'll rip off your leg and feed it to the coyotes."

I rolled my eyes and broke free from his hold, crossing my legs beneath me. "You weren't waking up, and I need to talk to you."

He let out a groan and tossed his head backwards. "If this is about earlier... Jeez, I don't actually wanna go to that party. And I was just messing with him. Didn't think he'd get so pissy."

I didn't say anything to that, just looked at Carter, but of course, he was still fast asleep, not bothered by our whispers. Then I gestured towards the kitchen before getting up from the sofa. Henry sighed but, a few seconds later, he followed.

"What's up?" He asked, crossing his arms and leaning back against the counter.

"It's gonna sound crazy."

Henry snorted. "Most of what comes out of your damn mouth sounds crazy, Madison. I'm used to it by now. Might as well just spit it out. Did Johnson tell you he wants a piece of the waitress, after all?"

"Ha ha. Very funny." I rolled my eyes. "Seriously, though... I think we should go to the party. Carter's gonna be pissed, but... I don't know why I didn't pick up on it before, but Jen said it was *'by the lake'*."

"Okay? If you're suddenly in the mood to go skinny-dipping with a bunch of entitled assholes, we can do that back home."

I shot him a glare. "Can you be serious for, like, five minutes? The party is by *the* lake. She acted like we should know where she meant. Like it's the *only* lake in the area. Ansel said their cabin was by a lake. I bet it's the same one."

As soon as I mentioned Ansel, Henry's whole vibe changed. He clenched his jaw and stood up straight, eyes narrowing to slits as he said, "Yeah, so? That fucker spiked you and then just left you in the middle of the night, in the damn forest."

"I wasn't in any danger, H. You know that."

"No, I don't. Whatever you might think, you're just a werewolf, Madison. You're not invincible." His voice got louder, so I had to spin around and check if Carter was still out, but he hadn't stirred at all. Henry, however, didn't seem to give a crap if he spilled our secret right then and there. "Yeah, you can find your way through the forest blindfolded. But he didn't know that did he?! And he *still* fucking left you."

Anger surged as my gaze turned back to Henry. "I'm very well aware of my shortcomings as a fighter, Henry. I know I'm not you. You don't have to remind me."

"You know I didn't mean it like that."

I bit back a smartass retort, because that would only escalate into a huge fight, and I didn't need that. Instead, I just sighed before continuing. "Look, I get it, okay? I know what you think about them. But I... I can't help but worry. I need to know if Colton's alright. Plus, Ansel and Jamie might be jerks, but I don't think they're gonna hurt anyone. Ansel could have last night, but he didn't. What if... what if there's more to it and that's why we met Jen? Why she invited us to the party? Maybe we're *meant* to be there."

"Like, some kind of divine intervention or something?" He scoffed.

"Well, no, not exactly. Or maybe. Dammit, I don't know, H. But think about it, okay? Does him drugging me even make any sense? I was fine this morning. No headache, no feeling sick... nothing. Does that sound normal to you?"

When I finished, quiet enveloped us as I gave him a chance to mull it over. He stood in silence, arms tightly crossed, his seething anger impossible to ignore. It quickly became obvious he had no intention of saying anything further on the subject, and I couldn't hold back the tired sigh that forced its way out as frustration set in. "Why do you always have to assume the worst of people?"

As soon as the words were out in the air, I wanted to claw them back. But it was too late. A shadow crossed his face as his expression turned dark, and it took every ounce of self control not to flinch under the look he shot at me.

"Are you serious right now? I *have* to, 'cause you never do! You think everyone's all rainbows and unicorns, but life isn't like that, Madison. That's just not how things go for us. The sooner you figure that out, the better. But until that fucking magical day finally happens, one of us has to be realistic, or else you'll get yourself killed! Maybe even both of us."

His words struck me like a gut punch, leaving me reeling. Immediately, I thought of Ryan, and all I could do was just stand there, open mouthed, as he struggled to catch his breath, his laboured breathing seeming to somehow echo throughout the room.

He read my expression. I saw it in his eyes, and I knew he regretted what he'd said. But it didn't matter. The words were out there now. They were tangible, like bombs ready to detonate. They couldn't be taken back.

"Hey, hey, what's all the yelling for?"

Carter's voice sounded from the lounge, followed by his footsteps crossing towards us. I kept staring at Henry, though. I was too scared to look at Carter, because I was sure I'd start crying, and how would I explain that? I couldn't tell him about Ryan. He only knew of a close family friend passing away. He didn't know any of the real details. I couldn't talk to him about Ben, or Vincent, or the attack. Not about the guilt I still carried. Not about any of it.

I had to get away. Just a moment, to pull myself together.

"Need to get ready." I mumbled – although it was so quiet and garbled, I wasn't sure either of them understood it – and then dashed into our bedroom.

A few seconds later, I heard the bang of the front door, right as I threw myself onto the bed.

"Knock, knock."

Carter didn't bother waiting for my response before coming in, but it wasn't until I felt the mattress sink beside me and his hand come to rest on my hip that I sat up. I inched closer to him, feeling the warmth of his arm as he pulled me in closer.

"So, Barton left. Kinda, anyways. He asked if he could borrow the truck, but he's just sitting in it outside." He chuckled softly. "Not sure he knows what to do with himself. You wanna tell me what the hell happened between you two?"

"He's a jerk." I grumbled. I knew it sounded childish, but I didn't care.

"Well, duh. Did you just figure this out?" He asked, giving me a playful nudge. "Why'd you let it get to you this time? Wait... Is this about tonight? Or that girl we met at the café? Because we don't have to go to the party. And I'm sure as hell not interested in anyone else. You know that, right?"

"It's not about Jen." I sighed, feeling myself relax as I lay my head on his shoulder. Just being next to Carter had that effect. "I actually kinda wanna go to the party. Y'know, to mark my territory." I prodded him in the side, making it obvious the 'territory' I was referring to was him. And when he grinned back at me – *that grin* – I felt those butterflies burst to life in my stomach.

"So what is it, then?"

I wanted to tell him so badly, but the words got stuck in my throat, and I couldn't find a starting point. Even I couldn't understand it, and I was the one experiencing it. There was just this voice in my head, insisting I had to find Ansel and talk to him. And it didn't make sense, so I knew Carter wouldn't get it, no matter how hard he tried. He would agree with Henry about staying away.

Suddenly, his arm around my shoulder felt like a vice, and I shifted away from him and off the bed. Just for something to do, I headed towards my hold-all, which was resting on the chair in the corner of the room, right beside the window. "It's not important." I said as I gazed outside.

"You're upset, Mads. Of course it's important. You can talk to me, you know."

Desperate to avoid his eye, I stayed facing the window, biting down on my lip before finally unzipping my bag. "I'm not upset. I'm fine. Promise. Let's just forget about it and get ready. We gotta go soon."

He stayed silent for what felt like an eternity, and I struggled to resist the urge to turn around. Without even looking, I could feel his disappointment, his hurt. It was like a black cloud hanging over the room, sucking all the energy out of it. But if I allowed myself to so much as glance at him right now, my resolve would crumble instantly, and what good would it do to give him half a confession? That wouldn't be fair.

With my lip still caught between my teeth, I focused on rummaging through the bag, pretending to search for something, until he muttered about needing to use the bathroom. Then came the sound of the door opening, and he was gone.

29

Not only was Henry angry with me, but now Carter was too. What a night this was shaping up to be.

I'd meant what I'd said to Henry. The more I thought about it, the less I bought into the drug theory. I just knew in my gut that something was off, and Ansel was my only chance to find out what was going on... which was why we were back on the road, headed to the only lake for fifty miles. Well, at least according to the map I found in Sean's kitchen.

It was a relief when I finally heard music and voices in the distance, because no one had said anything the whole ride over. But relief quickly turned to dread when Carter veered off the road and onto the grass, now serving as an unofficial parking lot, and I got a view of the throngs of people idling in splintered groups across a huge meadow.

How the hell was I supposed to find Ansel in this?

Carter parked the truck and let out a sharp whistle. "Holy cow. I didn't think there would be this many people."

It was the first thing he'd said to me since he walked out of our bedroom earlier, so I was happy to hear his voice. Maybe that meant he wasn't so mad at me after all.

"Me neither." I admitted.

Henry grunted in frustration. "Let's just leave. They won't even know we bailed. That waitress probably doesn't even remember inviting us."

As he said it, I looked out across the scene, taking it all in. There weren't too many cars, considering the amount of people here, but the lake hadn't looked too far from Rowland on the map. Those that *had* driven to the party had dumped their cars in this same area, just off the road, except for one pickup truck that'd parked about three quarters of the way to the lake. Someone had lowered the end panel of the bed and set up speakers and a couple of weak strobe lights that I doubted would last the night, but did, admittedly, add to the atmosphere. Just past that, a bonfire burned, a couple of partygoers lingering around it. That's where I spotted Jen, her unfairly perfect silhouette illuminated by the flames. Just the sight of her made me regret my decision to come even more, which was stupid, because I knew I had nothing to worry about with Carter. So why the hell was there a tightness in my gut all of a sudden?

While I watched, she bumped her hip against a guy with curly hair, flashing him a coy smile as she flipped her locks over her shoulder. Boyfriend, maybe? Either way, she obviously had a type, judging by the way she flirted with Carter earlier. Guys with curly hair, beware.

I paused for a moment, considering Henry's suggestion to turn around. What made me think coming here was a good idea in the first place? Even if I found Ansel or Jamie, I wouldn't know what to say to them. This was absolutely ridiculous. I should've given up when the police didn't care.

"I think H—" I started, but trailed off when I noticed Jen's gaze shift to the truck. The headlights were still blaring, the engine still running, and suddenly it was like we were on stage, under a spotlight. It was impossible to miss us. We had maybe thirty seconds to slam the truck into reverse before –

Right on cue, Jen squinted and raised her hand to block the light, and I couldn't help but cringe and mutter, "Shit."

I stared out the windshield, but I could feel Carter's eyes briefly flicker in my direction, like he was waiting for me to tell him what to do. But it was too late now. Jen had seen us, and though we'd likely never see her again after tonight, I couldn't bring myself to bail. Not when I knew she'd spotted us.

Letting out a sigh, I leaned back against the headrest, and Carter took it as his cue. He killed the engine without a word, and when the light was no longer blocking our faces, it only took her a second to recognise Carter. A smile spread across her face, and she eagerly started walking towards us.

"Here we fucking go." Henry grumbled.

Carter snorted. "This mess is all your fault, man. Or did you forget that?"

Henry turned a glare on me so, before he could say anything, I nudged Carter out of the truck. I wasn't ready for him to bombard me with questions, however justified they might be. If I couldn't even explain it all to myself, how could I possibly explain it to him?

"C'mon, it could be fun." I tried to sound upbeat, but my voice wavered as I lightly elbowed him. He didn't seem to notice, just let out a sigh and then got out of the cab, offering me a hand to help me down. "This is what you wanted to do, right? I know it's not Florida, and Henry is no substitute for Ethan." Inside the truck, Henry let out a grunt in reaction. "But—"

A figure approached, cutting me off, and I glanced past Carter to see Jen. She looked pretty much the same as she did at work, except for her outfit. She'd traded her café uniform for a striking pink halter-neck top, pairing it with a denim mini skirt that was embellished with buttons from the waist to the hem. With every step, her flip-flops slapped against her feet, until she stopped a little way from the hood, cracked open a beer, and took a long swig as she swept her eyes over us all. My shorts and oversized tee suddenly felt inadequate, and I couldn't help but squirm under her stare, my fingers nervously tugging at the hem of my shirt.

"Hey!" As she looked at Carter, a grin appeared on her face that made me feel invisible. "You made it!"

Carter cleared his throat. "Ayuh. Thanks for inviting us." He cast a pointed glance over her shoulder. "This is quite the party, huh?"

She looked around, her eyes jumping from one spot to another, before letting out a high-pitched girly giggle. "Oh, yeah. Literally everyone from our senior class comes to this thing, even last year's grads if they're around. Hey, come meet the guys! Trust me, you're gonna love 'em!"

I had a sudden urge to yank Carter away and disappear into the crowds, avoiding Jen altogether, but I resisted, because I knew that was just petty jealousy, and he didn't deserve that. Plus, it could help me out. Carter always was good at making friends, so maybe whoever 'the guys' were, they could keep him occupied while I searched for Ansel.

Still, while I tried to stay calm, my breath caught and my body tensed up as I watched her hand reach for his. But he quickly pulled back, and then I felt the gentle brush of his fingertips against mine, instantly relieving my anxiety. He grasped my hand in his and politely responded to Jen with a simple, "Sure."

She tried to act cool, but her eyes gave her away when they glanced at our intertwined fingers and then narrowed as she pursed her lips. But, just as quickly, her smile fell back into place.

She gave me a quick look before turning her attention back to Carter. "Are you into sports? You give off that vibe. You *gotta* meet Adam. He's really into football."

"Um, actually, I prefer basketball." Carter said, but I doubted she was listening, since she was already walking back towards the bonfire. Reluctantly, we followed her towards the curly-haired guy she had been flirting with, while I scanned the crowds for Ansel, Jamie or Colton as we walked. But there was no sign of them – not near the bonfire, at least.

Henry didn't tag along. I glanced behind me and spotted him lingering at the edge of the forest, grooming his hair while a group of girls whispered and stole glances in his direction. *Figures*. He didn't wanna come to the party, but Henry Barton wasn't gonna waste an opportunity to hook up.

The more I thought about it, the more grateful I was that he believed I was crazy for thinking the guys would be here, and that there might be more to the story. If he didn't believe me, then there was no need for him to worry. No reason for him to play bodyguard like he usually did. Which meant he was fine keeping his distance from me. It'd be so much simpler to search for Ansel if he wasn't staring me down and picking apart my plan. Now, I just had to sneak away from Carter too, at least for a bit.

That part might be tricky.

As we reached the group gathered around the bonfire, Jen's eyes locked onto the curly-haired guy, and she hurried towards him. Did she say his name was Adam? I couldn't remember, but since I wouldn't see him again after tonight, I guess it didn't matter much. *Maybe*-Adam glanced up, eyebrow cocked curiously.

"Who's the fresh meat, Jenny? Don't remember seeing these at Greenbank."

"Ugh, Adam, you know I can't stand being called Jenny." She rolled her eyes, let out an exasperated sigh, and playfully swatted his arm. "And that's 'cause they ain't from Greenbank. They're my new friends, from outta town. This is…" She glanced at us, her words trailing off. "Huh. I just realised I never asked your names."

"Well, you were kinda distracted." I didn't even realise I had said it aloud until both she and Carter gave me a look. A wave of warmth washed over my cheeks, and I quickly added, "I just meant that the café got kinda busy."

Her eyes narrowed, like she was trying to decide if she should call me out. But then she giggled. "I know, right?! It's been a crazy day, for sure."

When she turned her head, I let out a breath and leaned on Carter, while he reached out his hand to Adam. "Carter. And this is Maddie. We're just in town for a few days."

"Good to meet you." Adam said as he accepted the handshake. "Y'all want a beer?"

Carter looked my way, and I responded with a shrug, giving him permission to do as he pleased. I didn't love driving his truck, but he had given me a couple of lessons on driving stick shift, so I could do it if he had too much to drink. I owed him that much, at least, since I dragged him here. So, when Adam offered him a bottle from the chest cooler by his feet, he took it.

As Adam relaxed in his seat again, Jen made herself comfortable on his lap, running her fingers through his hair, and I had to resist rolling my eyes. He didn't seem to care about her attention, barely acknowledging her at all, despite her being all over him, so I still wasn't sure about their relationship. They didn't seem like a couple from their brief exchange. Exes, maybe? Was she trying to make him jealous by inviting Carter? Or was she hoping for a chance with Carter and using Adam to make *him* jealous? And... *ugh!* Why did I even care? I did trust Carter, didn't I? So why did I feel such a strong urge to grab her by her impeccably perfect hair and hurl her into the lake?

"Carter plays football, too." Jen's voice cut through my thoughts and brought me back to the group.

A rebuttal was on my lips almost instantly, but Carter beat me to it. "Uh, nope. I play basketball, actually."

She waved her hand like there was barely a difference. "Adam was the best player at our school, you know. He got a college scholarship and everything."

Adam rolled his eyes, and it half-answered my question. He clearly wasn't as into Jen as she was into him. It seemed to me, from the tight set of his jaw, that he didn't like her *at all*.

Before he could say anything to that, Carter butted in. "Oh yeah? That's awesome, man. Where to?"

"Fordham." Jen answered for him. Adam clenched his teeth more tightly together.

"In New York?" Once again, he directed the question at Adam, immediately intrigued by the mention of the city, and an idea formed in my head.

Since the campus tour, Carter had been subtly suggesting NYU as his top choice. He had his heart set on that place, but he was waiting for me to make up my mind before committing. Leaving him to talk to someone who already lived and studied in NYC was the perfect distraction. As much as I hated leaving him with Jen, I had to trust him so I could do what I came here for.

I cleared my throat, drawing everyone's attention my way. "You know, Carter is applying to NYU. How cool is that? You'll already know someone in the city!"

"*If* I get in." Carter said. "And *if* I go there, won't I have—"

"*When* you get in." I interrupted him before he could finish, acting like I didn't see the look he gave me. Because I knew exactly where that conversation was going, and I didn't wanna argue with him again tonight. "Hey, I'm kinda chilly," I said suddenly, capitalising on his temporary distraction. "Do you have a sweater in the truck?"

I knew the answer already. Once, a few months after we started dating, we went to the movies, and then the weather turned crazy on us while we were inside. We didn't bring jackets, so we ended up completely soaked when we finally got back to the truck. It wasn't his fault, but he still felt guilty because the pickup's heaters were broken that day, so I shivered all the way home. Since then, Carter always kept an extra sweater in there, just in case.

"Sure thing. I'll come with you."

I put my hand on his arm and flashed a smile, hoping it looked convincing. "No need. It's just over there, and Henry's around somewhere. I think I'll catch up with him – make sure he's not terrorising anyone. You stay and chat. I'm sure Adam won't mind answering your questions about life in New York."

Then I planted a kiss on his lips and dashed towards the truck before he could protest.

My skin tingled as I walked away, feeling his eyes on me. I desperately wanted to sprint off and disappear into the bustling crowd, but I resisted the urge and maintained a brisk walk all the way to the truck. When I finally got there, I grabbed his sweater from where he'd shoved it in the gap behind the seats - not because I needed it, but because he'd ask questions later if I wasn't wearing it - and pulled it over my head. Then I glanced at the bonfire, breathing a sigh of relief when I saw he wasn't watching me anymore. He was too busy talking to Adam.

I waited a minute to be certain he wouldn't turn around and spot me, and then I melted into the crowd.

30

I had no clue how long I'd been searching for Ansel, but it felt like forever, and if I hadn't lied to Carter about tracking down Henry, he would've definitely come looking for me.

What happened last night had him freaked out, and he was worried about me. I couldn't blame him for that. Which was why I had to catch up with Ansel and clear this up ASAP, so I could go back to just hanging out with my boyfriend, like two normal teenagers. Just the way I'd planned it.

Ugh! Jen said only the seniors and last year's grads did the bonfire thing, but there were way too many people milling around for that to be true. Clearly, word had gotten out, which shouldn't surprise me, really, since Jen had invited us – three complete strangers – after a thirty-second conversation. We probably weren't the only ones who ended up with an invitation just by stepping foot in Lil's Café.

Honestly, I had realised a while back that searching for Ansel was a waste of time. The problem was that giving up meant admitting Henry was right, and then confronting his stupid smug smile when I returned empty-handed. If not for that, I would've called the whole thing off a lot sooner. But stubbornness alone wouldn't make Ansel magically appear, and I couldn't ditch Carter all night.

I hadn't really paid attention to where I was walking – too busy studying everyone's faces to find the guys – and as I looked around, I realised I was by the the edge of the forest, on the far side of the meadow, where the trees cast long shadows that engulfed everyone in their reach. From here, the crowd hid me from Carter's line of sight, and Henry wasn't paying me any attention at all. He'd finally approached the group of girls he'd been eyeing, his focus solely on a petite blonde who was currently hanging off his arm.

At some point, I'd stopped walking, trying to decide whether to give up or turn back. That sense that I was supposed to come here, that there was something I was supposed to find, even if it wasn't Ansel himself, just wouldn't go away. Even now, when I'd all but given up hope, I still glanced around again, praying he would show up, even though I had been fruitlessly searching for what seemed like an eternity. Maybe one last look—

"Oh!" I blurted, blinking in surprise as a figure appeared right in front of me.

My breath caught, and for a split second, I thought it might be him. That I was right all along. But, of course, it wasn't. I didn't know who it was. I'd never seen her before.

How I'd thought it could be Ansel, even for the briefest of moments, I didn't know. The girl standing there, eyes boring into me, had black hair, so long that, even tied back in tight braids, it still almost reached her hips. The complete opposite of Ansel's buzz-cut. She'd paired her flowery summer dress with wedge heels that didn't seem suitable for the grassy meadow, and had makeup as impeccable as Jen's, a feat that, somehow, I doubted Ansel could pull off. But it was her expression that really dragged me back from my thoughts, and I suddenly realised how long I'd been standing there, right on the edge of their group, like some kind of creepy Peeping Tom. It had to have looked weird as hell, like I was eavesdropping. Or worse.

"Could you not?" She said, crossing her arms over her chest and raising an eyebrow at me.

"Huh?" The word slipped out instinctively, but I quickly followed it up with, "Oh. Sorry. I just... I'm just looking for someone."

"Well, they clearly aren't here, so can you move? You're freaking everyone out."

Her eyes swept over me as she said it, making me squirm, just like I had when Jen did the same – especially when her eyes stopped on my battered sneakers. As her friends laughed, I nervously shuffled my feet, feeling my face burn to an even deeper shade of red. I wished Carter were here. Even Henry. But that would probably make things worse. I'd dealt with enough people like them back home, so I knew exactly what they'd think if they saw me and the guys hanging out. It would just give them more fuel to judge me.

I wouldn't label myself as ugly, but I was undeniably average-looking. Still, Carter would always tell me I was beautiful. Whenever he said it, I would tease him about just wanting a kiss, although he denied it every time. Oh, he definitely wanted a kiss, and he always got one, but I knew it wasn't the only reason. He genuinely believed I was beautiful. Knowing that I couldn't see it myself, he just liked to remind me from time to time. He'd be doing it now, seeing how these girls were looking at me, if I hadn't ditched him. Maybe I deserved their derision, just for that. But honestly, why did I even care? Carter *loved* me. I'd never doubted that. And I'd never see these people again after tonight. Why should I give a damn what they thought? I didn't let it get to me when I overheard Carter's fight in the locker room that time, because that guy wasn't important. Neither were these girls.

Ugh, I was just feeling rattled. Letting people get in my head, because I was so exhausted and freaked out about everything. I should've listened to Henry. If only I could turn back time, I'd let him talk me out of this stupid idea. I just wanted to be on the couch, cuddling with them and pigging out on snacks while we binge-watched TV. Cosy and safe. But I couldn't. Not now. No matter how much I regretted it, I'd come here for a reason, and I couldn't bail just because some girl gave me a funny look.

"S-sorry. It's just... I thought someone might be here. A- a friend of mine. He's supposed to be staying close by. Maybe you've seen him around? His name is Ansel."

"Never heard of him. Who are you, anyway? Not to be rude, but this is a closed party, you know. Strictly for Greenbank seniors. Which I *know* you aren't. Actually, do you even go to our school at all? Because I don't recognise you, and I know *everyone* at Greenbank High."

Panic engulfed me, as if she had caught me doing something wrong, and for a moment, I thought about lying, but I quickly dismissed the idea after realising the truth was way more logical.

"Jen invited us."

"Us?" She repeated, quickly scanning the empty space around me.

"N-never mind. I was just leaving. Sorry for bothering you."

I took a few cautious steps, holding my breath in case she stopped me, because I really didn't want to make a scene... And then I heard a noise that made me freeze. My head snapped around to scrutinise the wall of darkness at the edge of the forest, but all I could see were the eerie, shifting shadows. Couldn't sense anything, either. The party was so loud that even the squirrels had bailed.

Great. Now I'm hearing things.

I let out a sigh and glanced back at Braids, when...

The sound again, this time clear and recognisable. A voice.

Hold up. Not just *any* voice... Ansel's voice.

The moment I heard it, my face broke into a wide grin, and all the anxiety in my stomach disappeared. I'd let Henry get into my head before, but I should've trusted my gut, because Ansel was right there. Just yards away from me, judging by the volume of his voice – which was all I had to go on, really, because the air was full of unfamiliar smells, making it hard for me to pick out his scent. But he was definitely nearby. That was what mattered.

Braids was still talking, but I had tuned her out, because I was too busy frantically scanning the treeline, hoping to catch a glimpse of Ansel. The woods were so close that the air was saturated with the sweet scent of pine, alongside the burning from the bonfire on the shore, but there was no hint of his trail beneath it. That meant I couldn't sniff him out, which was usually my go-to tracking method. It would make finding him more complicated, but still not impossible. I just had to head in the general direction his voice had sounded from, and hope I heard him again before I got too far along the wrong path.

After a quick check over my shoulder to be sure neither Henry nor Carter was watching, I turned back to face the forest, and...

A burst of bright red.

My feet slipped out from under me, and I stumbled backwards, the ground rushing up to meet me. "Holy crap, did you see that?!" I exclaimed after a second, ignoring the pain in my hands from where they'd shot out to break my fall.

I wasn't talking to anyone specifically, but Braids answered, her voice shaking a little with a hint of alarm. "See what?"

"Those eyes!" As I scrambled to my feet, I gestured wildly behind me. "Right there!"

Braids' face took on a guarded look, eyes narrowing at me. "There's nothing there. How much have you had to drink? Just a heads up, some kids went missing nearby not too long ago, so it's probably not a great idea to be out here by yourself."

"What? I haven't had... I mean, don't you see—" I trailed off, my focus shifting to the rustling of leaves in the woods. But it was just the wind, softly whispering through the trees. Braids was right. There was no one in the forest. It was completely silent.

What the hell?

Braids was speaking again, but I couldn't make out the words over the blood rushing in my ears. I definitely saw it, didn't I? Just like last time. The eyes. I was *so* sure...

"What the *fuck* are you doing all the way over here? Where's Johnson?"

I didn't notice Henry approaching until his voice cut through the fog of my thoughts. Or was it the sudden, tight grip on my arm that jolted me back to reality? I wasn't sure. Why was someone gripping me so damn tightly, anyway? And *who?*

My eyes struggled to focus, but eventually, I could make out Braids beside me, shooting daggers at Henry.

"Hey, back off."

Henry's eyebrows shot up, but he kept his distance from us, just out of Braids' reach. "Sorry, what?"

"I said, *back the hell off.*" It was impossible to ignore the coldness in her voice. Her eyes met mine then, and she held my gaze as she asked, "Do you know this guy?"

I couldn't think straight. My mind was still foggy, making it difficult for me to respond immediately. Instead, I just stood there, looking like a dumb idiot, while her friends stepped forward, forming a human barrier to stop Henry from coming any closer. It took me a moment to understand *why* they were shielding me from him, but then I gasped in surprise. "Oh! Oh my god, yes. We're friends. He's fine."

Braids didn't seem convinced, crossing her arms and pursing her lips. "You sure?"

"Yeah. Absolutely. And my boyfriend is around somewhere. Honestly, it's cool. I'm just tired. Sorry if I was acting weird before." I paused, struggling to find the right words, and settled on a simple "Thank you."

She never took her eyes off me as I spoke, like she was analysing every word for any sign of lying. But eventually she nodded, motioning for her friends to go. She stayed behind for a moment, glaring at Henry.

"Your friend here has had a lot to drink. Get her boyfriend and take her home, alright?" Then she spun on her heel and strutted away to rejoin her friends.

"Yes, ma'am." Henry called after her, before he snorted a laugh. "Making friends, huh?"

As Braids vanished into the crowd, my mind kept replaying our brief conversation, and I raised an eyebrow. "I'm honestly not sure."

The way she'd flipped from being – honestly – kinda rude towards me, to protecting me... it didn't make any sense. But it didn't really matter, I supposed. It wasn't like I'd ever see her again. It was nice to know there were still girls looking out for each other, though.

"So, just how much *have* you had to drink?" Henry interrupted my thoughts.

"Shut up. You know I haven't touched a drop, jerk." I jabbed him with my shoulder as I crossed my arms over my chest. "What do you want, anyway? Weren't you busy with some girl?"

His eyes narrowed slightly, and his lips curled into a sly grin. "Why? You aren't jealous, are you?" When he saw my reaction, he burst into laughter. "Jeez, I'm kidding. Lighten up. I noticed you were loitering around the forest and, if you remember, I promised to look out for you on this trip."

"And as *you* might remember, I told you I didn't need a babysitter."

"Recent events would strongly suggest otherwise, Madison." He said, and then sighed. "Also, the girl... well, let's just say she might not have been as single as she led me to believe."

I snorted and glanced over my shoulder at the girl he was talking about, seeing her surrounded by her friends as she sobbed into her hands. Just past her, a burly and shirtless dude ranted to another guy, his arms flailing in the air as he stormed off into the distance. When I looked back at Henry, I laughed again, because he had disappeared into the shadows of the trees.

"Ah. *Now* it makes sense. You're just over here so I can protect you from getting your ass kicked."

Henry scoffed. "Keep dreaming. I could take that guy with my eyes closed. I just didn't wanna cause a scene." I rolled my eyes, and he shot me a glare. "Speaking of boyfriends, where the hell is yours? Clearly, your plan to track down that jerk isn't working out, and this party is boring as hell. Can we just grab Johnson and get back to the cabin already?"

I turned a smug look on him. "Actually, that's where you're wrong. 'Cause while *you* were shoving your tongue down that girl's throat, I found him. Ansel *is* here! Ha!" And then, like magic, I heard Ansel again - no words, just a laugh, but definitely him. "Through here somewhere. I was about to go grab him."

As I nodded towards the woods behind him, Henry turned a sceptical look over his shoulder, his eyes narrowing.

"So you *were* sneaking off? I fucking knew it. After everything that went down—"

"I wasn't going far." I grumbled, feeling like a kid caught with one leg out of my bedroom window. "Can we not do this now? I really gotta talk to him, and if he hears you yelling, he'll bolt again."

Henry gritted his teeth in what I assumed was an effort to stay calm, and then he took a quick breath before replying. "I think you're too late."

"Huh?"

"There's no one there."

"Yeah, there is. I *just* heard him. Didn't you?"

He gave an eye roll. "No, I didn't. 'Cause he's not there. Whatever you heard, it wasn't—"

A coldness swept over me suddenly, and, without waiting for him to finish, I sprinted away, shoving back tree branches before they could whip against my face. I had enough scratches already after last night. But he was wrong. He had to be. And I'd prove it.

Behind me, there was a moment of stunned silence, before a string of curses filled the air, followed by his footsteps pounding after me. But I kept going. The world became a blur of green and brown as I ran, and all I could hear was my own breathing.

After what felt like forever, I stumbled upon a little clearing, and I brought myself to a stop as pain throbbed through my legs.

I wasn't used to running so fast in human form, and claws were way better suited to the terrain than sneakers. It felt as though I had run for miles. But it was fine, because this was where his voice had come from. Ansel should be here.

I looked around desperately, hoping for any sign, but there was only the rustling of leaves and birdsong in the distance.

The clearing was empty. No sign of anyone at all.

"I told you," Henry snapped as he caught up. "I fucking told you!"

"No. He's gotta be somewhere. I... I heard him."

Henry growled. "For fuck's sake, Madison. You're still doped up on whatever that asshole slipped you last night. Seriously, when are you going to accept that he's not the guy you think he is? That you *want* him to be?" His face relaxed slightly when I glanced in his direction. "Well, it's true. You can't keep doing this."

I opened my mouth to argue, but a tightness in my throat silenced me. What could I even say? As much as it sucked, he was right. Trusting my gut had only led me on a wild goose chase in the woods, chasing imaginary voices. So either someone drugged me, or I was having a complete mental breakdown. If I had to choose, I knew which one I'd want to be true.

"Okay!" I said, finally. "You're right. Is that what you want to hear? I should've listened to you this morning. I was wrong." I let out a shaky breath, my shoulders drooping with exhaustion. "I just... I didn't wanna admit it. I'm sorry. Let's just forget about it and head home, alright? I told Carter I was gonna find you, and he'll freak out if we don't get back soon."

I could see the hesitation in Henry's eyes, as if he had a *lot* more to say, but he ultimately decided against it. Instead, he only nodded, his footsteps falling in sync with mine as we retraced the path of destruction I had left during my rampage through the forest.

The silence stretched between us as we walked, the tension growing with each passing moment, until he finally broke it by clearing his throat. "Since we're gonna be back pretty early, we might actually get enough sleep to hit the slopes tomorrow. What d'ya think?"

I let a few beats of silence pass between us before I replied, and when I finally did, my voice came out more of a mumble, lacking any sign of actual interest. "Yeah. Sounds awesome."

It would've been comforting if it came from Carter, because that's what he did - if I didn't feel like talking, he'd try to distract me. To put a smile on my face. But when it was Henry, it was so fake that it just made me feel even worse, because it showed how worried he was about me. Henry always told me the truth. He didn't hold back at all, and he'd cuss me out if I needed to hear it.

But not this time. This time he was treating me like I was a bomb just waiting to go off. Like I really was crazy.

And, honestly? I was starting to think I might be.

31

Carter was still by the bonfire, perched on an overturned tree trunk, as we made our way across the meadow back to him. Jen and Adam hadn't budged from the deckchair, but a few more people had joined them, including a girl practically sitting on Carter's lap, giggling at every little thing he said. What was the deal with the girls in Rowland? Maybe I needed to keep a closer watch on my boyfriend.

My heart swelled when he turned around, like he sensed I was close by. I could tell he was looking for me by the way his eyes scanned the crowd. Even with girls all over him, he only had me on his mind. And all I ever did was lie to him.

When he didn't spot me, a flicker of disappointment crossed his face before he seamlessly reengaged with the conversation. Seeing that look, though, made me pick up my pace, suddenly desperate to be back with him, as if it had been forever, when in reality it couldn't have been more than thirty minutes.

"Boo!" I called as I reached him, throwing my arms around his neck from behind.

There was a split second of hesitation where he tensed, but then he relaxed back against me, chuckling. "Hey, you." He twisted around to glance up at me. "Thought you'd got lost."

The girl who had been unsuccessfully flirting with him shot me a glare and shifted away from him on the log, and I slid into the spot she'd vacated, tucking myself into his side.

"What'd I miss?" His arm snaked around my waist, and I instantly felt a wave of calmness wash over me.

"Ah, a bonfire classic." His face turned serious as he lowered his voice to a whisper. "Ghost stories."

"Hmm, we better get out of here then, or I'll be having nightmares tonight."

He smiled, a small grin that didn't reach his eyes, but it still made my heart flutter. "I'll keep you safe, don't worry."

"I know." I leaned closer and planted a quick kiss on his lips. Then I asked, "Ready to go?"

He glanced down at his watch and arched his brow. "Already? Took us longer to drive here."

"Yeah, sorry, it's just I... have a headache." The lie slipped out without a second thought, and instantly, a wave of guilt washed over me. "We can stay if you want to." I quickly added.

"Oh, really? Well, in that case, let's go. I'm pretty sure I have some aspirin in the truck."

We rose to our feet, and he reached for my hand, his fingers interlocking with mine. We were just about to leave when Jen's protest stopped us in our tracks. "You're kidding me! You're bailing on us already? Come on, Carter, don't leave us hanging! You promised us a story."

Hearing her say his name made my stomach tighten, though I still couldn't understand why. It was *my* hand he was holding. *I* was the one leaving with him tonight. What the hell made me so threatened by her? He had done nothing to make me not trust him. So why...

Then it hit me - it must be the thing Ansel slipped into my drink. Turns out, I did have some aftereffects. Feeling super paranoid. *Great.*

Carter's chuckle interrupted my thoughts. "Uh, that's not what I said at all. Havencrest is pretty boring. There're no stories to tell."

"Oh, c'mon! Think harder. Big Foot? Haunted lighthouse?" Jen said. "Every town's got *something*."

Right on cue, a coyote's howl echoed through the air.

"Werewolves?" Adam chipped in with a grin, making me stiffen beside Carter. Henry stayed quiet behind me, and I had to resist the urge to turn around and make eye contact to see if he was as nervous as me. Because what had Carter said before? Legends had to start somewhere. While I was off searching for Ansel, had he said something to the group? He'd never asked questions about what happened that night in the woods, with Vincent Lavoie, but I knew that was just because I asked him not to and, for whatever reason, he trusted me. Completely. But clearly, he had some questions, even if he was keeping them to himself. Maybe my explanation of him being all woozy from the blow to the head, imagining things, just wasn't cutting it anymore. Maybe he suspected...

No. Stop it. It was insane to even think about it. If he knew... if he had any doubt, he wouldn't be here. No way would he be at this party or spending a week in a cabin in the middle of nowhere with me, let alone holding my hand or sharing my bed. If he suspected what I was, he'd have run screaming a long time ago. And I wouldn't blame him.

Still... The silence was killing me as I waited for him to say something. Why was he taking so long, anyway? Was he *trying* to freak me out?

It felt like an eternity before he finally chuckled again. "You know that was a coyote, right? I've seen a few of those back home, but never a werewolf. Of course, that could be because they aren't *real*."

Jen let out a deep sigh, as if Carter had just said the most absurd thing imaginable, while I had to bite my lip to stop myself from exhaling in relief.

"Well, *duh!* That's what makes them freaking *legends*." As she spoke, she snuggled closer to Adam, rolling her eyes and wrapping her arms tightly around his neck, while swinging her legs out in front of her. She didn't seem to notice his attempts to wriggle out of her grasp, or the way his face contorted with annoyance. She just continued to chatter obliviously. "But if you're gonna be boring, then I guess it's *my* turn."

A collective groan came from the circle, but it was the guy with the mohawk, sitting across from Jen, who spoke. "You always tell the same fucking story, Jen. It's lame."

She hesitated for a sec, her face turning red, before muttering, "It's not lame."

"Yeah, it is. It's for kids. No one is scared of that shit anymore."

While they argued, I gently pulled Carter's hand and slowly backed away from the group, trying not to attract any attention. Jen would probably complain again about Carter leaving, and I just wanted to get the heck out of there.

Adam snorted a laugh, and she scowled, her cheeks flushing an even deeper shade of red. "Well, you should be!"

"Oh yeah? Why's that, Jenny?" Adam asked, and even though she had said she hated the nickname earlier, she didn't protest this time. She just stood up and crossed her arms.

"Well... just because! Because Lydia went missing a month ago, and the cops combed through these woods with dogs, but they didn't find squat. There's only one explanation for that."

In an instant, the air around the group grew tense, as if charged with electricity. Some people looked nervously at Mohawk, so obviously 'Lydia' had something to do with him, whoever she was.

"Yeah, and I already told you. They fucking ran away." Mohawk fired back and then chugged his beer.

I had no clue what was happening with them, but I was thankful for the distraction. Jen was so annoyed that she didn't even realise we were sneaking away. We were almost far away enough to vanish into the crowd. Just a couple more steps, and...

"Maybe. Or maybe the stories are true. Maybe it got them."

I couldn't pinpoint the trigger, but out of nowhere, a memory came rushing back, making me freeze. The missing poster in the Chibouwood store window. The girl with red hair... her name was Lydia. Was she connected to Mohawk? Who just *happened* to be at the party we'd come to, looking for Ansel? That was way too much of a coincidence.

My mind raced, and an icy shiver ran down my spine as a question slipped out of my mouth, earning a groan from Henry. "What are you talking about?"

Jen's piercing gaze met mine, her eyes shining with delight as she realised she had someone captivated, even if it was only me. "The windikouk, of course."

Ignoring the groaning from the group, I focused on Jen. Those red eyes haunted my thoughts, but maybe it was connected and I wasn't losing my mind after all. I thought I was meant to find Ansel at this party, but maybe this was why we were here. Maybe this was how I got answers.

"What's that?" I asked.

Jen's eyes practically glittered with excitement now. "Girl, how can you come to Berkton County and *not* know about the windikouk? You said you guys are staying in Chibouwood, right? You didn't see all the silver hanging from the doorframes out there? Silver stops it from crossing the threshold. If not, it might sneak in and yank you right out of bed and deep into the forest. *Never to be seen again!*"

"Christ, Jen. Knock it off, would you?" Mohawk grunted as he flicked ash from the cigarette dangling between his fingers. "Don't even listen to her, new girl. The windikouk is just a dumb story parents tell to make sure their kids don't stay out too late."

"If that's the case, why do they leave silver out? Huh?" Jen needled him. I couldn't tell if she actually believed the story, or she was just trying piss him off.

Mohawk inhaled a sharp breath. "Because people around here are fucking crazy. And as for my sister? She's just being a brat, throwing a fit because my dad said no to her dating that asshole. Who the hell is he, anyway? Some jerk from who-knows-where. I never even saw him around before she brought him home, and he was always messed up. The guy was on drugs or something, I'm sure of it. He's either gonna break her damn heart or mess her up just as bad. Whichever it is? We'll be stuck cleaning up the mess." With each word, his voice grew louder, more aggressive, while a cloud of dirt danced above his feet as he kicked at the ground. "Once she figures out that running away with him was a huge mistake, she'll come crawling back."

The silence that followed his words was thick and suffocating, as if the air itself had become heavy with their weight. It was Jen who shattered it, and a wicked glint danced in her eyes as she spoke.

"It's been over a month, Jax. I think that ship has sailed."

His eyes were like daggers as he looked at her, but she didn't so much as flinch. "Yeah? Well, I sure hope they're pleased with themselves, wherever the hell they are. 'Cus my parents are losing their minds. But let me tell you something – if William Porter ever shows his face around here again? He's gonna wish the windikouk *did* get him. Because that son of a bitch is dead."

32

We got out of there pretty quickly after that.

It was getting way too uncomfortable, and I didn't wanna be there when Jax inevitably lost his cool with Jen. I felt sick just *thinking* about someone I cared about being missing, so to have people making jokes about them being dead? Honestly, I doubted I could have held myself together the way Jax did.

Luckily, the drive home was way better than the drive *to* the party. The guys were back at it, teasing me about my terrible stick-shift driving, but I was too happy they weren't mad at me anymore to get upset. Of course, that didn't mean I wasn't gonna play them at their own game.

When we arrived at the cabin, I hit the brakes hard before jumping out of the cab without saying a word. There was a moment of stunned silence, where I could picture them exchanging glances, but eventually, the passenger side door creaked open, and their footsteps grew closer. I turned, arms crossed tightly over my chest, and shot them a glare. Henry cleared his throat and nudged Carter.

"Good luck with that." He said before striding away towards the deck. "Excuse me while I go find some silver for the door. Knives will do the trick, right?"

Carter made a noise somewhere between a laugh and a squawk. "Bro! You're seriously using that windy-whatever-it-was to get out of this? Whatever happened to 'leave no Silver Hawk behind'? I thought we were a team, man!"

"Haven't you heard? I'm a Golden Bear now." Henry called out while retreating, and Carter shook his head, his laughter lingering long after Henry vanished.

When he turned back to me, his eyes held a mischievous glint, and I felt myself instantly wavering. Especially when he stepped closer, his hands finding their way to my hips as we stood by the bumper. His touch set my skin on fire, and I responded by pressing myself hard against him.

"I've really gotta give you more lessons." He grinned down at me.

"It's not fair when you two team up against me." I tried to scowl, but a smile kept sneaking in. "And I wasn't *that* bad."

He chuckled and gave me a quick kiss on the cheek, leaving a cool sensation when he pulled back. "Let's just agree to disagree, babe."

I huffed. "Be grateful. If I hadn't offered to drive, we'd be stuck walking from Rowland. So I hope the next words out of your mouth are 'thank you'."

His eyes crinkled, twinkling even brighter. "Is it a bad time to confess that I only had one beer?"

I gasped, moving far enough away so I could shove him backwards and aim a playful punch at his arm. "*Jerk*! You had me drive home just to make fun of me?!"

"Well, not *just* to make fun of you. You're also *ridiculously* hot behind the wheel. Your clutch control needs some work, but you're very adept with a gear shift. Can you blame a guy for wanting to enjoy the show?"

As he grabbed my waist again, I pouted, even as I felt my cheeks flush. "Adept with a gear shift, huh?"

His face loomed inches from mine, his warm breath caressing my skin, and when he answered, his voice was a husky, barely audible whisper. "Very much so."

His body had a magnetic pull that drew me closer, although at this point, I wasn't sure how we could possibly *be* closer. Still, I pressed myself against him, and he sucked in a sharp breath. The sound of it, the reaction his body had to *my* touch, sent a rush of heat coursing through me. I rose on my tiptoes to kiss him, not even caring anymore that we weren't alone. I'd forgotten everything else. It was just him and me, and the hood of the truck holding us up. I paused mere inches from his lips, wanting to tease him just a little, but I couldn't resist any longer. I needed him. Needed the reminder that he was mine, and I was his, no matter the madness taking place around us. Carter was a constant. He was my anchor. And I needed it now more than ever.

Our lips brushed. Gently, at first, but that didn't last long. Soon enough, I was wrapping my arms around his neck, and his nails were digging into the flesh just above the waistband of my shorts, and...

A cough sounded behind us. I pulled back from him, biting down on my lip to suppress a groan. When I opened my eyes, I saw my disappointment echoed in Carter's expression, though he swiftly replaced it with a lopsided grin before resting his forehead against mine. His hands squeezed my hips again – silently promising we'd continue this later – and then he straightened up, moving to stand beside me, allowing me to see Henry under the porch light.

"Need to speak to you." Henry growled.

My eyes flickered towards Carter, but that only made Henry's expression harden. When he spoke again, it was more like a snarl.

"*Now*."

And just like that, everything changed. One minute we were all goofing around, and then it was gone, leaving me with a pit in my stomach.

"What's wrong?" Carter asked, beating me to it.

"*Madison*." Henry hissed through gritted teeth, completely ignoring him. Instead, he focused on me, his eyes ablaze with some emotion I couldn't quite place, waiting for me to go to him so we could figure out whatever was happening. Just me and him. The way it had always been. The way it still had to be, if I wanted to keep Carter safe.

Whatever it was, I didn't want to know. I knew that was selfish, and that Henry wouldn't interrupt if it wasn't important. But I just wanted to lock it in a box and forget about it. To go back to five minutes ago, laughing and joking with them both. But with every passing second, Henry's impatience grew, until he couldn't suppress it any further. He blurted it out... and once it was out, there was no taking it back.

"They were never at that fucking party. They were here. The whole *fucking time*."

"Who? What are you talking about?" Carter asked, but I didn't need to hear the explanation. I knew exactly who he meant... and the hairs on the back of my neck stood on end as the puzzle pieces slotted together.

I broke free from Carter's grasp and sprinted towards the deck, my heart racing. It seemed to take forever to reach it, although it was only seconds, and when I finally got to the door, what I saw made my stomach turn.

It was like a tornado had ripped through. The place was a complete mess, with drawers flung open and their contents strewn across the floor. In the living area, the drapes fluttered with the gentle night breeze, a smashed window coming into view behind them. Shards of glass gleamed ominously in the moonlit glow, while muddy footprints stained the carpet and sofa. But what really caught my attention was the smell. Because I recognised it.

Ansel and Jamie.

Moving further inside, I traced the rough texture of the wooden walls with my fingertips. The hallway was empty, but every door had been flung open, so it was obvious that someone had been there, looking for something. The thought of anyone rifling through our things made my skin crawl. Maybe that was silly, since they already broke in yesterday, but that didn't feel so bad, somehow. They'd been desperate, and they'd even used the spare key to get inside. No damage done. I might've done the same myself in that situation. If anything, Sean was to blame for leaving his key in such an obvious spot. It was asking for trouble.

But this... this was on another level. This was personal.

At the sound of footsteps behind me, I jumped and spun around, but it was just Carter. For a moment, he only stood in the doorway, wide eyed and his forehead glistening with sweat.

"Did they take anything?" His voice trembled as he asked, finally crossing the threshold into the kitchen.

I hadn't actually looked, but I was fairly certain they hadn't. They had no interest in robbing us. They were searching for something else - some kind of proof that we had hurt Colton.

When I shook my head, he let out a deep breath and then took a step towards me, enfolding me in his arms. "Okay. That's good. Don't worry. We'll figure this out, okay? Tomorrow morning, we'll go right to the sheriff's station and report it."

Just as I was about to reply, Henry showed up in the doorway behind Carter. "Screw the cops. Those assholes won't have got far. I'm going after them."

I felt Carter tense as he turned to face him. "Bro, we've been out for like three hours. Whoever did this was probably *waiting* for us to leave and then broke in the second we were gone. They'll be long gone already."

"*Whoever* did this? You're kidding, right? Because I know exactly who did this."

"No. You only *think* you know. There's a big difference. What makes you so sure, anyway?"

Henry glanced at me, and I shot him a pleading look, silently urging him to stay calm. He had a tendency to say things when he was angry. Things he couldn't take back.

His lips formed a tight line, sending a wave of tension through me, but then he rolled his eyes, let out a deep sigh, and carried on. "Seriously, who else would it be? George of the fucking jungle? This place doesn't get much foot traffic, in case you didn't notice. And those assholes trespassed on my territory once and got away with it. I won't let it slide twice." With a snarl, he turned and stomped down the porch steps, vanishing into the night, leaving his words hanging in the air.

I tried to follow him, but Carter grabbed my hand and stopped me. "Mads, this is crazy. It's pitch black out there. And last time..."

The memory of the previous night – Ansel ditching me, and everything that came afterwards – sent a shiver down my spine. I still didn't know what to believe, but if there was a chance it was real, I couldn't let Henry go out there on his own. Even if it wasn't, he was so mad I had no idea what he'd do if he found Ansel and Jamie. We really didn't need them reporting him for assault, just to make things worse for us right now.

My hand came to rest on Carter's cheek, and I noticed how his expression shifted – his eyes narrowing, and his jaw setting. Because he knew what was coming. Of course he did. We'd been here before – me lying to him, taking off with Henry and leaving him on the sidelines. But I had no choice, right? I had to keep them safe. *Both* of them.

The taste of blood coated my mouth as I bit my lip, so I swallowed hard before carrying on. "Carter, I have to go after him. He's angry, but I can get through to him. You stay here. I'll be careful, I promise. And it's only Ansel and Jamie. They just wanna find Colton. And I... I can talk to them, too. I can fix it."

I hoped.

"How could you possibly know it was them? It could've been anyone who broke in here! And even if you're right... what the hell makes you so sure they won't hurt you? You're tough. I know that. But... fuck. What aren't you telling me?"

I fought against the impulse to sneak a glance over my shoulder again. I wouldn't see Henry, anyway. The forest had engulfed him completely. But I could still hear him, his footsteps crashing in the distance, so I knew he was okay, and I could catch up with him... once I convinced Carter to let me go.

We locked eyes, and I let out a fake laugh that he totally saw through, but I kept going anyway.

"*Nothing!* But you know how Henry is, and I don't want him to mess things up even more this week by starting a fight. Lemme go calm him down, and everything will be fine, yeah?" When he said nothing, I added, "I've got this. Just trust me."

As soon as the words escaped my mouth, a heaviness dropped onto my chest, and I knew I'd made a mistake. But there was no going back. They were out there, just hanging in the silence like some toxic fog. His grip on my arm loosened and his face contorted into an expression that appeared out of place on his normally gentle features. It wasn't anger, but it was dangerously similar.

"Seriously? I *do* trust you. There's nobody in the goddamn world I trust more than you. Don't you know that already? Yet you still…" He cut himself off as he raked his hand through his hair. At the sight, that weight on my chest seemed to press down even heavier. He held my heart in his hands, squeezing it tight, and I couldn't catch my breath.

I wasn't ready for this. I knew it would happen eventually, but I thought we had more time. This week was supposed to be perfect. But I'd screwed it up, like I screwed up everything. And now I was about to lose him… and it was all my fault.

My head was throbbing, practically begging me to open my mouth. Just to say something, to do *anything,* to reassure him. But my tongue was as dry as a desert, and I couldn't speak. He was right there, the boy I loved so much that the idea of being without him made it hard for me to even breathe, and I was about to lose him… yet I couldn't think of a single thing to say.

I saw disappointment flash in his eyes when I stayed quiet, but then it was replaced by something far worse: hurt.

This was it.

"Madison," he started, and I couldn't help but flinch. He only ever called me Mads, or Stone.

He ran his tongue over his lips to wet them, and I had to focus on my breathing to keep the tears at bay, feeling every thump of my heart against my ribcage. It wouldn't be fair on him to cry. He'd feel guilty, and he had nothing to feel guilty for –

"I love you. And I trust you. But you… shit, you've gotta stop using that as an excuse to keep me in the dark all the time, okay? Let me help you."

I blinked, confused, my mind racing to catch up. Because that didn't sound like a breakup, right? Maybe there was still hope. I could try to fix it.

"That's not—"

"Not what you're doing?" He finished for me. "Yeah, it is. I'm not stupid, Madison. Or maybe I am, 'cause I'm so scared shitless of losing you that I just go along with it."

I couldn't handle looking at him anymore, so I redirected my gaze downward to fixate on the mess that littered the floor. As the silence suffocated us, my mind whirred with the urgency to break it, to find something, anything, to say, but it was as if my brain had stopped working, and suddenly I couldn't string a sentence together at all.

I wasn't sure how much time passed like that, until, finally, his fingers grazed my arm again. It was hesitant, but it was *something*. An olive branch.

I sucked in a breath, my gaze lifting to meet his hazel eyes that I loved so much. The eyes that made me feel like I was the only one he saw.

He smiled, but it lacked the warmth that usually accompanied his grins. "I'm sorry. Just forget about it, okay? Now's not the time. But you're out of your mind if you think I'm gonna sit here making s'mores while my girlfriend runs through the forest in the middle of the night... *again*."

"Girlfriend?" I asked, my voice little more than a whisper. I hardly dared hope. "You still want me to be?"

He rolled his eyes, but the corners of his mouth quirked. "Did you miss the part where I said I *love* you?"

A wave of relief surged over me at that, making my legs wobble, as if they might buckle under my weight, but I was too happy to care. If I ended up on the ground, I knew he'd be right there beside me, and then I could stay snuggled up with him all night. Under different circumstances, I would have done exactly that, but I couldn't. Not now. I had to chase after Henry.

"I love you, too, Carter. And that means I have to keep you safe. That's all that matters to me." I said finally, even though it killed me to do it. "So I'm asking you—"

Our lips collided suddenly, and his hands grasped my cheeks with a firmness that startled me, cutting off my sentence. It ended as fast as it came, but he stayed there, so close I could feel his breath on my skin.

"Stone, I'll do anything for you, you know that. Anything but this. So please don't even ask. I'm begging you. Don't put me in a position where I have to say no to you." His voice seemed to thunder in my ears, even though he wasn't speaking particularly loudly, yet I still found myself holding my breath, mesmerised by the intensity of his gaze. "You're a badass, and I know you don't need my protection. But guess what? You've got it anyway, even if I'm useless. So you can stand here and argue with me until Henry comes back carrying their decapitated heads on sticks, or we can go now. *Together*. Those are your options."

I wanted to argue and beg him to stay, but I knew he wouldn't listen. Sure, I could have waited for a bit, maybe even until later, when he fell asleep, and then snuck away without him knowing. But he was right – Henry could wreak all sorts of havoc in that time. Plus, what if he woke up and found me missing again? Then he'd come after me.

I had to decide quickly, because Henry was getting further and further away with every passing second. Could I really be sure that leaving Carter behind was any safer? What if Ansel and Jamie came back? They might not be supernatural, but that didn't mean they couldn't still do some serious damage, especially if it was two against one... and Ansel knew damn well he could get to me by going for Carter.

Was that their plan? To get Henry and me out of the way so they could take Carter hostage and use him to get information about Colton? What if...

No. I was being paranoid. Or I probably was, anyway. But if there was even a slight chance I was right... was I willing to take the risk? I already knew the answer, because I had asked myself the same question multiple times over the past two days, and it never changed. No risk was worth it when it came to Carter. So, I only had one choice... I just hoped I wouldn't come to regret it.

I gulped, then reached up and squeezed his arm.

"Okay."

33

I let Carter take the lead, mainly because I wanted him right where I could see him. I was probably just being paranoid, but I couldn't stop thinking that he might disappear if I didn't keep an eye on him. Just like Ansel did. And Colton, Lydia, her boyfriend, whose name I couldn't remember…

It felt like everyone vanished in these woods.

I let out a breath and watched as it danced in the cold air, until it disappeared, taking the thought with it. Freaking out wouldn't help, and it would only worry Carter. Better to focus on what I could control right *now*.

Henry had a bigger head start on us than I expected, and as we ventured deeper into the woods, the sound of twigs snapping and foliage rustling faded until I lost track of him completely. Carter's heavy, stumbling steps didn't help – he wasn't as accustomed to the wilderness as I was – but it didn't matter much. We didn't exactly need a map to find them; the broken branches and fresh footprints were enough. Even Carter, equipped only with a flashlight, could effortlessly follow their trail.

The problem was that, even with obvious tracks, Henry, Ansel, and Jamie remained frustratingly out of reach.

Before too long, Carter came to a stop and looked back at me, sighing. "We're getting nowhere, Mads. We might wanna turn back before we get lost, don't you think?" I glanced around at the surrounding darkness, anxiously biting my lip as he spoke. Carter spotted it – my nervous tick – and stepped closer. "Seriously, what's Barton gonna do? Kill them? I mean, he's got a temper, but that's going too far, even for him."

He was right, of course, but I'd rather Henry didn't get himself arrested for assault, either, even if he wasn't actually planning on killing them. That would just be the icing on the cake for this damn trip.

What was scarier than calling Dan and Sierra to tell them their son had been arrested, though, was whatever was lurking around Chibouwood, snatching teens as they roamed the woods. Well, assuming there was actually something out here. Henry didn't believe it, and I had given up trying to figure things out. My mind was a jumbled mess, like a tangled web I couldn't unravel. All that mattered to me now was getting all three of us home to Havencrest in one piece, but I was starting to doubt if that was even possible.

I didn't realise how long I had been standing and staring into space until Carter's touch on my elbow snapped me out of it, and he said, "Or we could go a bit further, if you're up for it."

He shrugged, like he couldn't care less, but I knew it wasn't true. He wanted to head back to the cabin, hop into bed, and maybe, if I was lucky, keep going with what we started earlier. I knew, because I wanted that, too. But he wouldn't force it, because Carter never did. Carter, who was the sweetest and most gentle person I knew, who always put me above everything and everyone else, even himself. Even when I didn't deserve it. Maybe *especially* when I didn't deserve it. Like tonight.

We had so much to talk about. But like he said earlier – now wasn't the time.

I nodded. "If that's okay?"

"Of course it's okay." Leaning in with a soft smile, his lips lightly grazed the top of my head, and I closed my eyes, inhaling and savouring the scent of the cologne that still clung to him. "Anything for you, Mads. You know that."

"He's gotta catch up with them eventually, right? The forest can't go on forever, even in Maine. So, unless they're currently racing each other on the highway..."

As I let out a breathy laugh, Carter smiled back, but his smile seemed feeble, and a knot tightened in my stomach.

"I'm sorry, Carter." I blurted out, and his eyebrows shot up in surprise, mirroring my own reaction, because I hadn't expected those words to come out of my mouth. Not now. But suddenly the floodgates had opened, and I couldn't stop the torrent of words from spilling out. "I'm sorry this week has been such a mess. It's not what I wanted. I just wanted to be with you. It's all I ever want. You know that, right?" I didn't give him a chance to respond before I hurried on. I was too scared to hear the answer. "You must hate me. When you mentioned going to Daytona with Ethan... I should've just said yes. I wish I had. And I'm just so sor—"

Just then, a sudden gust of wind rustled the leaves at my feet, filling the air with an overpowering stench that stopped the words dead in my throat. I turned, my nose homing in on the scent, and...

"No." It was barely a word, just a breath. "No, no, no."

"Mads? What's wrong?" Even though he was right next to me, Carter's voice sounded all shaky and far away, like he was talking through a tunnel. It took me a moment to figure out that it was just my blood pounding in my ears, messing with my perception, but once I did, I automatically reached for his hand. To keep him close. In a split second, his fingers tangled with mine, knowing exactly what I needed, even if he didn't understand why. "You sense something?"

All I could do was nod in response.

Blood.

The sickly, coppery scent of it tainted everything, overwhelming my senses and making it impossible to confirm anything other than just that – it was blood. *Human* blood.

Panic surged through my veins while my chest throbbed with pain, each breath I took coming out in panicked gasps. I opened my mouth to speak, but only air escaped, so all I could do was charge forward, dragging Carter along behind me. He called out to me, but it was all gibberish, and I didn't have time to figure it out. Eventually, he gave up and fell silent, except for the occasional grunt as he struggled to match my pace. But I couldn't stop. Couldn't slow down. Not when one thing consumed my mind: a memory. Ryan, slumped in his car...

No, god, please. Not again. Not him.

I couldn't hear him anymore. Could he really have gotten so far ahead? What if...

No. I couldn't think like that. If it was him, then I'd *know*, wouldn't I? I would feel it in my heart. Because we had a connection, Henry and me. A bond. He was my packmate, my best friend, *my* Henry. It couldn't be him. It just *couldn't*.

I inhaled sharply, trying to shake off the thought and redirect my attention to the path in front of me. The flashlight's eerie light pierced through the midnight darkness, its beam bouncing with Carter's every step, conjuring looming shadows that seemed to encircle us, like beasts waiting to strike. It made the forest dense and suffocating, the trees so close it was as if they could reach right out and grab us. To haul us away, ensnare us for eternity in their roots, like in Jen's bonfire story. Like seemed to have happened to Lydia.

At the thought, my hand instinctively tightened around Carter's. I felt the clamminess of his palms, saw the flashlight beam swinging, and yet I still kept glancing over my shoulder after every few steps to reassure myself he was there. That he was safe. But that meant taking my eyes off the path, so I didn't see the raised vine until my foot snagged on it, making me lurch forward. My fingers just barely found purchase on the rough surface of a tree trunk before I fell, but it was too late for Carter. My stumble knocked him off balance, and he gave a surprised squawk as he tumbled, dragging me down with him until we were in a heap on the ground.

"You okay?" I asked breathlessly, not waiting for an answer. Instead, I pushed away from him, but my feet slipped on the slick, damp leaves, causing me to flail and fall. I landed on top of Carter again, and he let out a grunt of pain. "Sorry." I muttered, before getting quickly back on my feet, more cautiously this time. Then I reached out and clasped his hand, attempting to hoist him up with me. But he kept slipping too, and I bit back a growl of frustration, turning to look for something to help, when—

Wait.

A shiver ran down my spine. Because, just like before... I couldn't hear anything. Only complete silence. No signs of life at all.

That wasn't possible. I thought back to minutes before, to before the blood, wracking my brain for anything, any sign that the forest wasn't as dead as the body we were tracking. Hadn't there been birds chirping in the distance? Owls? Rodents? There was definitely...

Except there wasn't. I just didn't notice because I was so focused on Henry and Carter. My familiarity with the forest tricked my mind into believing I could hear its usual soundtrack, because that's what my brain expected, when in reality, there was no sound at all.

We were completely alone. It was like the forest knew something we didn't, and it watched with bated breath, too scared to even make a noise.

How did I miss that until now?

"*MADISON!*"

Carter's sudden outburst caught me off guard, and I jumped, blinking at him in surprise. I took in his wide-eyed expression, the creases of worry on his face, and my cheeks heated.

I'd zoned out again, and now I noticed his hand clamped around my arm, anchoring me to him as he struggled to stand up without losing his balance. Once he'd straightened, he took a deep breath. "Madison, just stop! You're scaring the crap out of me. What the hell is going on?"

My eyes darted between his face, the surrounding darkness, and the leaves at our feet, illuminated by the still blaring flashlight, while I tried to come up with an answer that would get us on the move again as quickly as possible. "I- I... I don't know. Just please tr—"

The words came without thought, but I cut them off when I saw his jaw clench at the all too familiar line. He didn't deserve to be brushed off with the same old non-response. It was a cop-out, me once again taking for granted his willingness to go along with whatever I asked. But recognising that didn't change the fact I couldn't explain anything right now, and even if I could, where the hell would I start? He'd think I was crazy, drag me back to the truck and drop me off at the nearest psych ward, and then what would happen to Henry?

The truth was I hadn't expected this conversation to ever actually come up. Since our first kiss, I'd known I was on borrowed time, that I just had to try my damnedest to keep those sides of myself separate, the wolf and the girl Carter knew, until he inevitably moved on to live his spectacular life, doing whatever spectacular thing he decided to do. Because Carter Johnson could change the world if he wanted to, and I wouldn't be the thing that stood in his way.

But neither could I let myself be the reason anything happened to Henry.

I met Carter's gaze, feeling my heart break at the hurt in his eyes, because he knew what I was going to ask, and we both knew he'd do it. But I had this gut feeling it would be the last time. "I'm sorry. I know you're tired of hearing that, and I'm tired of saying it. I don't deserve your forgiveness. I know that. But—"

"What exactly are we talking about here, Madison? Because I don't know what the hell is going on with you. Forgiveness for what?"

"I—"

My mind went blank. I just stood there, my mouth agape, trying to form words that just wouldn't come. I mean, it was the middle of the night, and we were deep in the woods, tracking down a dead body. What was I supposed to say to make him happy? That would make any of this better?

Still, the suspicion in his voice cut through me like a knife, and I blinked back tears, wishing I could take back everything that had happened. But I couldn't, and it killed me. He deserved so much more – someone he could trust, who didn't lie to him all the time. Someone who could share their complete self with him.

I wanted to be that for him, but right now, my priority was Henry. It had to be. Because the alternative was unthinkable.

When Carter's hand found my waist, I expected the usual tingling sensation, but a coldness spread through my body instead. His voice turned gentle when he spoke again, but, honestly, it might've been better if he was yelling, because guilt pierced me like a knife to the chest.

"Tell me." His eyes were glassy, as if he was on the brink of tears and struggling to hold them back. "*Please.*"

His voice cracked on the last word, and it was a punch to the gut that left me winded. My throat constricted, but I still reached up to touch his cheek, and he turned his face into my hand, his eyes fluttering closed for a moment.

"I swear to you, I'll explain everything." Did I mean that? I wasn't sure, but I hoped he'd believe it. At least for now. "But we need to keep moving. I... I heard something before. A bear, I think." I continued, the lies like acid on my tongue. "We need to find him, Carter."

For what felt like an eternity, he said nothing. There was only the rustling of leaves in the breeze – the only sign of life aside from us. Then his shoulders slumped, his arm falling limply to his side, my skin icy where his fingers had been. He stepped backwards, and it was only a few paces, but it felt like a chasm had opened up between us, and I didn't know how to close the distance without falling in. He averted his gaze from mine, his eyes darting away as if he couldn't stand to look at me anymore, and my heart sank.

"Okay." He nodded once. "I get it."

I didn't know whether to feel relieved or terrified by that, but every second wasted was a second we couldn't afford, if that blood was Henry's. We had to *move,* so I could find—

The thought halted, and I cursed myself. How had I been so stupid? I'd been so wrapped up in panic that I'd ignored the small voice yelling at me to stop and think for a moment, reminding me I had *superhuman goddamn senses*, and I should use them. Then I'd know. Maybe that was partly cowardice, because if I didn't confirm it, then I could avoid facing the reality. I could stay in the blissful in between. The 'before', the time when everything was okay. But I couldn't just bury my head in the sand forever.

Raising my nose to the wind, I tried to find the scent again, but the breeze had shifted slightly since we fell, carrying the trail away. I breathed in harder, but it didn't help. The scent of pine, animal droppings, and the distant presence of a herd of deer surrounded us, but the trail I had been following was nowhere to be found.

And without it, I was just some terrified kid, lost in the woods. No help to anyone.

34

My hands trembled as I desperately looked around for any kind of marker that could lead us back to where we needed to be. But everything looked the same. Of course it did. What the hell else did I expect in the pitch black forest? There *were* trails, ones I hadn't noticed before, but they were all faint, like ghostly imprints of the animals who had wandered through here before us, and the thick vegetation covered the ground like a carpet, so there wasn't even a single print to direct me.

There was nothing. A complete dead end.

I'd failed him. Maybe the scent wasn't his, but it belonged to someone, and the creature that attacked them was still out there, and Henry—

"Shit, is that... is that *blood?*"

"What?"

My head snapped around at Carter's voice, my eyes following the path his finger traced until my gaze landed on the huge thicket before us. I studied it, taking in every detail, but there was nothing that stood out as strange...

Then he shone the beam of his flashlight towards it. And there it was. So blatantly obvious that I couldn't believe I hadn't spotted it myself.

In an instant, the sound of my pulse pounding in my ears faded to nothing, as if my heart had stopped beating altogether. The world around me faded away, leaving me in a vacuum of nothingness. Or perhaps it was me that was fading away, my mind lost in a different dimension, far from reality. Either would be better than this.

Because it *was* blood on the tree. Bloody fingerprints. And I knew the scent all too well.

Henry.

My hand instinctively found Carter's again, squeezing it so tightly that I felt the rough callouses of his palms scratching against mine. But he didn't say a word, and he didn't recoil from my touch, either. Like the forest, he seemed to know better. For now, at least, he was still with me.

No. No, no, no...

My mind screamed at me to turn back. As if that would turn back time, right back to arguing in the truck and messing around with Carter on the hood. Was it actually possible that was less than an hour ago? It felt like a different lifetime. A different me.

My body acted on instinct though, propelling me forward before I even realised I was moving, and then we were forcing our way through the thicket, wading through a sea of thorns, each step bringing stabs of pain as branches scratched at my face. I noticed Carter's outstretched arm, attempting to shield me from the worst of it, but they still clawed at us both. I hardly felt them, though. I was numb, except for the all-consuming pain in my chest.

And then finally, and yet still somehow all too quickly, we reached the other side, and...

The world seemed to stop and hold its breath in anticipation. And then, in a split second that sent my stomach into free fall, it happened - the moment that would forever divide my life between 'before' and 'after'.

The bright spring colours of the wildflowers caught my attention first, almost concealing the figure lying among them. It was difficult to spot amidst the tall blooms, their lush petals creating a beautiful canopy that shielded it beneath. The corpse's pale complexion blended in. It was strangely mesmerising; the crimson pools seeping into the undergrowth, the fragrant aroma of the flowers mingling with the metallic tang of the blood. It seemed almost unreal, like a meticulously curated display, a detailed masterpiece on a painter's canvas.

Except, it wasn't art. Neither was it a dream or a figment of my imagination; it was all too real.

I never thought that, by following the trail, I'd find anyone alive. I wasn't stupid, and they definitely couldn't have survived with all that blood loss. But even with that knowledge, I still wasn't ready for this, and nausea hit me like a wave, until I keeled over to empty the contents of my stomach onto the grass. Because what I was looking at... it wasn't a body. At least not entirely. In front of me, only a head and torso remained, severed at the waist, with the lower half missing except for a red trail vanishing into the trees.

I straightened up, using the back of my hand to wipe the saliva clinging to my lips... and that's when I saw it. My knees gave way, and without Carter's support, I would have crumbled into the pool of blood at my feet.

Thick black hair.

My chest constricted with fear, as if an invisible hand were squeezing my heart. I let go of Carter, and he didn't hold me back, although a small part of me wished he had. Wished that he'd insist we leave, and then I could call my dad to come and deal with it instead, so I didn't have to. I just wanted to be home, in my bedroom, hiding under my comforter and blocking out the world. I wasn't ready for this. This is what Henry had trained for. He was the one Ray took under his wing, not me.

I needed him. I needed him to tell me what to do. But he couldn't, and I felt so lost. Lost and alone.

Carter seemed too frozen in shock to react at all, so he stayed still even as I took a step closer to the body. The overwhelming stench made me gag, and my eyes watered until the forest became a blurry, disorienting mess of red and green hues. I blinked rapidly, trying to regain focus, until the world sharpened into clarity... and then a lump formed in my throat.

Up close, it was obvious. Henry was wearing his usual jeans and tee. But whoever this was, they had on a dress, so that meant...

Tears cascaded down my cheeks, a wail breaking free from the depths of my soul.

It wasn't Henry.

The sudden rush of relief was so intense that my legs actually did give way this time, and I crumpled to the ground. My hands tore at the grass, pulling out clumps with every racking sob until dirt bedded under my nails and my fingertips ached. But I couldn't bring myself to stop. The pain was the only thing keeping me grounded.

I wasn't sure how long I stayed like that, but eventually the sobs subsided to hiccupping breaths, until I could finally think clearly again. I scrambled backwards, desperate to create as much space between myself and the body as possible. When I was far enough away, I stood up, looking around for Carter, finding him standing to my left. Staring at the flowerbed, his hands trembling.

Guilt joined the tornado of emotions swirling around my head. As a werewolf, I was no stranger to death, but it still made my stomach turn. What must Carter be thinking? He shouldn't be seeing this. No one should have to see something like this, but especially not him. Not my sweet, gentle Carter, who always saw the good in everyone.

He wasn't even supposed to be here. He should be in Florida, hanging with Ethan and the guys, getting wasted, playing truth or dare, hooking up with random girls. Enjoying a crazy senior break. Not with me. And the worst part? I saw this coming. Not a mutilated body in the woods, sure, but I knew something would happen, something that would change him.

He never should've answered my call that night – the night of the snowstorm when Henry was at Pete's party. If he hadn't, then none of this would've happened. He'd be happy. Safe. Ignorant about how cruel the world could be. Now, because of me, my selfishness, his world would never be the same.

As I turned to face him, tears welled up in my eyes once more. I wiped them away, trying to hold myself together for Carter's sake... and then it hit me like a tidal wave, and if I hadn't already hurled, I'd probably do it again.

Recognition.

The body. Or what was left of it, in any case. The hair, the dress, those adorable pastel flowers, now ruined with blood... I knew who they belonged to.

Braids.

The girl from the party. The one who didn't even think twice before shielding me from what she thought was a threat. Yeah, Henry wasn't a danger to me, but she didn't know that, and she still had my back, even though she didn't have to. She didn't know who the heck I was. I meant nothing to her. She could've just walked away, forgotten about it, and had a great time at the bonfire. That's what most people would've done. Would I have done the same thing if the situation were reversed? I wasn't sure. But she had. She'd looked out for me, and now she was dead. And way, *way* too close to our cabin.

That couldn't be a coincidence. We only talked a few hours ago - maybe three at most. Was she still at the lake when we left? I tried to remember, but I wasn't really paying attention. I couldn't wait to get out of there after my plan to find Ansel bombed, so all I'd cared about was getting back to the truck. But either way... how had she ended up here?

It wasn't until Carter's arms enveloped me that I realised I was crying uncontrollably again. He spun me around so I couldn't see it anymore, and as he did, I felt his fingers tighten around me, and I knew he was struggling to keep it together, too. But he was trying. Trying so hard. For me. Like always.

I should've been the one comforting *him*. This was part of my life, after all. Death and destruction. I'd dragged him into it. Because I was selfish. Because I wanted him. I'd lied to myself, convinced myself I could protect him from all of this, that it was only a couple of months until he left for college and that would be it. I could have him until then, no harm done. But I was wrong, and now, when I should be the one protecting him, I was too weak to do it. His embrace was a cocoon of safety that I couldn't bear to break away from. I clung to him, tears streaming down my face, my fingers twisting and pulling at the fabric of his jacket. His reassuring whispers in my ear as he pulled me close were an anchor, while his hand cradled the back of my head, his warm breath tickling my skin.

"Shh," He murmured, "Shh. It's not him. Okay? Listen to me. Henry's gonna be fine. And so are you. I've got you."

We stayed like that, my body shaking with sobs and the weight of everything that'd happened up to that moment, until no more tears would come, and I finally lifted my head, leaving a soaked spot on the front of his jacket. Then I was back – back in the forest, back in the nightmare. No longer cocooned. No longer safe.

"Carter, I..." I started when I finally found my voice again, but my mouth was dry, and I had to swallow hard before I could continue. "I knew her."

I felt him shift his stance to look down at me, but I didn't meet his gaze. "What? How?"

"At- at the party. When I was looking for An- *Henry*." My teeth grazed my lip as I cringed, but Carter didn't seem to notice. "She was there, with her friends. And she... she..." I paused again, swallowing, and Carter said nothing, just waited for me to continue. I took a step back so I could look up into his face now, and he gave a reassuring nod, encouraging me to continue. "Henry came up while I was talking to her, and he was angry I was wandering around on my own, what with Ansel and Jamie and everything. And, well... you know what he's like. I guess she thought he was a bad guy. That I was afraid of him or something. She really laid into him. I didn't expect it, because at first, she was kinda..." I trailed off, allowing him to fill in the gaps, since it didn't seem proper to speak ill of the dead. Especially when the dead lay right *there*.

A cold sensation ran down my back at the reminder, making me shudder. Carter noticed and gave my arm a gentle squeeze.

"She was protecting you. Or at least, she thought she was."

Our eyes locked, and I struggled to catch my breath again. It took me a moment to collect my thoughts, and in the meantime, I simply nodded. But then I shifted so I could see the body once more and whispered, "And now she's dead."

I didn't even know her name, and as I stood there, looking at her remains, breathing in the putrid scent of death, I couldn't help but feel like this was all my fault. I knew logically that it didn't make sense, that I had nothing to do with it, but I was freaking out. Logic couldn't reason with me. My mind raced with questions while my eyes stayed transfixed on her like a moth to a flame, even though I knew it would bring me nothing but pain to look. It felt like some sort of penance to gaze upon it. Like it was the least I deserved.

Was I the last person she talked to? One of the last people to see her alive? Was it all some kind of message for me? A warning? And, if so... *why?* Nothing made any sense.

"We need to go back. Call the cops." Carter's voice was sharp and clear, cutting through the jumble of thoughts in my head. The words took a moment to sink in, but when they did, I jerked my head around to face him.

"What?! No way. Henry is still out there somewhere. We can't just leave him!"

"Don't you think I know that, Madison?! I'm going out of my mind here! But look at what happened to that girl. How the hell are we going to help Henry if we're dead? We don't have the first clue where he is or how to find him. We need the cops. They'll have tracker dogs and weapons. They can—"

"*No*. I can track him. I can do it." As soon as the words left my mouth, I sprinted towards the body, throwing myself to the ground beside it. I inhaled deeply, desperately, but the acrid smell of blood and death burned my nostrils, and...

"Madison."

Carter's voice was gentle but firm as I felt his hand on my shoulder, pulling me backwards, away from the scene. Away from the clues. Away from Henry.

That was nuts. I knew that, deep down. Knew there was no hint of Henry, no sign he'd ever been here, and that Carter was just trying to help. He was trying to console me, to calm me. He was human, and the cops were there to protect them. That's what he knew. It was all humans knew. But not werewolves. And right now, all I knew was my packmate was in trouble, and Carter was getting in my way.

"*No,* Carter. No cops. I'm not leaving. Not without him. *I* am his best chance."

"What the hell does that even mean?"

"It means—"

Suddenly, a twig snapped, causing both of us to whip around in surprise. I glanced around, heart pounding, feeling a surge of hope in my stomach. Maybe it was Henry. He'd smelled blood, abandoned the chase for Ansel, and circled back to investigate. To make sure I was okay. Because that's what we did; we looked out for each other, always, and above all else. He'd always come back for me. *Thank God.* Now we could go straight to the sheriff's station, together, just like Carter wanted. I didn't think it was a werewolf kill, but even if it was, I had little choice now that Carter was involved. There was no way to hide it. Sure, it wasn't ideal, but they'd probably put it down to an animal attack, anyway. A terrible but easily explainable tragedy.

There was at least some comfort in knowing her family could bury a body. They could mourn. That was something, and a helluva lot more than the man from the mountain. The one Ben purposefully lured Henry and me to, to help cement his place in our circle of trust. I never told them, but I kept an eye on the police investigation into his disappearance. His name was Greg, and the theory was he was tired of his debt-filled life and walked away to start a new one. Case closed.

I was so lost in my memories that I almost missed it – a flicker of movement out of the corner of my eye. It was a few yards from where the snapped twig had seemed to come from, and I held my breath as I tiptoed closer, anticipation building with each step. But then, my heart sank again, another wave of realisation hitting me.

Henry wouldn't try to sneak up on us. That was our rule – only ever in *our* forest. At Vineyard Manor. It was too dangerous to let our guards down anywhere else. If he thought we saw him, he wouldn't try to back off, either. Why would he?

Which meant it wasn't him. And I was stupid to think it could be.

No, it was probably just an animal, enticed by the scent and the promise of an easy meal. Sure, it was spring, and usually the forest would be teaming with creatures, but even on the best day, no animal would turn down a handout. Plus, we'd been here two days, and I hadn't seen anything more than a few deer or heard the occasional hoot of an owl. Something was making the wildlife move on, which would just make it even more likely for those that'd stayed to take their food wherever they could find it. It wasn't Braids' killer coming back.

Better to be completely certain, though, just in case.

I crept closer to Carter, my head turning to get a better look at whatever was there without spooking it...

And then I spotted him, crouched in the bushes. Our eyes locked, his wide and panicked, like an animal caught in a trap. I heard him take a sharp breath as he fell back, and the branch he gripped quivered and rustled as it settled back into place. But it was too late. I'd already seen him.

Ansel.

35

Our eyes locked, and in that fleeting moment, before he disappeared into the shadows, everything around us seemed to freeze in time. The air itself seemed to crackle, as if a lightning bolt was about to strike at any moment.

He was the first to move. The lightning struck, and his footsteps echoed like thunder, growing louder with each step as he bolted. And it was like waving a red rag to a bull. I didn't even stop to think, I just gave chase, my feet gliding across the forest floor with ease. The wolf growled inside me, and all I could picture was running through the forest at headquarters. The rustling of leaves as my claws scratched the earth, the scent of prey, the chilly wind brushing against my fur – the sensations felt so *real* I had to remind myself they weren't. That I was still human. And as much as I wanted to fully let go, I couldn't step back completely. Not with Carter right there.

Wolf or human, it didn't actually matter - Ansel didn't stand a chance.

In an instant, I pounced on him, and he grunted as my body collided with his, sending us both crashing to the ground. I climbed on him, pressing my knees into the dirt to keep myself stable while he squirmed beneath me, struggling to break free. It was a waste of time, though. As I held him down, I secured his wrists above his head, preventing any chance of him lashing out. He showered me with snarls and curses, and I reciprocated with equal intensity, baring my teeth and launching a relentless barrage of questions. I wasn't even sure if they made any sense. I was completely losing control. The line between human and wolf blurred, and she was pushing it further than ever before, desperate to be unleashed. But, in that moment, I couldn't bring myself to care. All I saw was red.

He'd killed Braids. Ripped her to shreds like she was nothing. And he'd do the same thing to Henry, Carter, and me.... I couldn't afford to show mercy. Not if I wanted everyone I loved most in the world to survive the night.

"Where is he? What the fuck have you done with him?" I demanded, gripping his wrists even tighter. He hissed in pain.

Despite his best efforts, he was no match for me, and the veins in his forehead throbbed with frustration. I could see the confusion in his eyes. Confusion, because he should've been able to shake me off easily, but he couldn't. We'd caught him. And now he was in a total panic.

"Get the fuck off me, you crazy bitch—"

In response to his words, I yanked his arms with such force that it momentarily lifted him off the ground, before I slammed him back down, knocking the wind out of him. As I trapped him again, he spluttered and coughed, struggling to catch his breath.

"If you don't tell me where he is, I swear I'll—"

"You'll what?" He spat in between wheezes. "Kill me like you did her? Make me disappear like Colton and Jamie? Like my brother? I know what you are. What you all are."

His words stopped me dead. Did he mean...? *No.* No way. The idea made me shudder, even as I silently reassured myself that there must be another explanation. He couldn't possibly know. How could he?

Then I realised what else he'd said, the meaning finally clicking into place: *'kill me like you did her?'*

"What the hell are you talking about? *You* killed her." I tried to snarl, but my confidence was fading, so it turned into a weak sneer.

Before he could even say a word, the sound of approaching footsteps diverted my attention, getting louder with each passing second. Then I heard Carter desperately yelling my name. His voice was all hoarse, so he must have been shouting for a while, but I was too busy trying to catch Ansel to notice. Guilt washed over me again, making my stomach twist.

I looked around, hoping to let him know I was okay, but I lost my grip on Ansel as I twisted. We realised simultaneously, and I scrambled, trying to recover my hold, but he saw it coming and dodged, and my hand closed around nothing but air. He bucked his hips, sending me stumbling backwards, and my hands instinctively shot out, meeting the rough ground with a jolt that stung my palms, but at least it saved me from crashing face-first. My ankle, on the other hand, wasn't so fortunate. It twisted under me, sending a sharp, shooting pain surging up my leg, and making tears well in my eyes.

Even with tears blurring my vision, I could still make out Carter's flashlight piercing the dark when he reached the clearing. I sat up, hoping to mask the pain, but he could tell as soon as he looked at me, and he broke into a run. At the same time, Ansel shuffled beside me, and a moment later he was on his feet. But I had anticipated it, so I leapt forward, wincing as my ankle shifted, but I was too slow, and he swerved me easily, leaving only a lingering breeze against my outstretched hand as he slipped away.

While he moved further backwards, frustration coiled in my stomach. Fortunately, though, he didn't make it very far. He clearly hadn't *planned* a murder tonight, or maybe he was just too cocky, because his outfit was totally useless for escaping the forest in a hurry. His sneakers grappled with the leaf scattered ground, causing him to slip and stumble with every step he took. He just about stayed on his feet, but only after he slowed down to barely more than a jog, so I knew I could catch him easily.

Forgetting about my ankle for a second, I tried again to stand, only to be met with another searing wave of pain. I bit my lip to hold back a cry, but a quiet whimper still slipped out. It didn't matter, though. It *couldn't*. Even if I'd broken it, I'd deal with it later, because I couldn't let him get away. He'd been lurking in the shadows by Braids' body, as if he'd been waiting for us to find it. There's no way he wasn't involved. It was just too much of a coincidence.

Even as I thought it, though, his comment from before echoed around my head: '*You'll what? Kill me like you did her? Make me disappear like Colton and Jamie? Like my brother? I know what you are.*'

I had no idea what his brother had to do with anything, but I was certain Jamie wasn't missing. He was just trying to mess with me, play mind games. Henry wouldn't abandon me unless he had no choice, and the forest was so quiet tonight that there was no way he'd have missed the commotion. No matter how much he wanted to track them down, he would've turned back if he thought I was in trouble. If he didn't, it was because he *couldn't*. Because wherever he was, Jamie had him trapped.

They must've got the jump on him somehow. He was strong, but not invincible, and he'd been so furious when he took off after them. Anger made you reckless, and even supernatural senses couldn't always keep you out of trouble. It was possible they'd somehow overpowered him, and were now keeping him hostage until they got whatever it was they wanted from us. I *had* to believe that was the case. That wherever he was, Jamie was there, too, standing guard. If Ansel was telling the truth, it meant something happened to Henry as well, and I couldn't - *wouldn't* - wrap my head around that.

"Madison? Madison!" As I was about to descend into panic, Carter's voice broke through, snapping me back to the present as he dropped to his knees next to me. His hands roamed over my arms, gentle but searching, before his gaze met mine. "Where are you hurt?"

"I'm fine. Just tripped and landed all weird. I just need to—"

I attempted to stand again, but as soon as I put any pressure on my ankle, the pain intensified and I dropped back, letting out a cry. Carter's hands caught me, his face filled with concern as I let out a sharp hiss and muttered, "*Shit!*"

Ansel was getting away. He was gonna escape, and I was gonna miss my best chance to track down Henry. All because I'd twisted my goddamn ankle. Unless...

"Carter, you've got to stop him. You can't let him get away!"

His eyes widened as he stared at me. "You can't be serious. There's a fucking dead girl back there, Madison. And you're hurt. No way am I leaving you here."

"He's the one who killed her. And he knows where Henry is."

"Then we'll tell that to the cops! Madison—"

"*Please.*" I clutched onto his hand. "Trust me."

Those words, yet again. His jaw clenched, and I braced myself for an argument, fully aware that I deserved it. I had asked too much of him, and I knew it. Yet, instead of erupting, he simply nodded, his defeated expression breaking my heart into pieces. But before I could even think about it, he was gone, running after Ansel. As he closed the distance, the crunching of his hiking boots on the fallen leaves echoed loudly in my ears. I could hear Ansel's heart pounding, his footsteps tripping as he pushed himself to run faster, knowing Carter was catching up. And even though my ankle hurt like hell, I had to be there when he finally did.

I spotted a tree stump on my right side and crawled towards it, using it as a support to pull myself up, before looking around for a sturdy stick that I could use as a crutch. Spotting one just out of reach, sticking out from the shadow of the trees, I awkwardly hopped closer, teetering on one leg, and clumsily bent down to pick it up, my fingers grabbing onto another tree trunk to stop myself from falling into the bushes. Sweat dripped from my forehead and my chest heaved from exertion as I straightened up, but I had no time to rest. I had to catch up with Carter.

An *'oomph'* resounded in the air, but I couldn't tell who had made it, so I tightened my grip on the walking stick, hobbling as fast as I could with my injured leg, wincing at every step. It took what seemed like an eternity, but I finally reached the clearing where the sound had originated but, in the darkness, all I could make out were two shadowy figures—one pinning the other against a tree. I couldn't tell who was who, so I cautiously moved closer... and then the one with their back to me turned around, and I let out a sigh of relief when I saw Carter's face.

Our eyes locked, his silently asking *'what now?'*, and I lightly touched his arm as I stepped up beside him, shifting my focus to Ansel. But before I could utter a word, Ansel cut in, directing *his* attention towards Carter, as if I wasn't even there.

"Please, man. Just let me go. I won't say anything, I swear. I know it wasn't you. It was her. Her and that psycho. You don't have to do this."

My muscles tightened, a sudden rush of fury burning through me. "Hey. Don't you talk to him, alright? Just tell me where Henry is."

At first, Ansel still didn't meet my eye, but when Carter continued his silence, letting me take the lead, it forced him to look at me... and it took everything I had not to recoil from the daggers he shot my way.

"*Fuck you.*"

He didn't even raise his voice, and somehow that made it cut deeper. The words left his lips, and they seemed to hang in the air, time standing still for a moment... until, without warning, everything exploded. Carter snarled and gripped Ansel's jacket, jerking him forward before slamming him back against the tree hard enough to make him gasp for breath. His eyes widened in shock, and...

That's when it hit me.

Oh my god. He didn't do it.

I couldn't explain what it was exactly. Maybe it was the look of absolute horror on his face or the unmistakable odour of fear that smothered him. Or maybe it was both. But one thing was crystal clear - he was innocent. Innocent and terrified. And suddenly I had no idea what to do anymore. He was my last hope. I'd focused all my attention on catching him, and forcing him to give me answers, because it was easier than admitting I was completely out of my depth.

I glanced at Carter, silently begging for his help, for him to tell me what to do. To step up and handle it for me, like Henry would if he were here. And I knew that wasn't fair, because if I didn't know what to do, then how the hell could I expect Carter to? He *wasn't* Henry. This wasn't his world.

But it didn't really matter, because he didn't even glance my way. His eyes were vacant, as if lost in a world of their own. Like he wasn't even here anymore. He had flipped a switch in his head, and I couldn't blame him. I wanted to do the same. I'd come face to face with death more than once, but Braids' body was like nothing I could have imagined. Something nobody should ever have to witness.

Carter... he was just too sweet, too gentle for all of this. He couldn't even bring himself to look when we passed roadkill, a common sight on the back roads connecting Havencrest and Silveroak. He needed me to be strong – I knew that. But honestly, I needed him just as much. I needed him to be my light, my anchor. Maybe that was selfish, especially since I always promised to keep him safe, to never expose him to the dangers of my world again. I would break both our hearts without hesitation to keep him safe. But this wasn't a werewolf kill. I didn't know much, but I knew that. And I needed him. I needed to know I wasn't alone.

Except, I *was* alone. At least mentally I was, because he'd checked out. And I was trapped on a life raft in the never-ending ocean, barely clinging on. All I could do was row and row, desperately looking for land, while it stayed maddeningly out of reach.

My throat felt parched and scratchy, but with no water at hand, all I could do was keep swallowing, and hope there was enough saliva in my mouth to keep the dry cough away. As I did, I tried to shake off the mental fog, to concentrate on Ansel.

"Where's Jamie? Does he have Henry?"

Ansel's fiery glare made me shrink back, and I mentally scolded myself for reacting.

"Why don't you tell me?" He snapped.

Before replying, I took a deep breath, feeling it fill my lungs and calm my racing heart. "Why were you following us?"

"*What?!*" He spluttered. "I *wasn't*. Look, I didn't even see anything. If the cops ask, that's what I'll tell 'em. I swear. C'mon, Madison. Just let me go. Please. I won't say a word."

While he was objecting, I couldn't help but notice how his tone suddenly switched. Not confrontational or sarcastic anymore. Now, he was coming at me from the same angle he did Carter – all soft and gentle. If he thought he could play me by acting all familiar, though, he was wasting his time. Yeah, I didn't think he was a murderer anymore, but that didn't make us friends.

It took a beat for his words to fully resonate, but once they did, a sickening feeling settled in the pit of my stomach.

"Did you just... I mean do you... you think *we* killed her?" His eyes narrowed suspiciously as I said it. "Oh my god. *No.* We just *found* her. We were looking for Henry, who was after *you,* because you broke into our cabin again, didn't you? Now he's gone, and you're here, spying on us."

"I wasn't spying." He spat, lips curling into a snarl. Pretending to be friends didn't last long, but I was cool with that. It would be an easier conversation this way, anyway.

Trying to appear confident, I rolled my eyes, while a wave of anxiety churned in my stomach. "So you say. But come *on*. You were lurking around a corpse. You gotta see why that seems kinda sketchy." Though he remained silent, the intense glare he directed towards me sent a chill down my spine. Still, I closed the distance between us slowly, each step creating a hollow thud in the tense air. "Ansel, seriously. Where the hell is Jamie?"

He met my eye, and for what felt like ages, he said nothing. But then he blurted, "I DON'T KNOW!"

His shout, so sudden and piercing, jolted me, and my heart raced up into my throat. The sound reverberated, echoing like a thunderclap. It even shook Carter out of his daze, and he shuffled his feet, his eyes blinking rapidly, like he couldn't remember where he was or how he got there. But if Ansel had hoped to startle him into letting him go, it failed.

"I... I don't know. Are you happy now?" Ansel said, his voice trembling slightly. He took a sharp breath before continuing. "He insisted on going back to your place. Convinced he'd find something about Colton. I tried to warn him... I fucking told him it was a bad idea."

"Why?"

"Are you serious?" He gave Carter's forearm a pointed look. I blushed as I followed his gaze. "This ain't the first time your guard dogs have had us in a chokehold, is it?"

"Can you blame us?" Carter said, and my knees shook when I heard his voice, feeling so relieved to have him fully awake and with me again.

Ansel gave him a death stare, but he didn't argue. Instead, he only said, "If you're going to kill me, can you just make it quick?"

Even I didn't expect the groan that came from me next. And then, out of nowhere and completely inappropriately... I burst out laughing. This whole thing was just crazy. How did my spring break turn into such a mess? How the hell did we end up here? It felt too surreal to actually be happening.

Ansel and Carter both stared at me, Ansel's expression unreadable and Carter's a blend of confusion and concern. It was enough to sober me, my laughter fading as I murmured an apology before clearing my throat. "For the last time, we didn't kill her. Did you see her body? The amount of blood?" As the memory resurfaced, a wave of queasiness washed over me, making me flinch, while Carter squirmed uneasily at my side. I fought back the taste of bile rising in my throat before I could carry on. "If we hurt her, wouldn't we have at least some of it on us? Same as you. That's why I know now that you didn't hurt her. I was... I was just in shock before."

Ansel's eyes narrowed, his lips forming a tight, thin line as my words sank in. He looked me up and down, then Carter, and his face changed as everything fell into place. I could tell he believed me by the way his eyes softened, and he slowly unclenched his fists... but there was a huge difference between admitting someone wasn't a murderer and actually trusting them. If I wanted him to talk, I had to make a gesture. Something to help him let his guard down. I was just hoping it wouldn't blow up in my face.

"I meant why did you go back to our cabin." I sighed. "But I guess it's not really important now. Your friend is missing, our friend is missing... so, chances are they're together somewhere, right? We're better off as allies, Ansel."

That suspicious gaze again... but this time he followed it up with a humourless laugh, his lips curling into a sneer. "Damn, if this is being your ally, I'd hate to see how you treat your enemies."

"Funny how I'm the only one who got hurt from our little run-in." I fired back, and he opened his mouth to retort, but then closed it again, his eyes narrowing to slits as a tense silence settled between us. I took a deep breath to calm myself before speaking again. "Look, we'll let you go. Feel free to run. But I wouldn't do that if I were you."

"Is that a threat?"

Ugh! I had to fight the urge to roll my eyes again, because he was really *not* making this easy. What happened to the cool, charismatic guy I met on the first night? I didn't know Ansel that well, but he was acting like a totally different person, and I couldn't tell which one was the real him.

"No, I'm trying to help you. There's something – maybe some*one* – out there killing people. Making them disappear. Colton wasn't the first, you know. I saw a missing poster in town. Some young couple disappeared a month or so ago, right around here."

I stopped to catch my breath and... did I imagine it, or did he just flinch when I mentioned the missing kids? He quickly bounced back, his face scrunching up again in that same old angry stare, so I brushed it off. Probably a trick of the light.

"All I want is to find Henry and get the hell out of here. And I know you want the same for Jamie, don't you? But you can't do it by yourself."

I let the weight of my words settle between us. He said nothing and instead looked around the clearing, purposefully avoiding eye contact with Carter and me. Carter glanced my way, waiting for my cue. I allowed a moment to pass, before giving a slight nod and, after a beat of hesitation, he slowly let go of Ansel's jacket.

It took Ansel a moment to realise he was finally free. Carter's arm fell limply to his side, and a deafening silence settled among the three of us, broken only by the faint rustle of Ansel's jacket unfolding. But I saw the gleam in his eye, a spark of understanding as everything clicked in his mind, and...

He took off running.

Carter's body reacted instantly, his boots scuffing the dirt as he made to follow him, but I quickly grabbed his arm and stopped him in his tracks. His eyes locked onto mine, searching for answers, his brows furrowed in confusion, but I simply shook my head. He still tensed, though, like he wasn't sure if he had misunderstood, but a moment later, he eased back into his place beside me, turning instead to watch Ansel as he moved away.

He didn't get very far. He stopped a few steps into the shadows on the opposite side of the clearing, the back of his head illuminated by the flashlight's beam as Carter pointed it at him. But I didn't move, and neither did Carter. We just waited.

And then a groan broke the silence of the forest as he reluctantly turned and started walking back towards us. He came to a halt just a few yards away, crossing his arms over his chest.

"Fine. You win. So, what's the plan?"

36

"Um..."

Shit. What was my plan? I talked him into staying and trusting us, without even having a *plan*?! How was I supposed to find Henry without one? I needed to —

"Maddie can track."

At the sound of Carter's voice, I spun around, meeting his gaze while a shiver ran down my spine. "Wh- what did you say?"

He looked at me, his head tilted to the side, and his eyebrows furrowed. "That's what you said before, right? That you could track Henry. By like... footprints, or whatever."

"Oh!" I chuckled nervously, relief flooding through me. "Of course. Yes. Sorry."

His touch was warm and comforting as he put his arm around my shoulder, and he smiled down at me. "So, it turns out it was worth it, losing you to the woods so much." He snorted a laugh, then turned to Ansel. "That's how she found the girl who... you know. If anyone can find Henry and Jamie, it's Mads. She's a good one to have on your side."

His eyes narrowed at Ansel as he said that, his grip tightening protectively around me. He was clearly referring to the curses he'd hurled my way, and Ansel gulped, so I cut in before it could escalate. "I wasn't tracking her, though. I had no clue she was here. It was a total accident."

I denied it, but Carter was right, even if he didn't fully get it. Okay, so maybe I couldn't get down and sniff the ground like an animal with those two watching, but I could figure something else out. I *could* track them. Just not in the way Carter thought.

As subtly as possible, I inhaled a deep breath. I still couldn't catch Henry's scent, but that actually gave me a clue to where he was, because no smell meant he was upwind. I just had to keep going in that direction, and sooner or later, I *had* to come across something. Plus, the darkness provided the perfect cover for investigating. I could stoop down, pretending to search for footprints, while secretly sniffing the air for any kind of a trail.

I nodded to myself. It was the best plan we had, so I straightened up with a surge of determination. "Carter's right, though. My dad's friend, Ray... his house is on this huge plot of land, with loads of woodland, you know? They're into hunting, and I tagged along a few times, so I guess I picked up some skills. You know, like how to spot prints and stuff."

Ansel shrugged, still trying to keep up the arrogant act, but I didn't miss how his voice faltered slightly, and he snuck a look at Carter as he said, "Didn't need the whole backstory. I just wanna find my buddy."

Carter tensed, his teeth grinding together as he clenched his jaw right in my ear, the sound reverberating through my skull. I peered up at him, and as our eyes locked, I smiled slightly, letting him know I was okay. I didn't care what Ansel threw at me, because I knew he was just scared. Carter's face softened, the sternness in his gaze vanishing. But he still rolled his eyes, silently mouthing *'asshole'* at me, while nodding at Ansel, and I chuckled as I stepped away from him to look around the clearing.

I moved to the edge and crouched down, running my fingertips through a mound of dried-up dirt, pretending to search for footprints. Then, a few seconds later, I stood up and declared, "It's this way."

There was no objection from either of them, and Carter wasted no time in rushing to join me in the front. "How about a piggyback ride?"

Propping myself up on my walking stick, I shot him a smirk. I was just thankful he was joking around with me again. "That's okay. We don't need you falling over as well, 'cause then we'd really be in trouble."

"You don't think I could handle it?"

"Oh, I *know* you can handle it." I laughed, a blush warning my cheeks as I remembered the day last year, when the Celtics finally made it to the playoffs for the first time in years. We'd been home alone at his place, and he'd been so happy he threw me over his shoulder and didn't put me down until we were in his bedroom...

Those damn butterflies burst into action once again at the memory, and I shook my head, trying to refocus. "I'll hold onto your arm, though, if that's alright?"

He immediately offered it for me to interlock mine with. "Ayuh, I can do that. Whatever you need."

Having the stick and Carter's help made walking a little easier, but it was still slow. Despite that, Ansel didn't seem to mind much. He followed us quietly; so quietly I could almost forget he was there, which was perfect for me because then I could pretend he *wasn't*. Still, the silence soon became suffocating, and I sensed my mind diverting to those dark places I couldn't allow myself to explore, so I turned my attention to talking with Carter as we walked. It was mindless conversation – I pointed out the different plants and flowers that we passed, and he listened, asking the occasional question. I could tell he was just as unenthusiastic as I was, but it provided a temporary respite from the chaos in my mind.

Before too long, though, Ansel became impossible to ignore. Sure, he wasn't actually doing anything, but I could practically hear his mind ticking constantly, and it was driving me crazy.

"You wanna say something?"

He raised his eyebrow. "Huh? No. Why?"

"Your thoughts. Seriously, they're loud as hell."

"That doesn't even make any sense."

I let out a sigh as I loosened my hold on Carter and bent down again. He handed me the flashlight, and I made a show of sweeping it across the ground in search of prints. Still no sign of Henry or Jamie. Or anything else, really. I straightened my back, retook Carter's arm, and continued hobbling onwards in the same direction, wincing with each step.

"Yes it does." I resumed the conversation with Ansel seamlessly, as if there had been no pause. "It means I can feel that you're tense. But okay, if you don't have anything to say, can I at least ask you some questions? It might help us find the guys, if we're on the same page about Jamie's... state of mind."

Ansel scoffed at that, but he didn't say no, so I took it as begrudging agreement.

"So, why *did* you come back to our cabin?" I asked, and when he didn't respond right away, I glanced at him again, just to make sure he heard me... and immediately regretted it when my stick got tangled in something. I almost fell, but Carter saved me from hitting the ground, however the stick broke in half when I yanked it from the vines that'd wrapped around it. "*Crap!*" I hissed and scanned the area for something else, but there was nothing long enough.

Ansel let out a curse so quietly that it was hard to hear, and I doubted Carter even noticed. But then, within moments, he shifted to my other side and put his arm around me. I hesitated for a second, but with few options, I reluctantly draped my arm around his shoulders, and then did the same with Carter, before mumbling a quick thanks. Ansel just grunted.

When we were on the move again, he finally said, "I dunno what Jay wanted. To look for clues or something, I guess. It's true, what I told you last night. Colton has done this before. He's been out of it since his cousin went missing. Wanders off, likes to be alone for a while. But he always comes back, y'know?"

My eyebrow arched in surprise. "His cousin?"

"Yeah. Well, really, they were more like brothers. Colton's family is... Let's just say it was rough for him growing up. He never really told me the whole story, but I know he left home as a kid and his aunt took him in at their place in Boston. He's younger than Asher, but they hit it off. Colton looked up to him." Then he just stopped, like he didn't know if he should keep going, before he sighed. "So yeah, that's how we became friends. Asher and my brother were tight. I don't really know how they met, to be honest, 'cause Asher didn't go to college. But to cut a long story short, they went camping together last summer with a couple of buddies. Actually, it wasn't that far from here - the campsite - just a few hours north, I guess. I suppose that's how my brother heard about this place."

He paused for breath, and I thought that was all I was getting, so I was about to respond when he rushed on. It was like, now he'd started talking, he couldn't stop.

"Anyway, from what I know, it was mostly college guys, but Asher was cool, so it doesn't surprise me they let him come. Everyone seemed to like him. It probably had something to do with him having his own car and being old enough to buy beer, but who really knows? It was supposed to be just a low-key guy's weekend." He paused again, as if in thought, before continuing. "Me and my brother... we aren't super close. I mean, we go to the same college, but only because my mom teaches there, so it's the only place we could afford. We don't really hang out or anything, so I don't know what happened. I didn't ask, and he never told me. But here's the thing... Asher never came home from that trip. And no one's heard from him since."

"*What?*"

"Shit." Carter whispered beside me. Then, a little louder, he said, "Anyone have any idea what happened? Did he just take off?"

"Beats me. There was a rumour he had a secret underage girlfriend somewhere, and they ran away together, but I don't buy that shit. I barely knew him, but man, Asher Mitchell could have any girl he wanted back home. No need to look elsewhere. And *definitely* not at some high schooler."

We continued walking in silence for a while, the only sound being the crunch of leaves under our feet, until Ansel unexpectedly snorted a laugh. "That's it? Just one question? Or has the cat got your tongue?"

Truthfully, I had so many questions I didn't even know where to begin. I opened my mouth, but no words came out. It was Carter who found his voice first.

"Why'd you tell us all of that? Assuming any of it was true. I thought you didn't trust us."

Ansel scoffed, rolling his eyes at him. "It's true. What difference does it make now? There's a madman on the loose, and if he doesn't get us first, hypothermia will. If we're all going to die tonight, what's it matter what I tell you?"

I took a deep breath, the air filling my lungs and helping me gather my thoughts enough to form a coherent sentence. "We're not gonna die, and it's not cold enough for hypothermia."

"Ah, well, isn't that a relief? Just the crazed lunatic to worry about, then. Although you don't seem very afraid of him, Madison. Is that because you know you're safe, huh? Because he happens to be your boyfriend?"

Carter's steps faltered, his teeth grinding together again, and my stomach lurched. But I refused to take the bait, because that's what Ansel wanted. Anyway, the insult didn't really pack the same punch as before. It was as if he didn't really believe it himself.

"But why did you wreck our place? What were you expecting to find?"

He let out a breath and I couldn't tell if he was impressed or bummed that he couldn't get a reaction out of me. Still, he didn't push it.

"Listen..." He said with a deliberate slowness. "I know it doesn't make it any better, but I stayed outside, alright? I was just the lookout. Jamie went in on his own. I don't know what the fuck he was trying to find. But ever since you bailed on me in the woods and we hightailed it—"

His words made me stop in my tracks, digging in my good heel to bring the guys to a halt as well. "Wait, what? *You* ditched out on *me*. I turned around, and you were just *gone*."

"Wow, Madison. Are you seriously trying to gaslight me right now? And here I thought you wanted to be allies."

I opened my mouth to argue, but Carter beat me to it. His voice slicing through the air as he turned to Ansel, his face twisted in a scowl. "Don't even try that shit. Alright? I should kick your ass for what you did to her."

"Oh yeah? Try it." As Ansel spat back, I felt his fingers loosen their grip on me, and the sudden shift made me lose my balance. I thudded down on my ankle, wincing at the impact. Carter's head snapped towards me at the sound, and his face reddened in outrage as his grip on me tightened even more. Then he turned a glare on Ansel.

"*Guys!*" I yelled and they both froze, eyes locked in a silent standoff. Luckily, it seemed like they were paying attention to me, at least for the moment, so I quickly continued. "Ansel, what do you mean I bailed on you? What... what happened? What did you see?"

"What do you mean 'what did I see'? I didn't see jack. Isn't that the whole damn point?" He snarled, not tearing his eyes from Carter as he said it.

"*Ansel.*" His name escaped from me in a sigh, and Carter grumbled a curse, barely keeping his annoyance in check. I reached out my spare hand to squeeze his, hoping it might calm him down a little. He didn't squeeze back like he usually did, but I still sensed some of his tension melting away. Once I was confident he wasn't going to explode at him, I went back to Ansel. "Can you just humour me? Please?"

Ansel's eyes narrowed, and I thought for a minute that he was going to say no. That he'd changed his mind about working together, and he was going to go off on his own to search for Jamie.

But then, finally, he let out a sigh, and his face softened into a slightly less hostile expression.

"We'd just left the creek. I'd told you about Colton, and then..." His voice trailed off, and a faint pink hue spread across his cheeks as he fidgeted with the knuckles on his right hand. I hadn't noticed it earlier, but he had bruises and scratches all over his skin, presumably from when he lashed out last night when we didn't find anything. "You remember that?" He added, almost sheepishly.

I nodded. Then, for Carter's sake, I said, "You said Colton had done it a few times. Running off. But never like this. Not in a strange place, in the middle of the night. So you were worried about him. About his state of mind." When I finished, he didn't say a word, so I asked, "Was that true?"

"Yes." His voice had a tinge of bitterness, though it was milder than before. "After that, you were walking ahead of me. But I could see you. We were talking. Then Colton yelled my name, and I stopped—"

"Hold up, what did you just say? You heard Colton?" I repeated, sure I'd heard wrong, but he nodded. "That's not possible. I didn't hear a thing."

Ansel just shrugged. "Honestly, I'm not really sure if I did either. It was so late, and I was exhausted. I mean, it'd been a really fucking long day, and I was so damn worried about him. I reckon I just imagined it. But it felt so real, y'know? Anyway, I just stepped away for a *second*. I was trying to find him. But then it just... stopped. Got quiet again. I told myself it was just in my head and went after you, but you'd disappeared. Just gone and left me."

It wasn't until Carter pointed his finger at Ansel that I realised he had let go of my hand. "Are you serious? She was fucking lost because of you. *Anything* could have happened to her, you asshole."

Ansel's nostrils flared as he fixed a fiery glare on Carter. "And that's my fault? Dude, what the hell was I supposed to do? Just kick back and wait in case she came back? It was the goddamn middle of the night. My friend was gone, and I was completely alone in the damn woods. I thought... Shit, I don't even know what I was thinking, but I knew me and Jamie had to get the hell away from you three and that damn cabin before it was too late."

"I... Okay, I know this sounds nuts," Seeing Carter's fists clenching, I quickly interjected, positioning myself between them both. "But seriously, Ansel, I didn't go anywhere. Like you said, we were talking, and you were right behind me, until you weren't anymore. You just vanished. I think... I think I was hallucinating, maybe."

A rush of heat flooded my face, a blend of irritation and shame, when Ansel scoffed once again. Who did he think he was, laughing at me like he hadn't just said the exact same thing? Hearing voices that weren't there wasn't exactly normal behaviour. He might have been hallucinating, too. Both of us. At the same time...

Did I actually believe that? Honestly, not really. But what other explanation could there be for all the strange things that had happened? A dead girl, people just poofing into thin air, and voices with no bodies. Oh, and don't forget about the creature I saw. Was it possible we were *all* drugged? Me, Carter, Henry, Ansel, Jamie, and Colton - we all had one thing in common: the cabin. Maybe something was off with the water. A squirrel could've gotten into the tank and contaminated it. I'd heard about that kind of thing happening - animals getting stuck in tight spots and not being able to escape, so they end up dying. It wasn't impossible, and it made a lot more sense than anything else.

But that still left Braids. A contaminated water supply didn't even begin to explain how she ended up here, a few hundred yards from our cabin, ripped to pieces.

We had resumed walking, as if we all instinctively understood that standing idle was a waste of time that we couldn't afford to lose, but I couldn't pinpoint when it happened. I couldn't make sense of much anymore. It felt like all I had collected was scattered puzzle pieces of information, but they refused to fit together into a coherent explanation.

Then it hit me – a question. One I couldn't believe I hadn't thought of before now.

"Ansel... How did you know we wouldn't be home tonight?"

There was a brief pause, a fraction of a second too long, before he said, "Huh?"

I came to a sudden halt, pulling my arm away from his grip and shifting all my weight onto Carter. Then I hopped around, positioning myself directly in front of Ansel. He glanced away, mumbling something inaudible over the soft rustling of leaves, and then crouched down by a thorny bush. When he reached inside, a sharp hiss of pain escaped him, but he pulled back holding a stick that appeared almost identical to the one I had broken earlier. I reluctantly took it from his hand, but it didn't distract me.

"Tonight. You and Jamie came back to the cabin to see if you could find any clues about Colton. You wouldn't have done that if you weren't absolutely sure we wouldn't be there."

I heard Carter behind me sharply inhale, and I knew he had just reached the same realisation. There was no chance they'd come back, just the two of them, after they took off like that. Especially not when they knew Henry was there.

But Henry wasn't around anymore, was he? Someone had made damn sure he was out of the way.

Who the hell were they working with?

Ignoring the throbbing pain in my ankle, I forced myself to stand up straight, my hands clenched tightly. I inched towards him, and...

"Whoa, hold up!" At the sight of my clenched fists, Ansel's eyes widened in alarm. He shifted his gaze to my left, and I could sense from his gulp that Carter was ready to fight, too. Ansel's heart pounded while he raised his hands in surrender, his breath fast and shallow. "Look, I have no idea what's going on in your head, but I didn't do anything to the big guy, I promise. How the hell could I? I just..."

Suddenly, his words trailed off, his lips clamped shut, and I could feel the tension in the air as I tightened my fists, the cracking of my knuckles piercing through the silence like gunshots. That seemed to spook him, because he rushed into an explanation. "I know a guy from around here, okay? Not well, but enough to talk to, y'know? Anyway, he knew I was in the area, so he hit me up. Told me there was some bonfire party and that I should drop by. I told him no, it'd be weird since we don't know anyone. Then he said there'll be other out-of-towners too." As he paused, his lip caught between his teeth, and the pungent smell of his anxiety overwhelmed me, making my stomach churn. "We just... we took a gamble on it being you three."

I didn't know if I believed a thing he said, but, besides his racing heart, there were no obvious signs he was lying - no flicker in his eyes, no trembling in his voice.

"How?"

"How?" He repeated hesitantly.

I gritted my teeth, trying to contain my frustration. "*How* do you know someone from here? You said you're from Boston, didn't you? You said you'd never been here before."

"I *am* from Boston. And I've never been here in my life. But I already told you, my brother has. He knows people round here. The dude I talked to? He was buddies with him. That's all. I didn't lie."

His brother again. Seriously, why the hell did this guy keep coming up every five freakin' minutes? How did he fit into all of this?

"*Was?*" I didn't bother to wait for an answer. My attention abruptly shifted, a question pricking at the corner of my mind.

But... *no*. There was no way, right? Ansel would've *said* something... wouldn't he? Why would he keep something like that a secret? It made zero sense. I was just being crazy. Trying to find links that weren't there.

But if that was true, then why were my hackles standing on end?

My instincts kicked in, and I moved to stand in front of Carter. My heart pounded in my chest, my blood rushing in my ears, but I gulped it all down as I asked, "Ansel, what's your brother's name?"

I could sense Carter's piercing gaze penetrating the back of my head, his bewilderment matching Ansel's, but he stayed silent. Nevertheless, his hand lingered on my hip, exerting a gentle yet insistent force as he tried to manoeuvre me aside and position himself in front instead. But I didn't back down, and finally, he gave in and moved back, still behind me, but a little to the side, so I could see him from the corner of my eye. Where he could rush forward if necessary. It wasn't as far back or protected as I wanted, but I couldn't afford to argue with him while also keeping an eye on Ansel, so I let it slide.

"My brother? Why?" Ansel asked, his voice subtly rising in pitch.

"Just answer the question."

His eyebrow shot up, but he must have picked up on the urgency in my voice because he didn't make a snarky comeback. "Well, technically, he's my stepbrother. But my mom married his dad when I was a kid, so we basically grew up as brothers, and—"

"*Ansel.*" I pleaded.

He parted his lips to respond, and I held my breath, my senses heightened with anticipation. But as soon as he spoke, a wave of confusion engulfed me. His voice sounded different, and the words... they made no sense.

"Madison?! Where are you? *HELP!*"

It took a painfully long time for me to process that the voice wasn't Ansel's.

37

No, no, no, no—

It couldn't be. It just couldn't. He was okay. He had to be.

But I knew it was. I'd said it a hundred times - I'd recognise his voice anywhere.

Henry.

As I spun around, his name tumbled out of my mouth. Squinting, I frantically scanned the trees, my heartbeat thundering in my ears, desperately looking for any sign of him. But the forest had already fallen back into silence, as if his voice had never disturbed it.

Had I just imagined it?

"Mads?" Carter's touch on my arm was gentle, his voice soft, like he didn't want to startle me. "You doing okay?"

No. That was my honest answer, but that wasn't what came out of my mouth. At first, nothing did. Then, after a few seconds, I coughed and finally blurted out, "Yeah, sorry. I just thought I heard—"

"MADISON? ANSWER ME!"

His voice echoed, creating a disorienting effect as it surrounded me from every angle, so I couldn't pinpoint where exactly it was coming from. But he sounded like he was getting closer.

"HENRY?!" I cried out, and then my feet began moving on their own, before my head had even had a chance to catch up, the sound a magnet pulling me in. "Where are you?!"

Silence.

Frustration surged through me, and I unleashed a torrent of curses as I spun in circles, desperately searching for any clue. I didn't stop until I felt Carter's firm tug on my arm.

"Madison? What's wrong?" The worry in his voice was enough to make me tear my gaze from the trees, and I looked at him, *really* looked at him, for the first time all night. I saw the deep creases etched on his face, the heavy bags under his eyes, and the weight of guilt settled in my chest all over again.

"You didn't hear him?" I asked, trying to push it to the back of my mind, because I couldn't think about that right now. Not while I was already so worried about Henry. The emotional trauma I'd inflicted on my boyfriend would have to wait.

His eyes darted between me and the trees, his brow furrowed in confusion. "I didn't hear anything."

Anger tightened my chest, and I could feel an argument about to explode out of me. I wanted to make him listen, to make him understand that I wasn't crazy. But I clenched my jaw, biting down on my tongue, refusing to let the words escape, because as I glanced at Carter, I reminded myself that he was just like any other person. He didn't possess superhuman hearing that could hear a pin drop from a mile away. It wasn't his fault that he hadn't heard Henry's shout. I had to remember that, even during a total freakout.

Taking a deep breath, I pushed aside my irritation. My emotions were getting the best of me, but that was no justification for lashing out at Carter. I had to be patient, understanding. The way he always was with me.

It was tough to stay calm, though, with Ansel's words playing on repeat in my mind. *'Then Colton yelled my name'.* He'd said he thought he imagined it, because there'd been no sign of him... the same thing happened to me yesterday when Ansel and I were out looking for Colton's pack. I was sure I heard Carter calling me, but he wasn't even back from town yet. He arrived right as I made it back to the clearing. But his voice... it'd seemed *so real.* Just like Ansel had said.

Just like Henry's voice did now.

I wanted to chase after him. To follow his voice, even if it wasn't actually him. At least then I'd know. But I couldn't, not with Ansel and Carter around. I had to be on my guard for them. It wasn't just me anymore.

I forced myself to stay still, my ears on high alert, hoping to catch even the tiniest sound. Anything to prove it was real. But I couldn't shake this nagging doubt in my gut, no matter how hard I tried to ignore it.

I knew Henry. Our thoughts were so in sync, it was like I could read his mind, so I knew he could be wild and impulsive, but he wasn't dumb. He wouldn't scream and yell, because that would just attract all the predators around and make things worse. Plus, if he was truly in danger, he would want me as far away as possible. Because that's what Henry did – above anything, he put my safety first. And it drove me *insane*.

Henry always had my back, no matter what. It was in his blood, as if his entire existence revolved around keeping me safe. He never expected the same from me, or from anyone, really. He never let himself rely on anyone. Never asked for help. That's how I knew it wasn't him. It couldn't be.

My throat burned with bile and my heart pounded against my rib cage as the realisation sank in. God, I really was losing my mind. And wherever Henry was, I couldn't help him.

A harsh scraping noise pierced the stillness, abruptly snapping me back from the edge. I spun around, my body automatically moving forward to defend Carter, and...

As soon as I laid eyes on it, a wave of icy dread washed over me, making my heart constrict. From the darkness emerged a pair of crimson eyes, their eerie glow sending a shiver down my spine as they locked onto mine. And then it hit me. I couldn't say exactly what it was, but suddenly I knew – it wasn't just any ordinary animal, and it had an aura unlike any supernatural creature I'd ever seen, as well. It was something else entirely. This... this *thing*... it just oozed evil, the blood lust emanating from it so strong I could almost taste it.

It was a hunter. And I was its prey.

My fingers tightened around Carter's hand, refusing to release their grip as I shifted my gaze from the creatures to search for Ansel. Making sure they were both behind me. They still hadn't noticed it, and I needed to get them both out of there—

The creature timed its move perfectly, choosing that very moment to prowl forward, stealing the air from my lungs and leaving me unable to utter a single word of warning. For a moment, I couldn't move. All I could do was stare. It was still mostly hidden by the darkness of the night, but I could just make out its face, catch a glimpse of its features. It was identical to the creature I had seen during my vision near the creek last night. But now I knew it wasn't just in my head. It was all too real.

I backed up, pulling Carter with me, when...

The creature snarled, its teeth bared and saliva dripping from its yellowed fangs. That's all it took to get me moving. I twisted around, dragging Carter by the hand, and finally found my voice again. Just a single word.

"RUN!"

My heart was pounding so hard it echoed in my ears, matching the rhythm of my feet on the ground. The noise drowned everything out, the forest morphing into a chaotic whirlwind of colours and shapes as we sprinted through.

It was impossible to tell if the creature was giving chase. Not without looking back, and I couldn't do that. It was way too risky and, honestly, I was scared of what I might see. What I'd *do*. I couldn't afford any distractions while I was leading Carter, especially with him still holding my hand. If I stumbled, we'd both fall.

We had been running for what felt like an eternity, and there was no way of knowing how far we'd gone. There weren't any obvious signs to guide me, and I probably wouldn't have noticed them anyway. All I cared about was getting away from that thing, so I just kept running... and running. Until I couldn't run anymore.

Almost out of nowhere, something sprung up in the path in front of me, forcing me to a stop. A tree, I figured, that'd emerged from the darkness too quickly, but before I could react or change direction, Carter crashed into me from behind, sending me stumbling forward. He caught me just in time, and I hardly even noticed the impact. But honestly, even if I fell on my face, I probably wouldn't have felt a thing. My mind was a whirlwind, desperately trying to absorb every sound and strategize my next move. I couldn't think about anything else right now.

I righted myself, ready to set off again... and that's when I finally realised what had stopped me, and it wasn't a tree at all. That I mistook it for one, even for a second, just showed how freaked out I was. But when I looked up, instead of the usual vibrant browns and greens of the forest, all I saw was a dull, monotonous grey.

We had run so far that we had reached the foot of a mountain, its peak disappearing into the dark, cloudy night sky. As I looked around, there were no visible signs guiding skiers to the slopes or any apparent ski lift mechanisms leading up to the top, so it clearly wasn't Chibouwood Heights. I had no freaking idea where we were. Or how to get back home.

My eyes darted from tree to tree, frantically searching for any clue, but all I saw were their eerie shadows stretching ominously across the forest floor, reaching out their claws to drag us into their depths. Whichever path I chose would be a blind jump into the abyss, with no clue where I'd end up. We could find ourselves back at the clearing where the creature was waiting. Or worse, if that was even possible. But, really, was I certain that creature was the only one in these woods? There might be an entire pack of them, whatever they were. An entire pack heading our way, ready to rip us limb from limb.

And I'd dragged Carter into this. He was going to die, dismembered and left to rot like Braids, and it was all my fault.

It was like invisible hands were squeezing my throat. I couldn't catch my breath, and panic started to take over. But I couldn't let it get to me. Not now. Not when Carter still had a chance. When he still needed me. I had to be strong for him.

I dug my nails into my palms as the world around me blurred, but no matter how hard I blinked, my vision wouldn't clear. I couldn't make sense of anything. The guys were talking, asking me questions, but I couldn't understand a damn thing, their voices all jumbled up in my head. My knees shook as I stumbled forward, lost in my thoughts, and then someone grabbed my arm, but I was too freaked out to care, and—

Something caught my eye, and a spark of hope ignited inside me. There, at the base of the mountain, was a large, dark hole in the rock that seemed to stretch endlessly underneath it.

A cave.

My heart pounded harder, if that was even possible, as I cautiously took a step forward. As I did, a cool, crisp breeze brushed against my skin, raising goosebumps on my arms, and every sound, every movement, seemed magnified, as if the world had hushed to a whisper in anticipation. Just like it had earlier. With every step I took, the sound of my footsteps filled the air, creating a steady thump that echoed through the stillness of the woods. The scent of earth mixed with the damp and musty odour from the cavern, making me hold my breath as I paused, straining my ears, listening for even the faintest hint of that haunting, dragging sound. But there was only silence.

Glancing over my shoulder, a wave of fear washed over me, my breath hitching in my throat. And...

Nothing. No piercing crimson eyes staring back at me.

My knees almost gave way from the overwhelming relief, but I couldn't drop my guard just yet. Instead, I directed my attention forward, straining my eyes to see what lay inside the mouth of the cave. Thanks to my werewolf vision, I could effortlessly see the rough rocks even in total darkness, and when I inhaled, the smell of wet stones and bat poop hit my nostrils. Then I held my breath to listen again, but all I heard was an overwhelming silence.

I didn't wanna think about why even the bats had ditched the place – we didn't have many other options to choose from. So, I just reached back and grabbed Carter's hand, squeezing it tight when I felt his palm in mine again. Then I dragged him into the cave with me as I yelled, "This way!"

As we pressed on into the darkness, nobody spoke a word. Not until I stopped when we were about halfway in. Far enough away from the opening but not so far that something could leap from a dark corner and attack. I let go of Carter's hand and took a few more careful steps forward to be sure there was nothing lurking in the shadows, and then I turned around to face them.

They both came alive at the same time.

"Madison, what the hell is going on?"

"What the *actual fuck?!*"

I shifted my gaze towards Carter, focusing all of my attention on him. "I'm sorry. I just... I had to get us away from that thing. We should be safe here. At least for now. Until—"

I choked on my words as soon as I saw Carter's face. I glanced at Ansel, feeling a knot form in my stomach as I saw the same expression reflected there. Disbelief. Astonishment. *Fear.* Ansel's eyes said it all, and I knew exactly what was going on in his head. He thought I was out of my mind. He was inching away from me like I was a bomb, and he wanted to get as far away as possible from the inevitable explosion. But why? Was he seriously scared of me, when I was the one who'd just saved him? *Twice*, if you counted letting him tag along with us when we found him by Braids' body. I could've just left him to rot. Maybe I *should* have.

Carter was scared too, but in a different way than Ansel. I could read his thoughts just by the way he looked at me.

He wasn't scared *of* me. He was scared *for* me.

It was written all over his face - he thought I was crazy, too.

I gulped, feeling the bile burn in my throat. "Wh-why are you looking at me like that? You s-saw it, right?"

His Adam's apple bobbed in his throat as he swallowed, and then he slowly moved towards me with his arms outstretched, like he was approaching a skittish animal. When his fingers brushed against my arm, I jerked away, but he didn't seem to notice. "Mads, babe, listen to me. There was nothing—"

I scrambled backwards, my heart pounding in my chest, desperate to escape his grasp and retreat into the dark depths of the cave. He just needed some breathing room. Maybe then he'd see things more clearly. At least, that's what I told myself, but it wasn't true. Not entirely, anyway. The truth was his look was so full of pity that it burned, and I couldn't stand to be near him.

Rage swelled in the pit of my stomach. "There *was*, Carter. Okay? You just didn't see it, because I got us out of there so quickly. I'm not *lying!*"

A flicker of hurt flashed across his face, but he quickly hid it. "I'm not saying you are! But I know you're exhausted, and you've been so jumpy lately. I don't know what's going on with you, but maybe it's got something to do with why you're…"

"Why I'm *what?!*" I snapped. "I'm trying to keep us all alive!"

The sound of Ansel's laughter filled the cavern, bouncing off the walls and drowning out any trace of Carter's reply. "Oh my god, you're crazy. You've lost your damn mind. Jesus Christ. I'm outta here."

He turned to leave, but he didn't get far. Carter's hand moved so fast it was a blur, grabbing his jacket and stopping him in his tracks.

"Hey, give her a break, okay? Her best friend is missing."

He was trying to make up for not believing me, trying to calm me down, by defending me to Ansel. I knew that. And he was worried about me. *Really* worried. With everything that had happened since we arrived in Chibouwood, could I blame him for that? After all the secrets and lies, the sneaking around?

If I had been thinking straight, I would've known the answer was a hard no. *Of course* I couldn't blame him. But my right mind had abandoned me hours ago, leaving only rage, and now my words were full of it. I was like a loaded gun, anger building up inside me, aimed at my boyfriend.

"I don't need you to fucking defend me! That's not why I—"

I didn't get to finish my sentence, because Ansel cut me off.

"So is mine! Fucking *both* of them! But you don't give a crap about that, do you? And I'm thinking she might have had something to do with it after all."

Of all the things he could've said, that was the last thing I expected. I opened my mouth to argue, but it was as if my words evaporated, leaving a bitter taste in my throat. Not that it mattered. Even if I had managed to utter a word, the force of Carter's fist connecting with Ansel's nose silenced any sound that could have escaped my lips, the vibrations echoing through the cave. As his body crumpled to the ground, the pungent scent of blood wafted up, instantly replacing my anger with disbelief.

There was a moment of complete silence, and even Carter seemed shocked by what he had just done. Ansel snapped back first, his hand trembling as he tentatively reached for his face, wincing as his fingers made contact with his nose. But it seemed to spark something in him, because he jumped to his feet, and there was only a split second of hesitation before he charged right at Carter.

Instinctively, I jumped backwards out of the way, but as soon as my brain registered what was actually happening, I cursed before rushing closer. I tried to circle them, to find an opening to cut in and break it up without winding up with a broken nose myself, but it was impossible. Now the adrenaline had worn off, my ankle throbbed again, even worse than before. My movements were more like a hobble, way too slow to stand a chance when the guys were a wild tangle of limbs. Grunts and huffs echoed around me as they exchanged blow after blow, and I had no option but to let them fight it out while I stood on the sidelines, pleading with them to *stop*.

I didn't see how it happened, but at some point, Carter gained the upper hand, and he slammed Ansel against the wall, making the whole cavern shudder. As the impact reverberated, a thick cloud of dust billowed down, making him cough and struggle for breath as he sucked it in. It made him weak enough for Ansel to take charge, and before I could even give a heads up, Ansel threw a punch so strong at Carter's stomach that he doubled over in pain. Then he clasped him tightly around the waist, and for a split second, I couldn't make sense of what I was seeing. Was he trying to give him a hug? But then I realised, and I shouted a warning, but they were both too lost in the fight to listen. Ansel grunted, his muscles straining as he heaved Carter off the ground... before he hurled him against the same wall.

Instantly, more dust rained down, settling on everything like a thin veil. But they didn't notice. Or maybe they just didn't care.

They were so caught up in the chaos that they didn't even hear the low rumble coming from the depths of the mountain. But I did, and a chill ran down my spine. My throat tightened, and in that moment, the fear was so intense that I couldn't even move.

It'd followed us – that creature. Snuck in another way, and now we were trapped. If I turned now, I'd see those blood-red eyes, filled with malice and hunger, and it'd be the last thing I ever saw.

I swallowed the lump in my throat and forced myself to turn anyway, my heart pounding so hard it felt ready to burst right out of my chest, and...

Nothing.

Thank God. Relief washed over me, and I turned to the guys, my voice shaking with desperation as I yelled, "Guys! Enough! *Please!*"

No reaction. I was like a ghost, just a whisper drowned out by their rage.

As if to prove it, a sudden gust of wind swept into the cavern, carrying with it the unmistakable scent of blood, sweat, and adrenaline. Another loud thud followed it when one of them crashed into the wall again. There was no way to tell which was which anymore.

And then that rumbling again, like thunder in the distance. But it was louder now. Moving closer.

A tremor shook the ground beneath my feet, causing a shiver to travel up my spine, but as I looked up at the cave ceiling, all I could see was a haze of dust. I was about to bail, grab Carter and make a run for it, take our chances in the forest. But then the grey cloud shifted, and suddenly I could see perfectly.

And that's when it hit me like a gut punch.

It was already too late.

I tried to yell anyway, to scream a warning, but another tremor shook the room and eclipsed my voice. Then the sound of a body colliding with the wall echoed through the air again, and in that fleeting moment, time stood still. But it was only for a second before the ceiling came crashing down in a storm of rock, and there was nothing I could do but scream his name.

38

Something sharp struck the top of my head, sending a surge of pain through my body, so intense that I stumbled backwards, gasping for air. It was dizzying, like a lightning strike in my brain, and for a split, blissful second, I had no idea where I was. Oblivious to the chaos that surrounded me.

It didn't last. In an instant, the fog in my mind dissipated, and the booming sound of thunder bombarded me as large pieces of the ceiling tumbled down. The air was thick with a suffocating haze of dust and debris that made my eyes water and my nostrils burn. I squeezed my eyes closed, but there was nothing to do about my nose, no option but to breath it in while I raised my arms to brace my head and rolled away. Only a second later, a boulder crashed down right in the spot I'd just occupied.

My breath rushed out in a gasp, and with it I inhaled a mouthful of musty air that made me cough and splutter, worsening my already hoarse throat from screaming for Carter before the ceiling collapsed. I wasn't sure if he even heard me. If he was alive. And there was nothing I could do about it.

Huddled against the furthest wall of the cave, the sharp edges of the rough rock dug into my back. As the cool stone brushed against my skin, it seemed like the walls were tightening around me, making it hard to breathe. And, truthfully? I hoped they would.

At least then I wouldn't have to sit there, cowering helplessly like a child, wondering if Carter was trapped beneath a mountain of rubble just feet away from me.

But the walls stood firm, leaving me to endure the clamour of thuds and scrapes. With every shard that broke off and sliced through the air, my face, scalp, and legs became targets. But I welcomed the pain. It was the least I deserved.

My ears kept ringing even after the ceiling stopped crashing, so I didn't realise it was over at first. I just stayed there, squished against the wall, head between my knees. What was the point of moving? Carter was right under it when the first rock fell. I hadn't been fast enough. I hadn't warned him in time. And now...

"MADISON?!"

My head shot up so fast that I felt a sharp twinge in my neck, but I didn't care. I leapt to my feet, rushing towards the wall of debris, his name on my lips. Initially a whisper, but then the words tore from my throat, fighting their way out as if my life depended on it.

"Carter? CARTER?!"

My fingers frantically clawed at the jagged rocks, desperate to pry them away and get to him. But even my werewolf strength didn't help. The rocks had wedged together so tightly that there was no way to break them apart. With each desperate attempt, I stumbled and fell, a stinging pain shooting through my fingertips as they became raw and bloody, until I eventually had no choice but to give up.

Sweat pouring down my face, I looked up at the massive pile of rocks... and once again, it took my breath away.

The debris had formed a delicate jigsaw puzzle, fitting together perfectly to uphold the cave's stability. It was the only thing keeping *everything* from collapsing. If it budged even slightly, the entire structure would crumble, leaving us trapped underneath.

No chance of breaking through it. No way for me to get out.

But Carter was on the other side. The side with the exit. He wasn't stuck. He was safe. That was the only thing that mattered.

"MADISON? Are you okay?" His voice was hoarse too, as if he'd been screaming for me the whole time I was screaming for him, but we couldn't hear each other over the chaos.

I nodded without thinking, then remembered he couldn't see me. "Y-yes. Yes, I'm okay. Are you?"

"We're both fine. We'll try to clear a path, alright?"

"NO!" I shouted. "It's too dangerous. This wall is the only thing stopping the whole place coming down."

There was silence for a moment as he thought about it. Then his voice called back, "I don't care."

Ansel squawked in panic, but I replied before he could protest. "Well, I do, Carter. Henry is still lost somewhere out there. You gotta help him. It's no good us all dying in here."

"Don't even joke about that, Madison! No one is dying!"

The desperation in his voice struck me like a dagger, leaving a sharp ache in my chest, and my voice wavered as tears welled up in my eyes. "Carter, listen to me—"

"*NO*! You listen to me! We don't have a choice, okay? I don't give a damn if it crushes me. I'm getting you out of there."

I was about to argue, but I quickly realised it wasn't worth it. It was a waste of breath since he wouldn't listen, and I didn't know how much air I had left. Could air still pass through the stone barricade? Honestly, I had no idea, but it didn't really matter. If the situation were reversed, I wouldn't listen to reason, either. I wouldn't accept there was nothing I could do but wait for him to suffocate, or starve to death, and I didn't want to waste what little time I had left arguing with him. If I was going to die, trapped in this freezing, rocky tomb, I wanted to tell him I loved him, and how sorry I was for everything, how I hoped his future would be filled with —

A sound cut off the thought. It was soft, like a melodic tune playing far away...

"Give me a second!" I yelled, a spark of hope igniting as I turned back into the cave, even as Carter shouted frantically at me to wait, to stop whatever I was planning.

At first, just shapes appeared as my eyes adjusted to the darkness, nothing but a monotonous sea of solid stone. But if I strained my ears, listening past the persistent ringing, I could faintly hear it... *yes*! Water! I could hear running water.

There were no signs of water at the cave entrance, and as I delved deeper, it became clear that there were none on this side either. But I could hear it, whooshing around nearby, so there must be a secret passage, a hidden tunnel, that connected this cave to the maze of the mountain. Probably an entire network of caves. One of them would surely lead me back to the forest. If I could just find...

Then, my eyes caught sight of it, and now that I knew it was there, it seemed impossible that I hadn't noticed it earlier. Hidden within the wall there was a narrow crevice, and up close, the whooshing sound was much clearer. At first glance, the opening appeared too narrow to pass through, but as I knelt down in front of it, I realised it was spacious enough for me. Just about.

As I straightened up to return to Carter, a smile spread across my face.

"Carter! There's a way out. A tunnel. If I go through, I'll bet it connects to another cavern. I can get back to you that way."

He didn't reply immediately, almost like he didn't understand what I'd said. I was about to say it again when he finally spoke. "No way, Madison! It's way too risky. We can figure this out. I can… I can get help."

The smile slid from my face as I sighed. "That'll take too long. And Henry might not…" I trailed off, not daring to finish the thought. "I hear water. If there's freshwater somewhere under here, then it'll probably wind up outside, eventually. I just need to follow it and I'll find another way out. I'm sure of it. It's at least worth a shot."

"What if you get trapped? I've seen documentaries about stuff like that, Madison. People get stuck in cave tunnels, and they suffocate. It's not worth it. Barton would tell you the same thing if he were here."

Annoyance surged through me in response to that. Not because he was wrong. He wasn't. There's no way Henry would allow me to crawl through some random hole in the wall and go explore the freaking inside of a mountain. I was annoyed because he used that as an argument, making it seem like Henry had authority over me. Carter had always believed in me where Henry didn't. And he chose *now* to turn against me?

"I can fit." I snapped. "Or are you suggesting I'm fat?"

"Are you serious?" Carter groaned, and I heard him kick the toe of his boot against the ground in frustration. Something – probably a stone – ricocheted off a distant wall a few seconds later. "*No.* Jeez. As if. I'm just being realistic, for god's sake."

"So am I." I retorted, and I knew how pathetic and brattish I sounded, inwardly cringing at it, but I still couldn't force myself to back down.

He was silent for another beat, but when he finally spoke, it was the last thing I expected him to say.

"Would you let me do it?"

"Wh-what?" I spluttered, completely thrown off by the question.

"It's a simple question, Madison. If it was me on that side of this fucking wall, would you be okay with me going through a random passage with no idea what's on the other side? Knowing there's no way to get to me? If you tell me you'd be okay with that, then I'll shut up. You're way smarter than me, Mads. We both know that. So, if you can honestly say that it wouldn't bother you if it was me, and that you're sure it's safe, then go ahead. I trust you."

My mouth was like a damn goldfish, opening and closing over and over. But no words would form. Which was exactly what he expected, wasn't it? He already knew the answer, and for all the lies I'd told to keep him safe, there was no way I could lie convincingly about that. If the situation were reversed, I'd come up with another plan, even if it meant tearing the wall down chunk by chunk and getting crushed in the process. I wouldn't care, so long as he was okay. But what other choice did I have? It was that or sit here and wait to die, knowing that the beast could appear any time. I'd seen what it did to Braids. I wouldn't let Carter suffer the same fate. No freaking way. I wanted him as far away as possible from this forest.

A lightbulb went off in my brain then, and I sucked in a breath.

Could it actually work?

He said he'd go get help, and wouldn't that be the best move? Maybe not for me, but it would at least get Carter out of the forest. Away from that creature. Whatever it was, it didn't seem to give a damn about him. Every time it showed up, it disappeared as soon as someone else joined me. And he hadn't even seen it just now...

Then it hit me - the reason nobody else saw it. Hadn't I already decided that it wasn't natural? That it felt paranormal in some way? I pulled the image to the forefront of my mind. It had always stayed mostly hidden, careful about what it revealed to me, so I hadn't seen much, but the piercing gaze of its haunting eyes was etched into my memory. Crimson, threatening, like pools of blood. Fangs the size of elephant tusks. I'd never seen anything like it, but something was bugging me, some itch of recognition that I now realised had been there since that very first night.

I'd heard a similar story, about a creature that only revealed itself to its victim. I couldn't remember the details, or even where I'd heard it, but if I had to guess, it was probably from Ryan. He might have been a professor of history, but he always had an interest in myth and legend. He used to say they were all a *part* of history, all the stories passed down through generations. I could see him in my mind so clearly, *hear* his voice as we roamed around Vineyard Manor, all fired up recounting tales from his research. He even kept records of all the supernatural creatures he came across while studying - the ones the pack knew about, the ones we had encountered, and even the ones only mentioned in those old stories.

'*I'm making a compendium, Maddie. Our very own 'Liber Monstrorum', if you will.*' He'd said, the day he finally showed me what he'd been working on for months, locked away in a backroom at headquarters.

I had no idea what '*Liber Monstrorum*' meant, and Ryan never explained, but I knew what a compendium was. It was like an encyclopaedia, but on a specific subject. In Ryan's case – supernatural creatures. *Damn,* I wished I had it with me, or that

I'd studied it more when I had the chance. Maybe it would tell me what to do.

Still, I definitely remembered *something*, and it meant I *wasn't* going crazy. Carter hadn't seen it because it didn't *want* him to. It posed no threat to him. Whatever the hell it was, it was after *me*. Using Henry as a pawn to get to me. A trap to lure in its prey.

And I had no choice but to play along if I ever wanted to see my best friend alive again.

"Okay." I said finally, trying to ignore the guilt that loomed like a spectre over my shoulder.

Carter's response was almost immediate. "Okay?"

"Okay, you win. Go get help. Go back to the cabin and grab the truck. You'll need to head into town to use your phone. Then you can call mountain rescue." *By that point, I'll have sorted my own escape, and he'll be miles away from any trouble while I go save Henry.*

I heard him let out a sigh, and I couldn't quite decipher if it was a sigh of relief or one of disbelief. Most likely the latter. I'd given in too easily, and he saw right through it, so now he wouldn't leave. *Damn it!* A tight knot twisted in the pit of my stomach, and I was glad he couldn't see me, because I knew my face would give me away.

"Do you think you can find your way?" I asked, hoping to divert his attention.

Ansel finally spoke then, and I'd never been more grateful for his interruption. "I've got my cell. No bars, obviously, but the compass is still kicking. That might help."

I might not have been able to see him, but I could practically hear the gears turning in Carter's mind as he thought it through. Then, uncertainly, he said, "You're sure this will hold until we get back? We can still knock it down. Somehow."

"It'll be good." I insisted, even though I couldn't be sure. I just had to convince him to go. "Just... make sure you don't get lost, alright? Your best option is to get to higher ground. Look for something you recognise to help you navigate. We came in from the west side of the cabin, so if you can figure out how we got *here*, finding your way back will be a breeze."

His voice was closer when he spoke again, like he was right up against the barricade. I inched nearer, too, my hand flattening against the cool stone, as if I could feel him through it.

"I hate the thought of leaving you." He murmured softly, barely audible.

"I know."

Silence enveloped us as I imagined a different scenario - our hands intertwined, my forehead resting against his instead of the cold rock. Then, finally, his voice trembling, he said, "Promise me you won't go through that tunnel the second I leave."

I released a breath, watching it instantly freeze into a cloud of mist in the cold air. "Carter..."

"Madison." He pleaded. Full name again. He seemed to only use it when he was mad or worried, and it made me cringe. "You gotta promise me. Or I swear I'll tear this thing down with my bare hands. I don't care if it kills me."

I bit my lip, the taste of iron flooding my mouth, but I swallowed it back as I crossed my fingers behind my back.

"I promise."

39

I waited until their footsteps faded into the night, the silence becoming my only company, before I turned and cautiously crawled into the narrow crevice.

It was tighter than I'd expected, and I had to back out and remove my jacket to make myself smaller, leaving it on the cave floor. The cold air bit at me without it, but as I contorted my body to slither through the opening, feeling the jagged rocks scraping and slicing at my bare skin, I found it numbed the pain a little. Then finally, after what felt like forever, I made it to the end, using my hands like feet to drag my body into the cavern ahead.

The darkness made it difficult at first, but once my eyes adjusted, I saw it was larger than the one I had come from, but otherwise pretty much exactly the same. Except that no moonlight seeped in to illuminate the way forward, other than the tiniest sliver spilling over from the first cavern, a thin beam that'd fought its way through the wall of rubble and into the crawl space.

My stomach knotted. No moonlight meant no way out.

It shouldn't surprise me - when has luck ever been on my side? Still, it was damn frustrating, because it meant I had to delve even deeper into the heart of the mountain. Further away from Henry. From Carter.

Carter would forgive me for lying. Sure, he'd be mad, but only because he was so worried about me. If I got myself out of here unscathed, he'd be so relieved to see me safe that he would immediately forgive me. Just like he always did.

Yet I had to admit there was a part of me that wondered if it would push him too far this time. That this would be the moment his patience finally snapped. But I buried the thought, relegating it to the part of my brain reserved for all the things that weren't crucial to our immediate survival. Anything else could wait, I told myself, as I anxiously retrieved my cell from my pocket, hoping it still had enough battery to be of use, because even werewolf sight couldn't work with no light at all. I could see for now, but the further I journeyed into the mountain, the fainter the light would become, until it would eventually fade away entirely. Getting around with my messed-up ankle was already going to be difficult, let alone doing it blindly.

Clutching the phone tightly, I raised it up, waiting for the screensaver to spring to life – a silly photo of Carter and me with my dad from Christmas, all three of us wearing matching plaid pyjamas. When the screen stubbornly stayed dark, though, a sinking feeling of disappointment settled in my stomach. Frustrated, I jabbed at the button on the side, desperately trying to bring it to life, but after several tries, all that greeted me was my reflection on the screen.

It took all my self-control not to throw it across the cave and smash it against a wall. But I resisted, angrily shoving it back in my pocket as I kept going through the cave. The further I went, the faster the light faded until, just like I thought, it disappeared entirely. After that, it was a clumsy battle in the dark. Each step hurt like hell as my ankle wobbled on the scattered stones until, eventually, it gave out and I fell to the ground, cursing as new cuts and scrapes joined the ones I already had on my skin.

I couldn't take it anymore. The panic and stress of the past few days erupted into a single, piercing scream that echoed through the air, bouncing off walls like thunder. Even after my lungs were empty, the eerie echo of it persisted, surrounding me as I lay exhausted on the cold ground.

Shit. Now what? I had no choice but to drag myself back to the first cavern and wait for Carter to bring help, even though I really hated the thought of just sitting there, waiting to be rescued. Especially with Henry still out there, and that creature...

I interrupted that thought, because I knew I wouldn't have the energy to escape this cave if I let it take over. Besides, the creature was stalking *me*. It wouldn't kill Henry if it was using him as a trap to get to me. I had to believe that. But I felt so useless, stuck, with a messed-up ankle, waiting for humans to come and save me. I was a freaking werewolf, for crying out—

Suddenly, I bolted upright, my veins pulsing with adrenaline, which was swiftly joined by a prickling sense of annoyance. But, this time, I couldn't be mad at anyone but myself, because I had been such a damn idiot. I was a freaking *werewolf*. Okay, so Changing wouldn't completely fix my ankle, but it'd speed up the healing process. Plus, having four legs instead of two would not only ease the strain on the injured one but also enhance my eyesight, sense of smell, and agility. With Carter gone to get help, there was nothing stopping me from putting my special skills to use.

I didn't even bother taking off my clothes. It was too cold for that, and I wouldn't be coming back to collect them, so why worry if they got torn apart? I took off my boots, though, but only because the leather material was too tough to split apart easily, and I didn't want my paws to become stuck in them with no way to get out.

Hissing at the biting cold seeping through my cotton socks, I lowered myself to kneel on the ground, palms flat in front of me, and closed my eyes. Within moments, a tingling sensation spread through my arms and legs, as if a thousand needles were poking at my skin. Anticipating the first wave of pain, I steeled myself, but it crashed over me like a wave with barely any warning, forcing a scream to escape my lips before I could stop it. I could only hope that Carter and Ansel were already too far away from the cave to have heard..

The Change never got easier. It was an agonising torture, as if my flesh was being ripped off and my bones pulverised. That's why some shifters avoided doing it until they absolutely had to. But, to me, the pain was worth it just to experience the incredible freedom of being a wolf. It was a feeling like no other.

Soon enough, the screams of pain morphed into a howl, and when I looked down at my hands, I saw paws instead. As I raised my head, the cavern materialised before me, its colours muted in shades of grey and black. The remnants of my jeans and shirt fluttered down to the ground, and the heat of my breath formed a mist that tickled my snout while I panted, as exhausted as if I'd just ran to the top of the mountain and then fallen over the edge, hitting every outcropping of rock on the way down. But then, just as quickly, it was over.

Arching my body, I extended my front legs and felt the hard rock beneath my claws. Then I took a step forward.

Despite effortlessly manoeuvring through the winding labyrinth beneath the mountain in my wolf form, I didn't seem to be getting anywhere. In fact, I was sure I was going in circles as I clambered through cramped passageway after cramped passageway, the click of my claws on the ground grating on me more and more with each dead-end.

Okay, I supposed I hadn't technically hit any *dead*-ends yet. Even so, each chamber mirrored the last, and it felt like the mountain itself was taunting me by offering the hope of a way out, only to send me on a constant loop through its maze of identical tunnels.

There was one stark difference in this cavern, I noticed, as I moved further in – water. I'd finally tracked down the running water I'd heard, so at least I hadn't imagined that. A small waterfall trickled down from somewhere above, flowing into a stream that meandered along the ground until it seeped into a tiny crack in the wall, too small for even a wolf to crawl through. Still, it offered a glimmer of hope. If I could somehow follow the trail of the water, it might eventually steer me towards freedom.

I took a moment first to lap up a drink from the stream, then stretched again, feeling some of the tension release from my muscles as I shook off the fatigue. Then, keeping my muzzle inches above the ground to avoid the dust and dirt, I started forward again.

There'd been no scent to follow so far. Except for bugs, it seemed like no animals had ventured into these caverns in months, which struck me as odd, but I wasn't an expert in zoology. It *was* spring, and well past hibernation season. It was also possible nothing had discovered this cave, since I had no idea how deep under the mountain I'd travelled, so there was absolutely no need to panic about the fact I was the only living thing down here...

A few yards to the left of the stream I spotted another opening in the wall, much larger than any of the crawl spaces I had come across so far. I took a cautious step forward, my pace slowing as a twinge shot through my leg. Changing helped, as expected, but the pain wasn't completely gone, and crawling through tiny spaces wasn't making it any easier, so I was relieved to find I could walk through this tunnel without having to hunch down and drag my body through. It also gave me a chance to look around. Not that there was much to see. Stone walls. Stone ceiling. Stone floor.

Once we got home, I was never going mountain hiking *again*.

Just then, something caught my eye, and I paused, my attention drawn up towards the ceiling again. On either side of the tunnel, there were deep grooves carved into the walls. Knife marks, maybe? They looked fresh, like someone made them recently, maybe in the past few weeks or even days. But there was nothing else, no scents or footprints, to suggest anyone had passed through here, so—

I stopped dead as realisation hit me, and my stomach dropped. There was only one thing that came to mind that could leave gauges of that size in solid rock. Only one thing I could think of that didn't have a scent, or at least not a consistent one. I thought back to that first night, seeing the eyes in the forest. There'd been no scent then. But then before, with Braids, there was that awful stench. How was that possible?

It wasn't possible. And yet, it was the truth.

Despite the unsettling sensation that washed over me, I forced myself to keep going, feeling my hackles rise and my muscles tense. As I entered the adjoining cavern, I noticed a faint sliver of moonlight that grew brighter with each step I took into its depths... and the relief that washed over me was dizzying.

Moonlight! Moonlight meant a way out. It meant salvation. And it also meant it didn't matter one bit what'd left those markings, because I'd figured out how to escape, and maybe I could find Henry and make it back to the cabin before Carter got back with help, and—

My eyes landed on something, and I froze, then snorted when I realised what it was – a pile of white twigs on the cave floor. Goddamnit, I was frightened of *sticks* now? That was a new low.

Shaking my head, I crossed towards them, but the closer I got, the more tense I became, until I was close to enough to see them properly... and then I dropped back with a yelp of surprise.

Because it wasn't twigs at all. It was a pile of *bones.*

Okay, it was just animal bones. No big d—

The thought cut off as my eyes landed on something else, sitting slightly to the side of the pile, as if a gust of wind had blown through and rolled it away. A skull. A very clearly *human* skull.

There was a moment where I completely lost all sense, where I felt all the blood drain from my face, certain I was looking at Henry's bones, before I realised how ridiculous that was. Henry had been missing for less than two hours. The human body didn't skeletonise that quickly.

My legs weakened then, and I turned, trying not to barf, and...

That's when I saw it. The smell hit me at almost the exact same time.

Blood.

A dark trail of it stained the ground, leading from the cave entrance to a shadowy corner. Staying rooted to the spot, I followed it with my eyes... and immediately wished I hadn't. I wished I could turn back the clock, to before the image burned itself onto my retinas, and never come in here.

Just visible in the shadows was a pair of legs, ending with feet gracefully strapped into wedge heeled sandals, perfectly painted toenails pointed up towards the ceiling. From my angle, the dark obscured it such that I could almost pretend it wasn't what I knew, in my heart, that it was. But there was no denying that smell, and the familiar taste of bile surged up in my throat.

The missing half of Braids' body. Which meant I had found the creature's lair.

40

Oh my god. Oh my god. Oh my god...

As it sank in, I felt as heavy as a block of lead, unable to move even though every part of me was screaming to run. To get the heck out of there. But I didn't. I *couldn't*.

It wasn't bravery that kept me from running away. If the creature came back, I'd bolt. But for now, it was way out in the woods, so I had a chance. A shot at finding clues that might lead me to Henry.

As I ventured deeper into the cave, the silence was broken only by the echoing click of my claws against the ground. I stayed as far away from Braids' dead body as I could, since I doubted it could tell me anything I didn't already know. It had only been a few hours since I talked to her, so I knew she hadn't been dead for too long, and I could tell, even from a distance, there was no scent from the creature. I wished I couldn't smell *her*, either, but the strong odour of blood, urine, and the first signs of decomposition were impossible to ignore, painting a vivid image in my mind.

Honestly, I was glad for the opportunity to keep my distance. To look anywhere but at her. The sight of her mutilated body, soaked in blood and torn in two, filled me with overwhelming guilt. Guilt for the fact I didn't even know her name, when I was probably the reason she died. I could've sworn I heard something in the thicket where she and her friends were hanging out, but I brushed it off as me being paranoid. Even Henry agreed there was nothing there. But I should've checked it out anyway. What if we were both wrong? What if, even then, it was that creature stalking me? Maybe I could have saved her.

Since I had no idea what it was, I also couldn't tell if it had any level of intelligence. Even in my wolf form, I was still aware of my human thoughts. We had a choice to fully surrender ourselves to the animal or not. If that thing was supernatural like I thought, maybe it was the same. Maybe it saw us chatting, thought we were friends, and took her. Another trap for me, just like with Henry.

Except Henry wasn't dead. *Yet.* But she was.

Why?!

I couldn't answer any of the million questions swirling in my head. Worse, I couldn't even allow myself to try. The *why* didn't matter right now. Only the *how* – how I could put an end to it. Anything else was another dark path I didn't have time for.

Blocking out the flood of thoughts, I shifted my focus to the pile of bones, the last avenue I had left to explore.

I wasn't eager to approach that either, but at least, being bones, they were probably several years old. It gave me a bit of relief to think of them as evidence, not a real person. That was the only way I could do what needed to be done. I didn't touch them, but I moved closer to take a deep breath, even though I knew it wouldn't help. I'd watched enough CSI to know that I needed a real lab to figure out their age. My nose didn't stand a chance. But I didn't know what else to do, and that at least felt like doing *something*.

Lowering my muzzle to the ground, I inhaled, and...

Oh my god.

I hadn't expected there to be a scent, but there was, clear as day. A human one. And unless skeletons could magically put themselves back together and wander around, the scent belonged to someone else. Someone who was very much alive in the last couple of days, at least.

When that realisation hit, my body reacted instantly. My hackles stood on end, while a deep growl resonated in my throat, even though I was still alone. But it was so unexpected that it made me uneasy, and suddenly I couldn't shake the feeling I was being watched, as if there were eyes hiding in every corner, every shadow, just waiting to pounce. I strained my ears, searching for even the faintest sound of movement or any signs of life, but there was only silence, broken occasionally by the skittering of bugs and the steady drip of the waterfall in the adjoining cavern. Definitely no one else close by. Nobody to come running at me with a spear or something equally as deadly. I huffed at that, and let myself relax a little, but I remained on guard, ready to react at any hint of movement.

The smell coated practically every inch of the cavern, forming a tangled web of intertwining trails. They all belonged to one person, but some were more potent, fresher, than others. That meant whoever it belonged to had been in and out of this cave for weeks.

What the hell did that mean? Whoever they were, were they controlling that thing? Maybe they *were* the beast. Some kind of shapeshifter.

I dismissed that idea almost immediately. There weren't any shapeshifters with no scent at all. At least, none I knew of. I ran through a mental list: werewolves, obviously, but also were-coyotes, berserkers, skin-walkers... As far as I knew, their scents didn't change, no matter what shape they took.

Maybe I was wrong. Maybe this wasn't the creature's lair, and instead, I'd accidentally found the hideaway of a – *totally unrelated* – psycho murderer. Honestly, that wouldn't surprise me. With my luck, it was almost par for the course that I would come looking for one monster, only to stumble upon a completely different one. But now I was here, there was only one way to be sure.

The trails all pointed in the same direction, beckoning towards the deepest, darkest part of the cave. I hesitantly stepped towards it, still on edge, even though I'd already confirmed the cavern was empty except for me, but, to my relief, nothing came hurtling from the shadows. Empty food wrappers littered the ground surrounding an unlit campfire, while an abandoned sleeping bag lay nearby. Bugs skittered across both, and I squirmed in spite of myself, which was ridiculous considering there was half a corpse behind me and a skeleton to my left. Still, as I looked at the sleeping bag, crawling with ants and who knew what else, my stomach turned. If whoever left it behind planned on returning, I hoped to God they also planned on bringing a new one back with them.

Apart from the pest-infested camp, the only things left for me to investigate were two rucksacks in a corner, leaning against a wall. I went over to them and, after making sure they weren't full of bugs too, used my teeth to drag them out into the light. It was a struggle to open the zips, what with my lack of opposable thumbs, but I eventually managed by gripping them with my paws and biting at them. Then I clamped my jaw around the bottom of each bag, lifted them off the floor, and shook them until everything fell out.

It was a wasted effort. Neither of them divulged much, just a deodorant spray, a half-empty toothpaste tube, two toothbrushes, more dried food packets, and a change of clothes in each. Basic camping essentials. Other than that, the only thing that stood out was a notebook. It had fallen open to a page with a note, written in a messy handwriting that was impossible to read, but I could make out the faint outline of a drawing on the back. I used my muzzle to nudge it gently, and the page obediently flipped over. As it did, something slipped out from between the pages and floated upwards, carried by a gentle gust of wind. I didn't give it much thought as it fluttered in the corner of my vision.

I turned my attention back to the notepad. I was right – on the other side of the page was a black and white sketch, beautifully shaded... and it took my breath away. Because on the page, staring right back at me, was the creature.

Whoever this camp belonged to... they had seen it too. Maybe they'd taken refuge here, thinking they'd be safe until someone came and rescued them. That sent a chill down my spine, because it was way too close to my own situation right now, waiting for Carter to bring help.

Suddenly, I didn't want to look at it anymore. I lifted my paw, ready to slap it away, when...

That same memory resurfaced, persistently tugging at the corners of my mind, just like it had done before. Ryan and his damn *'Liber Monstrorum'*. Why did it keep haunting me? It was completely pointless and, frankly, annoying as hell, because I couldn't remember any of the damn details, so—

My heart stopped as I looked at the sketch again, closer this time. And it was as if someone had finally hit 'play' on a movie, the footage streaming crystal clear in my head.

I saw Ryan in his study at headquarters, the warm glow of the desk lamp casting a soft light on his face as he examined the papers scattered across the polished mahogany desk. A smile involuntarily spread across my face as I recalled the sound of his voice, as clearly as if he was standing right beside me.

"Now these creatures, Maddie... they're just fascinating. Native American origin. There've been no proven sightings, of course, but I've included them anyway, because you never know, right?"

"Right," I had agreed, and he had flashed me a grin. *"So... what exactly are they?"*

"Well, many legends exist. All the tribes have their own variation. But they all concur on one point, which is they are the epitome of evil. Cannibalistic creatures, you see. Though, I personally find that to be an oversimplification. Many notorious criminals have served jail time for that specific offence, and not one of them transformed into a wendigo, did they? I think we would have heard if an inmate transformed into a giant beast and began tearing people apart. That kind of thing makes headlines."

I'd raised my eyebrow. "Yeah... I mean, I guess so. Unless they kept it under wraps."

Ryan had nodded thoughtfully. "It's certainly possible. Yet, all the stories suggest no cell could ever imprison something as powerful as that. No, I think there may be a genetic component to consider as well. Similar to us. I was bitten. But in your case... That's simply who you are. You inherited the gene from your dad. Perhaps it would be a similar story if, of course, they were real. It would explain why there has never been any evidence of their existence. Only stories, passed down through generations. Because they've learned how to control it and trained their young in the same. Like the pack. It's a shame we'll never know for sure, though. It would be absolutely fascinating to study."

I'd laughed. "You and I have very different opinions on what's fascinating, Ry. I think I'll stick to books for learning about the," I'd *paused, leaning over the table to pull one of the loose pages towards me, squinting as I read the words. "Windiko... windykoo... wind..."*

As I'd struggled over the name, Ryan had chuckled, playfully nudging me with his shoulder. He'd gestured towards a different paragraph on the page. "That name is the most commonly used. I'd suggest you stick with that. Much easier."

I'd read it, nodded, and then said, "Wendigo."

"Yes. That's it."

Ice crept down my spine. I *knew* I recognised it from somewhere. A goddamn *wendigo*. Even Jen had brought up the legend at the bonfire, but she'd called it the 'windikouk' – and it suddenly dawned on me it was the very name I'd struggled to pronounce that night in Ryan's study.

Different names, but the same creature.

It wasn't just a legend.

Then another memory came back. Driving into Chibouwood on the first day, Carter pointing out the statue in the square and asking if it was a werewolf. I'd laughed, because it looked nothing like a real werewolf. It was some hideous thing, standing on two legs, with huge antlers. But now... now I couldn't understand how the hell I hadn't figured it out sooner.

Except... they weren't *real*. They were an urban legend. Even Ryan, the smartest person I knew, hadn't truly believed they existed. Yet, they obviously *did*. I'd seen one with my own eyes.

And for some reason, it was fixated on *me*.

I wracked my brain, but apparently it had abandoned me now, because I couldn't recall anything else useful.Nothing about how to *kill* it.

Nausea burrowed into my stomach when I looked back at the notebook. The sketch didn't really match any of the images Ryan had showed me, but he'd also said there were different versions of the legend. That might explain why I didn't immediately make the connection - apart from the horns, it looked nothing like the statue. And yet, somehow, I knew it was the same creature.

Now I was sure what it was, I *really* couldn't stand to look at it any longer, so nudged the page until it flipped over again. The next sheet revealed more of the messy, scrawling handwriting. I squinted, trying to decipher the jumbled mess of scribbles, but nothing made sense. It was even worse than Henry's, and that was saying something. I could make out 'dear', right at the beginning, so I figured it must've been a letter, but the name written next to it was mostly unreadable. If I had to guess, I'd say it began with an A, but, truthfully, I couldn't be certain. It could just as easily have been a B or an R, and even if it *was* an A, it didn't really narrow it down much.

It turned out not to matter, because at that moment, the page that had slipped out finally fluttered down, its corners catching the light as it delicately settled on top of the notebook. Only, it wasn't a page, but a photograph. One of a guy confidently smirking at the camera while a girl leaned in and planted one of those mock, over-the-top kisses on his cheek. I narrowed my eyes at the image, because the guy had a familiarity about him, as if I'd met him before, but I was almost certain I hadn't. There was just something about his eyes. The image was too small to be clear, but they looked to be green, and that fact tugged at something. Something I couldn't quite hook onto.

As if it might help me identify him, I glanced at the jumbled pile of belongings on the ground before me, and then, with reluctance, turned my gaze back to the lifeless bodies before finally returning to the photograph, and...

The sudden jolt of recognition took my breath away for the second time in what had only been a matter of minutes.

I *had* seen their faces before. The day we arrived in town, walking to the coffee shop with Carter. The derelict storefront, with its windows that were more like notice boards, because they were so covered with posters. But there'd been one fresher than the rest. One with a photograph of a young couple. *This* couple.

The girl had the same flaming red hair.

Lydia.

It was as if a floodgate had opened, and memories came rushing back one after another. The mohawk guy from the bonfire, Jax, the one Jen was antagonising, had said she was his sister. Once again, my head instinctively turned to the pile of bones.

There was only one person's scent present in this cave, and looking at the photo, the skeleton was way too petite to belong to the guy. *Will*. I could see the poster in incredible detail now, like it was right in front of me. Lydia and Will. *Missing*.

Was it even possible for a body to decompose so completely into a skeleton so soon? They'd only been missing for a few weeks. I knew piranhas could strip a cow down to its bones in minutes, but there were no piranhas in a cave in Maine, for god's sake.

But I knew in my gut it was Lydia. Wolves, in a feeding frenzy, could completely rip flesh from bone like that. That creature could definitely do it. Unless there was another explanation. A less terrifying one. Well, less terrifying for *me*, at least. Had *Will* killed Lydia? Was this all just a crazy coincidence?

Even as I thought it, I knew I was clutching at straws. Trying to think up an alternative ending where my best friend and my boyfriend *didn't* end up a pile of bones, discarded and forgotten in a cave under the mountain. Because if Lydia's death was a crime of passion, and Braids had just been in the wrong place at the wrong time, then I had no reason to freak out. But there was no way that was true. Too many stars would have had to align for everything to have happened like that, purely by coincidence. The photos I'd seen showed a happy couple, their smiles bright and genuine. Sure, people could snap out of the blue, and Jax had said he suspected Will was on drugs... but as much as I might want it to, none of the evidence pointed to him being a murderer.

Ugh. I shook my head to clear the thought away. It wasn't important. Not right now. It was up to the cops to figure out the details when they received an anonymous tip later, leading them here, so they could finally take Lydia home. That was all I could do for her now.

There was nothing else to learn from the contents of the rucksacks, and I didn't have the time to waste packing everything meticulously back inside. Instead, I sent out a silent apology for the mess – even though it kinda made the place look better, all things considered – before turning towards the cave opening, and...

A piercing shriek cut through the air, so shrill it felt like someone had stabbed my ear drums. Instinctively, I fell backwards, trying to shield myself from the noise, but it echoed through the cavern, attacking me from all sides. But then, just as suddenly, it stopped, leaving behind an unsettling silence that squeezed my chest, as if the air itself was waiting for something to happen.

Then something *did*. Something far more terrifying than that screech.

A sharp, agonised cry. One I recognised all too well.

Henry.

41

No. Please, god, no.

My legs were already moving without me even thinking, but somehow, I knew I was heading in the right direction. Acting on pure instinct, I sprinted through the woods, nature's vibrant colours blurring as they hit my face. But I didn't care. The twinge of pain in my hind leg was still there, but I didn't let that slow me down either. I needed to reach him.

A surge of energy washed over me, making my senses more heightened. I was almost there. Fuelled by adrenaline, I effortlessly leaped over a dense thicket, my paws barely grazing the foliage, before crashing into the other side with a resounding thud. Then I looked up, and...

Nothing.

I was in an empty clearing.

How was that possible? I'd heard him. I'd heard Henry, hadn't I? But he was nowhere—

Like a brick to the face, the realisation washed over me, chased by a swirling sensation of nausea. *Shit*! The creature. The *wendigo*. It had imitated his voice again, and I fell for it. Walked right into its trap... *again.*

I clenched my teeth, holding back a growl, on high alert for any hint of the dragging sound that meant it was coming. But there was nothing, and yet my instincts kicked in, as if the wolf was trying to tell me something my brain couldn't grasp yet.

And then I heard it, and my blood turned to ice.

It came from behind me, but as I turned to confront it, it shifted, coming from another direction instead. And then suddenly, it was everywhere, coming from *every* direction. Trapping me.

Did that mean there was more than one? Did they live in packs? I had no clue. I couldn't remember anything else from that day with Ryan, no matter how hard I tried.

I gulped, my heart racing... and then I *smelled* it. The stench of death.

With a snarl, I spun around, my eyes scanning the dark treeline for any sign of the creature. For those horrifying red eyes. But there was still nothing.

It was taunting me. I wasn't sure how I knew that, but I did. It led me to this place, but now, wherever *it* was, it seemed content to observe me silently, as though I were a caged animal on display.

But I refused to just wait around and accept my death.

After taking a small step forward, I hesitated, listening, waiting for it to make its move. When it didn't happen, I drew in a deep breath and took another step, and then another, until...

A branch snapped. I whirled around, but there was still nothing there. Yet the sound just kept going, like dominos falling, one after the other, like the thing was moving, going in circles around the clearing. Around *me*.

I circled with it, my body tensing as my senses tried to pinpoint the source of the noise until, just as quickly, it vanished. And without it, that haunting, deathly silence settled in.

What the hell was going on?!

Was that it? Was it gone? Done playing its games – at least for now? Or was I just totally losing it? Probably both. Or neither. Either way, I couldn't just do *nothing*, so I cautiously kept moving. I wasn't sure where I was aiming for. I couldn't lead it back to the cabin. But maybe I could figure out how to get back to the cave. At least it couldn't sneak up on me in there. That would be my best chance. Probably my *only* chance.

My blood was no longer ice. It was like a tidal wave flowing through me, so I didn't hear it. Not until I felt hot air on the back of my neck. And, by then, it was already too late.

Claw-like fingers wrapped around my body, their grip squeezing the breath from my lungs... right before hurling me across the clearing.

If there was any breath left in my body, it abandoned me the second I hit the cluster of trees. But I was alive. *For now.*

My vision was blurry, and I blinked to clear it while swallowing back the fresh wave of bile that rushed up my throat. I wasn't sure if that was from the impact or the sight of what stood before me. Whichever it was, it didn't really matter. I only wished the impact would have knocked me out. Then I wouldn't have to look.

Because there it was. Whatever you wanted to call it: creature, windikouk, wendigo... it was all the same. It was death. *My* death. I knew that now, even as I tried desperately to scramble out of the way.

It was the first time I'd seen it up close, but I knew, if I somehow survived the night, that the image would stay etched in my memory forever.

Those red eyes bore into me, and I couldn't tear my gaze away. They had me hypnotised as it moved, agonisingly and tantalisingly slowly, towards me. A whimper escaped my lips. Because I didn't stand a chance. Not at all. The thing was huge. It was at least twice the size of Henry, with fangs that glinted like daggers. Massive antlers, covered in dried blood and with tattered pieces of leather clinging to their ends, protruded from the top of its head. Or that's what I thought at first. As it came closer though, I realised how wrong I was. It wasn't leather. It was hunks of *flesh,* and I had to take panting breaths to keep down the vomit threatening to spill out of my mouth at the sight.

Its long, bony arms scraped across the ground, and that dragging sound I'd heard before made me cringe as it came closer. I snapped and snarled at it, trying to ward it off, but it didn't care. Didn't even seem to notice. It just kept coming, and I forced myself to my feet, ignoring the pain that shot through me as I straightened. Then, right before it lunged, I darted to the side. It stumbled, emitting a low, angry grunt, but quickly regained its footing. Still, it planted a seed of an idea in my mind, and I could feel a surge of hope building up inside me.

It was enormous, no doubt about that. I was a mouse, and it was a hawk. It could rip me to shreds... but only if it got a hold of me. Being small had its perks. It made me quick on my feet. Every time I beat Henry during our runs back home, he would complain about it. He said it wasn't fair, that I beat him because I could dodge obstacles more easily, being so damn small.

He was right. And maybe it wouldn't work here, but it was at least worth a shot.

I planted my claws into the ground as the beast turned to face me again, because I didn't want to bolt right then and there. I knew I couldn't outrun it, no matter how fast I was. Wendigos were hunters. There's no escaping them if they're dead set on catching you. But maybe...

The creature growled again, irritated by my game, but it didn't matter. If I could just tire it out by playing long enough, I could bring it down. There was no other choice.

It made to lunge again, and I held my breath, waiting until the very last second... then I feinted left, spinning away from it, the ghost of a smile on my face.

And that's when I saw him, standing on the edge of the clearing, staring at me with wide, unblinking eyes.

Carter.

Oh my god. Carter!

What was he doing here? He was supposed to be heading to town already. Far, far away from this mess. Yet here he was. But I didn't have time to question it, because at a movement from the corner of my eye, I swivelled... just in time to see Henry launch himself at the wendigo.

It saw him, but it seemed too bewildered to act, and the next thing I knew, Henry was on top of it. It quickly recovered, though, pulling back its lips to reveal a row of jagged, yellowed teeth that snapped at him. And all I could think about was how I needed to do something. To shift its focus from Henry to *me*. Give him the chance to get the hell away from here and take Carter with him.

A deep growl rumbled in the back of my throat. It started as a warning, but then turned into a desperate howl when the creature didn't react. That got its attention. The creature's gigantic head jerked, and it stopped for a second, like it couldn't quite figure out the sound. Then, with deliberate slowness, it turned its massive body towards me, its eyes emitting an intense red glow that stopped my heart.

Despite Henry's relentless assault, the creature continued to inch closer to me, its shuffling movements sending a shudder through my body.

I could hardly see Henry now. Just his hands flying up and down behind the creature's head. But it was a waste of time. He had to know that. It didn't want him. It wanted *me*. And I wished I was in my human form so I could tell him, scream at him, to do the one thing I knew he wouldn't ever do, no matter how much I begged. He had to leave me behind. To save himself. He had to let me *go*.

My mouth opened; a howl ready to burst from my throat. He'd know what it meant, and—

A blur of grey shot past me, diverting my attention.

Everything happened so quickly after that. I heard a clunk, and it took me a moment to grasp that it was a rock hitting the wendigo's head. As I turned, I saw Carter, his eyes wide with disbelief, his fist frozen in mid-air, and I realised *he* had thrown it. To distract it. But it just made it focus on him instead.

Fear churned in my stomach as I saw its lips curl again, those rancid yellowed teeth coming into view as its narrowed eyes fixated on Carter. As it swerved towards him, it bucked and threw Henry off its back, letting out an ear-piercing screech that sent chills down my spine. Carter backed up fast, but he wasn't looking, so he didn't see the root sticking up from the ground behind him. I tried to call out a warning, but all that came out was a whine, and I cursed myself as he stumbled over the root, falling and rolling backwards.

I didn't even stop to think about it. I just launched myself towards him, desperate to protect him. To put myself between him and the beast. But he yelped and scrambled away, and I froze, pain stabbing in my stomach as I took in the terror on his face. Terror... directed at *me*.

But then it hit me. I wasn't *me*. Not to him. He looked at me, and he didn't see his girlfriend, because *she* was still trapped in the cave where he'd left her. All he saw was a wolf. A wolf that was advancing on him, teeth bared in a snarl.

Fuck!

I stumbled back, my paws tripping over each other, while my mind raced to determine the perfect distance between us – enough to show surrender, yet close enough to protect him if needed. From the other side of the clearing, Henry hurled another rock that whizzed dangerously close to my head. He dropped to grab another one and took aim again, nailing the wendigo right between its horns. The roar that came next was more irritated than angry. It did the job, though, taking its attention away from Carter once again.

The creature slowly made its way back towards Henry, its movements more sluggish than before. It was confused. All it's other victims... they'd been alone. That couldn't be a coincidence. It must have stalked them, striking only when they were by themselves. Alone and defenceless. It had no clue what to do with the three of us.

We could use that, couldn't we? Coordinate something? I could pounce right now. A sneak attack while its back was turned. Because it didn't know which of us it wanted to taste more.

As if reading my mind, it stopped in its tracks, and I watched as it raised its head, nostrils flaring, drops of saliva dripping from its open mouth.

I'd said it, hadn't I? It was a hunter. A hunter that had already selected its target: me. The ambush had momentarily diverted its attention, but Carter and Henry were only distractions. I looked into its eyes now, and I saw a determination that nothing would hinder.

My blood ran cold. I didn't want to die. Didn't consider myself brave, heroic, or anything along those lines. In fact, I was absolutely terrified, but it gave me some relief to know that Carter and Henry might escape while it came for me. If I had to, I'd gladly sacrifice myself to save them. No hesitation. They were all that mattered to me. My two guys. My favourite people in the world. If that was the only way, then—

I was so caught up in my thoughts that I didn't notice the whir of movement behind the creature until it was too late. At first, I assumed it was Henry and readied a bark of anger, thinking he was still trying to draw its focus his way, but my heart dropped into my stomach when I realised who it actually was.

Carter was right behind it now. He'd snuck up so silently that I hadn't seen him even get up off the floor, let alone grab hold of the massive stick he now held in his hand. He thrust the weapon at the creature, only about half of the jabs connecting as he flailed wildly. But with every stab, I heard the snap of splinters breaking off, and smelt the distinct scent of fresh blood. It didn't stop his attempt, despite his hisses of pain confirming that the rough bark was cutting into his palms. Once again, the creature didn't seem to care. Or so I thought, until it spun around, emitting a low growl as its eyes burned with rage, fixating on Carter once more.

I couldn't explain it, but the atmosphere suddenly turned thick and suffocating. It hummed with an electric charge, a palpable tension that lingered in the air, like the calm before a storm.

That's when everything became clear.

Until now, the wendigo hadn't been trying to kill us. No, it'd been content playing with us, feasting on our terror as if it were an all-you-could-eat buffet. Sure, the guys fighting back had provoked it, but it wasn't actually *angry*. Just irritated. But now it seemed like something had suddenly switched. It wasn't playing anymore.

Once again, Ryan's voice echoed in my head, narrating as an image of Lydia's remains materialised - a stack of bones inside the cave.

'They are the epitome of evil. Cannibalistic creatures, you see.'

Will hadn't killed her. He was totally innocent. It was this *thing*. The wendigo. It had taken her life, ripping every shred of flesh from her body. And Braids... oh god, it killed her too. Would've devoured her as well... until Ansel and Jamie came tearing through the forest. Disturbing its hunting grounds.

Now, it wasn't just hungry – it was angry. No, *furious*. And I finally had to accept the truth I'd been desperately avoiding: there was a good chance we wouldn't all make it out alive.

It raced forward, almost as if it knew what I was thinking, leaving me no time to catch my breath. I just acted, rage lighting a fire in me – rage for what it'd done to Lydia and Braids. For Colton, Jamie, and Will. But mostly for what it planned to do to us. To Carter and Henry. They were all that really mattered to me.

With a growl, I launched myself at Carter again. I didn't give a damn if I scared him. He'd get over it. Better to be scared than dead. As my weight pressed him down, I glanced upward and my eyes instantly focused on the creatures. Carter's heart thumped beneath me, its steady and deafening rhythm echoing in my ears, but I didn't back off. I couldn't. My body was the only barrier between him and those razor-sharp fangs, and I refused to budge. Not even an inch. Not with that thing bearing down on us.

"MADISON!"

Henry's voice pierced through the clearing, conveying a terror that was unfamiliar coming from him. There was also a plea in the way he said it, and in it, I heard everything he *couldn't* say. Understood, just from the way he said my name, what he wanted me to do. Was *begging* me to do.

He wanted me to abandon Carter.

Henry might come across as cold, heartless, and uncaring, but he wasn't. Not deep down. If he really believed we could save Carter, that we could all get out of this alive, then he wouldn't ask me to give up. *He* wouldn't give up. He'd fight like hell to save him, not just for me, but because it's the right thing to do. Which meant he thought it was impossible. That if I stayed, I'd only die alongside him, because I wouldn't be able to save him.

In my gut, I knew he was right. I didn't stand a chance. But what he didn't - *couldn't* – understand, was that I *didn't care.* If Carter died, or if either of them did, it wouldn't matter if I survived in this forest tonight. I might still breathe and exist, but that's all it would be – existence. I'd rather die, ripped apart, than live without them.

The thought twisted in my stomach, causing nausea to rise in my throat again, and I clenched my eyes tightly shut, hoping to block out the pain in my chest. But only for a second. It was long enough, though, and I didn't see him moving. Not until it was already too late. But then there he was, leaping at the creature, his human form lacking the grace and agility of a wolf, but hitting the mark anyway. The creature's head turned, and a deafening roar shook the ground beneath us. Its eyes held a mix of curiosity and caution, as if it couldn't comprehend what had happened, and I held my breath, until...

It happened so fast that I didn't have time to process the details, but suddenly, Henry's feet were dangling in mid-air. For a second, I just stared, my exhausted, petrified, *broken* mind desperately trying to figure out how the hell he was *flying*... but then my brain caught up with reality, and my heart sank as it hit me.

He wasn't flying; that was impossible. But I wished he was. I wished he had secrets he'd never shared, not even with me. Anything would be better than this.

The creature had him firmly gripped in its claws, and it was tossing him around like a rag doll, while I stood frozen, unable to do anything but watch as it raised its massive arm... and launched him into the sky.

Time seemed to bend, slowing down and speeding up at the same time, while I helplessly watched Henry's body being flung across the clearing before crashing into a tree. There was a sickening crunch and then, almost in slow motion, his body slid down the trunk and landed in a heap at the bottom. Motionless.

I couldn't hold it in any longer. My anguished cry echoed through the air as I dug my claws into the earth, preparing to pounce towards him. To do something, *anything,* to help him. But then I heard something that paralysed me. A whisper so quiet I wasn't even sure I hadn't just imagined it.

"M-Madison?"

For a painful moment, I couldn't muster the courage to meet his gaze. But he deserved better than that, so I had to force myself, feeling my throat tighten up with a lump that wouldn't go away even when I tried to swallow. Carter's eyes were wide, bloodshot. *Terrified*. Despite my weight pressing down on him, he fought back and strained to lift himself up, propping himself up on his elbows, until he could see me clearly. Until he could lock eyes with me.

For eighteen months, he'd gazed into these eyes, telling me how beautiful they were before he kissed me. Staring into them as he listened to me talking, like there was nothing more important in the entire world than whatever I had to say. Some days, they were the first thing he saw when he woke up in the morning. He knew them. He knew they were mine.

This was the moment.

I saw it – right when the light bulb turned on in his head. The second his world changed. I hadn't realised I'd loosened my grip, but his mouth fell open, and then he scrambled backwards again, his face draining of all colour. And he might as well have taken a knife and plunged it deep into my heart.

He was scared of me. Disgusted, even. He looked at me like he didn't have a clue who I was.

He sprang to his feet, and my heart was practically in my mouth as I noticed the rock clutched tightly in his fist. I didn't know what to do, so I backed up. I knew it put me closer to the wendigo, and I could smell its foul stench wafting through the air, making me want to gag. But it wasn't attacking. *Why* wasn't it attacking? Was it just enjoying watching my heart crumble? It didn't matter. What mattered was that, for now, it was still, and now I had to show Carter I wasn't a threat. Not to him. I would *never* hurt him. It was *me. Madison. His Madison*!

Another piercing screech suddenly broke the silence, making my hackles rise. Was it that creature, or was it me? I honestly couldn't tell. Nothing made sense. Carter's lips moved, but his words seemed to dissolve into thin air. But while I couldn't hear him, I could *see* him. Could see the way his arm raised, that rock still tightly clutched in his fist. I recoiled, bracing myself for the blow... only to find him pointing his finger at something behind me.

I didn't have time to react. Something slammed into my back, making me stagger forward and gasp for air, before being abruptly yanked back. Then, suddenly, I wasn't on the ground anymore. I closed my eyes tightly, attempting to shut out the world, but my nose remained exposed, and a foul blast of decay and heat grazed my face as the wendigo's clutches tightened around me.

Knowing you're about to die is a strange thing. I expected I would lose my mind. Scream and cry and beg for mercy. Instead, a calmness embraced me that felt like being wrapped in a cosy blanket on a snowy night. My senses went numb, kinda like what I imagined it would be like to be drunk. I'd never been drunk before. Now I never would be.

No!

At that moment, a fierce determination surged through me. There were so many things I hadn't experienced, and I couldn't change that. But if I was gonna die here, trapped in its bloody claws and suffocating in its disgusting smell, then I wouldn't let that creature's disgusting face be my final memory on this planet. I wouldn't give it that kind of power.

Keeping my eyes tightly closed, I searched through the memory box in my head, recalling moments that brought a bittersweet smile to my lips. I saw the vibrant colours of the Easter egg hunts the guys used to organise for Henry and me on the sprawling grounds of Vineyard Manor. I heard the excitement in Ryan's voice when I finally agreed to *consider* studying history at UMaine. I felt the exhilaration of our runs through the woods, side by side with Henry. Tender moments shared with Carter. Our first time together, and every intimate encounter that followed. That afternoon, the three of us huddled together on the sofa, the piercing sound of a crack ringing out through the cabin...

Wait. *What?*

Startled out of my daydreams, my eyes flew open automatically, but I immediately clenched them shut again, so tightly that I could almost imagine my eye sockets flattening. I wanted to go back to that peaceful place. Carter's arms wrapped around me, my fingers tangled in his hair, our lips locking...

A searing hot pain burned through me as something grazed my leg.

"*FUCK!*"

A voice rang out. It sounded like Henry, but not quite.

The weight of realisation crashed over me, jolting my eyes open once again. But this time, I didn't fight it.

It had sounded almost like a gunshot, but there was no way that could be true. Carter wasn't carrying a gun. I doubted he even knew how to hold one properly. And Henry... Henry was knocked out. Just knocked out. I couldn't believe anything else.

My eyes darted around, my ears on high alert as I tried to find where the noise had come from. But all I could see was the creature's face, and all I could hear was its heavy breathing that felt like it was scorching my skin. Yet, the noise - unmistakably a gunshot - had triggered a reaction inside me. Help was here. I didn't know who, or why, or even *how,* but I didn't care. I bucked and snapped and snarled at the creature, scratching at its pallid skin. Yet wherever my claws caught flesh, no blood oozed, and it continued to slash its jaws at me until...

Another crack. And then I was falling, the ground rushing up to meet me as the creature's arm went limp. Not before our eyes met once more, though, and in that split second, time stood still.

Because I was no longer looking at those deadly crimson eyes, so full of evil. They were now a striking shade of green, like lush fields on a sunny day. And my breath caught in my throat until another shot went off. A piercing, agonised screech followed, assaulting my eardrums with its sharpness. And then I really was free falling, the world spinning around me in a chaotic blur. I heard someone yelling my name, that not-quite-Henry voice again. And maybe Carter's as well. Or was I imagining that?

My body collided with the ground, a searing pain racing through me that left me once again struggling to catch my breath.

And then everything went black.

42

Every inch of my body ached, and I couldn't see. That was my first thought.

The second was that I was dying. Or maybe I was already dead. But then a voice cut through the fog, shouting my name, and soon a face materialised in front of me. It kinda looked like Henry, but not exactly. Then Carter was there, too, his face pale and ashen like a ghost. Without warning, a piercing scream escaped my throat, and tears streamed down my face, scalding my cheeks.

I'd failed. I'd failed them both.

Then the world faded to black again.

When I finally came to, my head throbbed, and my mouth felt as dry as sandpaper. Still, I jolted upright and struggled to pry open my heavy eyelids, as if sleep had glued them shut.

In that hazy state between sleep and wakefulness, a single thought consumed my mind, and a name escaped my mouth. "CARTER!"

"Shh... hey cub. Cub, calm down. He's fine. Henry's fine. You're all fine, okay? Just take a breath."

A gasp caught in my throat, and the sound that followed was more of a strained cry than a word. "Dad?"

Finally, my eyes popped open, but I was still half asleep, so I had to blink a bunch to see clearly. As my vision returned to normal, my eyes locked with a pair of warm, chocolate brown ones, mirroring my own, except for the delicate wrinkles that graced them. He smiled a gentle smile, and for the first time in a week, I felt truly safe. Before I knew it, tears were streaming down my face, my body convulsing with uncontrollable sobs.

"Dad!" My voice trembled over the word. He leaned over and pulled me in, his hand softly caressing the back of my head, like when I was a child and used to climb into his bed after a bad dream.

"Hey, shh. It's okay, cub. I'm here. Everything's going to be okay."

I wasn't sure how long we stayed like that. The crying felt like it would never stop, and when it finally did, I couldn't catch my breath, my chest hurting. Even when I pulled away, Dad kept hold of my hand, instructing me to take deep breaths and, eventually, it returned to a normal rhythm.

I glanced around the room, soaking in the familiar sights and sounds. Sunlight filtered through the small, open window, casting a soft golden glow on everything, while the air carried a delicate aroma of pine, the distant sound of birdsong, and the faint murmur of nearby voices.

I was in the cabin. In mine and Carter's bedroom. But there was no sign of Carter, and a sudden rush of panic hit me like a punch in the gut. Immediately, my mouth flew open, but it was as if Dad saw it coming. He could see it all in my face, and he knew my mind was already going crazy.

His hand extended towards me, gently brushing away the tear that had settled on my cheek, as he reassured me, "Carter is fine. He was here. He wouldn't budge until he knew for sure that you were alright. But..." He shook his head and sighed. "It's been a shock, Maddie. For everyone, but especially him. I finally convinced him to go home, though, so Jackson took him this morning. I know you guys have a lot to catch up on, but for now, I need you to just focus on getting better, okay?"

I just nodded. It was all I could manage, because a wave of relief washed over me that brought tears to my eyes once more. But the feeling was short-lived, because a thought struck me, and I quickly threw off the covers, desperate to get out of bed.

Before I had a chance to stand up, my dad intercepted and pushed me back down.

"No, Dad, you don't understand!" I warned, trying to fight against him, but it was useless. He was way stronger than me. "It's a wendigo, Dad. There's a wendigo out there. And it... it's—"

"Dead."

His calm, hushed tone didn't lessen the impact of his words, which sliced through my frantic shouts. I froze, my body going slack in his arms once more. "What?"

Dad sighed, settling back down on the edge of the mattress. "I didn't want to have this conversation until you were feeling better. But I guess that's on me for forgetting who I was dealing with." He said sternly, but a smile played at the corner of his mouth. "I suppose you won't go back to sleep until you hear the entire story, huh?"

"No." I said, a hint of doubt seeping into my voice.

It wasn't that I didn't trust what he was saying – my dad would never lie to me, even if it was a matter of life and death. If Carter and

Henry weren't okay, he wouldn't have said so. Even so, the image of the wendigo lingered in my mind, its twisted form haunting my thoughts, making it difficult to imagine how they *could* be okay. How did we all make it out alive? How was Dad even here?

He rolled his eyes up to the ceiling. "Y'know, some days it's annoying how alike we are, cub. Stubborn as hell."

He sighed again, and then he told me everything.

They knew about the wendigo. Or they had some idea about it, at least. But no one would have ever guessed what it really was. Ray heard about a couple of teenagers disappearing in the north from one of the pack living nearby – one of the former rogues who had decided they wanted to settle down somewhere. The disappearances wouldn't have been a big deal, but they all vanished from the same spot, around the time we heard about a rogue passing through our territory. That made Ray suspicious. Since he was the closest, he asked Sean to check it out.

"The cops searched the mountain with cadaver dogs but didn't find anything, but Brandon and Sean did. Way deep under Mount Ciney. Those passages have been closed for years 'cause someone got trapped and nearly died. There's no way any human could've made it there. It was completely by chance, too, because there wasn't even a scent. It was like these kids had gone out one day and then just... poof." Dad made a motion with his hands, as if a cloud was vanishing into thin air.

"Anyway, unless he used some sort of cloaking spell, it couldn't be that rogue. And I can't imagine any witches coming to the aid of a werewolf like that. Plus, he popped up in Florida a few days later. But there was just... nothing at all, Maddie. You haven't met Brandon, but he's one of our best trackers. If there was even a smidge of a hint, he would've found it. So me and Ray, we started digging through the archives for any clues. He never finished it, but Ryan's book—"

"Liber Monstrorum." I interrupted him, blushing when Dad shot me a quizzical look. "That's what he called it. It was the name of this old book he was studying, and that's where he got the idea to keep the records from. He showed it to me once. That's how I figured it out. But I couldn't remember anything else, Dad. Anything helpful."

Dad's face softened as he patted the back of my hand. "It's not your fault. Not even a little bit. It's mine, for letting you come here. But we never could've imagined... I mean... a wendigo? They're just a myth. And Mount Ciney is at least two hours from here on the highway. You should've been safe."

He inhaled sharply, his face turning crimson as his hands clenched into tight fists, and I could hear the rapid thumping of his heartbeat. His gaze became distant, and I knew, for that moment, he wasn't here anymore. He had stumbled into the shadowy abyss of his thoughts, the same place I had fought to avoid throughout that night, because imagining Henry's lifeless body would have destroyed me. Dad was picturing that now, I could tell. *My* lifeless body.

After a moment of silence, he released his clenched fists and took a deep breath.

"Dan really thought he was doing you a favour, you know. Letting you and Carter look after this place. He's devastated. I mean, if something happened to you, Madison... Shit, you're all I got. My little girl."

His hands were trembling so hard that the bed started shaking, so I reached out and gave him a reassuring squeeze. It was all I could think to do to pull him back, to let him know I was okay.

As much as I could be, considering everything. Dad pulled himself together, swallowing hard and wiping his teary eyes with his shirt sleeve before going on.

"When you guys didn't check in yesterday, I dunno... guess I just got a bad feeling. Call it fatherly intuition. I checked the place online, and that's when I found out about those two kids. They vanished right *here*. In Chibouwood. I got Sean on the phone, and he swore he knew nothing about it. Said he hadn't been into town in weeks, hadn't seen anything weird before he left. Must be a coincidence, he'd said. But I just knew something wasn't right. Felt it in my gut. I wasn't gonna just sit around and hope for the best, so Dan and I headed up here early last night. I guess Ray told Sean to get his ass back as well, because he beat us to it. Just in the nick of time, thank goodness."

The gunshot. It wasn't from Carter. It was Sean. But how?

It wasn't until Dad replied I realised I had been talking aloud.

"Ran into this young fella when he got back. Someone called Ansel?" He offered, waiting to see if I recognised the name. I inhaled sharply, nodding. "He told Sean you were trapped after a cave collapsed, and that Carter had gone after Henry after telling *him* to find help. Sean didn't hang around. Grabbed his gun and then chased after you all."

"I told him to go for help." My voice was barely above a whisper, but I wasn't really speaking to Dad anymore. "I didn't want him anywhere near it. Why? Why would Carter risk himself like that?"

"You'd have to ask him that, cub. But I think we both have a pretty good idea why, don't we?"

I just brushed that off, not wanting to dwell on what was being implied. What it meant for the three of us. Instead, I asked, "Wait, you said the wendigo was dead? How? I thought—"

"Oh, you know, that old cliché." He smirked mischievously as he dug into his pocket, and when he withdrew his hand again, something silver glinted between his thumb and forefinger. He turned it over, and the sunlight danced off its surface, making me squint.

"Silver. Like Jen said." I whispered softly.

"Who?"

I waved off the question. "It doesn't matter. Why did Sean have silver bullets, anyway? Aren't they our kryptonite?"

"Glad to see you haven't lost your sense of humour." Dad's warm and infectious chuckle elicited my first smile since waking up. "Sean's a werewolf, living all by himself in the woods, miles away from the rest of the pack. I guess he's not taking any chances." He glanced at the door and then lowered his voice to a conspiratorial whisper, leaning closer to me. "And between you and me, he's kinda weird."

I snorted a laugh, but it was half-hearted, because now that I was fully awake, I remembered something else. The image of those red eyes shifting to a vivid green flashed through my memory. Right after the gunshots.

Realisation hit, and I gasped. "Dad! Oh my god. The wendigo. It was… it was…"

Dad patted my knee, giving it a gentle squeeze. "Yes. Dan saw the pictures in town. It was that young man. Will. He… he turned back when…" Dad trailed off, his voice breaking slightly.

"I think… I think Will might have been Ansel's brother." I whispered.

Dad cleared his throat. "Maybe. We'll never know, cub, because your friend didn't stick around. Can't say I blame him though." He shook his head and then let out a long breath. "Alright, that's it for questions today. I've gotta go help Dan and Sean with the clean-up. Recover that poor girl's body. When you're feeling up to it, we'll go home, but right now, you should rest, so—"

Someone cleared their throat outside the bedroom door, cutting him off, and I turned my head towards the noise. Dad's lips were pressed together as I glanced at him, trying to be serious, but I caught a glimpse of a smile. Then he let out a tired sigh and mumbled to himself as he reluctantly got up, before saying, firmly, "Five minutes, alright?"

That was all Henry needed. The bedroom door creaked as it swung open to reveal him standing in the hall. Bruised and battered, yet alive and kicking. In a split second, he morphed into a blur of motion, hurtling across the room towards me. When he dropped down beside me, I flung my arms around him, and as Dad slipped quietly from the room, tears fell once more, wetting his chest. But for once, he didn't complain, and we clung to each other like that until I dozed off again.

43

"Can I take a break yet?"

I peeked over the book I was holding, catching sight of Henry sitting at my bedroom desk, his textbooks haphazardly strewn about.

A few days had passed since we got home from Chibouwood, and Henry had been spending a lot of time at our place ever since. He kept saying it was impossible to study at home, what with a toddler in the house, but I knew better. He was here whenever Dad wasn't, and stayed just long enough after Dad got home to not make it obvious that they didn't want to leave me alone. That would irritate me, if not for the fact I really didn't *want* to be on my own.

Dan had stayed behind to help Sean search for any trace of Colton, but so far, they had found nothing. With the information I gave them, they found the rucksacks in the cave before we left, and now Ray had them locked up somewhere at headquarters. If there were any clues in that notebook that I missed, my dad and Ray would find them.

Jamie turned up the next day, alive but dehydrated, disoriented, and with a nasty infected gash on his arm. He couldn't even remember his own name, let alone how he got separated from

Ansel. But I had a good idea. The wendigo could tell he was desperate to find Colton, so it imitated his voice to lure him even deeper into the forest, just like it did to me. If Sean hadn't taken it down, I had no doubt that Jamie would've been its next prey.

I wasn't completely certain, but I had a feeling that was why it targeted me. It fed off negative emotions, and I had an abundance to provide. Mostly guilt – for Carter and everything I didn't tell him, and for Henry, for hurting him. For Ryan. But I also had this lingering sadness that was always with me, knowing those secrets would eventually tear Carter and me apart. My soul must have been a siren call to that thing.

Except for a few texts, I hadn't heard from Carter since that night.

Part of me wanted to get in the car and just drive to his place. Force him to confront it, to talk to me. But that wouldn't be fair, and I knew I had to give him some time. He knew everything now. He knew I was a werewolf. After all the effort I put into hiding the secret from him, to keep him safe, he finally found out what I was, and the world didn't end.

It was different, though.

I sighed as I met Henry's eye. "That depends. What's the square root of sixty-four?"

"I'm not studying math."

"Wrong answer. Keep studying."

He sighed while I went back to reading, but then he came and sat on the end of my bed. "Mads, we need to talk."

I gulped, but kept my head buried in the book. "What about?" I asked casually, even though I knew he wouldn't buy it. Right on cue, he grabbed the book from my hands.

"I spoke to Johnson. He's doing okay with... y'know. And I made it clear he can't tell *anyone*. He gets it." All I could do was nod, and Henry let out another sigh as the room grew quiet for a minute. Then he said, "You were right, y'know. I didn't wanna admit it, cause... *fuck*. It's embarrassing. But Cali... it's harder than I thought."

Before I could control myself, my eyes widened in surprise. Henry, admitting he was *struggling?* That I was *right?!* It was unheard of.

He noticed my surprise and chuckled. "Yes, alright? It's tough. But it's not just about work or basketball. I just... I really miss home. I miss *you*. I'm all alone down there. Nobody to save my ass."

I mustered a half-hearted smile in response. He didn't need me. He was just trying to make me feel better, because once again, my stupid decisions nearly got us killed. If only I had called the cops when we found Ansel, Colton, and Jamie in the cabin, maybe things wouldn't have gone down the way they did.

"I just get you into trouble. You're better off far, far away from me."

"I was the one who took off into the forest, Madison. You tried to stop me. I just... I saw red, and I was an asshole, and you got hurt. Because of *me*. So I... *fuck*. I'm just really sorry about that."

A wave of warmth spread across my cheeks. "I guess we're even then." I mumbled. But we weren't. We would never be even. I hadn't saved Henry at all. He could have run when the wendigo came for Carter and me. He didn't. He saved me. *Again*.

"Even? Oh, c'mon, Mads. I've been a jerk, I know that, but... jeez. I've never kept score. And I never will. Not between us."

Henry had told me about how he followed Ansel and Jamie's trail until it split. That's probably where the two guys separated, just like Ansel said. Thinking they had divided to loop back, he tried to get back to me first, but he found Braids instead. What remained of her, anyway. Not far from there, my trail vanished without a trace. More tricks from the wendigo, I figured. At some point, he ran into Carter, who was searching for *him*, and that's when they heard the commotion between me and that thing. With no time to get Carter to safety and then come back for me, he'd told him to stay put. Carter didn't.

'He wanted to protect you,' Henry had said, with no hint of his usual scorn.

No one had seen or heard from Ansel since that night. I wasn't sure if he knew about his brother, about what he was, but I didn't think so. I got the sense he really was just out there following his trail. Trying to track him down. Considering everything that happened, it's no surprise he suspected us of being behind his disappearance.

Honestly, I wasn't sure if it was better or worse that he didn't know Will was dead. But I hoped he would be okay. I really hoped so.

My mind drifted back to Carter then, and I felt a pang in my chest. We had never gone this length of time without seeing each other before. Until now, the weekend he spent checking out colleges in New York with his parents was the longest. Just like Ansel, I was starting to think I'd never see him again. That he was just going to cut and run. Disappear from my life without another word.

Then, as if he knew I was thinking about him, my phone buzzed with a text message.

> *Meet me at our place.*

I glanced at Henry again, and he rolled his eyes, but I saw the smirk behind it as he said, "Go."

He was already there when I arrived, leaning against the hood of his truck, arms over his chest and legs crossed at the ankles. His unruly curls, as defiant as always, poked out from beneath the vibrant orange beanie, and I took a moment, before he realised I was there, to just watch him. To drink him in.

He looked amazing... and it just made the knot in my stomach tighten.

"Thank you for meeting me." I said, stepping out of the car and making my way towards him across the otherwise empty parking lot.

He turned to face me, his lips curling into a smile that didn't quite reach his eyes. "Sorry it took me so long. I just..." He trailed off, and I nodded. He didn't have to say more. I understood.

We walked in silence, our arms naturally falling by our sides as we did. I ached to take hold of his hand, to feel his fingers weave with mine. But I didn't. Neither did he.

When we reached the footpath that meandered beside the river, we finally stopped, turning to meet each other's gaze. It was Carter who spoke first.

"A lot of things make sense now. Henry helped me fill in some blanks. Y'know... *after.*"

I bit my lip, suddenly remembering what he'd said in the forest that night: '*you sense something?*' Not hear or see. But *sense*.

"When did you figure it out?"

Carter let out a breath. "I didn't. Not really. Not until... well, you know. But there was something somewhere, I guess. Something that didn't add up. I just never would've thought..."

"Carter, I'm so sorry. For everything. For putting you in danger like that. I get you must hate me, but trust me, I hate myself more. I just... I thought I could keep you safe." My words came out in a rush, and when I was done, he just opened his arms and enveloped me in a hug. Tears streamed down my cheeks as I buried my face in his chest, feeling his fingers brush gently through my hair.

"You think I could hate you? Nah. Never, Stone." As my sobs faded away, he chuckled, but there was a hollowness to the sound. It felt forced. But then he added, "None of what happened was your fault, Madison."

I straightened up, brushing away the tears and sniffles with my sleeve, the fabric rough against my skin, until I finally mustered the strength to meet his gaze. "It was. Of course it was. You wouldn't have been there if it wasn't for me. You wanted to go to Florida. I should've just said yes."

"I totally understand why you didn't. Why you couldn't."

Another sob escaped me, followed by an uncontrollable hiccup. "I should have told you. I *wish* I'd..."

I trailed off as another one of those maddening, gentle smiles crossed his lips. "I wouldn't have believed you, even if you had."

I swallowed, the lump in my throat refusing to go away, even as I dared ask, "So you're not mad at me?"

My heart raced as I held my breath, my eyes locked on my feet, waiting anxiously for the answer. A surge of air escaped from my chest the instant he replied, momentarily stealing my breath.

"No. I'm not mad. How could I be? You warned me. Right from the start. You told me you had secrets. I accepted that."

My head shot up, not daring to actually believe my own ears. Still, when his deep, hazel eyes locked with mine, I felt a flicker of hope. Maybe, just maybe, we could get past this. He knew everything now, and he didn't hate me. He wasn't angry or frightened. Not running away. Maybe we could—

Carter's cough stopped my train of thought.

"But..."

With a single word, everything changed. Only three letters. And suddenly, darkness engulfed my world.

"You can't even imagine how tough this is for me. But I... I need to say it, so please, just let me, okay?" He paused, waiting for an answer, but no words would come. Finally, I mustered a small, barely noticeable nod, but it satisfied him. "Shit, Mads. I thought I knew you inside and out. But... fuck. You're a freakin' werewolf. How am I supposed to react to that?"

Stepping back, I could feel the scorching heat of shame spreading through my body, making my cheeks burn. I'd never felt that before. I'd always been proud of what I was. But in that moment, I wished I could just let it all go. All I wanted was to be human, be Maddie, and belong to him. But it was impossible. That wasn't who I was.

"You think I'm a monster."

At my words, his eyes bulged, almost popping from their sockets. "What? No! Mads, I could *never* think that. It's just... how do I even say this? *Shit!*" He cursed and snatched off his beanie, desperately running his hands through his hair. "It's just... shit, Mads. You've got this whole other side to you I never even knew about. This entire *world*. A few days ago, werewolves were just something on TV. Now my girlfriend is one? And I might be able to get over that, if it weren't for..."

When he hesitated, I urged him on, asking, "For what?"

His shoulders slumped, and he turned to face the lake, his elbows resting on the metal barriers that bordered the embankment. "You know, with all the secrets and everything... I thought you were gonna tell me you were hooking up with Henry."

It felt as if he had slapped me across the face. "Carter, I would *never*—"

"I know! Or I know that *now*. Your dad explained about it, about that *thing*. The... the wendigo. He said they have powers. That they can manipulate people, make them see things that aren't there. Mess with their emotions and stuff." He paused for breath. "You know I trust you, Mads. I never lied about that. But I think there's always been some jealousy. I always knew there was a connection between you two. Something I could never be a part of. I didn't expect *this* but—"

"I don't understand." I cut in. "If that's what you thought, if you really thought me and Henry were..." I trailed off, unable to bring myself to say the words out loud. To make them tangible. "Why did you go after him? I told you to leave. You weren't supposed to be there!"

"C'mon, Mads. I heard him yell. Or I thought I did. Turns out that wasn't real either. But I couldn't just bail. I mean, I thought I'd be helping him escape a bear or something, not *that.*" He shuddered. "What kind of person would I be if I knew he was in trouble, and I just walked away? You love him, Madison. I'm not blind. And I... Look, I know Barton doesn't like me very much, but I still care about him."

There was a momentary pause, where my thoughts seemed to vanish, leaving me speechless. But then I said, "You're right. I do love Henry." He flinched at my words, though he tried to hide it.

"He's my best friend. No matter what, he'll always be my best friend. My pack mate. That's a strong bond. But that's *all* it is. Whatever else, whatever the wendigo made you feel... it's not real. I swear to you!"

"I want to believe you. I do. But isn't that the whole point? I have no clue what's real and what's not anymore. And I can't help but feel you just didn't trust me enough. I know it's selfish and I hate myself for it, but it really hurts, Mads. It hurts like hell to feel like that."

The pain was like a sharp knife piercing through my heart. "I never wanted you to feel like that. I... I *wanted* to be honest with you. I was just trying to keep you safe. And I was selfish, and I'm so sorry for that. But I swear, Carter, it was all real. Everything between us. I *love* you!"

"And I love you." The words came out in a strained whisper, his voice faltering. "So damn much. I always have. That's why I think we should take a break."

And there it was. Even though I had been expecting them all along, those words still hit me like a punch to the gut. They were like a black hole, casting a shadow over every aspect of my existence. I wished it would swallow me up, too. Take me to a place where it wouldn't hurt so much.

Carter was still talking, but the rushing of blood in my ears drowned out his words. I had to take a few deep breaths to clear my head enough to listen.

"—for the best. I just need some space to process everything. You have no idea how hard this is. How much I want to tell you everything is okay. It's been killing me not talking to you for the past few days. Even now, all I wanna do is kiss you, Madison. But I can't. We can't. I just... I just need time."

"So what are you saying?" I asked, finally finding my voice.

He gulped, and his eyes filled with tears, shimmering like glass as he turned to look at me again. "I'm saying that I'm going to NYU in the fall. They sent me an offer, and I decided to accept it. And I know you don't want to go. That you never wanted to go. I shouldn't have pushed you in the first place, so I'm sorry for that. But it's probably better this way. To put some distance between us. At least for a while. Until I can..." He trailed off, leaving it hanging.

I opened my mouth, but the words seemed to dissolve on my tongue. I wanted to scream at him, to shake him, beg him for answers. *Until when?* How long did I have to live without him? Because I wasn't sure I could do it. He was everything to me. I had no idea who I was anymore without him.

The silence lingered, only interrupted by the far-off chirping of birds, their cheerful song clashing with the ache in my heart. Time seemed to freeze until he finally whispered, "I'm really sorry, Madison."

"You don't have anything to be sorry for." I said, if only because I couldn't let him walk away, blaming himself when this was all my fault. He was perfect, and he loved me. And I totally screwed up. I was to blame. Not him. Never him.

He gave a slight nod, and our eyes locked, the look heavy with unspoken words. He turned then, taking his first step away from me, and I wasn't ready. I couldn't let him go. His name involuntarily burst from my mouth, and he stopped, his dull eyes meeting mine. I could see the wet tracks on his cheeks, where the tears had started to flow.

'That day... the day we got to Chibouwood? You said you wanted to be the one who saved me sometimes. Well, you did. You saved me, Carter.

More than you could ever imagine. Through all the craziness in my life, you... you were everything. I'll never forget that.'

That was what I wanted to say, but now, with the distance between us, the words wouldn't come. All I managed was one.

"Goodbye."

A sad smile appeared on his lips. "See you around, Stone."

And just like that, my heart shattered. All those times I thought about this moment, him going to college, forgetting about me, and eventually losing him, because of what I was... I never really understood how much it would hurt. This boy, who had been there for me through everything, who loved me even when I was at my worst, who trusted me without hesitation, who made me laugh when everything was falling apart... he had become a huge part of who I was. Now, there just existed an empty space where he used to be.

I knew I deserved it. But I wasn't sure how I would survive it.

There was nothing else to say, so I turned, my heart thumping as I fought the urge to sprint to the car. His gaze never wavered as I walked away. I could feel the heat of it burning into the back of my head. I longed for him to call out my name. To tell me to stop, that he'd changed his mind, made a mistake. And I'd run to him, and kiss him, and tell him over and over how sorry I was. How much I loved him.

But he didn't. He stayed silent as I walked away, and with each step, the knife twisted deeper.

Somehow, I stumbled my way to the car. As I pulled out of the lot, I avoided looking at him and focused my gaze straight ahead on the road. Time seemed to warp, and next thing I knew, I was home, but I couldn't remember how I got there. It was all a blur.

Dad was home when I got back. I saw him through the window to the lounge. He peeked out and greeted me with a wave, but didn't come to the door to meet me. Henry must've told him where I was, and he figured out what was going to happen. He knew. Not like me, who was dumb enough to think it might be alright.

I made it to my bedroom without interruption, closing the door behind me before sinking onto the edge of my bed. Then my eyes landed on it, and another stab of pain jolted me – the framed photo of the two of us before the homecoming dance he'd talked me into going to. I'd always avoided dances, but I felt safe with him. Like I could conquer the world.

I picked up the frame, feeling the smooth surface beneath my fingertips as I traced the lines of his face. And then I couldn't suppress it any longer. The dam burst, and I curled up under the comforter, hugging the photograph to my chest, and sobbed until I fell asleep.

44

I spent the next few days in bed, only getting up to use the bathroom. Even my meals were brought to me on a tray and left on my nightstand. At first, Dad tried to coax me out by leaving it on the kitchen counter before heading out for work, but when he came home to find it untouched, he started delivering it to me. I ate a little, but only to keep him off my back.

Henry came back a couple of times. At first, he would try to make me talk, but I guess he got annoyed when I refused, because he soon stopped coming over. I couldn't blame him. Aside from the fact I was so miserable to be around, he had finals to study for. He never said what he wanted to do about Berkeley, so I figured he was heading back as planned. When he was gone, I'd be all alone anyway, so I might as well get used to it now.

The day I finally dragged myself out of bed and into the shower, the house was empty. Dad had left for work hours ago. I'd woken up to the sound of him leaving, but just turned over and gone back to sleep. I wasn't back at school until next week, so what was the point of getting out of bed? Truthfully, though, I was starting to get cabin fever. I needed to run. To clear my head, if that was possible.

Some days, Dad got a ride to work with a buddy, so he'd left the car at home today. I couldn't help but wonder if that was on purpose, though. Like he had a feeling today was the day. But it didn't really matter. I grabbed the keys, their weight heavy in my hand, and then I made the familiar journey to headquarters.

The forest was quiet. Peaceful. It was nothing like the chaos swirling in my mind, and I felt out of place at first. Like I didn't belong. It hadn't even been two weeks since I was last here, but everything seemed different now. *I* was different. But I soon got back into the groove, shook off the rust, and ran until the sun went down and my stomach growled. I didn't feel like hunting today, though, so I returned to the clearing to Change. Maybe I'd grab pizza for Dad and me on the way home.

It was incredible the difference a run could make. I hadn't felt complete since that day at the riverside with Carter, but being out here, I felt a bit better. A little more like me. Stronger, since the forest had given me a chance to think more clearly.

After Changing, I sprinted to the house, finding the spare key under the plant pot. Since the lights were off inside, I knew Ray wasn't home, which was a relief because I didn't want to talk. I wasn't ready to face anyone yet.

The only noise that broke the stillness of the Manor was the low, steady hum of the refrigerator. As I flipped on the light in the hallway, its warm glow spilled down the corridor, but though my stomach continued to rumble, I didn't head to the kitchen. Instead, as if an invisible thread was tugging me along, I headed down the hall towards the den, stopping at the second to last door. The door I hadn't opened in over eighteen months.

Ryan's study.

Holding my breath, I gingerly pushed open the door, hearing the hinges squeak, and then stepped into the room.

Since Ryan's passing, no one had tended to the archives, so I prepared myself for the musty smell of dust and stagnant air. But then I remembered what Dad said about him and Dan searching through the records to learn about the wendigo. I was the only one who couldn't bring myself to come in here.

Stepping inside, the first thing I saw was the mahogany desk from my memory. Except it was tidier, because it wasn't littered with papers. Just one book, set neatly in the centre. I knew exactly what it was, and as I crossed towards it, the worn-out wooden floorboards groaned beneath my feet.

As I neared the table, I traced my fingers over the book's cover, then shifted my attention to the spine. I hesitated for a moment before lifting it, and my breath got stuck in my throat when I noticed a piece of paper sticking out of the top, a single word visible.

Maddie

I grabbed it with shaking hands, immediately recognising the unique penmanship. It felt heavy in my hands, and I almost didn't want to open it, because it felt so final. The last thing from him.

Dad must've known it was here, but he hadn't said anything. Hadn't wanted to pressure me to come in here before I was ready. Was I ready now? I wasn't sure.

Pushing aside my doubts, I unfolded it and felt a mix of anticipation and nervousness as I began to read the words on the page.

There is no one else I would trust more than you to continue this work if, for whatever reason, I should be unable to do so myself. Your greatest strength lies in your brain, and I have no doubt you'll make me proud.

Always,

Ryan.

P.S. While I still recommend a history program, might I also suggest you consider anthropology? I think it could be more to your liking. There are some books on the shelf if you are interested. Reach out if you have any questions.

Clutching the note to my chest, tears welled up in my eyes once more. It felt like crying was all I did these days, and I was tired of it. It was time to move forward. If Sean hadn't arrived when he did, I might have died last week. I would not waste my second chance, knowing that Ryan didn't get one. I had to do this for him. To honour his memory.

Feeling for my phone in my pocket, I pulled it out, my new one firing up way quicker than the old one, which I'd left behind with my clothes in the caves. A sudden wave of pain twisted in my stomach when the screensaver popped up. I still couldn't bring myself to change it. That felt final, too, and I wasn't ready for that.

Swiping quickly away from it, I opened the messenger app, my thumb gliding across the screen as I searched for a name. Then I began typing out a text message.

> *Hey. Decided to apply to UMaine... How do you feel about coming to Orono for winter term?*

My finger hovered over the send button, my lip caught between my teeth. But, before I could talk myself out of it, I hit send, the satisfying click of the button lighting a spark of excitement, before I stuffed the phone away again. Then I tucked Ryan's book carefully under my arm, his note securely hidden between the pages, and turned towards the doorway, feeling lighter than I had all week.

THE END

Dear Angel,

I'm sorry. I had to go.

You were right. I didn't want to admit it, but Asher... shit, he's dead, A. We got in a fight about some girl. It was so stupid, but then he fell. I swear it was an accident. But something happened after and... I didn't know what to do.

I'm scared, bro. I don't know what's happening to me. ~~There's so much blood.~~ I keep waking up ~~covered in it~~ and I don't know where I am. ~~Mom said my dad was. My other family, the one I never met, they're fuck~~ I've been a shitty brother lately and I'm sorry man. ~~It's like them old stories mom used to tell us. About us~~ When I'm better, I'll make it up to you. Somehow.

This is a mess. I wish I could talk to you. Ur so much smarter than I am. Always have been. Maybe you'd even know what to do, but I can't risk it. You're my little bro, and it's my job to keep you safe, remember? I don't know how I'll even get this letter to you. I probably can't. Maybe Lydia can when she goes home. I never asked her to come with me, you gotta know that. If she gets this to you... just, I dunno, keep an eye on her for me, ok? ~~I never should've~~

Just wanted to let you know, I'm not dead. But, A, don't come looking for me, ok? I'll reach out when I can. Just need to figure some things out.

I love you, bro. Tell mom I'm sorry.

Will

Dear A,
I told her to run. I'm sorry.
W.

ENVY

Acknowledgements

Wow!

If you told me back in 2020 that in four years time, I would have published not one, but *two* novels, I wouldn't have believed you. And yet here we are.

It's been a hard road to get here, and it's taken a lot longer than I ever expected it to, so for that, I apologise. Sadly in 2022, we lost our dog, Nala, to cancer at the age of five. I went to a really dark place after that, my mental health being at the lowest it has ever been. Working on this book, getting to escape with these characters once again, has been the only thing to keep me going at times. But it wouldn't have been possible without the support of an amazing group of people.

Firstly to my husband, Paul. Thank you for your unwavering support, through my good days and my bad ones. For being my sounding board for ideas, even though you had no idea what I was talking about because you don't read! And for the fantastic sketch of the 'creature' – you took the image from my head and put it to paper, and it's perfect!

To my parents: thank you for always believing in me. If not for you getting that first draft of Discovered bound, I doubt I would be writing this acknowledgement today. Mam, I know you don't read (you're as bad as Paul!) but I know that as long as my dad is around, I will always have at least one fan!

To my beta readers, Jenna, Rebecca and Rebekah, thank you for your time and effort in making this book as perfect as it could be. I have asked you numerous questions, sent you draft after draft, and you have given me so much support through this entire process. Your insight has been invaluable and I cannot thank you enough. And to Ann-Marie, Alicja and Somyr, for giving me the kick up the backside I needed whenever imposter syndrome was getting me down. I'm sure I would have given up a long time ago without your support, so thank you.

And finally to *you!* Thank you for believing in me, and for reading my work. I know this took longer to be released than any of us hoped for, but I cannot thank you enough for your patience, and for loving these characters as much as I do. Reading your reviews and feedback makes me happier than you know. To see that people connect with Maddie, Carter and Henry... it is a dream come true. And I'll let you in on a secret – Maddie has one last adventure to share with you, so watch this space!

I truly hope this story was worth the wait. Our little wolf pack may be small, but you are mighty. Thank you for making my dreams come true.

Emma

Playlist

1. Walking On Cars - Somebody Else

2. Walking On Cars - At Gunpoint

3. My Chemical Romance - Summertime

4. Picture This - Unconditional

5. Picture This - Take My Hand

6. Dermot Kennedy - Something to Someone

7. The Maine - How Do You Feel?

8. Uncle Kracker - Smile

9. Picture This - Smell Like Him

10. Parachute - Without You

11. Picture This - Addicted To You

12. Parachute - Kiss Me Slowly

13. Parachute - Had It All

14. Dermot Kennedy - Kiss Me

15. Lewis Capaldi - Forget Me

16. Tom Grennan - All These Nights

17. New Rules - Love You Like That

18. Why Don't We - Just Friends

19. New Rules - RIDE

20. Mayday Parade - Kids in Love

21. BANNERS - Tell You I Love You

22. Lewis Capaldi - Leave Me Slowly

23. Taylor Swift - cardigan

24. NateWantsToBattle - Monster Inside

25. Colbie Caillat - Fallin' For You

26. Taylor Swift - You Are In Love

About the author

E.M. Taylor is an author of young adult supernatural books. Growing up, she devoured all things otherworldly, from Harry Potter to Mona the Vampire, and would rush home from school to watch Sabrina the Teenage Witch, wishing she too could be blessed with magical powers.

Reading fulfilled that wish. Whether it was running with the werewolf pack in Kelley Armstrong's Bitten, or moving into the Glass House in Rachel Caine's The Morganville Vampires, books offered an escape from reality, and a world of adventure, inspiring Taylor to pick up the pen herself.

Aside from writing, she works in pensions administration, and spends her free time playing video games or attending conventions... but mostly watching Julie and the Phantoms or The Hunger Games on repeat. She lives in Hartlepool with her husband.

Also by E.M. Taylor

Junior year wasn't supposed to be this deadly...

Discovered

A stand-alone young adult mystery
Coming 2025

Oakridge Farm

Printed in Great Britain
by Amazon